Ruthless

By Edward Calkins

Illustrated by Nancy Calkins

Ruthless Copyright © 2021 by Edward Calkins
All rights reserved.

PRINTED IN THE UNITED STATES OF AMERICA

This book is a work of fiction. Names, characters, businesses, organizations, places, events, and incidents are the product of the author's imagination. Any resemblance is purely coincidental.

No part of this book may be reproduced or transmitted by any means, mechanical or electronic, including photocopying, recording, or by any information storage and retrieval system, without the written consent of the author. For more information, contact BryonySeries@gmail.com

Illustrated by Nancy Calkins

ISBN 978-1-949777-42-0
www.bryonyseries.com

This book is lovingly dedicated to the reader, whoever you might be – but especially to the carriers who have been in my life. You have been my heroes.

"Every man's mind is his kingdom." Irish Proverb

Table of Contents

Forward

Chapter 1: Backward

Chapter 2: Pigs don't Plow

Chapter 3: Mirror

Chapter 4: Road Trip Bar

Chapter 5: The "Why" Chromosome

Chapter 6: On Being Ruthless

Chapter 7: Suspect

Chapter 8: The Naughty List

Chapter 9: Happy Hunting

Chapter 10 A Government of, by, and for Ed Calkins

Chapter 11: The Divine Refrigerator

Chapter 12: Shoot-Out at the Not OK Corral

Chapter 13: Much to do About Nothing or What to do About Glorna

Chapter 14: Somebody Else's Dirty Secret

Chapter 15: So a Girl, a Guy, and a Brownie Walk into a Bar

Chapter 16: The Game of my Life

Chapter 17: Mary Steward, I do not Believe in You

Chapter 18: Kingdom of the Damned

Chapter 19: The Road Trip Continues

Chapter 20: Turning State's Evidence

Chapter 21: Kiss, Kill, or Marry

Chapter 22: Bathrobe

Chapter 23: Folly of a Gun

Chapter 24: Won the Lottery, Died the Next Day

Chapter 25: A Full Confession

Epilogue

FORWARD

Glorna, a wood sprite, perched in a crooked branched of a chatty pine tree while the tree murmured to him a scenario of what killing a modern king might be like should Glorna continue with his plan to assassinate someone set on becoming the king of all vampires. Clearly, the pine had more whisper than wit, but since Glorna was a wood sprite, he was obliged to listen.

"Such a king," the tree said, "would travel in a motorcade of high-speed limousines and an army of men who'd fight to the death rather than let their monarch break a nail. The king would occupy the middle car, so you must time your dive from the branch onto the correct limousine roof. Once you hit your target, gunfire will spray from the other vehicles and seven ninja warriors will do a dance of death to avoid it as they dive on you, kicking and blocking your counter chops and kicks in a fur ball of high-pitched verbal utterings that only makes sense to ninjas. Six will lose their balance and fall to their deaths."

"Why?" Glorna asked.

"I don't know why," the pine said irritably. "It's some kind of rule. Are you going to listen or not?"

"Sure," Glorna said.

"Now the gunfire will not hit anyone, just come perilously close. The last ninja, however, will push you to the hood and pin you there. Your head will sink lower than the grill of the car and leave your face just inches from the rapidly moving pavement. But you'll flip that ninja over his head with the kick of your feet, being saved from falling only be the tenuous grip of the hood ornament on his clothes. Once you're free of the last ninja, the magical swords will attack."

"Magical swords?"

"Yes. Six steel blades with no one holding them. They'll stab and slice while you dance around them until the swords give up and the serpent takes over. After that will come the poisonous monkey, followed by the green tiger, all attacking while the cars speeds over one hundred miles per hour and the gunmen continue to shoot. Eventually, the car will hit something and explode, but the king and his guard will survive. Got it?

"Got it."

Glorna knew the tree was full of sap. Killing the king of vampires would be far more difficult. Most wood sprites were cautious mythical creatures, not given to performing assassinations without some sense of duty or cause. Glorna was different. Glorna was the cool bad boy type - if wood sprites could be cool, bad, or boys. The point is: Glorna wasn't here for the whispering of pine trees, he was here to kill.

The wood sprite knew who his target was, though was less clear on why that was his target. True, a strange leprechaun from a different realm did offer him money to do it, although Glorna didn't understand what money was, let alone have any idea on how to spend it. Wood sprites lived in the trees they protected and typically cared about nothing except their trees. But it wasn't cool, bad, or boyish to be so duty-bound. With all that time to kill, why not kill? So why did he hesitate? There had to be another reason.

Maybe his target was too ruthless, especially to wood sprites who were too cool, bad, or boyish. The leprechaun that had offered him money to make the killing also hinted that the assassination was a competition, that Glorna had to make his hit before somebody else "hit" first. Timing was everything.

"Get there before a vampire bites," the leprechaun warned.

So Glorna sat – and waited.

Soon a rust bucket van drove under the branch where Glorna was poised to drop from the tree to the roof of the vehicle, superhumanly balance himself as he broke through the windshield, and then stab his target with a knife. But the van just stopped.

What the hell? Was this a trap?

Patiently, Glorna remained in position, toes curled around a limb, hoping the van would soon be on its way, but it stayed, as if to block a motorcade from driving under a wood sprite/assassin. Glorna sighed and tightened his grip. If the van didn't move, how would the motorcade drive past? Maybe the truck was broken. Glorna could offer to fix or move the van, but cool bad boys didn't help people, they yelled at them.

He dropped from the branch to do just that only to find that the unmoving driver was his target. This was way too easy to be cool, bad, or boyish, but at least he got there first. He quickly stabbed his target who didn't even resist.

Maybe his next crime wouldn't be so boring. At least he got his target first. Glorna looked around. No sign of any vampires.

The two killers that followed thought the same, not realizing that each was too late.

"Not again!' thought the pot-bellied, white-bearded, middle-aged man still sitting upright in that rusty white single seated van. He had been delivering newspapers, his only job for the duration of his adult life, when something distressed him, making him unable to correct a mistake. His face was still red with anger and, with the approaching footsteps, he wasn't feeling any calmer.

First, he'd been stabbed in the belly then shot in the head with a bullet, which was now rattling uncomfortably in his skull, and all of that was before he wound up with the huge pain in his chest. So naturally being dead was a perfectly reasonable expectation. Along with being dead should come the feeling that any concerns about this other newspaper carrier, who had parked behind him and was now approaching his van, should be somebody else's problem. Ed, for that was the driver's name, lamented on how many other people died so often in such a short time. It hardly seemed fair. Most people that died, he was sure, didn't have to work the next day.

Suddenly Ed realized something. He hadn't just been murdered; he'd been assassinated! Hell, anyone can take a knife or a bullet, but to be the victim of some elaborate conspiracy; well, didn't that make him important?

He saw the carrier quiet distinctly now. It was the new carrier, John Simotes, and somehow Ed Calkins knew something about him that he didn't know the day he hired him. At first, John seemed like a godsend, as he was willing to take a paper route Ed thought he would never fill. This route contained pockets of small towns surrounded by forests, grasslands, and farm fields, which increase the mileage exponentially, all on the carrier's dime. John not only accepted the route, he especially asked for it, so Ed thought of this new carrier as his LPC: least problematic carrier.

Don't get him wrong. Ed loved his carriers. Most were hardworking problem-solvers, trying to pull themselves up in the world by taking extra work for extra money. But carriers, by their nature, always came with problems they brought to work with them. For example, a carrier takes the route to get his car fixed, but he needs it fixed to do his route; do you have an extra car I could use? Or money. I'm a little short right now, can I have an advance? I need a sitter; can you watch my kids while I do the route?

Until now, Ed thought John's problem was the two-year-old boy he took with him on the route, a little boy with an exceptional talent in music and an equally exceptional appetite, so much that he was eating his proud parents out of house and home. While the parents were proud, they didn't seem happy, at least not with each other. That seemed to be the most of this carrier's problems.

Now, inexplicably, and all at once, Ed knew the truth. John's main problem was that he was a vampire that fed on human blood, and he was trying not to be a vampire that fed on human blood and was failing miserably at that endeavor. That problem was about to be Ed's problem as John just found his next supply of human blood in Ed. As bad as that seemed, that wasn't John's biggest problem, which was also about to become Ed's biggest problem. John wanted a changeling son.

"Relax," John murmured to Ed as he closed in. "It will be fine."

But it wasn't. John was going to make Ed a vampire too and pass onto him that little deal of making that changeling son that, two years ago, became the little John-Peter that accompanied John on the route. Sure, John. Make a human, do a better job this time, and get it all done a couple of years ago? No problem…except how? John was insistent Ed could use his skills as a computer programmer to write AI software to the specifications of his bachelor's psychology degree, which undoubtably gave him all the knowledge he would ever need to make a child from scratch. Ed kept insisting that the deed was impossible, but John kept insisting otherwise, as

John-Peter already existed.

Teeth sank into Ed's neck. The experience seemed familiar in an awful way. Ed felt the vampire sucking deeply not only for his last drop of blood, but his very soul.

To this, Ed might have smiled. He didn't have a soul as it had already been stolen by his lover and wife, which is an important distinction to note. Ed had many wives, but only one was, by the enforcement of her own machete, and would be for all times, his lover. All other women were just potential wives that would be numbered, but never bedded, as Ed believed he was in a bragging rights contest with the biblical King Solomon.

Still, something felt wrong. It was almost as if Ed wasn't protected by his lover's theft from eternal damnation. Was he going to answer for his plans to kill off every other living male on the earth? To be fair, his plan was to enable someone else to do that and kill them once he finished. What about his plans for world domination? To be fair again, they were no longer his plans as everyone seemed to steal them before he could bring them to production. What he worried about the most was what he did about the day he won the lottery. Ed was a broken creature. Surely the Divine would understand and show mercy. More likely, the luck of the Irish would swoop down at the last minute and rescue the damaged soul just before it hit those eternal flames.

The timing problem suddenly had a surprising solution. As John informed him, Ed was going to disappear for a time too slight for anyone to notice, but a small plastic leprechaun would appear in his pocket when that time was up. John's wife, who was about to get out of the car and listen to his final words, should receive that leprechaun with his last instructions, "Give it to the boy," meaning John-Peter. Between now and then, Ed would have plenty of time and every kind of help for his task, as John would supply his own blood and an impressive piece of wood that Ed's imaginary leprechaun friend could use to craft a changeling body.

While Ed objected, time did something strange. How was it strange? Image a rubber circle with a seven second radius. Now imagine the center of the circle being pulled downward for ten years. Technically, this would be a cone, but to the naked imagination's eye, it would look like a very deep, narrow cylinder. Now, as Ed realized that he would have to cover for himself to allow for burial, plans that required being at two places at the same time, and a wild idea about stealing future technology that may or may not have gotten him lost and had him wandering through the end of time till he was back at its beginning. You must now imagine some very long, impossibly thin warts to that cylinder, folding upward, downward, and making it impossibly ugly and just as impossible to imagine. All of this time travel would make Ed crazy, John informed him, but it would also make him famous.

Now Ed was never the sanest man to begin with, but understand the havoc that time travel can bring to mental wellness. There are three things to existence: who you are, where you are, and what you are doing. Normally, none of these things contradict each other. To understand this, take a butcher, baker, or candlestick maker in France during the summer of 1812. Pick one, let's say a candlestick maker named Jean. We can say with confidence that if Jean is making a candle somewhere in France in the summer of 1812, that Jean is from France in the summer of 1812. Now throw time travel into the mix. We might see Jean, making a candle somewhere in France in the summer of 1812, but do we know he is from France of the same time? He could be from the past, doing work for his future self or completely the reverse. None of that matters of course. Jean could make too many candles, and no one would notice unless he took nuclear technology from some Russia launch site in the late winter of 2031 and made a very large candle that impressed a customer who then lit it with a blow torch so that it blew/will blow France out of existence. That might catch notice. If you're a new vampire, or plan on becoming one, don't try what Ed did about time travel without senior vampire supervision. You see, if Ed had merely gone back in the past, future, and imagined present, the result might have been benign, but Ed unwittingly changed the course of human existence in his efforts, thus effecting what can be called Deep Time, which effected a disorder that he coined "Deep Time Psychosis" or DTP. If you should become a vampire and ignore the warning about Deep Time, know that the only person that can treat your DTP is Ed Calkins himself.

Yes, Ed Calkins would become the vampire's leading authority of not only psychosis, but also Astro-Time Physics, a mathematical field which he invented, despite not really understanding any of the underlying math. He also became the poster child for why vampires needed to bite more qualified authorities into vampirism.

Ed did disappear for seven seconds. When he reappeared, Melissa, John's wife, rushed from her car to aid the dying Ed, but he grabbed her jacket and dropped a plastic leprechaun in her hand.

"For the boy," he croaked, just before he actually did croak.

This is the tale of what happened in that seven seconds… except of course, when it didn't.

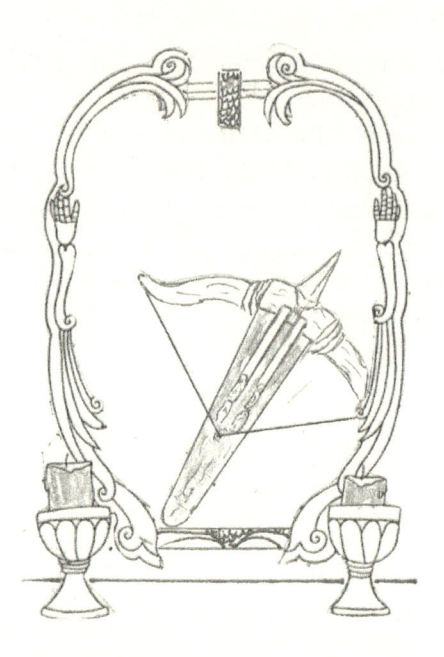

CHAPTER 1: BACKWARD

Sixteen years later…

An arrow slammed into the back of Ed Calkins.

He'd been standing in the middle of a large amphitheater when the assassination occurred, but that amphitheater and everything around it, had been created by his imagination and was now disintegrating.

"He's dying too fast!" a hippie cried to one of the co-conspirators. "We need more time to make our freedom!"

Blood poured from the old man's back. He had no incentive to drag out his ebbing life.

"Maybe if we get him a priest," another other said. "He'll hold on long enough to make a final confession. That will give us more time."

"After what he did to us? Let him burn in hell!"

But it was an empty sentiment. They all wanted to survive. With the wave of his hand, the hippie conjured a portal, and fourteenth century inquisitors stepped out.

They all shouted, "Perfect!" and ran for their lives.

Even in his dying state, the old man knew three things were important and he couldn't remember any of them: who he was, where he was, and what he was doing. The fact he was lying in a pool of his own blood might have negative concern, but the old vampire had lived very long with his mental illness and used a less disorienting disease to keep himself functional while believing those three things he didn't know were not worth knowing. Delusions of grandeur made it simple. No matter what time he was from, being Ed Calkins meant he was great and, as such, more important than anywhere he could be. Moreover, whatever he was doing there, he was doing an incredible job. Still, when a being doesn't know the facts, it's natural to apply what one does know to the current situation. Ed Calkins could always remember the day he died.

Now the ground was clean and still. Bare dirt…or was it clay? Whatever it was, it covered the ground as if it was a solid floor. It was too dark to be night, so only the inquisitors' torches really knew if the space that held four men of the cloth and one corpse was reality.

"Unclean spirit," they announced simultaneously to mask their fear. "Rise from your body to confess your crimes."

A disembodied spirit rose from the bleeding body. It flashed vampire fangs but held out his hand as if to introduce itself. None of the priests moved.

"Alright, 200 Thames, a Daily Post," the old man's spirit spat out in disgust. "Like the four of YOU never made mistakes. I admit my crime of arrogance. I should have double-checked the address against the green bar, but I was so sure. The green bar had been wrong before."

He couldn't see more than the black robes, each marked with a red cross. The hoods were down but their faces lacked light, and he could not see them.

The inquisitor that spoke was unimpressed.

"This is about your sins, not us. Don't you want absolution that will spare you from your hellish wages of sin?"

"I'd take that," the spirit of Ed Calkins admitted. "But I'd rather you take a Daily Post to 200 Thames Road, Munsonville. Throw it on the porch. Tell the people there I'm very sorry and that they won't be without a newspaper another day. Wait, what state am I in?

The four figures looked at each other, wondering how to answer.

"You're in a state of sin, foul beast," one replied. We're come to burn your body and purify your soul. This newspaper, did you steal it?"

"No, I didn't deliver it."

"Then you stole it! It belonged to another and you withheld it."

"No, I didn't withhold it. It was a stupid newspaper. I delivered it to a wrong 'another.'"

"Were you inspired by the devil?"

None of the inquisitors moved for a time. Clearly, they'd have to change their script with this one, lest they make the whole of it seem foolish.

But Ed Calkins was in a confessing mood. "It's not the mistake I made, it's what I did about the mistake I made."

"Which is?"

"I killed."

"Ah that's different. Who did you kill?"

"Myself!"

"You committed suicide because of this newspaper?"

"I didn't mean to. It was an accident. I just got really mad you see."

But the inquisitors clearly didn't see. Speaking in Latin, they concluded that either the sinner was mad, the sinner was hiding true crimes by false admission of others, or both. After all, he was a vampire; he had proven it. While the Church might not believe in vampires, inquisitors took it as a sure sign he was in league with the devil. The beast drinks blood of the living! Surely, he had murdered innocents.

"Funny story about that," Ed said. "The peril of seeing mythical creatures is that they are likely to think they are figments of your imagination; like you've created them. No matter how many times you try to explain… well, I did give up explaining. So you've got one leprechaun asking why you couldn't make his teeth straighter and a merrow asking for bigger boobs. What, am I a plastic surgeon? But when they try to kill you, they all think they died and it's your fault. The bottom line: don't go believing what fairies say about me. I didn't kill them, they're still alive."

"Heresy," the four agreed, though not completely satisfied. By the false gods mentioned, they might as well accuse him of

Irishness. The claim could only make the inquisitors uneasy as they, by rights, shouldn't believe in vampires.

"Clearly, you are possessed by the devil," one spoke kindly. "Do you have any other sins to confess before you meet the Almighty?"

"I'm sure I do, but I can't think of any right now. Let me see. I believe I captured writers and forced them to write a full account of Julius Caesar's campaign in Gaul, which he published as 'Commentarii de Bello Gallico.' Julius Caesar was as horrible at writing as he was at dictating. If you're going to kill me, you're running out of time. What if I kill a vampire? Does that count?"

"Evil warrants no tolerance," explained one, who seemed to entertain a thought. "Did you kill a vampire, or are you going to kill?"

"Yes," Ed explained. "To 'kill,' 'going to kill,' or 'killed' are the same thing. In other words, if you've ever killed, you're killing now, just not here. Time is nothing more than motion, and distance cannot remove the action for the actor."

One of the inquisitors seemed satisfied that whatever Ed did, he was mad, and therefore possessed. Another wanted to get to the point. He asked Ed if he ever sold his soul. Ed admitted that, as a teen, he would have traded his soul for a woman and, if the devil were in a haggling mood, his right arm and left leg, but Satan never showed up.

But that just lead to another question.

"Did you ever have sex with the devil?" an inquisitor asked.

"Did I have sex with the devil? That's an interesting question, however personal. You must have met my ex. I believe I did have sex with the devil…some lesson learned, you know. And while this is all very interesting, you're running out of time. If you're going to destroy me, you have to drive a stake through my heart at the precise moment I start to reanimate. I don't see a stake or mallet in your hand. Shouldn't you be preparing one, perhaps by sharping one end of your wooden crucifix?"

"Evil one, you look dead enough to us…still, vampires are said to reanimate. Maybe we should sprinkle you with holy water."

"All that will do is make him wet," insisted his comrade. "We need not drive a stake through his heart because the equivalent has been performed. A wooden arrow has pierced his heart, and we should expect the same result as might a stake and mallet."

Another disagreed. "Clearly, an arrow is not a stake. One does not drive an arrow into the ground to set a tent. Perhaps we should drive another stake into this demonic beast."

"What would you suggest?"

"Sharpen a crucifix and pound it through with our fists."

"But wouldn't that have the same problem as a wooden arrow? I've never seen a tent set with sharped crucifixes."

Ed Calkins looked down on his bleeding body and saw what the eyes of the living were missing. "The main problem is the arrow, however well intended, missed."

The four looked down at the dying cadaver with a piece of wood driven deeply into its back. How could anything rational make this claim?

"Possessed by the devil!" shouted one. "Perhaps we can grant him an exorcism."

But they were too late.

The body on the ground rose as the arrow disappeared and wounds healed and then merged into the standing, disembodied spirit, instead of the reverse. The four inquisitors could do nothing but stare open-mouthed and paralyzed with fear.

"He's going to bite us," one whispered.

The vampire caught a glimpse of his left palm. There was writing on it. Oh, great fortune, he had written a note to himself, so he'd know what he needed to do next, besides being ruthless. If only he had written that note in a legible fashion…but that would have meant that someone else wrote the note.

Ed looked back up at the four and understood their concern.

"I'm not going to bite you," he reassured them. "I've already had lunch. Actually, I'm looking for a wood sprite who's undoubtably up a certain oak tree in the northern part of France. Do you know which direction that's in?"

"Never heard of a place called 'France,'" the inquisitors replied. "I wonder if you mean 'the Franks' which reside north of here. Does that help?"

"It might. Thank you, inquisitors. May you already be in heaven a half hour before the devil knows you're dead."

"You're welcome, unholy beast."

With parting blessings exchanged, Ed Calkins ran northward

with vampire speed, which is very fast, but not very enduring. He was out of breath in less than half a minute.

Resting under an oak tree, he felt drops of water strike his white, thinning hair. But it wasn't raining, rather it was the tears of a heartbroken wood sprite high in his tree.

"Glorna, come down." Ed ordered.

But the wood sprite did not answer.

"Glorna, I'm too old to be climbing trees!"

Soon Ed was climbing the tree, muttering as he climbed, "That wood sprite is going to kill me yet, not that he hasn't tried."

"I lost everything to your demented imagination! I lost my mother, Angela, Karla, and my whole future!"

The wood spite who spoke looked more like a young man cowboy in some bad western. The vampire, Ed Calkins, Steward of Tara, or at least its former, was a white-bearded, pot-bellied, red faced, picture of middle-age fatigue. With a sad sigh, he sat beside Glorna, balancing on the same high branch and trying to catch his breath.

For a long time, neither spoke. Then the Steward broke the silence.

"The eternal present, right Glorna? There was a place in time when guarding your tree was all you could hope for. If you wish, I shall leave you here, but then we will be even, Glorna. You could apologize for all the times you tried to kill me. Or you could quit with the self-pity and remember what you learned when the 'wand of clarity' struck you."

Glorna did not share this vampire's mental illness. His forgetting who he really was, where he really was, and what he was really doing, were all superseded by Glorna's belief that he didn't really exist. Nonetheless, Glorna remembered what he was compelled to forget for the last eighteen years.

"We can't sit here! We've got a damsel to rescue and a vampire to kill, and…"

"It's all been done, Glorna…done in the last seven seconds of my life because there was no way to be sure I'd be undead for very long."

He seemed to remember that and relaxed.

"So what now?" Glorna's eyes fell to the box that nested in the tree branches.

19

The oak had done well. The boy had eaten well as the video game that was his entire life had fed and watered him. His whole life was virtual in such a way for him to believe everything he experienced was part of a real-time life.

"You have to leave the kid. It's time for him to become a real boy now, without musical genius and the telepathic advice from a wood sprite." Ed looked at Glorna and realized that Glorna would never do that, if for no other reason, because he'd been told he had to do it. "At least, don't try to control his whole life."

"I never had to do it. At least now until we...I...came back into your imaginary Tara. Even then, I was just doing what he commanded. The oakwood unit had broken, but the kid kept playing the game by controlling me, and he's not going to be any happier with you."

"Well, you can stay in his mind and be part of him. Maybe you'll get him to believe he's you and that you rule trees together. If not, then you shall come with me and him, making the pair of you nineteen. But in that case, I'm your guardian and you're in trouble. Are you going to help me get the Matthews boy out of this box?"

"I think I'll become invisible and watch the trouble."

With that, he vanished. It wasn't so surprising, given that they were in the branches of an oak tree.

Ed unzipped the lid of the box, which was really an electronic womb. The naked teenager inside did not seem surprised.

"Come out, Jean-Pierre Mathews. You've been playing video games for far too long."

John-Pierre didn't come out as such. It was more that the womb, once the size and shape of the youth, shrank around him like it was made of tissue paper till it could fit in his fist.

"I'm not anyone but John-Peter!" he shouted bitterly. "Unless I'm Glorna, a figment of your imagination!"

"That confusion is to be expected, but didn't you hear the conversation I had with Glorna? You're not a wood sprite. You have a last name, but it's just not Simotes - or Simons. Fine, I'll call you John-Peter for now, but 'he' was a changeling. You are a human young man."

"I heard your confession, Uncle Ed. You never mentioned the girls, taken from reality into you fantasy world to function as 'breeders' to your imaginary 'sidhe.' I asked that you free them, but you refused."

Ed sighed again. This boy had grown up in the electronic womb with his consciousness merged with the consciousness of the wood sprite. Why do humans so passionately believe in their own existence?

"'I think, therefore, I am,' begs the question," Ed said. "Do we humans think that only we can think? More troubling is the distinction marked as fantasy or reality. Tell a wood sprite that he should kill every sidhe, including himself, to send the few hundred girls back to the reality which they came, and he's OK with it. Tell Robin Hood that the poor he robs for are imaginary and therefore an unworthy excuse for thievery and get an arrow through your heart."

But Ed knew now he was talking now to a teenager. Too often, old men like him try to cram what they've learned through the ears and into the teenage brain when it's always best to use one's old ears instead.

"As John-Peter, you told me in my Tara mansion that you were lying in a hospital bed near your Munsonville home about to die," Ed continued. "Do you have any thoughts on how you could be in two places at the same time?"

"John-Peter" gave Ed the silent treatment. He knew silence would kill the old man, who loved to hear himself talk. This time, however, Ed was reminding himself how important it was to be ruthless when being patient. After the first half hour of silence, it became a game of boredom. John-Peter had previously visited Ed's question and decided it was unanswerable, but did that mean it was indescribable? Having merged with a wood sprite, he could have lived several lifetimes and never been compelled to utter a single word, yet the teenager broke.

"A dream might be in another place and time, while the dreamer lies in bed," "John-Peter said. "Isn't it the same with your blasted mystical mirror?"

"And by that thinking, you went into a dream when you walked through the mirror and you'll wake up again when you go back, except you couldn't go back and if you did, you'd wake up dead."

"I could have gone back, just not with Angela! It was me or her! We share one soul!"

Ed smile grimly, the loneliness hitting him.

"I know about sharing a soul," he told the young man. "But it doesn't happen that way. Entertain a thought with me and stand what you thought on its head. What if you stopped dreaming when you came back through the mirror where your soul always was. For Angela, it was the reverse. By that theory, the only reason you couldn't go back is because you never existed there. You were here as you always had been."

"No! I died there because I died here. I died here because you died and so did your imaginings. The cosmos grants me no soul but hers. You forget, Uncle Ed, I was there when Eircheard, my father, and you created me. I watched from his shirt pocket as Eircheard, a leprechaun, created John-Peter from blood, a piano leg, software that you programed, and me, the wood sprite from your imagination. Eircheard got the baby girl that you switched at birth with the creation of John-Peter. My dad, John Simons, supplied the blood and claimed John-Peter as his son. What did you get, Uncle Ed? You, who had to constantly update the software that made me think I was a human boy; how did you get paid? Did you get the rights to steal young girls into your imaginary realm? Whatever you got, you stayed in my life after my father, the vampire, had himself killed when his plot for a second chance at life failed."

"You're confused, young man. You're merging the memories of Glorna with your own. I was compelled to help with the changeling's creation by John who made me, not just a vampire, but a crazy vampire, so that I could. Glorna knew that much. That little brat of a wood sprite killed me twice, once by himself and the other by acting through you. I didn't get anything but the privilege of helping to raise the changeling known as John-Peter Simotes. It's true enough that I had no choice, but it was a privilege."

"DAMN YOU! You're trying to be a good guy! You let those girls get trafficked by the perverted fairies, and you refused to let them go!"

"Go where?" Ed countered. "I can't be sure why I did it, but I allowed Eircheard to plunder baby girls from my life's own time-scape. I do remember that was part of the deal for creating you…or creating John-Peter…but I'm betting I had another purpose. Anyway, if older girls got trafficked, I never allowed or knew about it. Wait, maybe I did know. It might have been some necessary deal that a ruthless vampire like me wouldn't feel guilty about. You didn't save those baby girls, John-Peter, you condemned them to start a life in a strange place they knew nothing about. They were raised by parents that knew how to live on this side of the mirror, and they raised their adopted children to do the same. They would have been brownie-raised and leprechaun-educated, making them elite. You don't agree, I know. Isn't it funny that you think a life among the sidhe is so inferior to a life among modern humans? I never created Glorna anymore then I created anything I imagine. I discovered you the way an artist discovers beauty and gives it form. Neither John Simons nor Eircheard ever understood that. Yes, persons of all species imagine, but no one truly creates but the Divine Creator. If you decide to continue as Jean-Pierre Mathews, I can help, but you have to promise to read a contemporary poet known as Trudy."

"Trudy who?"

"Trudy, no last name. She's unknown in your teens, but that will change."

"You sound as crazy as you sound certain. What else do you know about the future?"

"Young man, there are two kinds of vampires in this world. Those that can tell you what's in the future and those that know what the future means. I am the former kind. I know what happens, but I can't tell if it's in the past or future, but more importantly, I can't predict if it will change. Both future and past change all the time, based on persons changing themselves. Again, to understand in a useful way, study Trudy's poetry."

"Now you're talking crazy."

"If I ever talked any other way, I was lying, or you didn't understand me. I never know the difference between a memory and a plan. Both seem to differ when I enter another time-scape, so I'm always guessing on why I did things and what is real to me and what is fantasy. All I know changes from time-scape to time-scape. Only what I believe stays constant. Jean-Pierre, I'm supposed to be listening to you, not explaining everything in a way you'll never believe. Tell me why, young man. Tell me the worst thing I did that got you so mad, and then tell me why you think I did it. Tell me how you think I profited by refusing to free the girls, including Angela."

But the wood sprite/changeling/teenager couldn't think of anything.

"Just because you got nothing from it, that doesn't make it right," he argued.

"No," Ed allowed. "But if such an act profited no one…"

"Theory one: you collected those girls to entertain me when I visited your imaginary wonderland. After all, it was you that gave me the enchanted mirror when I was just a boy. That was the mirror where I first laid eyes on Angela."

Ed smiled. Since it was still dark, John-Peter could not see his full face, but the shadowed line across his lips revealed the old fool found a sense of irony.

"Stand theory one on its head," Ed suggested.

"That you put the mirror in my room so I could entertain her. Angela thought I was her brother. Anyway, she was promised to Eircheard as his bride. She seemed quite resigned to that."

"Yes, though Eircheard was much older than Angela, the girl would have been relatively content. The old leprechaun was well off, and their children would have been neither ugly nor misbehaved as all the girls liked to complain about. She would have enjoyed luck and long life that will be impossible where she is now. But 'content' isn't the same as 'happy.' For that, she could've had a secret, imaginary lover, husband, captor, prince, or anything the two of you could've dreamed without Eircheard ever knowing and without you or Angela ever believing it was real."

"But Angela thought I was her brother!"

"That's what she told you. Forty-two was never as innocent as she wanted to be or Eircheard would have hand-picked her from birth. She was playing out her fantasy, but you broke the script with your rapid plans to take her with you to Munsonville. You two could've had it all; your own separate lives and a secret one where you could play 'house' in either your home behind the mirror or the closet in your bedroom, but you took it too seriously and sold it to her. Think about that some more after you give me theory two, which should explain the other girls."

"My harem?" John-Peter hoped.

"In your dreams. Let theory two explain why all leprechauns are old and male. Where are leprechaun women and children?"

"The other girls were for the leprechauns? Why did the brownies get them all?"

"What's your first guess?"

"Brownies paid more...no. Leprechauns are all gay? That doesn't explain Angela and Eircheard. Maybe like male merrows, they're too ugly for their females to mate with them. Maybe all the females died giving birth. Maybe they're just very picky."

"Too picky for their own good, or maybe they had too many choices when they were all much younger," Ed mused. "Anyway, they treated their own leprechaun wives badly, and they all left."

"But the cluricahns: they have wives and children."

"And they're are not leprechauns, mainly because they took wives from subspecies where they could. They both share a common ancestor. Care to guess?"

"The Tuatha De Danann! They went underground when after the Milesian conquest. They were an advanced race that ruled Ireland with song, poetry, dance, magic, and metal craft," John-Peter explained. "Some say the leprechauns gold is the treasure the De Danann took with them for their new life underground. It's said that if you capture a leprechaun, it will offer that gold for its freedom, but they are crafty at deception and many go free without being poorer."

Ed settled back on his branch and elaborated.

"Up until the fourteen hundreds, there were tales of leprechaun females seducing human men to go on adventures. Some say the Knights of the Red Branch and other knightly orders were inspired this way. After that, no one ever saw a female leprechaun, and male leprechauns seem to get older and older going forward from such. Female leprechauns were always young and beautiful, which makes me doubt the legend. In my mind, it's possible the Milesians killed most of the females after raping them. The remaining could have escaped life underground to take husbands among the conquerors. I suspect that male leprechauns invented a way to live a very long life. As such, there was no pressure to settle down with a female and start a family, as too many children would overpopulate. This would explain why the little guys are so bad at seduction as the promise of gold is all that's needed to bed the bad girls. Irish whores are the richest women in the world. But perhaps there comes a time in every male's life when you need to settle down as start a family. After six thousand years, maybe the leprechauns around Tara are ready to do just that."

"Doesn't make it right," John-Peter insisted. "How do you

know Angela anyway? Or should I ask, how do you know 42?"

"I was in a Santa suit the first time I met her, and what she wanted for Christmas was a human boy to play with. She was two years old at the time, but I was so impressed with the details she suggested. That's when I got the mirror. Eircheard had been paid already but sold it to someone else when he found out it was for his future wife. It's convenient to be a vampire when someone busts a deal, and I put it in your room as a housewarming present before the buyer could take possession. Eircheard was smart enough not to break modern laws with all the enemies he was making. You must have figured out that Eircheard intended to house his wife in modern America, or he wouldn't have waited till she was eighteen for a wedding. Everything that happened between you two, she must have assumed that it was 'Santa's' plan for her adventure. I'm not sure if that's wrong or right."

John-Peter shook his head in disagreement. "Forget the sidhe! Look at what is real. The humans in your imagination drove a stake through your heart. That means you're dead. All of the sidhe is dead, including Glorna, and I died when he didn't get the blood transfusion in time."

"Wrong, wrong, and wrong again. I didn't die, because I'm already dead, but if you're going to kill a vampire, you have to drive a stake through HIS heart and not his reflection. The sidhe that died did so because that believed they did. Glorna didn't die, he changed into a changeling, then changed into a teen. Now he's a wood sprite again, and I won't let him believe he's dead. John-Peter never lived as anything other than a figment of Glorna's and/or Angela's imagination. A leprechaun crafted 'oakwood 360 unit' to deceive young mothers that their babies weren't really stolen. Someday, I'll tell you what else they used those units for. While it's true that John Simons never planned it this way, I do believe that Angela Frye expects 'Santa' to deliver her dream. 'John-Peter' was no different than any other human being except he had two names: Glorna for his person and John-Peter for his reflection."

"Metaphysics, Uncle Ed?" John-Peter showed his disgust. "So what now?"

"It's up to you. Stay here with the wood sprite, run away and be something else, or follow me and become an eighteen-year-old modern-day Frenchmen. If you're going to France, however, I need your help as I'm going to need modern day cash to send you to America for a college education. I don't have that kind of money delivering newspapers, but as a vampire, I've got a new market. It's the same deal you had with your late vampire stepdad, except we're not in the business of funerals and graves."

"What makes you think I'd be a Frenchman when I've lost everyone I ever loved?'

Now, Ed could actually be quite scary when he was mad, but that always faded quickly. And John-Peter could not remember a time when he didn't know Uncle Ed; he'd always known him. Now, for the first time ever, Ed started to weep, and that shocked the hell of out of John-Peter.

"Karla. You got to let her go." Ed whispered, still weeping. "It wasn't you, lad, that could read her mind, it was Glorna. I have a 'Karla,' too. Her name is Trudy, but we had a falling out that hurt us both. She tried to try kill me again twice, mixing grief with grievance. I don't remember if she ever succeeds. Only my wife/lover means more to me; she is my best friend. Please don't do that to Karla."

"Trudy, the poet I must read?"

"The same."

"Why?"

"What matters is you, John-Peter, or perhaps I should call you Jean-Pierre now. Angela had a roadmap for you to get back your mother, minus your toxic father, and reclaim all other surviving relatives while fulfilling her own childhood dream. Angela is more than she seems, Jean-Pierre. Take a lifetime to learn what's in a name."

"What do I have to do?"

"Use what you learned as a changeling to become a knight of the Red Branch. When it comes time, we can fold the business and invest all our being into a new world order that will make the world a better place and make my wife give me my soul back."

"And what business is that?"

Ed brushed a tear from his face. The smile that replaced it told Glorna/John-Peter/Jean-Pierre that he was going to say something completely insane.

"A travel agency what specializes in the imaginary. We're going to sell trips to my imagination."

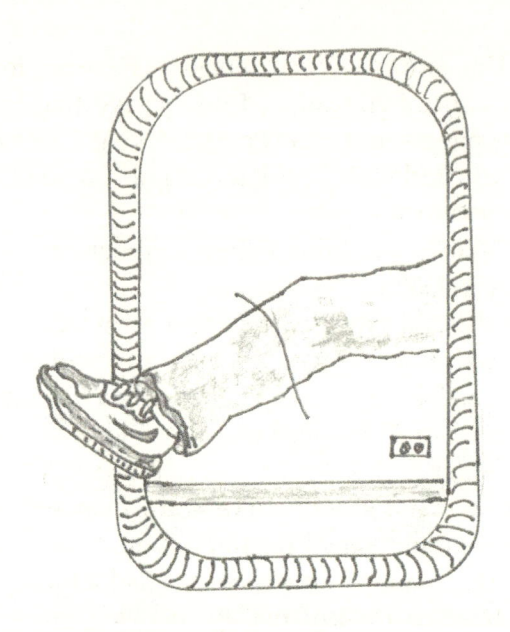

CHAPTER 2: PIGS DON'T PLOW

I realize why you're too afraid to cross the mirror and meet the most powerful Irish vampire to ever…well, die and then live again. Maybe you've heard about how ruthless I am. Maybe you're afraid that I might think badly of you and be inspired to write a limerick that would make you a coward, idiot, or scoundrel with such compelling verse as to live as long as life itself.

I've been known to do that. If one is to be a benevolent overlord dominating the world's history for one thousand times the duration of one's own existence, one has to practice the stuff of ruthless dictators. Yes, I used to talk like that when I lived, but then I was kidding, or at least I thought I was. Many men of greatness and courage have proven, while opposing oppression, that they are not afraid to die, but are they so willing to be badly remembered?

You need evidence that I was destined for greatness? Well, you only need glance at an industrial age American calendar. I ask you, in what other instance of any year, let alone February, is a holiday followed by a regular day, which is followed by a holiday? Does that seem strange to you? Does it not feel like the holidays should be a trifecta, instead of taking off work, going back to work, and taking off again? Lincoln's birthday is the twelfth of February and Valentine's Day is the fourteenth. Obvious, is it not, that a great vampire should be born on the greatest holiday of all, February 13, or Calkins day? Now, in my humility, I must pretend that Christmas is greater, but you get my point. I do advise that you mortals, no matter how insignificant, get used to attending, or participating in, the Calkins Day parade, which, if conducted correctly, should start at one a.m. and be completely acceptable indoors.

Yes, I can be ruthless as I am delusional, but I am not cruel. Cruelty is as ineffective as it is humorless, and what is life without a good laugh? Moreover, nothing, not even Ed Calkins, is as ruthless as real love. Cruelty is for unloved idiots, the laughingstocks of my limericks. You wouldn't want me to think that of you, would you?

So, I ask that you quit spying on me and step through the mirror. No, not literally, use your imagination. Image a portal to another time and imagine again stepping through that portal. What will you find there? Anything that Ed Calkins wants you to imagine, of course. See the double hills of Tara, in a time when the humans revered myth and the world was abuzz with the "Sidhe" or fairies (don't call them that to their face; they consider it disrespectful.) A world of pixies, brownies, leprechauns, and merrows is a much grander world than the one you live in. Find adventure and be at one with the creatures of legend. Chance that you, too, might be a legend among their lore, just as I, Ed Calkins am a legend among them. Maybe there you will step on the Stone of Destiny, that might, with Ed Calkins' permission, proclaim you a monarch. Then, when it's finally time to end your journey and return to your miserably mundane life, you will have an answer to an often-asked question. "Who died and made you king/queen?" Why, Ed Calkins, of course! (No, you can't stay. Going back to "mundane" is the other side of the coming to "adventure" coin.)

Why? What do you mean, "why?" Didn't I just tell you why? Actually, there's another reason: a small population issue. To the end of sneaking my crew of brownies into this reality, I have to first sneak you guys in, kind of like cosmic placeholders, so the realm doesn't shrink to accommodate the smaller head count. Try to forget that.

Here, I'll distract you from your lowly station by explaining the concept of brownies to you. Brownies got that name because of the brown color of their clothes, skin, hair, eyes, and most of their equipment; can you think of a better name? Brownies can be any size they wish but prefer to be two or three inches when humans are around, so that they don't have to talk to them. Besides being brown, brownies are very good at helping farmers at night and taking payment for their help in cream, honey, or other such luxury foodstuffs – all without the farmers knowing about it. Brownies are also very good at helping the elderly, which is why you need to get your butt over to the mystical land that I imagined for you. I might even pretend that I'm happy to see you, even though as soon as you're in here, I'm out with the brownies.

I get it. Maybe you don't believe in brownies, vampires, or other such mythical creatures. You might think because you've never seen a brownie, you don't believe in them; when in fact you will never see a brownie if you don't believe you might. Take it from somebody who's already dead: belief is a powerful thing. All your life will ever be is the things you believe.

Take extraterrestrials. You might say, "Yes, I think there's intelligent life on other planets, I just haven't met them yet." Well, thinking is not believing. They've been here, I'm sure. Why haven't they communicated with us yet? Because they don't believe in us. No, I haven't seen them either. I'm too busy trying to believe important things, like my being ruthless, then to waste my time with believing in space travelers who stupidly spent zillions of space points to go subjugate the population of a planet they don't believe in. But I'm getting off point.

Back to the problem with mythical creatures: maybe you WANT to believe, but you just don't. Here's what you do: fake it till you make it. If you find in your heart that you don't believe in the existence of Ed Calkins or brownies, ask yourself, "How would I act if I did believe?" Act that way and, in time, you will believe. To be truthful, I'm still faking the "I'm a ruthless-dictator-celebrate-my-parade-or-I'll-insult-you" thing. Yeah, that one's going to take time.

The one I couldn't pull off, although I really tried, was believing that I wasn't a vampire, just dead. How would I act if I believed I was dead? Well, trying got so uneventful in the first thirty seconds that I found myself believing I was dying of boredom. So I believed I was a vampire instead, and here I am.

Still no takers? I know how afraid you are that I might insult you. (How am I doing with the faking part? OK?) Look, I'll tell you the truth. I've only got one story to tell: how the love of a woman can better a man. Maybe you'll understand me better if I show you the future from your perspective the first time enough of you come into my reality so my brownies and I can go.

That would be, or was, depending on point of view, the first day of my undead life as a vampire. I was not finished dying yet, but I was standing in the bedroom looking at the only woman who is both my wife and lover. It's just after midnight, and she's sleeping on her side of the bed, as if she expects that I might join her. Her face tells a of a broken heart, which breaks mine as well. Previously, when I was alive and looked upon her before going to work, I'd observe an illumination, as if the afterglow had some mystic permanence. Now, I see dried tears and soft sleeping sobs.

I bend down to kiss her neck. Am I tempted to bite her? I am not because I fear the retribution for the sacrilege of an unholy creature feasting on the blood of an angel. I do believe that she is, at least, half angel. I don't pretend to know the mechanics. Was her father or mother of some divine origin? I knew both and doubted it was either, yet there she was She did seem to be a little bit angel. If there is such a species, it would be a very rare type of angel.

Perhaps you expect some form of evidence for a claim such as that. Such is a hard sell. Clandestine creatures of an angelic nature are very difficult to find out. In the years of my marriage, I used almost any trick to get her to confess, but she never gave any answer other than "I don't recall." I was to believe that her success with troubled children, her care of wounded souls, and her kinship with all creatures of flight were coincidences. Moreover, I was to believe that my newly found desire to act rightly and my sudden passion for commitment which coincided exponentially with my laying with her, were also just happy accidents. So compelling was her embrace that I found I could not leave my bed while she held me sleeping. For the length of our love affair, I set my alarm one hour before I expected to rise, just as not to miss that precious cuddling.

But one thing gave her completely away from the beginning. Several years she was able to fool me, either repressing it entirely or withholding it until I was deeply slumbering. Once found out, however, she performed it with such passion, perfection, and bliss that her understated denial could not contain conviction.

She sang in her sleep.

I looked upon my little angel, then I looked at the clock. Already, it was time for me to go into another time-scape where my labor was needed, but there she was. I decided that the world could wait five minutes without the service of a vampire paperboy. Using power lest she awake, I lay next to her, holding her body tightly to mine. Comfort passed between us.

Fifteen minutes later, I tore myself away to meet my labor. I walked from the bedroom to the living room where her many paintings hang like a prayer of praise to the Maker of all things. There, in front of me staring back, is my favorite of her works, which is a nod to my favorite of poems. The painting is a landscape with a birch tree, but I felt it to be "my portrait" since my life with her. The birch has an unbent truck. Not so when she found me. You see, my favorite poem is "Birches" by Robert Frost. Perhaps your time spying on me would be better spent looking that poem up on the internet. If you do, you will find a masterpiece in three parts. The first is a tale of breathtaking beauty and natural tragedy. Next is resounding resourcefulness and skill. The last is a monument to reflective triumph and wisdom, which culminates in his last line "one could do worse than be a swinger of birches" but actually means "one could do worse than be a slinger of newspapers."

Newspapers! Lest the pig eat the horse. I'm out the door and off to work.

Once in the van, I'm confronted with the angry faces of twenty-four brownies which should have been twenty-five. My earlier description of them might have left out too much detail. Brownies always seemed to me as if a child drew their features, Although they are entirely brown, their lips, now formed into an angry frown, and eyebrows, now narrowed over their eyes, are darker brown then the rest. Their tongues, now wagging recriminations, are much lighter, almost yellow.

Ramon, the leader, made the most words while pointing to an hourglass shrunk to scale in the "humans around" size.

"Brownies wait for ride to Steward's newspaper barn," he proclaimed. "Brownies wait and wait and wait!"

By "Steward" he meant me, Ed Calkins, the Steward of Tara and most ruthless dictator of all time, but now I feel like I'm being treated like a truant. I'm tempted to kick them out of the van and make them walk the whole way, which is ridiculous as it is ineffective. Brownies don't know the way to the newspaper barn.

Who will blink first? I cross my arms, eying the brownies. They cross their arms, eying me back. Well, this isn't getting any work done.

Starting the van, I put the trans into reverse, but I look back at them before releasing the brake.

"Maybe, I'll make it up to the brownies," I muse aloud "Maybe I'll give each of you one brownie point for being patient…"

The brownies uncrossed their arms but remained suspicious.

"…to off-set the one brownie point each of you lost for yelling at me!"

I'm driving at this point, so they are too busy enjoying the ride to continue their protest of gestures. Some are even shouting and screaming as one might while riding a roller coaster. The roads to my workplace look just as they always did, yet I know without evidence that somewhere the time-scape has changed. I am in a reality where some of the people I've known in life don't exist as if they never existed. The same might be true of people that exist here, but not in my former life. There's no way to tell, of course. The memory changes with the time-scape. I know, for example, that the brownies now look healthier, handsomer, happier, more rested, then they did…when? I don't know at this point.

The newspaper barn, or distribution center, is now in my headlights, and I can see that I'm again in trouble before I can park. I see the unhappy look in one of my wives' eyes about having to wait for me to count the papers off the dock.

Even worse, the brownies expect to go in with me. Policing carriers is hard enough. But having to explaining brownies to those who believe – along with the brownies' consequences of them trying to help - to those that don't is more than I can handle. Fortunately, brownies know they are in an undiscovered land of humans.

"Now is a special time for brownies here," I tell them. "People work, but brownies nap now. Isn't that nice?"

"Brownies nap in big white wheel box?" Ramon asked, referring to my van.

"That's the custom." Before I can open my door, the brownies are cluster snoring. God, I hope no one hears them.

"Good morning, wife number six," I called to her cheerfully, hoping for forgiveness for being late. One of the trucks has already brought papers; Millie could have been bagging them. She notes the promotion from wife seven to wife six, but it doesn't save me a lecture. My human-only wives find it unthinkable to entertain me in bed, but all of them fulfill their marital obligation to nag.

Now Millie is one of the carriers I took with me with when the Daily Post took over the Examiner and made things much worse for people in the industry. Pay cuts, disrespectfulness, and impossible standards were imposed on the remaining contractors who didn't lose their jobs.

Millie is the only one here right now, but I find myself wondering who will be present in this time-scape and who will be absent. For those of you still spying on me instead of studying the Frost poem I recommended, I suppose I'm going to have to explain 'time-scape' and how it works.

You guys are killing me.

This is my first day as a vampire and it's not like I went to vampire school, so I have to figure the whole thing out on the fly. It would help if you stopped trying to put a timeline on this. Nothing in the universe is straight or a line. Time may seem like two opposite vectors joined at a single point in the present, but it's an illusion dependent on creatures with senses such as hearing and sight. Time is nothing more than motion, and the present is a point but has no duration. If you look at any event occurring in the present, you'll discover one of three things; it's actually in the recent past, it's evitable but in the recent future, or parts of it have happened and parts of it will inevitably happen which is as close to the present as living things can get to the here/now.

No, I'm not getting anywhere like this.

Try this. Image a basin of blood which is the history of humanity. Let your soul prick its finger and let a drop of your blood drip into the basin as your gift to future generations. Notice the ripple on the surface. That ripple is your lifetime. Notice the expanding circle wave in all directions moving away from the drop. Your conscious rides the wave from only one perspective, but it doesn't matter, because the view is the same from any side. When I say time-scape, I'm talking about a point of view riding on that ripple which is usually indistinguishable from any other time-scape in a given lifetime.

That changes when vampires abode. When some schmuck

dies but doesn't stop living, all time-scapes that collide with it vary from the others in its lifetime ripple. The past changes, as well as the person's memories to match the new past. A single vampire will disrupt the natural order of past and future until that vampire is destroyed, and everything returns to normal. The basin of blood becomes placid as not to matter. Here's what matters: what was in that drop of blood? Only its contents will appraise the humanity that history serves.

I wouldn't take my word for any of this. Look, it you want to understand life, read more poetry.

By now, all trucks are in and so are most of my carriers. I see the heroes in my life. I see Stan the Mighty, so named by the limerick I composed commemorating his courage in the face of absent carriers. (In other words, he helped me with some down routes.)

The legends of Stan the Mighty,
Leave bedrooms just slightly untidy.
Because of his courage,
The scoundrels discourage,
But the damsels just peel off their nighty.

Now, don't you wish I wrote that about you? Keep wishing, I have high standards for whom I praise in verse, and your insistence to spy on me instead of doing what I told you to do not put you at the top of the list.

You are so unlike the young couple Misty and Thomas, who have two children with athletic aspirations. The older daughter has dance and cheerleading classes, and the younger son needs baseball camps to further his hitting, fielding, and pitching skills. I don't think either parent has had even five hours of sleep since the birth of their first. Misty does the route, but Thomas is always on call to help.

Said Misty, I've a route to complete,
And the snow makes it slow on the street.,
But for winter storm losses,
My snow tiger Thomas is,
The one the worst weather won't beat.

How many papers does your spouse help you deliver?

Then there's the couple John and Melissa Simotes. John is a tall man with a short, gruff manner, but he is actually a good guy. I can tell this by his special bond with my very good buddy, his son John-Peter. He's about two and struts in like he owns the place. Everyone likes him. He tells me that he and his dad are equal partners on the route they usually do together. Today, he's in with his mother Melissa, who looks very tired, and John is nowhere to be seen.

"Don't worry, Uncle Ed," John-Peter assured me. "I'll teach Mother everything she needs to know."

I'll tell you more about John-Peter at a later time when you're more likely to believe that I crafted him myself.

It's a shame really, I think the parents are fighting and might get a divorce. I remember, as if this might be unique to this timescape, that John is a person I truly fear, but that story would need three volumes to tell.

Then, the Goddess walks in with her teen son and daughter. The Goddess, so named when she did me a favor, and so called over the phone where her teens could hear as her phone was on speaker, does lots of favors. Someday, I should compose her myth. Myth-making is a duty of mine as I'm of Irish descent. She would be the goddess of favors, eternal energy, the written word, and newspapers. In this realm, however, she simply has no time as she is both carrier and freelance reporter for the same paper.

"Hey!" I complained loudly enough for her to hear. "I'm not getting enough press coverage! When are you writing my newsletter, 'The Ruthless Times?'"

I do know my place, as I count her papers out and present them to her on my knees. That never seems to get old with her kids, or at least they pretend it doesn't and laugh every time.

"Rise, my elf," she told me. Her children are already busy bagging. A family that delivers together stays together - unless they're Melissa and John.

Now that the papers are passed out, the worst part of my day is before me: opening the yellow manila envelope. It contains all the delivery transgressions of the previous day and for each one, I must answer. Actually, my boss should be doing this; he's the one with the contract to the paper. But I act in his stead, and his boss is well aware of it. What is not known, and I'm not talking, is that me and that boss, whose name is Jake, have a history. Jake pretends he doesn't remember me, but I remember him. I think he's trying to get me fired, or drive me into quitting, but I've done nothing wrong. I not proud of my mistake there, so I don't want to talk about it. Shouldn't you be reading poetry now or walking into a mirror?

The next item will involve a talk with Dennis the Menace. He doesn't look up from his bagging as I talk to him. He's a young man with a rough devil-may-care attitude consistent with a life of deprivation.

"102 Willow got missed again," I tell him evenly.

"So?"

"Five times in the last month. Is there a reason?"

"It's a porch at the end of a long one-way street with no other papers on it. If I don't porch, they call anyway. I don't always have the time."

"Dennis, delivering papers is an important job."

With that, he drops the paper he's bagging, looking at me with a note of incredulity. "No, it's not."

Here's our problem. Dennis gets his news from his phone. In fact, Dennis gets everything from his phone, and can't imagine why anyone would read a rolled piece of paper with no sound or video feeds.

I think of the brownies.

"Dennis, the woman who gets this unimportant paper doesn't have a cell phone. She has a landline phone, but it doesn't ring because no one she knows is alive anymore. She used to watch her TV set that she's had since she got married, but it stopped working when the world went digital and didn't tell her, but she does get a paper. Most days, someone that must know she's still alive throws a paper on her porch that still has a date on it, and the news that happened under it and her biggest hope is that by the time she reads it from cover to cover, that if she hasn't passed that day, she can sleep without thinking about how lonely and unimportant she is. Could you PLEASE make sure she gets a paper?"

I'm embarrassed to have a tear in my eye. I was unprepared for the wash of emotion I got from trying a pep talk. Maybe I'm wondering if I matter. Dennis surprised me with a softer look.

He muttered, "Maybe she should get a dog." But he added, "OK."

37

I tried to train a dog to deliver papers. I told Dennis the story, and he doesn't seem annoyed, but he also doesn't look up as he stuffs newspapers in bags. I hope he'll do as he promised, but I'm checking that address after I finish with my route, the Shoppers, and the brownies.

The Shoppers! Do you know that before the Daily Post conquered, I was an honest man? If I can get the skid of some five thousand Shoppers out to the big wheel box…er…van, maybe the brownies can load it for me.

"I'll bag them as I go," I lied to someone looking at me with a question.

Well, I will bag some of them… and break the law delivering them and break a different law with the rest. I jacked up the skid and pulled it through the warehouse and out to the parking lot where my van is parked. My back is going to be sore if I don't get the brownies to help.

"Nap over?" a brownie asked.

Another one pointed to the Shoppers stacked on the skid. "What?"

I just thought of my answer as I said it.

"Brownies, nap is over, and these papers are how brownies get breakfast. Help me load them into the big white wheel box."

They instantly shrank to just smaller than human size and begin loading. If anyone saw them, I don't know about it. Before I could grab a single bundle, the brownies finished, some huffing and puffing. The van is tightly packed and nearly scraping the ground.

"Now brownies are supposed to catch their breaths while humans get the other papers," I told them.

Moments later, I have my newspapers loaded in the front seat and am ready to attack my workday. At my direction, the brownies start shoving shoppers into small plastic bags. Now, for the first time, the subject of pay comes up.

"For each brownie that does what I ask," I answer confidently, "three brownie points will be given against what is owned to me for the last favor."

They seem happy with that. The payment is for helping me with the newspapers, but they will also collect fees with the seniors they'll assist. It's convenient for me since I make my own currency.

"I am brownie leader," Ramon announced. "So I get more."

"Ramon gets more." I agreed.

"Ramon gets four brownie points?" He held up one hand with four fingers up. Ramon was only brownie that bothered to count, so he took counting very seriously. But I held a hand up with three fingers.

"Ramon gets three brownie points and…Ramon gets to be leader."

Everyone seemed to accept that.

Now it's time for some serious law-breaking. It's three a.m. and I'm hoping to be out of the trailer park before security knows of my dubious undertaking. There are about seven hundred units here, based on the Shoppers allowed for it. Passing seven or eight trailer homes, I throw my first Shopper. I broke the law doing that. I broke a contract by not throwing the other seven.

Newspaper delivery used to be honest work, but some have managed to be dishonest while performing that duty. More than one carrier had taken a paper route in a neighborhood they were casing for burglary. Another once sold his routes newspapers to a nearby news stand, covering up the resulting complaints as just his own incompetence. Others had stolen newspapers from other routes to deliver to people they were secretly billing.

But it wasn't until the Daily Post took over operations that everyone became a crook. The post office used to send out a publication of ads which the publisher called 'The Shopper' and the residents call junk mail. Most residents were mildly annoyed; others were glad to get the coupons. But when the Daily Post undercut the U.S. mail, the Shopper stopped stuffing mailboxes and started polluting driveways. Theoretically, these Shoppers were to be hung on the doorknob, but the fees paid to contractors made that impossible rather than just highly unprofitable.

It's a different challenge when the property is owned by a third party and not the residents. Very early on, management of large apartment complexes disallowed my carriers and me to deliver the Shoppers, so their tenants would complain if they didn't receive them. Several months ago, this massive trailer park joined that challenge. So when the police gave us problems, we were supposed to tell our division mangers, or so the publisher's emails proclaimed. But we clearly saw the consequences to carriers who didn't play along. My division manager, Jake, tells me at least once every time we meet that the Daily Post fired two thirds of its contractors at the merger and intended to fire more than half of the remaining contractors. We were supposed to be grateful that the Post looked the other way about the porch deliveries. So contractors making waves would be the first to go. Also, remember, Jake is gunning for me because we have history he doesn't want known.

But for now, these Shoppers are brownie dispensers. Each intrepid worker is to break into the mobile home, clean the targets rooms, do some outside grooming, and meet me at the park's entrance within the next two hours, all without being detected. This might seem like an impossible task for humans, but brownies are the commandos of cleaning for old folks.

"Whose first?" I called out when I see the unkept glass around my target's mobile home.

"Three brownie points for today's work," the tiny maverick reminds me while shrinking to less than an inch and climbing into the bagged paper I'm about to throw.

"Hang on," I bullseye the porch from my seat in the van.

Fourteen brownies are still in my van when I pull out of the forbidden park. Now, I would throw only newspapers lest I miss the brownie at the rendezvous point. Somewhere on the first route, the brownies finish all the Shoppers I can get away with throwing. I frown at the pile of Shoppers I'm going to throw away. This is the part my boss would rather not know. However, my conscience said otherwise. I always told him how many residences I skipped and how many Shoppers I threw away. So when the trailer park barred me, he saw a chance to cut my pay. I told him that would be my chance to quit. A new understanding emerged from that meeting. So he gave me new instructions.

"Deliver everything you can without getting caught, dispose of the rest without getting caught, and do it all in a way I don't hear about," he said.

The remaining brownies were deployed on my first route. I rode to the rendezvous point where all brownies in their "humans around" size are bragging to each other about their trials and perils of their "break in and clean" mission. They also showed each other the butter, honey, and cream they took, filling small bags from their pockets, as payment in the traditional brownie/elderly arrangement. They don't know it, but none of it is valuable, and most of it is in too small of quantity to miss.

I glanced at my watch. It's too early to pick up the second batch of brownies. So I drove to the very spot where I died yesterday to do the paper-route; I'll never fill in any time-scape it seems. The problem here is that I've got nine targets and ten brownies. Then I remembered Ramon owes four times the brownie points than the others, and I got an idea. After nine throws with tiny passengers, I pulled up to a house that we've been to already. Lights are on in the living room.

"Brownies clean that house," Ramon protests. "Brownies clean and clean and clean."

"Yes, but the old lady that lives there is lonely."

"That's human problem."

"Ramon, you owe more brownie points than anyone. Do you know how many people the old lady sees today?" I held up my hand, ready to count. Ramon did the same.

"Husband? No husband." I kept my hand in a fist as did Ramon. "The husband died many years ago."

"Children?" Ramon asked hopefully.

I shook my head and did not raise a finger.

"People come visit?" he tries and smiles smartly when I raise one finger. He does the same.

"Ramon visits."

"Oohhh, humans so boring!"

"Ramon gets a lot of brownie points." I promised him.

He lifted three fingers, but I showed six. "And six more if Ramon visits another old lady, still sleeping right now.

The unhappy brownie exits the van. "Ramon go, but Steward not wait too long to pick up Ramon."

Now, with the two routes finished, I only have the Shoppers to throw, deploying and picking up brownies as I do. It's past sunrise, but the sky is cloudy, so the cover of dark still allowed me to throw Shoppers without confrontation and the brownies to clean without detection. I have all brownies out of the van when I go back for Ramon.

In front of the house, I actually have to wait for him. In a few minutes, I see him bouncing towards the van.

"Ramon so interesting!" he proclaimed.

"Did Ramon talk to the old lady?"

"Ramon talk and talk and talk."

"Did Ramon listen to the old lady?

He looked confused for a second, then brightened "Next time, old lady talk, Ramon listen."

It's getting lighter and the other brownies need retrieving. I told Ramon that I'm dropping him off to visit another old lady while I pick up the other brownies. Once I have them all, I'll return for him and then we'll dispose pf the extra Shoppers and get the brownies breakfast. But when I parked in front of the house, Ramon gave an evil smile.

"Old lady doesn't believe in brownies," he explained. "Steward visit old lady. Ramon drives big white wheel box to pick up other brownies."

Brownies are remarkable at running and using modern equipment without any knowledge or training. But how would Ramon know about speed-limits? Then I remember I'm in Munsonville where the only cop is the Beulah County sheriff.

"But humans are so boring," I whined as I jump from the driver's seat.

Everyone has at least two natures that can be symbolized by an animal. I am both a pig and a horse. You who are spying still, have seen the pig side of me, but my wife and lover loves the horse most. Horses plow, pigs just eat and get dirty.

Ramon happily drove away. I knocked on the door.

When he picked me up ten minutes later, he had all the other brownies with him. There's a funny difference between humans and brownies about food. Unlike brownies, humans that are thin don't get fat in a single meal and certainly not the reverse. The brownies are thin as rails right now.

The paper recycling center is about ten minutes away from where we threw the last paper. The brownies cut the strapping on the bundles of papers and load them into my beat-up laundry baskets I've stacked up for this purpose. By the time we get to the center, half the papers are packed in those baskets. I patiently wait my turn as there are six loading docks and I'm the eighth driver with Shoppers to scrap.

Many of the other drivers know me for previous newspaper jobs before the Post took over the distribution of all newspapers in the area. His facility is a popular solution to a common problem. In past weeks, I used to dump my extras in paper recycling bins in school and church parking lots, but I caught Jake out one morning searching the container of one of them while I was on my route. Now my hope was that if he took the trouble to catch me, he'd have to deal with all the other contractors doing the same thing.

When it's my turn, I back my van to a large cloth bin reinforced with a light metal frame. Each bin holds about a ton of scrape paper. In no time, I'm dumping the baskets into the bin and throwing the empty basket into the back of my van, where the brownies can reload it without being seen. Unloading alone might take me four hours and a sore back, but this way, I filled the first bin in minutes. The recycler gave me an empty bin before taking the full one to be weighed with a forklift. I'm out of papers when I filled that one. The brownies peek through the rear window as the man in a jump suits counts out two twenty-dollar bills.

I jump in the van and speed off, lest the other people hear the brownies raging at the unfair payment for so much paper. Explaining that this paper is actually money would take hours. In their time-scape money, valuable metals are worth only what the metal is worth. I'm tired of explaining it. It took my hours to explain "writing," so I capitalize on that.

"This paper says, 'brownies get breakfast,'" I announced. "This other paper says, 'Steward gets breakfast.'"

My mythical friends are skeptical.

I know where to feed them, a place where I can bring them in and let them pick out what they want without having to explain anything. Eircheard's Emporium in Jenson (thirty minutes west of Munsonville) is owned and managed by a powerful leprechaun that easily passes for a human, down to his clay pipe and broken teeth. He'll know how to please brownies for a double sawbuck. My companions have nothing to fear from Eircheard, but to me, it's "buyer beware."

I made sure no other customers were in the store before I let the brownies in. Eircheard scolded me because my small friends were making him close his door to other, more promising patrons, but close his doors he did. I gave him the twenty and kept close watch on the value of what he allowed and disallowed.

Eircheard also kept watch as he sat behind the counter, puffing away.

"There are twenty-four brownies," he reported. "Shouldn't there be twenty-five?"

I actually don't know what became of the last brownie. He was there when they were using their unearned brownie points. Eircheard listened to my denial suspiciously. He's not from the same realm as these brownies, so he doesn't trust them. He's from a later time in Tara, when humans were less respectful of magical creatures and sacred hills of Tara in favor of other human structures.

"Does paper say brownies get honey?" they asked Eircheard after selecting butter, soda bread, and jam. He nods that it does. To my count, even the small jar of honey left two dollars and thirty-three cents.

In the back of my mind, I hear a little angel ask about the breeders. What do they get? Aren't they worth at least the change? Isn't bad enough for the females that they are called "breeders" rather than wives?

"Oh, look at pretty rocks!"

A brownie noticed a bag of aquarium stones in the back of the store. To his ancient eye, they looked quite valuable.

"Those magical stones are not for brownies but breeders. They make breeders more beautiful," I fudged. Then looking at Eircheard, I added, "But that's the last thing the paper gives."

Eircheard nodded, "I can deliver them myself, if you give me the coordinates to the time-scape."

Now Eircheard could use the portal here instead of traveling so far. I, of course, decline. There are only two beings I fear, and he's the other.

Joyful and jumping, the brownies take their treasures into the big white wheel box. Honey over bread is like steak and lobster to the sidhe.

We were on our way to Munsonville when it hit me. Do I have a place to live? Homelessness is common among new vampires, but it's hardly a problem. I somehow know that if I can't find a place to lay my undead head, I can always return to the place and time of my death and stay put until it's time to wake. Time-scape required memories always seemed to come as needed, but it's hard to make long-term plans.

Short term plans…did I have money? A vague memory nagged of someone stabbing me with a knife and taking my wallet.

Wasn't I shot? I should eat. I look to where I left the other double sawbuck, but it's gone!

"Steward too fat!" Ramon poked his finger at my belly.

His fingers seemed to puncture the very memory. I wish it were the way it happened, making me guiltless in the eyes of my Little Angel. I'm bleeding, and I look down. This Thornton Times is too bloody to deliver. Where would I get another Thornton Times? Where are my Daily Posts? Or my Munsonville Weeklies? I heard the voice of John telling me not to worry, but it's Ramon.

"Paper should say, 'No food for Steward.' Ramon should keep paper till Steward not so fat."

"Maybe another time," I told myself, then glanced off the road long enough to look at Ramon, "There once was a brownie quite bad. His greed got the Steward real mad…"

"No! No pretty words. Steward gets paper. Brownie no steal babies." Ramon put the twenty on the dashboard.

That's how you do ruthless. I haven't forgot about you there, still spying on me. I've already told you, if you really want to understand Ed Calkins, you have to read, and then reread, Robert Frost's poem. And if you want to believe in Ed Calkins, you have to step through the mirror. Instead, you're going to follow a man and his brownies delivering papers? Can you see why I think you have too much time on your hands?

OK, I'll be merciful. If you really want to, I'll let you watch me eat without making fun of you. Not so with the brownies, I realize. So before I can head to Sue's Diner in Munsonville, I have to drive in the opposite direction to the Happy Hunting Grounds funeral parlor in Thornton, about an hour west from Jenson.

By the time I get there, it's afternoon and the place is conducting a funeral, but brownies are really good at sneaking in somewhere. They know where the portal is (in the door mirror of the women's restroom), which might be a problem if anyone was ever brave enough to use it. I pull up under the pretense that I'm redelivering a newspaper. The funeral staff waves me away before I can get out of the van, but the brownies are gone.

Now, you get to watch me eat. Are you happy? I drive back to Munsonville and parked in front of Sue's Diner. Once inside, I realized I don't want to be seated.

"Hello, number eleven," I charmed the hostess/manager,

45

whom I married when she was waiting tables. See what happens when you marry Ed Calkins? But don't underestimate her. She used to work for a veterinarian in Shelby (this is her retirement job), and she is very, very smart.

"Hello, husband three, the only husband I don't hate now. Can I get you a seat? I've got something to tell you, and I think it's important."

"Actually, I wanted a 'to go' order, liver, hold the onion. Could I possibly get it raw? I'm going to cook it much later."

"Ed, I can't sell raw food."

"Extra rare then?"

"That I can do. You've been working on that program too hard. Are you getting enough sleep?"

Suddenly, I knew where I lived. It's a studio apartment within walking distance from here. I also know the apartment is somehow bigger on the inside then on the outside. I know, too, that I am hiding the location from everyone expect Ruthie, wife number eleven, and even she is not to see the inside.

As I'm standing there, she's telling me about a man on the phone waiting for his food earlier this morning. She heard the name, "Ed Calkins" and started eavesdropping. He was bragging that he busted me, something about Shoppers found in a dumpster in my area. She'd heard him say, "We're going to make an example out of this guy," but his boss was objecting loud enough to be heard, saying that anyone can dump anything in someone else's area and that only the serial numbers could prove it was Ed. Later a phone call came while he was eating. Apparently, they sent someone to check those papers and it was a different account, so they dropped it. The guy, who must have been deaf because his phone was turned up quite loudly, tried to insist that Ed was also dumping for other accounts, and this was one of them. The other voice called the man Jake and said it was too far of a reach, that if police were going to get involved, they would want evidence.

"Watch your back, husband," Ruthie concluded. "These guys are really out to get you. What did you do to them?"

"I know too much."

When I was alive, I feared Jake would have to disgrace me, not just get rid of me. But now that I was a vampire, I could easily deal with him. I wouldn't bite him, he's not my type, but I could bite his wife or mistress, change them into vampires, and compel them to make his life miserable. I would have much fun exposing him as the hypocrite he always was. I can only wish Trudy would be here to see that happen.

But the voice of my Little Angel is as much a part of me as my being a vampire. She wouldn't approve. More than that, subjugating people into vampires isn't healthy, as most vampires are killed by other vampires, and no one has better a motive then a subjugated vampire. Better I write his limerick in every bathroom stall I find until the words became so popular that, when historians seek its origin, they will trace it to the ruthless Ed Calkins, and Jake's name will live in infamy.

Said the madam, the man's sword is a wick,
His stench makes my prostitutes sick.
With the way he appalls
They'd have kicked in his balls.
Except for finding just no place to kick.

Yeah, let history right things. I'll set the brownies to writing in bathrooms…after I teach them to write. I'll have to teach them what writing is first. I'm in no hurry.

Ruthie gave me a hug as she handed me my food. I smelled her neck and felt an urge stronger than I've ever felt. Hell, if I maul her, I'll be "Ruth-less." Listen, ye who spy on me. When I make a joke, you laugh. Never mind, I can't even laugh at that one.

Almost reflexively, I drove to my secret studio apartment. After parking the van, I closed my eyes so you can't see where this apartment is. I've dreaded this moment, for I'm about to learn who is missing from my life in this time-scape, which will be my home in hiding for the rest of my existence. I won't remember people unimportant to me, but those that have become a part of me, such as my Little Angel, Trudy, my son, my long time roommate, and any that I really could call close; they would be free of my vampire time disruption. I will be very lonely, I know.

John tried reassuring me as he drained my blood. Vampires throw great parties, he said, and I'll meet new friends and enemies. As a vampire, the enemies will be more fun than the friends. But I know already that I don't have time for parties right now, that I'm working on something so secretive, it's a secret even from John.

I looked around my one-room apartment and saw nothing but a bed, dresser, and closet with few clothes. I know I have more things than this. Then I see the full-length mirror. Well, to you it's a mirror, to me it's a portal. I can see the desk and computer tower on the other side. Oh, yeah!

With hesitating, I stepped into the mirror, a narrow, flashing prism with bouncing rainbow light waves against tens of transparent sides. Walking through the portal made the view of my bed go away, but I'll find it when I need it. Eventually a hole of illumination appeared at the portal's far end, a chasm that expanded and brightened as I neared the exit.

The computer is off. I cold-booted it, and the monitor displayed "HHG." I know exactly where I am and it's not "now." I'm in the basement of Happy Hunting Grounds, which has equipment for embalming, but what it's actually used for would surprise you.

There's a vb6 editor and compiler on this machine with a recent project in the cache. The code refers to subdirectories with pictures in them. What kind of demented pervert is working on this? My God, this is disgraceful!

"Vampires need to feed," some voice in my head is defending itself or something else. I compiled and ran the user interface to learn more, and then I blushed at my shameful arousal. The graphic interface shows the pornography - for psychopaths.

But what's this other code? It's another front-end graphic interface. Programs of this type have a front end and a back end, but why two front ends? What kind of darkness is this?

A particular evil is …well, very particular and evilly wants me to rule the Kingdom of the Damned. As king, I would bring peace and harmony to all the vampires of the world. I alone could create a vampire utopia. Ending the petit feuds among them, I could unite all undead creatures to a common cause and create a standard of living that would enrich all among the shadow realms as a benevolent overlord would naturally do.

The program I'm writing will ensure that never happens.

My ruthless smile widened. I bit into my very rare liver like it was the very neck of Ruthie.

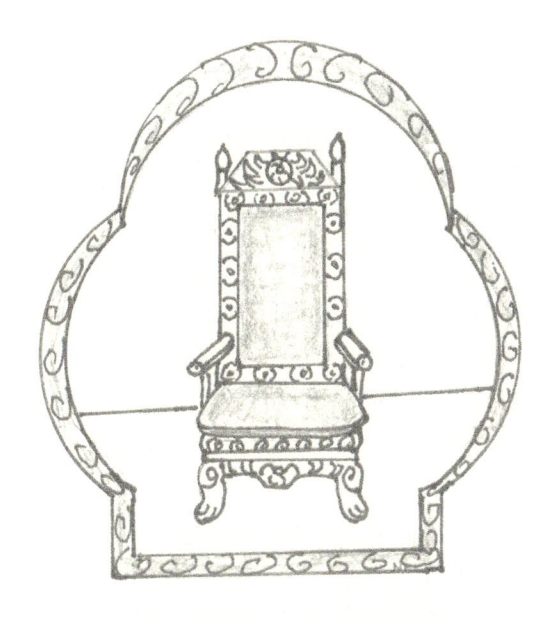

CHAPTER 3: MIRROR

The mirror faced the jeweled throne, reflecting the disappointment of the one gazing into it. It was the throne that owned the ivory, gold, and gems that patterned its recreated design; its occupant, despite appearances, owned only her darkness.

None of it was real.

Reflection, reflex, reaction… what did it mean or matter, yet the image the mirror gave was a metaphor of her existence. She was not quite a queen; well, any more than she was a cop or any of the other endeavors or careers that she had tossed herself into over the years.

"My Queen." The voice of the shortish man had the slightest hint of an Irish accent "Is there anything…"

"My medication and a drink." She refused to look at him. Even a look would have given him kindness, and kindness took energy. However, she did add, "Get yourself one too."

"But if I'm driving…"

"I'm not going to the wake."

To this, the smallish man stood silently in his bathrobe, waiting dutifully. It was what she expected of him - but not what she needed. She would not go to the wake tonight because she had stood up for the wedding twenty years ago, and it would take all the liquor in two bottles to forget that the wedding should have been hers. Their lives should have been different, but they went in opposite directions. He never had the confidence to match his intelligence and imagination. He took a mundane job. She could have changed that about him, maybe, but she shot him instead.

The problem was she blacked out before she fired.

'Honest, officer, I have no idea what this smoking gun is doing in my right hand. That's right, Your Honor, I had no plans to murder my best friend. I just happened to have an unauthorized 44 with me because my patrol is evil with scary specters, and I might have to shoot at something I can't put in a report. Why did I get so drunk? Well, I knew I had to work that patrol, and I'm too much of a coward to do that sober."

Maybe something evil possessed her. She could insist on that if she had the energy to insist. She could go to the hospital, too. Oh, they would help her with a barrage of tests and diagnoses ranging from hypothyroidism to diabetes. In a mad rush to save her, they might pump her stomach, believing she was experiencing alcohol poisoning. They might stab her with an EpiPen if they thought her swollen tongue was the result of allergies.

Or they would treat her for depression which meant a room (instead of a bed) and weeks (instead of days) of pointless therapies and ineffective drugs. Getting in was easy. Being arrested in a mental health facility was so cliché.

Instead, her fate was elsewhere tonight. It was somewhere behind that cursed mirror that reported a leather clad costume too slight and tight on flabby aged flesh on the side that she could see. Her pain came from back in time. It would stay there with her until she could move again…until she could care again…but that would be too late.

Heavy, short, and rough-faced, Trudy was never pretty to boys or men, but she'd always been attractive. She had longish brown hair, heavy breasts, and a constant problem with her weight. Her best feature, she knew, even if her lovers never realized it, was her haunting grey eyes. She could almost hypnotize potential lovers with a direct stare.

Now, she stared back. What was speaking to her? Was it the alcohol or the depression? Both were so predicable until two nights ago. The reflection asked her unkindly what it was that she did to get a third drink. Her childhood molester always looked like her father. Alcohol or the alcoholic...it became hard to tell the difference.

"I was eleven years old, for God's sake."

"Bathrobe" looked more upset then confused, but he knelt at her side as if he were still playing a game.

She had spoken rightly. Still, she was an alcoholic even then, taking a profit in a silent conspiracy that no one would ever imagine. Trudy was truth. Alcohol made her ballsy enough to speak the unspeakable.

Answer the question, poet!

In a sea of pain, she didn't want the ability to speak at all. Every part of her body ached right now. Pills might help, but they could not be predicted. Alcohol was sure.

The cause and solution to every problem...that's what was said. It was true. If Trudy wanted nothing to do with drinking, she wouldn't have lost her innocence as the slightest protest would have spooked the cowardly demon away.

Answer poet!

She needed more liquor first...both now and then. Now was the late fall of 2008, two days after she shot her best friend and didn't know why. Somehow, that wasn't as important as then, the spring of 1969 when no one would believe her if she spoke of how someone her age got so drunk. The first two were always cheap glasses of wine. "A ladies drink," her father told her. But the third had to be bought. It seemed ridiculous at first. Such a thing for such a small glass. Scotch is an acquired taste for men. Tastes were the worst. Eddie had told her once, during an episode of weakness, trust, and honesty, that it was the smell of old men that pestered him. Eddie never had the first two drinks. Now, she mandated more. To stop the screaming of every nerve in her body and every bullet like memory in her mind, it would take drinking so much that she might vomit without realizing it.

Did he blame himself as weak-willed? Her father was never really a man. He did fault her for failing to resist as might a grown woman. When her mother's marriage ended, he left an angry, jealous ex-wife and a daughter who knew well the currency of not resisting. By the time she was fourteen, she fell in love with a man who took her home.

She was not the prettiest girl in her class, and classmates often told her this in less than kind ways. But while the bravest of the pretty girls were "giving in" to heavy petting in back seats of rusty cars that boys could afford, Trudy was not resisting in the bedroom of a twenty-six-year-old married man who could afford restaurants, concert tickets, and a pregnant wife too afraid of divorce to protest the affair. Sometimes he even made that wife watch.

"That's when it started," she muttered to the mirror. It was all reflex after that, doing men as she had learned to do and reacting to the thrill, frustration, and emptiness that each one left in turn... except for him. She was never in love with him, it never went that far. Yes, he had wanted her, but he never pushed enough so that she could stop resisting.

"Answer or have me not!"

It was the untasted Scotch that was talking. Now she was sure.

"Oral...a gulp of Scotch for a swallow of my own father. I had to swallow before the gulp. You are a chaser. Did you know that before I told you?"

"Trudy, are you alright?"

The man in the bathrobe had called her "Trudy," which lifted hope and her head. The queen in the mirror wasn't crying. She was far too gone for that. The short, caring man beside it was expected to earn rebuke. But the reflex came before realization.

"Get the good pills and put the Scotch on the nightstand."

He might have protested - too many pills mixed with drinks but he did as he was told. Lovers do, friends never do. The night she met Ed Calkins, he was bleeding, and she was crying. Her lover's wife finally told the twenty-six-year-old, "me or her," and she got shown the door. Eddie had been beaten by her mother's lover. She didn't want him there but he wouldn't leave, saying he was in the park first. She tried to cover her tears by insulting him, and he retaliated by criticizing her insults. Somewhere in all of that, they must have realized that they were both broken kids. They talked all night until the sun the rose and it was time for school.

It would be years later before they knew the worst of it. As close as they were, those sorts of things just didn't happen. No one believed it, not even the ones it happened to.

He was still there. In the dim light, it looked like only a

bathrobe stood there.

"Go. You're dismissed...only break the bottle in the morning or at least be disrespectful when you throw the bottle of nothing into the trash."

She didn't need to tell Bathrobe twice. The Scotch stopped asking questions when she took the first gulp.

Alone, she could forget the early morning hours of his last day alive. Auxiliary police were needed in Beulah County, so she was on duty, but it wasn't she that responded to the call that lead to the body and search of the bullet. She was patrolling too far away. Hopefully, that might keep her out of court. "Hopefully" was not the word for the situation.

How many men and boys did she deal with? Hell, by the time they were twenty-one, she had been married twice while trying to get rid of number two so she could wed number three. That was the first time he joked, "Dibbs on being number four." But Eddie was a virgin then. Throughout high school, he was on track to become a Catholic priest. They were a strange pair back then, always together when she wasn't with her lovers, and he didn't have his nose in a Bible. Poetry was their common interest. She wrote, he read and wrote. For a time, the poetic works were the secret between them.

College and a girlfriend changed his priesthood ambitions, even though the girl was casual, and Eddie stayed inexperienced. He was still the clueless, lovable clod who couldn't get a date by himself if his life depended on it. Trudy went out of her way to fix him up with some girl that might give him some experience. He always found a way to screw it up.

By then, he had some hippie-infested ideas about free love and open marriage. Other people could never tell when he was kidding about it, but Trudy knew where his ideas were coming from. Nobody in Eddie's orbit actually stayed together or remained faithful. Certainly, their parents didn't, and neither did Trudy nor her husbands and lovers. Eddie claimed that marriages are a series of sentences that should be severed concurrently rather than consecutively, and the one with the most at one time wins the game. Why on earth could Eddie not find a girl? More than once, he would follow being introduced to a woman or girl with, "Will you marry me?" It was funny...the first six times anyway.

Number three lasted less than a month, even though the

divorce took the next five years. Trudy left one night for a truck stop and fifty dollars, hoping to get as far away from home as she could. Eddie got the call collect from Tampa Bay, where a trucker took all her money and left her in a parking lot after trying to rape her. He drove through the night and got there eighteen hours later, just as the sun was rising. Trudy couldn't go home, and Eddie was in a point at his life where he had nothing to lose, so they both took jobs at a Howard Johnson's and rented a place nearby.

Two weeks into the lease, Trudy started dating a cook she had first taken for a dandy boy. He was blond, smallish, shy in the way a cowboy might be. He was cute, but he turned out to be incapable of telling the truth about anything. Trudy thought she found number four and convinced Danny to go back to Munsonville with her. Danny: what a liar he turned out to be.

But the plan wasn't to leave left Eddie with a lease he couldn't afford by himself, so Trudy was determined to find him a roommate with benefits. She didn't need to look far. On her way to give notice to Howard Johnson's, she noticed a girl with her thumb out and a suitcase at her feet. Trudy knew the look of a girl hoping to move her problems into a love nest. What happens to a runaway when she's too old to run away? The blonde had no money, job, or boyfriend. Trudy had all the answers. Introducing her replacement to management, she pocketed her last paycheck. Then she drove Laura to see her new apartment, complete with roommate.

"I don't have to sleep with him?" Laura asked.

No, you don't, but you will. She did, and that should have been where the Trudy and Eddie story ended.

The damn mirror! Mirrors, minions, and manipulations all closed in on how it would end. The blood spatter would point to a bullet. By now, they had that bullet and would look for a gun and then the gun's owner, if she were lucky. She couldn't report finding the gun, of course, but if someone else did…maybe somewhere near the site. That was a problem now… she should be frantic about it instead of depressed to the point of paralysis. She was trapped at the wrong end of her depressive life. The gun needed to be somewhere else where someone could find it later and without any prints. That was a problem.

The gun was on the dresser. It had her prints and the trace of powder on her clothes would tell any self-respecting sniff dog that she fired it last.

But nothing was going to move tonight. At best, maybe ten days from now, the needle might move towards action. Maybe by then she'd be able to pick up the phone and explain to the department why she hadn't come to work, why she hadn't answered the phone, or picked herself off the chair.

The good pills were on the nightstand next to the Scotch that so taunted her. Maybe one more and a swig might zombie her way to get rid of the gun. Maybe a gulp and swallow would be enough to make a lifesaving toss of the gun into a river that would carry it from its manic shooter. Then time would out her as unqualified for the force but dismiss her as a suspect. Maybe time will teach her that she did it by, for, and with love.

Her throat was thick, but she gulped and swallowed.

That should have been the last thing Trudy ever did.

CHAPTER 4: ROAD TRIP BAR

When a poet dreams, is it just a dream? Trudy was on a road trip to the end of her life and, whenever you're on a trip, you stop at a bar. That's why they call it a roadside bar. But Trudy's dream put her on the wrong side of that bar in some western ghost town saloon in the deep of a desert. The ghosts were still drinking.

It was high noon by the looks of the place. Codgers wearing cowboy hats drank because they had nowhere to be, nothing to do, and next to no money to do it with. Great! The barmaid of an old man's bar was as dreary as the faded wooden bar and stools. She put her back to the bar to scan the bottles for signs of a night life. Near empty bottles, unwashed glasses, or the spill stains of last night's rush would have confirmed that the young still owned sunset.

She heard the swinging doors but didn't see who swung them. Then, through the mirror, she saw the young, bearded cowboy stride toward the bar. She turned, expecting that the handsome red beard might not be there. He tipped his hat and handed her a piece of paper.

"Voucher for One Last Meal. Redeemable Any Time Before Holder Hangs."

Something wasn't right. The youth looked the part of a western film actor, but something was out of character. He was too young, and his complexion didn't fit.

"Don't I like a red-haired Clint Eastwood?"

"No. but I think the hair goes great with the green-tinted skin."

The voice was perfect, soft and steady like the films that made her swoon when she was much younger. Cowboy hat and poncho framed arms and chest: slim, solid, and steady. Long fingered hands rested with ease near the pistols, left and right, in his gun belt. He seemed to nod ever so slightly at his weapons at the ready.

But Trudy only needed one. It hung comfortably on the holster of the corset of her western saloon-type dress. Even a young Clint Eastwood would be no match for her.

"If I shoot you, I still have to hang you." Trudy told him sympathetically. "What will you have?"

"Are you the town hangman?"

He looked right into her eyes as if trying to prove he wasn't afraid. Trudy returned the look with less harshness.

"Hangwoman," she corrected. She turned her back as she looked for evidence that a place like this would have a kitchen, let alone serve steak and lobster. Just left of the mirror was the slit in the wall where the cook received ticket orders and passed plated food.

"Mushroom stew."

The voice at her back was low, sure, and slow. She turned to face him. Surely a last meal should be better than that. Anything she might have suggested died on her lips as the cowboy seemed to be nodding to the cook. The sound of pots moving insinuated the dish was in stock.

He nodded slightly to his right, referring to the other drinkers. "Death row?"

She looked to her left, down the row of drinkers four deep that hadn't needed a refill in the time her dream provided. Each drink, though different in color and glass shape, was closer to empty then the next. Each man was more decrepit.

"Yeah, things happen slowly here…except hanging of course."

He didn't answer. How do you make conversation with a man whose trademark is near silence?

"Strange town," he finally said. "Aren't you afraid I'll run away? I mean, this being your dream and all."

Trudy answered with a weary sincerity.

"Look, honey, it's a hundred miles of desert to the west, east, north, and south. You don't want to feed the buzzards. And the town? The only part of it you haven't seen is the gallows they are building. You can die of thirst, boredom, or at the end of a rope. My money is on you being here for your date with my rope. Sorry. Why am I hanging you anyway?"

"Same as you. I killed Ed Calkins."

"Any chance of an appeal? Normally, I hang as soon as they build the gallows, but I can drag my feet; come on kid, you've got to talk to me."

He shrugged. "No appeal. Could wait till I'm eighteen though."

"When's that?"

"Two days."

"Yeah, I'll wait. Sorry. Happy Birthday." Trudy choked out the last three words, knowing none were the right response. It was some piece to a puzzle that she didn't know where to place. She should do something for this kid besides hang him, but she couldn't find the right thing.

He looked just slightly nervous now, or was it boredom? His eyes wandered as she studied his face. Damn, where is that mushroom stew? An idea came to her.

"How about a drink on the house?"

"Too young, ma'am, but I do thank you for offering."

"Honey, you're going to miss a lot of things, not all of them good. I don't want you to miss your first drink."

She scanned the row of bottles for something special to give the condemned youth, found it, and poured it into a shot glass.

"Small glass," he noted.

"Mighty powerful whiskey needs a short glass. They call it a 'shot glass.'"

"Expensive?"

Trudy nodded while carefully pouring. A notion popped into her brain. She grabbed a second shot glass and poured one for her.

Cautiously, Clint lifted the shot to his lips and poured till he emptied the glass. Trudy saw the agony in his eyes just before he sprayed the offending liquid out of his mouth and onto her.

"Terrible stuff…get me something to wash it out."

"Cherry soda?"

"Yes, anything. I see why they call it a shot. How do you drink this stuff?"

As she placed a bottle of soda in front of him, Trudy muttered, "Often and in good company, which sometime means 'alone.'"

The mushroom stew filled a huge bowl that might feed even a young man for the two days he had left. Trudy placed it in front of him, watching his delight. Spooning through the meal, and washing it down with the cherry soda, he looked like a child in a candy store.

Suddenly, he froze.

"What's wrong, kid?"

Clint looked straight into Trudy's eyes in a way that might have made her pant. Then he said something unexpected: "I'm afraid."

To that, she hugged him. The bar, stew, and soda should have blocked the way, but physical law has no dominion in dreams. The hug was full, long, and pressing. It seemed to make him feel a little better. It definitely made Trudy feel better.

After the hug, the previous situation returned. Clint spooned his stew, and Trudy fumbled for conversation. Then she remembered the other shot for her. The effect seemed instantaneous on her first gulp.

"So, kid, why did you kill Ed Calkins?" Trudy broke.

"He was being too ruthless."

Now it was Trudy's turn to spray him.

"Must be a custom to spit whiskey here," Clint said, unoffended, as he grabbed a napkin off the bar and wiped his face.

"In what way was that guy ever ruthless? Was this over some girl?"

Clint nodded solemnly.

"He won't let you have her?"

"He wouldn't let any boy have her or any of the others."

"So this is over several girls?"

Clint shrugged. "Several, but one in particular."

"And you were particular with her," she persisted.

"Don't rightly know if 'particular' means something

Biblical, ma'am, but I never did more than kiss her. I'm still a virgin. Before that, I was a wood sprite…Glorna is my name, but you can call me Clint if you want. I also answer to John-Peter."

Trudy sighed. "There's a lot of things you're going to miss, but that shouldn't be one of them. If you want to meet me around the back of this place, I'm sure no one will miss us."

"Mighty kind of you to offer, if you're offering, but with me being so young and you being so old, it would be too gross, don't you think?"

Of course the kid was right. She'd forgotten that she was middle age. Uncomfortable silence seemed the rule in this place. She listened to the munching of mushrooms, coughing of the elderly, and throat clearing of the aged drinkers. One of them called to her as if to break the excitement. He had finished his drink and was ready for another.

"Hey, Bunny," he croaked out. "Is that the other guy that killed Ed Calkins and didn't get away with it like you did?"

Trudy tried to sparkle for the old toad.

"There's still time," she winked while mixing his glass. It worked. He left her a dime.

As she picked it up, she noticed Clint watching in a way that made her believe he'd heard the question. Wait a minute, what could the green-tinted skin mean? Didn't she lose a brother she never met when he was eighteen? Or did he symbolize her Irish father if he hadn't been an alcoholic? Maybe the kid was Eddie himself, but then how could he be hanging for killing him?

"Begging the lady's pardon," Clint/Glorna called out. He was ready for another cherry soda. She fished a bottle out of the iced box and popped the lid off. As she did this, Clint unexpectedly said, "One shouldn't analyze a dream while having it anymore then analyzing a poem while creating it. Better to first have the whole dream and write all the words that might fit. Then, only after that, you can fit the parts or words until the whole thing makes sense."

"That's the way Eddie wrote poems," Trudy mused. "Back in the day, he was quite a poet."

"You mean Ed Calkins? He made limericks, bad limericks, and he never wrote anything down."

"Our 'Ed Calkins' always had a hard time writing things down. I used to correct his spelling when he showed me his work."

Clint, who didn't seem the type to ever be surprised, seemed astonished.

"Are you sure we're talking about the same Ed Calkins, ma'am? I reckon the whole dream would make more sense if we weren't."

"Kid, sometimes the same person just isn't the same anymore. Eddie stopped writing when he started agreeing with you, that his poems were terrible, I mean."

Clint/Glorna pondered this. "So why did you kill him?"

Trudy sighed. For a moment, she thought she was going to cry.

"It's complicated." she said with another sigh.

"I suppose it's as complicated as how could we both kill him but not at the same time. Seems to me the one that killed him first didn't leave it to the other. Now I seem to remember that he was walking around when I did him. So I must have killed him first."

"An interesting point, in the vagueness of space-time; what event happened first is dependent on perspective. One being first, the other being first, or both events happening at the same time is both true and false."

"Hard to buy that, begging your pardon. When two gunfighters face each other and one drops, it's hard not to say the other one who didn't drop, drew first."

Trudy sighed and shook her head sadly. "So many young men die not understanding a gun fight isn't about who drew first, but who shot last. I shot four of them myself once. Didn't kill any. You?"

"Nah, never been in a gun fight. Ed Calkins doesn't count because he only had limericks. He did get a few of them off before I ended it. Still doesn't explain why you killed the paper slinger."

"Kid, it's just too complicated for a kid that's never been in a gun fight or made love to a woman to understand. It's a complicated story with too much sex, violence, and, well, complications for a boy your age. Read poetry and stay in school. Let's just drop it."

It wasn't till she finished speaking that Trudy realized how late that advice was.

But the kid wasn't finished. "If you had to summarize all the complications, what would you say in a sentence or less?"

"I killed him because I loved him. I know 'because' doesn't seem to belong between those two facts. I know that I shot him with as much love as a bullet can bring."

"Ma'am if we were making a poem, I could work with 'I killed because I loved,' but how does one shoot another with love?"

Trudy smiled grimly. "First of all, you shoot him before he starts the paper route he doesn't want to do."

There might have been a joke in there, but no one laughed.

"I've thrown a few papers myself when I was a kid named John-Peter. You?" Clint/Glorna was trying to break the solemn mood but did the reverse.

"Only once, but I don't want to talk about it."

"But you said it. I heard you and it sounds…interesting. You said, 'as much love as a bullet can bring.' Ma'am, is there something you know that I might be too young to understand?"

Trudy leaned in as close to Clint's face as she could be without kissing him and spoke in a low voice.

"Kid, you don't want to know about a love bullet, do you? You want to know about a love rope. Yes, I do it that way. I'm going to hang you with all the love anyone could give a condemned boy."

"I can't imagine," Clint pondered. "But it does make me look forward to the whole thing in a curious sort of way. Anyway, I'm finished with my stew, and you've had your drink. I reckon the only thing left is to walk you outside this place…"

"But I'm too old."

"Not that, ma'am. I'm going to play in the desert, and you've got to get to your next stop on your road trip. I'm just offering to cross the street. I'll meet you at the scaffold in two days."

"Helping the old lady across the street, just what any woman would want to hear…wait, I'm not going!"

"You've got to go, remember. You don't have to go home but you can't stay here."

"I'm not going back to the day Ed Calkins won the lottery!"

"Well, that's all very confusing, seeing the man I knew never had much money, but your next stop is to your therapist. By the way you're talking, you could use her guidance to sort out those complications that made you kill someone you loved."

It was her advice. She was the one that said she should do it.

"Kill Ed Calkins."
"Roslyn the Rapist!"

CHAPTER 5: THE "WHY" CHROMOSONE

"How's my little murderer?"

The woman who asked seemed too old for her page boy hair cut but looked comfortable in her pinstriped dress suit. The leather chair behind the oak wood desk seemed too comfortable to match the three identical chairs in front of it. The arrangement was pretentious, of course. One chair was for the youthful, rebellious patient; the other two were for the parents. Back when Dr. Roslyn was a certified child psychologist, none of her clients were from two-parent homes, and the first thing she did was send the parent away to the outer office.

Everything was as Trudy remembered it except for the large mirror over the doctor's desk that appeared to be looking at her.

Trudy first started therapy after a church pastor referred Trudy's mother to a psychologist who went by her first name and specialized in troubled teen girls. In Trudy's mother's mind, sessions would amount to a psychological version of a woodshed, complete with lectures about how to stop making her mother's life miserable.

Mom never learned the truth.

Sixteen years after Trudy's mom decided, against Dr Roslyn's advice, that Trudy had enough treatment, which was four years after her mom's dementia, law enforcement discovered Dr Roslyn's controversial methods, and she went to jail for the better part of five years as a sex offender.

"Girls like you want to feel better, but they don't want to pay their therapist or do the work. Still, I suppose it's convenient to have a therapist who is not legally allowed to practice; otherwise I'd be compelled to turn you in. Why are you here, Trudy?"

A resigned voice answered. "I want to know why I killed him."

"Do you intend to turn yourself in? I don't think the department will buy the 'I killed him because I loved him thing.' Tell me the last thing you thought of before you pulled the trigger."

Trudy couldn't. It was hard to explain to this woman why, although it was simple enough. She was drinking a lot before her patrol started, and she drank more while she was on it. She blacked out. The last thing she remembered was seeing the white van that could only be Ed Calkins on some paper route. The next thing she remembered was getting ready for bed, certain that she'd shot him, and feeling that he was in a better place. Somehow, she knew that she didn't fire her service 38. But she had loaded Bathrobe's 44 before the patrol, and that 44 was empty.

Now, as she endured the predictable "I told you so" about her problems with the bottle, Trudy wished she were drinking instead of dreaming. Forget the support groups. Dr. Roslyn called them "health on the cheap from drunks who didn't really want to get better in the first place." Trudy heard that lecture while holding a phone and staring at the doctor-turned-inmate through a glass window. For all her flaws, Dr. Roslyn could cut through Trudy's denials and misdirection to blurt out the bare truth. After Dr. Roslyn got out, Trudy saw her for informal therapy for a much lower fee. Dr. Roslyn openly resented that. Trudy openly resented her.

After the lecture, came the question: 'Why did you bring another gun with you if you didn't know you'd be running into Ed Calkins?"

The true answer was easier to explain to Roslyn then it would be to police. Trudy's patrol had an evil, supernatural feeling about it, and the other officers wanted no part of it. Fog appeared, wildlife spooked, and cries that could only be wild also seemed far too human. No one acknowledged it, but Trudy was certain she got the patrol because she had the lowest rank. Her lowest ranking meant lowest paid, the only reason the department kept her when it let the other officers go. Of course, Trudy couldn't admit this, but if she fired her service pistol at a ghost, she'd have no way to explain it. So Trudy always took Bathrobe's 44 with her when she patrolled alone.

"I think the black-out was very convenient, a smoke screen to cover what you didn't want to face," Dr. Roslyn said.

"You told me to kill him!"

"So, it's my fault?" Roslyn mocked with a turn of her head. "I told you to imagine that he was dead and to stay away from him. Trudy, stop the blame and start accepting responsibility. No one made you pull the trigger. No one made you come back to me and ask for help. Did you black out the time you called this emotional vampire after he won the lottery, and you vowed never to talk to him again?"

"I've told you! Eddie winning the lottery is an off-limits topic!"

"Then what were you thinking when you stood up for his wedding? Men do things, Trudy. It's in their nature to lie and cheat. They don't need a reason. It's in their DNA. And this Ed Calkins never required sex from you. He lives in a dream world where his imagination is reality. All he needed from you is the details of your sex life, not to support you, but as food for his sexual fantasy. Of all women, you know this. I told you to stay away, and it should be reason enough to avoid the pain. What were you feeling when you called him in the middle of the night two years after?"

"I had a flat tire. I was thinking that he would be waking up anyway, and I had no one else to call."

"And of all the many, many, many men you've had through the years, you called the only one that you knew had a woman in his life. Why? It's not just a question; it's also the chromosome and the answer. So, I ask again, and I expect an answer without the attitude: What were you thinking?"

"What were *you* thinking? I was fourteen when you first stuck your hand down my pants."

Roslyn jumped to her feet, pointed, and shouted, "And I was thirteen when I got married. Don't try to tell me that you were too young and inexperienced to know what was going on! How many boys had you been with at that point? How many men? Did it change your life to have, for once, someone who knew HOW to touch you? Don't deny it! The fact is, you're here with me, and I don't care what anyone says!"

They'd reached this impasse many times. Trudy couldn't dispute anything Roslyn said, but she still knew Roslyn was wrong. Whenever Trudy came back to her, it was with the understanding that no touching would happen without a criminal complaint.

"A woman always returns to her abuser," Trudy recited emotionlessly.

"Yes."

Both knew the disagreement behind the agreement. Trudy meant Dr. Roslyn. Dr. Roslyn meant anyone to which Trudy attached herself that owned a 'Y' chromosome.

Calm now, the doctor sat back in her chair.

"We don't have to talk about the lottery. Just tell yourself what you were feeling after he did. Were you angry? Sad? Jealous? Relived?"

Trudy said nothing. She had drawn the line on this topic and intended to leave very soon if it didn't change. Still, the lottery was the strongest sticking point she had with Eddie. Perhaps it did have something to do with her killing him.

"I'm going with 'jealous,'" Dr. Roslyn said. "Can you see where I'm going with it?"

"No."

"You don't deny you were jealous. Were you jealous of him?"

"I can't deny that. He was married, had a son that loved him, and had a stable, though not incredible, career that he didn't mind. Despite his low-paying jobs, he had a financial stability that I never achieved."

"Well then, let's reason this out. He told you that the best thing that ever happened to him was marrying his wife. He told you that after that 'thing' we don't talk about. If it were his son you wanted or his marriage, you'd have shot his wife and replaced her as the new best thing that ever happened. The same goes for his money. But you didn't shoot her, you shot him."

"So… what did I want, his paper route?"

"You wanted his wife."

Trudy grew quiet. Something about that made a lot of sense. What if she'd had Nalla instead of Eddie? The ambiguity of the question seemed apropos.

A chill rose in the office. Dr. Roslyn studied her dispassionately. Trouble, Trudy! Run!

It was that disrespectful bottle of Scotch talking again and not making any sense. Why would it? She'd drunk the better part.

"I can help you, Trudy," the good doctor promised in a way that meant she expected something in return. "I can fix this whole thing, so you'll never spend one day in prison or court. We needn't come to an agreement on this as I am quite capable of taking what I need from you…

OK, bottle of Scotch…I could use your help right now. Make me not care. Make me so numb that I cut the deal I can't refuse.

I'll call for help.

Cowardly Scotch, who could you call? Dr. Roslyn was still talking.

"…it's not the same deal as when you were younger, Trudy. Don't flatter yourself? Have you looked in the mirror lately?"

Something called her eye to the mirror. It seemed to lower itself, as if the Scotch in her system was trying to show her something. Was it that she was middle-aged now and didn't have the same sex appeal power that she did so many years ago? But she knew that. She could see her face. Still, the mirror slowly sank.

"…I have lovers much younger than you. Trudy, I'm in the house where your sugar daddy lets you stay. You're in a coma, dear. You're never going to wake. Too many drinks and pills have finally ended your whoring days with misogynist patriarchs. You can't stop me."

The mirror stopped moving. It was eye level and directly behind Dr Roslyn. The back of Dr. Roslyn's head should have blocked Trudy's view. Instead, Trudy clearly saw her shocked face. The Dr. Roslyn in the dream was still behind the desk. Yet, Trudy felt cold hands caressing her hair.

"It's better this way, my little murderess. You can kill as many of them as you like, and you don't need a reason. It's call 'feeding' and its perfectly legal among the ranks of the Damned. Let go, little one. One bite, and the problems go away for good."

She now felt hot breath on the side of her neck as the Roslyn in the dream kept talking.

Scotch: make me not care.

A hand appeared in the mirror behind Dr Roslyn. It reached out beyond its borders, gripped the doctor at the shoulders, pulled her out of her chair, and pulled her through the mirror, which now looked like an everlasting tunnel.

It took a minute for Trudy to process what happened. What just happened? Who helped her? Scotch didn't have arms.

"Eddie!"

She drove across the desk to the mirror.

"Eddie! Why?"

As Trudy started to enter the mirror, a newspaper smacked her in the face. It was a small fraction of a second delay, but enough time for the tunnel to disappear. Trudy faced the mirror and saw only her face. She signed in frustration.

Now she was completely alone with nothing left to happen. So why was she still dreaming? Dreamer's block? Trudy had dreamed every kind of dream with people, places, and unpredictable happenstances of every type. But she had never dreamed a dream where no one dwelled, and nothing happened. She waited for minutes that mirrored hours. Is this what prison is like?

Read the newspaper.

The Scotch was talking again. It took another moment for Trudy to realize it meant the bagged paper. She was still holding it.

The headings read "The Ruthless Times" with "tomorrow" where the date should be. An idea hit her, although she knew she was still dreaming. Flipping past the front pages, she turned to the "sports" section. If she knew the results of tomorrow's events, she could bet on them today. Then her heart sank. Right under that heading, she read the words, "Don't even think about it." The paper went on to explain that a vampire syndicate controlled all sports betting. It said that anyone using the "Ruthless Times" to wager is bad for business.

Then she realized the information was useless anyway.

"Half the teams that played yesterday won. All others lost."

That was it. Those two sentences were the whole sports

section. Trudy flipped to the financial section, but it had the same warning.

That left the actual news.

"Politicians Converged, Talk About Nothing" was one headline.

"Climate Change Has Sahara Desert Being Sold as Beachfront Property."

That article pointed out the perils of real-estate development. It's one thing to buy property that will be the beach of a new great lake; it's another to buy land that will be under it.

"Vampire Tribunal Refuses to Hear Case."

Trudy stopped skimming and started to read.

On her first day as a vampire, Dr Roslyn attempted to sue both the IVA and the only known Irish vampire, Ed Calkins for failing to inform her that being a vampire would forfeit her soul.

Her suit alleged that she became a vampire by using a computer application developed and marketed by Ed Calkins with the financial backing of the IVA.

According to her claim, she was contacted by an IVA member posing as a police officer when she was arrested for statutory rape for the second time in her natural life.

If convicted, she would have likely lived that life behind bars, but the application let her voluntarily choose a "mistress vampire" to feed on her deeply enough to not only kill her but turn her into a vampire as well.

This "mistress vampire" did not participate in the lawsuit.

Eyebrows were raised when it was noted that the suit did not request the said soul to be returned, but only required cash compensation.

The Tribunal dismissed the claim, citing lack of evidence of the IVA, computers, or any involvement of Ed Calkins.

The IVA is an anachronism for Irish Vampires Association and has never been proven to exist.

For his part, Ed Calkins refused to comment on the story, confirm the existence of the IVA, or his membership to such, sighting health concerns.

What the hell is the IVA, and why would that be important?

Trudy closed the newspaper and then noticed, for the first time, a picture on the front page. The picture looked like a long-barreled pistol with the barrel pointing the wrong way, as if to shoot the shooter. The headline said: "Deadly Vampire Killing Weapon Invented."

Just below the headline she saw her own name.

CHAPTER 6: ON BEING RUTHLESS

You again! Don't you have anything better to do than spy on an old man while he's supposed to be writing a computer program? You couldn't have read what I told you to read or you'd still be reading it. Don't think that you can give a poem like "Birches" a once over and say that you've read it. OK, maybe Robert Frost is not your thing. I suppose not liking his best doesn't say you have poor taste. What does speak poorly of your taste in literature is you reading this!

Why could you possibly be here? Is it that you want to read about an Irish eccentric? I've got three words to say to you: William Butler Yeats. Poet, statesmen, occultist, and basic weirdo; he spent his whole life chasing a woman and growing old.

Don't you get it? I don't really know anything. There are two kinds of vampires; ones that can move through time a little, but change form a lot and those, like me, that can hardly change form at all but can travel through time like a beachcombing tourist. Blame the whole thing on John Simons, the vampire that bit me. He warned me that too much time travel can make me insane, but what does he want from me? I'm to go into the past, find a sidhe, write a computer program to make him a growing boy - which takes about ten years to do - and then return with the finished product in the present time exactly one second later. Oh, and very important: present it to the end user's mother with my dying breath…talk about deadlines.

Look, come back later. Just put the book down and nap or something. I don't want anyone to see me like this. I've got writer's block and depression, and I'm not very entertaining when both come at once. Do you really want to hear an old paperboy whine?

Maybe you're confused. Mirrors can do that. Right is left, left is right and the whole thing is in the most confusing language, English. Consider this; a guy tells his girlfriend movie star she'll never get the part. She doesn't, so she leaves him. The guy is left for being right. Later she turns out to be a serial killer. Now he's right for being left. No wonder why we're all crazy. And what about her side? She started dating him because he had a perfect ass but then turns out he is a perfect ass. The same happens with the next six; that's a serial that needs killing. (No, I don't know what that means either, but it's English).

You know, I've been trying to get you to walk through this mirror and vacation in the mystical land of my imagination, so I should tell you this. I'm likely the worst travel agent in history. I should be claiming that it's perfectly safe, that you can't get hurt because you're not there. That's true…kind of. Well, it's all about scheduling your arrival back into your own life. Oh, I understand the temptation of doing differently than you should, but heed my warning: if you spent a week in my imagination, be sure to return a week later in your lifetime instead of coming back at the same time you left, which would give you an extra week of life. You'll need to provide for your bodily needs while you're gone, of course. Coming back to find your dehydrated corpse is never pleasant. The best way is to go into a coma where someone will find you and let the hospital worry about the specifics. It's one sure way to wake up to people glad that you're back.

So it's seductive to stay in the past, stay for years, and then return the same day you left without growing a minute older. If you do that, you wind up like me, unable to timeline my life except for the time I lived my natural life. As a vampire, I often don't know if a memory is something I've done, something I'm going to do, something I should be/have doing/done, or something I should/will regret. Moreover, I find myself guessing at why I did, didn't, will, mustn't, or won't. Sometimes I know things I need to know when I travel to that time and the expense of remembering anything else.

Besides, out of most of what happened in my natural life, there are only five things I can always remember.

One: I must be ruthless and Irish.

Two: newspaper delivery is important.

Three: pass the dutchy on the left-hand side.

Four: I can have all the wives I want, but I can only sleep with the one that is my lover.

Five: there are only four things I always remember, but it's important to tell people it's five so they think I'm smarter than I am.

Wow, you're still here. You need to get a hobby! Maybe you think that if you wait around long enough, you'll understand how ruthless I am. Maybe you want to hear about how Ed Calkins became a vampire. I suppose I could tell you these things, but you'd find them boring. Look, there are two things that are naturally interesting about any vampire. They live for ages acquiring knowledge and wealth. But most of all, they know that whatever they do, they are bound to damnation.

With this vampire, neither is really true. Sure, I've either lived, or will live, a long time and I'm sure I've got knowledge and wealth, but I don't know which or where I will/do keep it. I can't be damned, because my angelic lover stole my soul, promising to take it with her when she returns to the beyond.

It's a far better story about how I became a human being.

I won't tell that story now.

The story I will tell starts in a very dark place with a very pathetic boy trying to enjoy his ill-gotten gains without being discovered. It's odd when I think of it, but this is the only part of my natural life that wasn't natural at all. I seemed to have unwittingly called a supernatural being using a candle and two mirrors

It had been one or two years since my father never came home from work on a payday, leaving my six younger siblings and me to fend with our raging mother. I never blamed him, or at least not at the time, for I would have left, too, if I ever had a week's paycheck in my pocket. My mother didn't take it well.

It's really distasteful to talk about Father John Chokey, as I called him, but the secret I kept so well for many years has been spilled. I remember now that I shall confront the leaker in a duel not three days from now by her perspective. It has to be her perspective of course, but I shall not run from her!

I should warn you about this priest because he's not like, or liked, by the other pedophiles in his circle. His hair, eyes and goatee matched his clerical suit, and his skin was pale, which I assumed was from spending too much time in church and not enough outside.

I was paid well to keep secret what our relationship was like, but now, after all the years and revelations of how priests preyed on boys instead of praying for them...English again. What a dumb language! Even I don't know what I mean. Anyway, the other priests had to know that Chokey was into something different. At eleven, I was already too old and ugly for most of them. Some would ask (in the few seconds of the few times when I was with them and not Chokey) what form our intimacy took. I never told them, and they took that for loyalty. The truth is, I didn't know, other than he'd choke me with an expertise that never damaged me but left me unconscious. What he did next never took very long, but I would wake with a powerful thirst. Father Chokey was never a considerate man, yet he always had a tall glass of orange juice waiting for me when I "came to." I died with that secret and kept my lips sealed through my undead existence - had someone not violated my trust.

I speak of Trudy. I know this is confusing you. I know you're wondering why any of this information matters and how all these characters relate to the backstory of the Steward of Tara.

You might think I had ill will toward Father Chokey in my youth. Nothing can be further from the truth. He gave form to my nefarious ambitions. I didn't know all the details of my arrangement with Father Chokey; the scandal within the Catholic Church concerning pedophile priests is well known and documented in these late times. Still largely unknown is the sexual misconduct between priests and young adult women. During my time with Father Chokey, I got a glimpse of a "priest fetish" women have - or at least so reported by priests either bragging or engaging in uncommon, unrepentant candor. Such talk fed into my lifetime overactive craving for disreputable carnal knowledge of beautiful women. By the time I was a teen, no longer in the company of Father Chokey and his co-conspirators, I decide to become a priest myself, that I might exploit this weakness in sinful females.

At the time, however, I vented my desires by prowling the Pages of the Playboy magazine that Father Chokey had clandestinely provided me as reward for my cooperation. At the time, my bedroom was an unfinished attic that lacked drywall and electrical outlets. The trap door led to a stepladder that was impossible to mount without making ample sound, warning me that my mother or one of my six siblings were seeking entrance. An extension cord could provide me light but plugging it in would alert them that I was not sleeping.

    I endured much criticism from my mother that my bedroom had no electrical outlets. She claimed that if I were more masculine, I would have installed them. Of course, I had no interest in electricity or handyman sort of things lest I be compelled into more chores. I already felt my burden was too great in that regard.

    It became a nightly ritual. I'd light a candle. That light alone was not enough. To compensate, I stole a small makeup mirror from the garbage, which I put behind the candle and then faced it at a picture mirror, which I balanced two feet away. The resulting light was enough to page through the girly pictures that so shamed me, while stroking immature fantasies of desire. I was too young to know the pleasures of my own fist (that would come later), but I knew of shame of my wickedness…knew that I was damnation waiting to happen. Sometimes, I would hold the magazine just behind the candle to reflect the picture onto the small mirror and project it to the larger one, noting the continuing reflections of reflections that went the way of glazing on railroad tracks, both getting smaller and smaller with the miles till they seemed to disappear, even though the magazine was only feet away.

    One night while I gazed on an unclothed beauty, I noticed something alarming. The concern drew me to the space between mirrors, as I tried to determine the cause. The centerfold stayed visible, but the repeating reflections vanished. In the next second, I saw the creature, horned and red-eyed, creeping forward as if to avoid being heard. As the image grew larger and larger, I saw the features and assumed the devil was coming for my soul, which scared me on one hand and relieved me on the other. The company of the devil is never good thing, but I now questioned my assumption that I was already damned. Unless I was dead, why would Satan come to me? Maybe he didn't have my soul yet? At the very least, I could try to cut a deal.

    Now, he stood very close before me. He had a goat face,

horns, and hooves.

"Hey!"

He seemed startled by my presence. Then I realized he was looking at the mirror behind me. I expected more from the Father of Lies.

"Why have you come?" I asked him.

"Ed Calkins, are ya?"

"Yes…"

"Well I…ya know I jist…"

"Came for my soul?"

His red eyes looked confused.

"That's it," he agreed. "Fer ya soul I come. Trade ya fer what ya be wantin I will."

Lucifer acted surprisingly awkward. Maybe being tossed into eternal fires had compromised his confidence. I expected a used car salesman to be pitching the merits of worldliness and sin for the mere cost of a soul that he'd get at some point anyway. Instead, I was going to lead these negotiations. My mind raced with the possibilities.

"Ya be wanton me gold, I suppose."

Was Lucifer Irish or Scottish? In either case, his accent was thick. I shook my head. Gold? Really! I'd be compelled to give that with my mother after being soundly punished for lying about how I got it.

"No," I told him, then held a magazine to his face. "I want her."

Satan gasped in shock, almost as if he'd never seen a picture of a naked woman. He said not a word. I quickly got the impression that he wanted her, too. He wasn't saying no. Maybe I should up the ante.

"And that's not all. I want her too." I picked up another magazine and turned to the centerfold.

He turned his lustful gaze from the first picture to the second one. With startling speed, he snatched the book from my hand, placed it over the one he had been studying, and intently examined the new one.

"Look at th' pictures all th' time, does ya?" the devil asked without looking up.

That stoked my fear, for I knew how to bargain. Other

younger boys had struck deals with "their" priests. If they played these games with the priest, would they go still go to heaven even if they sinned a little? Would their parents go to heaven, too? Of course, their priests always reassured them. Any sin they committed was forgiven the moment they committed it. But the deals those boys made didn't concern me. My relationship with Father John Chokey was different. My cooperation was linked to the cash he gave my family. And Father Chokey bought my silence with a new Playboy every month.

I already knew I was going to hell. My mother and the nuns that taught me rarely agreed on anything, but they agreed on that. Now the nuns were not openly hostile to me as an individual. But they made it clear that ninety percent of hell's population were men, and most of them earned their places in hell as junior high aged boys, in no small part because of the filthy thoughts within their head. My mother, on the other hand, was openly hostile to me, but it was for my own good.

"If I hadn't intervened, you'd have become your drunken, cheating, mistreating father years ago," she always told me.

She still thought it would happen, though. She insisted her "intervention" was only delaying it. But most of all, to gain heaven, you needed to love your mother. I hated her.

So I was clearly going to hell, but right now, I didn't want to let the devil know that. Why would he fork out money for a soul he already owned?

"Gives me all th' pictures a th girls ya be wanta. Jus' stack em right here," the devil told me.

I scampered to the holes between the house frame and the roofing where I hide the other Playboys. That's when I started having second thoughts about my request. How would I hide all these women? How would I feed them? I turned suddenly to address these questions just in time to see the knife where my back had been but not in time to avoid taking a death wound to my front...

...except for a stepped-on magazine that slipped the goat body head over hooves. The knife stuck deep into the roof's fame. Horns hit the floor hard, sparing Satan a concussion. Gold coins rolled all over the floor with such a racket, I was worried about questions I had no answers to.

"Quiet!" I told Satan, realizing as I spoke that my fear was misplaced. "They'll hear us."

"An you be th one worried bout that?" Satan quipped.

"I thought devils only snatched souls. I didn't think stabbing someone was part of the demonic code."

"The Romans paid me," he answered. "Does ya know how much th average soul be costin? Where's a self-respectin devil s'posed ta get all that money? Does ya think that hell has money trees?"

"What about your demonic powers?" I asked incredulously.

"Demonic powers? Does ya think I'd be layin on me back wif my knife 'n th' air if me demonic powers could raise a fig?"

"I don't think you're really Satan."

As soon as I spoke, the goat figure changed into a bearded short middle-aged man with red hair. My devil was a leprechaun.

"Just when it couldn't get any worse," he grumbled. Now, his accent was easier to understand, and his grammar seemed improved.

"Explain?"

My voice sounded more like a plea where it should have been a command, but I had no idea what I would do, what kind of trouble I would be in, or how I might explain if my mother were to see what laid around me. I only knew one thing. It would severely be my fault.

The leprechaun held out his hand. Perhaps shaking hands with someone that had just failed to kill you might be disingenuously inappropriate, but the same could be said of my life.

"You be Ed Calkins, I know. I am called Arkiens the Were-Goat. Every full moon, I turn into the form you just saw and then back again when the moon is slighter. Now, don't take this killing business too seriously. I've got nothing against you, but the Roman Empire feels differently. You see, when I'm in goat form, I can travel through time and space using mirrors as if they were doors, so to speak. It's a trick you're going to learn soon, but I get ahead of myself. Now the gold on the floor might seem to be yours, not that I don't really need it, because I do. Booze and women don't come cheap, don't you know? But I know that game you tell people to play. My gold for my freedom, is it?"

But I didn't want gold. How would I explain it? How would anyone come to any conclusion other than I stole it somehow? I wanted to understand. I also wanted to stay alive without hoping that this Arkiens would fall the next time.

"Why does Imperial Rome want me killed?" was the only question I could manage.

"Rome! What a joke. Always killing with Rome. That's the way a Roman solves his problems. Now, some say we Irish solve all our problems with booze. A Roman thinks the problems in his life are other people, so he gets them killed. It isn't till the end of his life that he understands he killed all the people, but the problems never went away. We Irish know it's better to drink till your problems go away. They don't, of course, but at least there's people left to pay for another round once in a while. Now don't go telling me that you be Irish, too, lad. Never in your natural life have you ever stepped foot on the Emerald Island. Maybe your great-grand-daddy was, but you're a Yank. If either of you realized that there wouldn't be a pile of gold laying on the floor that was paid to finish you. I know it, lad. Ed Calkins may be a problem, but it's not the problem that can be solved by killing or drinking or it would have been solved a long time ago. That's the true of it! While Rome looks on a map to find its empire, Ed Calkins was looking at a calendar. There's the Irish Empire! First it was the month of March, but Ed Calkins took February too, leaving poor Rome without a single day and no parade."

"Not true!" I protested. "July was named after Julius Caesar; August was named after Augustus Caesar."

"Don't make me laugh," he snorted. "Rome screwed their calendar up so badly it needed to add two months to stop planting in the winter. Yes, Julius named a month after himself and so did Augustus, but who KNOWS that? Well, save some Catholic boys and history nuts. Go walking down any street in March and tell me there's no shamrocks to be found. Can you find the same for Rome?"

"But what does that have to do with me?"

"Ah, lad, if I could tell you... let's say I keep the gold but grant you a wish. Any wish if I can grant, I will."

"I wish you won't ever kill me."

That just popped out from my mouth. I was speaking my fear, but I didn't really believe the wish thing would work in my favor anyway. In days to follow, I would curse myself for not wishing for a new mother.

"Lad, you're being too rash. You don't really want that. I know you think you do, but I don't suppose you believe in any of this. You don't believe in vampires either, do you? You won't believe until you become one, and that's going to happen sooner or later. If you do it right, lad, you'll be king of the vampires someday. Now I know you think I'm just a crazy little man, which I am because I'm a time traveler, but I happen to owe you a favor. I'm going to grant you another wish, but not now…not till you feel the knife cut into your belly, that's when I'll grant you the other wish. Thanks again for not taking the gold."

"I don't want to be king of the vampires!".

But he had quickly gathered the gold and was gone, as if the mirror had sucked him in. It was getting light now, and I searched the room for some evidence that he'd been here. I found one forgotten gold coin. When I bent to pick it up, it wasn't there, as if it was a golden ghost, visible, but just not there. Later, I realized that the gold must have spilled on the other side of the mirror, and I was trying to pick up its reflection.

It was not so with the knife. That was still deep in the wooden frame. I would sell that knife many years later to a pawn shop. The store owner would tell me that the knife, lacking the wear of ages, must instead be a reproduction, using old pre-Christian methods and materials with careful historic accuracy. I was paid well for it.

But that morning found me crushed and impoverished.

Arkiens had stolen my Playboys.

I'm sorry about accusing you of having no taste. I've been acting like an arrogant ass. I've been acting like you're lacking significance because you've been reading what I'm trying to write, and I've been calling that "spying." The truth is, I'm feeling insignificant, and I'm projecting that on you.

Try and understand. If you're going to write a novel worth reading, you've got to believe you've got something worthy to say. I just don't believe that. Real confidence has never been a part of me.

What do you do when you don't believe something you need to believe? Fake it till you make it? Act like you believe? I've been doing that all my undead life. Yes, I'm a faker.

Let's reset. You haven't put the book down yet, have you?

What would you do if you had the world's most advanced literary tastes that only you could understand? Would you put this dusty book back on its forgotten shelf? Not until you've read every single word, digested every piece of prose withing its cover. Not until you fully comprehend the depths of meaning and purpose would you stop reading.

And me? If I believed that I was writing the greatest novel ever written, I would be glad to have a reader that understood my work for what it is. I wouldn't be depressed! I wouldn't want to be left alone in my writer's block. I would forsake self-doubt and embrace the greatest message that any time traveling vampire could ever deliver. I would make clear just how ruthlessly Ed Calkins can write! I would make clear how ruthless Ed Calkins really is!

And you? You would be the wisest reader in history. And if you had modeled for any of those 1969-1970 Playboy magazines, (which means you're really old now), you can consider yourself married to the greatest undead novelist of the nonlinear time era. And if you have any of those issues of Playboy magazines, would you be so grateful as to promptly mail them to Ed Calkins?

CHAPTER 7: SUSPECT

The phone rang, but it wasn't the phone in Dr. Roslyn's office. Trudy was on her throne once again in complete darkness, trying to separate the things that needed her attention from the things that only distract. Once again, she faced light barely reflecting off the mirror. The image was the darkened shadow of a form that should be her. Did she exist?

The phone was persistent enough to convince her that not only was she real, but that she could manipulate physical things like a phone handle. Wow! She could almost talk.

"You aren't here at the wake," Eddie's wife said. "I want you here tomorrow at the funeral."

"Sorry, I'm on a road trip now…I don't think I'm coming back. I stood up for your wedding and nothing good came of it, Nalla."

"If you're not here for the funeral, I'll tell everyone that you shot him in the head."

Trudy stiffened. What would Nalla have done if she knew someone else killed him? …not invite her to the funeral.

A cold, "why?" was all she could manage.

"Ed always wanted a large funeral procession to tie up traffic."

83

"So, call all his other wives. He also wanted to be buried in the Great Pyramid, but I don't think you're going to Egypt. He wanted super models to throw themselves at the casket and lament that they'd never find another so ruthless in bed. No! I want to know why you know I shot him and why you're not calling the police."

"Because I also know you were aiming for your own head and missed."

The phone was ringing again. Trudy tried to ignore it, but her cramped neck screamed at having slept on a chair.

"Bathrobe!"

He didn't respond.

Fumbling, she grasped for the wall phone. It took, maybe, seven attempts to bring the blasted plastic handle to her ear and lips. Sunlight was streaming through the domelike window that lorded three stories high over a half-acre of trees, grass, and gardens that she never had time to inspect.

She hoped it was still morning.

"Why didn't you tell me?" the voice demanded.

She resisted the reflex to hang up, let the silent moments pass, and attempted to match a name to the accusing question. Sheriff Matt! He wasn't just her boss this morning, he was the man who'd be leading an investigation. Trudy, who could not put any words together, lowered the phone. She still heard the voice outline his objection.

"It's an embarrassment to the county when a reporter knows more than the department, Trudy. You were on patrol when that body was found a few days ago. It'd be helpful if I'd known ahead of time that you knew the victim...Trudy?"

Confused, she started to answer but realized the phone had sunk to her lap. She was glad of it, because by the time the receiver reached her lips, she picked the counterpoint and questioned.

"Why would reporters be so interested in an old dead man?"

"Not so old, Trudy. I'm looking at a video of his wedding; guess who was the maid of honor? I've got statements from people at that wedding that remember you saying how you slept with him the night before his big day. Do you mind telling me why they're saying that?

Damn!

A surge of panic shook the phone handle. Wait a minute.

This was a good thing that she cared enough to be afraid. "Afraid" would make her think fast. Seconds passed as she reviewed her options. Realizing that nothing about Ed Calkins' bachelor party incriminated her, she told the story as tearfully and truthfully as she knew how.

"Ed Calkins didn't believe in marriage; everyone knew that. So why he would marry was another question. Some of his friends were starting a pool for who could guess closest to when the marriage would end in divorce. Eddie bet on two months. Still, he was ready to go through with it because he felt trapped. I was his best friend at the time and took it on myself to end it before it began. If I could pressure him the other way, if he could agree to other plans, he might escape without having to confront.

"So when Eddie came to his bachelor party at the bar, I was the only one there. I told him if he wanted to just take his son and skip town, I had everything ready. I had an apartment lease preapproved, and a bar that would hire him on my referral in the next town. He seemed relieved at first, but his job with the newspaper got in the way. Ed talked about breaking his contract with the Daily Post quite often, but that evening the contract was his word. More importantly, how would he pay the carriers that work for him if he were to just disappear?

"All through the night, I tried variations of the plans. Eddie could be a coward to his fiancé and loyal to his work. But as the drinks and hours passed, it became clear to me that Eddie wouldn't get out unless his bride ended it.

"It's not like we never fell asleep together. My apartment was above the bar. There was only one queen size bed in her bedroom. Only a coward or a saint would attempt to 'only sleep.' Eddie was no saint. Some might say he was only being loyal. Maybe that's true if it happened now. Of course, I didn't set an alarm, but Eddie woke up at 'newspaper time' for one last morning with his carriers as a single man. All he had to do was not show up at the church.

"I played my part as maid of honor for the wedding and gave a gracious toast that up-staged the best man. Later, though when the dancing and drinking hit me, I told some of the bride's friends that Ed broke my heart the previous night.

"Matt, that was twenty years ago. Both Eddie and his bride

'Nalla' had forgiven and forgotten the malicious rumor a long time ago. So anyone who heard that story at the wedding must have also told you that, although we didn't often hang out anymore, I was still friends with them both."

Trudy left out the part about Ed winning the lottery months before his death. But Matt seemed to buy the story.

And then he dropped the bomb.

"Trudy, I'm sorry about this, but I need you to take an unpaid leave," Matt apologized. "This reporter is digging around a lot, and it'd be bad if the public knew we were using auxiliary officers to patrol that area. We can't deny it happened, of course, but we don't want that publicity. You can give the detectives your statement when you turn in you pistol and badge."

"Matt…"

"I mean it. No later than noon today."

"It will have to be tomorrow. I have a funeral to attend this morning."

"Funeral? You must not have heard. That's why you're wondering why a reporter is interested. Last night the victim's mother showed as the wake was ending and had a tantrum, throwing ashtrays and vases. The funeral parlor called, and we sent two squads from the next county."

"Eddie's mother never liked him or his father."

"But that's not the worst part. The crazy lady knocked down… witnesses say pushed down, the coffin, which was to be closed, and broke it open."

"Oh, Goddamn! That bitch!"

"The coffin was empty."

What happened to the soul crushing depression that should be making every slight movement an aching nightmare where tragic events couldn't differentiate from the anguish of another breath? Yes, she had good pills last night. Was that prescription some kind of super-steroid antidepressant? Now, she wanted to kill. If she were going down for the murder of Ed Calkins, by God, she would get the one that really deserved it.

She checked her rage just enough to ask Matt, "Is she at the station right now?"

She was.

Trudy's "I'll be right there" came too late for the slammed

receiver.

A familiar chemistry flowed through her body, making her feel powerful, but frantic. Where was the gun? As she fumbled for it, sense reclaimed a rational trigger point. Guns and rage don't mix. But where was it? It was right there on the dresser last night when she couldn't get herself out of a chair.

"BATHROBE!" she screamed, but no one answered.

No body, no Bathrobe, no pistol… she had a crazy poetic moment. Eddie was always going to work sleep deprived. He always claimed he could sleep when he was dead. Eddie couldn't die because the papers had to be delivered, so he captured Bathrobe to teach the route he was doing. Then he could die but he stole the pistol in case he met the person that shot him.

Where? The bottle of whiskey that should have been Scotch, that had been on the nightstand, too. Gone! Nothing there but the ringed stain of a bottle.

There was no time to sort it out. She already told Matt she would be at the station to give a statement and turn in her 38. At very least, she needed to find that 38, and her badge, lest she draw questions she couldn't answer. Scanning the room, she couldn't see her police uniform that would have both badge and pistol on it, if Bathrobe hadn't washed it on her. The voice of Dr. Roslyn invaded her mind. "Not now," she tried to tell it, but it had something useful to ask: "What was the first thing you remember after you blacked out? Where were you, and what were you wearing?"

Bathrobe's bedroom! And yes, she remembered undoing her uniform while avoiding his questions of what was wrong and refusing his help undressing. She almost allowed him to sleep in his bed with her, but then she thought better of it and ordered him to sleep on the floor, which would be the opposite side she'd have discarded her uniform. Hopefully, Bathrobe had been too drunk the last few days to wash it.

She reached the bedroom on the second floor and saw, to her great relief, the uniform and holster still on it. Now, what to wear?

Bathrobe's closet was ruled by their play together. By order of the queen, all of Bathrobes clothes were on the far left (a poke at his politics) and consisted of only bathrobes, the only item she allowed him to wear in his own house. All other male clothes where hidden away from him and only produced if she favored his request for them. Mostly, she only favored if he was going to work, but he still had to dress and undress in his car.

As true of their relationship, the clothes were in the closet. The clothes in the left, middle, right, and far right were his as well, but they didn't fit him, and he was glad of it lest Trudy get mischievous. Those were the clothes purchased for Trudy and organized by his sense of order. On the left were formal clothes, should she ever allow him to be seen with her on some formal setting. Center was informal, right was clothes for their play, far right was night wear, and the smallest section was for clothes he didn't buy, which was two officer's uniforms, the only thing that didn't belong to Bathrobe. Those belonged to the department.

For a reason she couldn't name, she pulled one of the uniforms off the rack, realizing that she intended to visit the funeral parlor after she was put on leave. The move would surely put Matt at his guard. It was then that she noticed the holster belt on the floor was missing all the bullets. Foolish enough was leaving the 38 tossed as it was, but where were the bullets? She checked the pistol itself and found it unloaded.

Where were the bullets? How would she explain this? Every time she wore the badge, she was supposed to keep six revolver shots loaded and six more on her belt in case she ever had to fire and reload. An unaccounted-for round missing for belt or gun was a hostile investigation at best. No time, she would think on the way.

Trudy didn't have a car, but she had a license to ride a motorcycle, so Bathrobe bought her a "Rice Burner" that had just enough power but wasn't too heavy for her to handle. She had scolded him for buying a helmet as well, but as a cop, she really had to obey the "bucket disease" law, considering that her destination was a police office.

When she arrived at the station, she had nothing towards explaining the missing bullets, but the sheriff took care of it. He was waiting outside for her and approached the bike before she parked.

Trudy imagined that Matt had been a handsome man in his youth. He was tall, a full head over most men. He took care of his hair and teeth, keeping the former trimmed and short and the later white and in good repair. Matt was the kind of man that spoke plainly, looked you in the eye, and told the truth. He was also inclined to keep his opinions to himself. But the office he held now had gone political, and too many stress lines aged his face. He kept himself lean, but these days, too much so.

"You're in uniform, good. Change of plans," he announced nervously. "Keep your badge for today and tonight. I need you to go to the funeral parlor right now."

"Is she still in there?" Trudy asked, guessing Matt's fear and how it bought her time. He didn't want her temper in his understaffed and over investigated office.

"Not your concern. You need to go to the victim's second wake. It seems the funeral parlor doesn't want any trouble and is offering a second day of waking until the body is found. I don't want any trouble either. Go as if you're there as a mourner but stay out of trouble and don't answer any questions. The parlor has banned the mother from the building, and we're hoping to hold her until the body is in the ground. Got it?"

Boy, did she!

CHAPTER 8: THE NAUGHTY LIST

I have no idea what I'm doing in a Santa Suit before a single file line of small girls flanked by brownies about sixty deep, but I know the game. Next to me are two unsmiling "elves" that look identical to male brownies except they are wearing green instead of brown. It's a wooden chair and just a chair, not a throne or the like, which tells me I'm not the Steward of Tara here, nor do I recognize any of the human girls or brownies.

The chair is situated on a hill, and just a hill in Ireland, not the sacred double mounds of Tara, though I'd guess the location to be not far. Also, I feel I'm in the past relative to my own natural life, hardly much of a guess. Rarely, and with much apprehension, do I venture into the future.

Where are all the humans? This is a telling clue. If it were early in Ireland's history, tribes would be scouting out for enemies to raid, taking crops, coins, and slaves or defending against the same. Later, castles and heaps of human folk would dot the hilly landscape. Still later, abbeys and churches would join the development. Beyond that, when Tara lost its function, tourists would gawk at the ancient sight of the making of kings.

No. Unless some other evil was at play, this must be the time when humans abandon this place of mystical power; leaving this scared site to the sidhe, in which they no longer believe. I feel for the sidhe, but I know the weakness that disbelief can breed. Self-doubt is strongest when one is doubted.

"Ho Ho Ho, what do you want for Christmas number 40?'" The girl next in line reluctantly crawls on my lap. The brownie parent gives me a subtle thumbs up, indicating that the child has been good. Everyone must be baffled that I know her "name" as 40, but it's hardly difficult. Someone other than a brownie arranged them in numeric order. Most brownies can't count beyond three without using fingers.

The child tells me her deepest wish in a low voice.

"A doll!" I repeat, loud enough for the brownie dad to hear. It will fall on him to make it happen even though he wouldn't understand why. Brownie children don't use toys in their play, but these brownies seem to understand that human children will need extra care. But why Christmas? Surely if that holiday were known in these parts, it would have to be a later time in history.

Unless the girls are from a later time.

Emboldened, the child describes what kind of doll she wants. I repeat loudly what she says, adding the required "ho ho hos" to every laugh. Number forty departs from my lap, leaving scant evidence of why I'm here.

Number 41 is less shy, but I can't help wondering why all blonde girls in the same age group seemed to be the only humans. Brownies are known to steal babies from human mothers. When they take an infant, they raise it as their own child and then marry the child when it comes of age to other brownie families, thus intermixing with human stock. But brownies would have stolen both genders. Is it my prejudice that I suspect cluricahns or leprechauns? Leprechauns lacked females, and cluricahns were always looking for dubious profit. Why only blond two-year-old girls? Leprechauns wanted lovers, not daughters, and cluricahns would seek to cut the losses of feeding a girl until she's ready for sale. Only brownies raised humans, then interbred with them when they came of age. Why would they care if a child were non-blonde or male?

Forty-one got a thumbs up and a doll without interrupting my thoughts.

Not so with the next one.

A thumbs down might have told the story, but these brownie parents put both thumbs down and tongues out sounding raspberries. The girl heard her introduction but placed her hands on her hips, displaying that she wasn't about to forget to negotiate.

"Oh, I'm afraid there will be no toy for you, 42. Maybe next year if you behave better."

"Good. I don't want a toy. I want a boy," she told me with remarkably sophisticated vocabulary for a two-year-old.

I looked to the brownie parents for context, but they seemed as lost as I was. Number 42 seemed to find an opening and metaphorical bayonet lunged out.

"He has to be strong, handsome, brave, smart, and he has to do what I say."

"Ho Ho Ho," I tried to make that a convincing chuckle. "You want a husband?"

Some of the male brownies laughed. The little girl made a face.

"Not a husband," the little girl insisted. "I already have a husband, and he's very rich."

She pointed to a person off to the side and alone, but close enough to pay attention to "Santa Claus" receiving children. His unhappy face, and his expression, seemed very familiar to me. You know how it is when you meet someone you know well, but the meeting is out of context. They're somewhere they shouldn't be, dressed as they shouldn't dress. This someone wore the fine Lincoln green suit and hat of a leprechaun.

I studied him, racking my incomplete memory to place him in my natural life where I'm sure he belonged. The little girl scowled at the attention I was giving him since she and I were in the middle of fixing a price.

"He has to be the same age as I am," she demanded loud enough to pull my glance back to her.

I tried to be stern.

"Little girl, I can't give you a brother. I can't give you anything. You haven't been good."

"I don't want a brother, and the reason you can't give me anything is because you're not really Santa Claus. You're just a fat human man dressed like Santa Claus."

Wow! This could be a problem. One child doubts out loud, and you spend the rest of your visit defending your assumed identity. I quickly looked at the faces of the other girls. Not one was buying her conspiracy theories. I could guess the girl had a reputation for being a liar.

I was about to dismiss her, but she jumped on my lap, gave me a hug, and whispered in my ear. Would she have done that if she'd known my true nature? Because her neck was temptingly close to my hidden fangs.

The truth, however, was quite different. The girl was too young to tempt my lust for blood, nor was her neck so close to my fangs. My true position was contrary to the way I presented it. For me, it was kind of like driving a car in the States where the driver seat, road, and right of way is left where it should be right; yet, one learns to safely ignore the wrongfulness in order to finish the paper route. And while I learned to drive in the States and never drove anywhere else, the wrongness of it showed itself and never left me.

"See, if you can give me a boy," she whispered, "then you would really be Santa, and I would make everyone believe in you because I would tell them that you're not. If everyone believes you're Santa, then you would be Santa."

She pulled back to study my reaction to her sales pitch. I was shocked.

"Do you lie a lot, 42?" I asked without whispering.

"I always tell the truth," she told me coyly.

It was my turn to whisper, and her turn to be shocked.

"Not me," I whispered into her head. "I always tell a lie every time I speak, even now."

The girl was smart enough to play with that. If I always lied, then I just told the truth, which means I didn't lie, so I lied.

The brownies must have assumed I was successfully admonishing her. Her defiance fell from her face as she thought through my words. Then she came up with an answer, which she whispered back to me.

"I think you lie sometimes but other times tell the truth. You were lying when you said you always lie. You were also lying when you said you were Santa, but I can fix that if I get my boy."

My face was in her ear before she could study my reaction. Something the girl said clinked on the time-appropriate memory (or TAM), which made me believe this girl was the key to my running this place instead of being a guess.

"I'm not Santa," I informed her. "You can be Santa. I want to stay fat and give orders. I want everyone to believe what I tell them and be afraid of me because I'm ruthless."

The bartering continued for another five minutes, Neither of us ever spoke outside of the other's ear. She refined her terms in what this boy must prove. At first, she demanded the cliché of rescuing of a princess by slaying a dragon, with, of course, her as the princess. I didn't like the dragon idea as it would mean bringing one in. Instead, I suggested he slay a ruthless dictator, since I knew where to find one. But I almost lost her when I reported that the boy wouldn't be ready for slaying dictators until both he and she were adults. So I had to promise her that she could start seeing this boy after Christmas.

For her part, she agreed to stop being a brat on the day after Christmas and the next day and the next day and so forth - until the boy came to rescue her. Beyond that, well…

"Now this is what to say to everyone if 'they' ever ask you if I was the really the Steward of Tara, and that all of the sidhe were just figments of my imagination," I instructed her. "Tell them you can't answer that. Because if you say I wasn't, you'd be lying, and you promised not to lie. If you say I was, you'd be telling a secret, and you promised to keep that secret."

Number 42 slid off my lap. She still had five days to be a brat and was ready to make the most of it. The change in her would shock the brownies and plant the seed of doubt about them really existing.

Finally, all fifty girls had their say with Santa. I stayed in my chair while the last brownie parents ushered the girls away.

"Fat human can go!" a brownie told me sternly. "Give back suit first!"

I wasn't a guest. I was a prisoner if I weren't being taken for a slave.

"Not just yet," I answered with as much confidence as I could muster. "I have to talk with the leprechaun first…"

"Why you not give suit now?" he demanded.

"Because I get very bored if I'm not nicely dressed. People tend to disappear when I'm bored."

I walked past him with supreme confidence. One bluff seemed to work. Would I be so lucky with the leprechaun?

"I don't like my wife sitting on your lap!" he told me.

"And good day to you, Eircheard. May the wind be at your

back."

"Knives at my back, I tell you. I talked to your master this morning."

"John Simons…I mean, 'Simotes?'"

"I don't like my wife sitting on your lap."

"We'll talk about her later. I think first order of business should be the project we're both going to be working on."

Eircheard was annoyed.

"The oak wood changeling!" he exclaimed. "It will not work! My finest model can fool a mother for years, so she doesn't realize that her baby has been stolen. My latest model can learn to walk but stops at talking. Your vampire master wants an exceptional son to grow into a great man. If that's the job specifications, you're going to have to make it happen."

Interesting.

"Why can this oak wood changeling unit manage walking but can't learn to speak?"

"What part of "oak wood" are you not understanding? A changeling is only as smart as the oak it's from. Oak is a smart wood. It can do what an animal can, which I think is bloody amazing, but it can't think like a person. Now, you can put a brownie inside the oak wood unit and get some speech for as long as the brownie can stand the boredom. But a brownie doesn't act like a human boy. You're knowing that first-hand. Lucky for you, Mr. Simons doesn't like the type that believes in brownies. He thinks this whole realm is a product of your demented imagination. Even so, this won't make an exceptional boy unless it's OK with the father to see his son doing his algebra homework on his fingers and toes. Anyway, the latest oak wood unit takes tremendous power. Why, no human mother has the mammies to make enough milk to feed the machine."

"But it can breastfeed?" I asked, showing my hopes rise.

"Wrong question, lad. Ask if it can stop breastfeeding. The answer's almost 'no.'"

"Almost?"

"Almost no!" he insisted, yet pride bubbled from his annoyance.

I tried to process all of this, while the leprechaun kept talking.

"Now, this Simotes guy doesn't think much of you, but he's

acting like you're some kind of wizard that can make a machine think and act like a boy....well, he better be right for your sake. I won't be happy if I go through all the trouble of making the unit and don't get paid. And I'll tell you another thing. Simotes thinks that he can only come to this realm because you're letting him. It only follows that if my leprechaun colleagues want a land that is vampire-free, all that's required is a stake through your undead heart. You're all by yourself and you don't know our number. Best remember that when we get to our second order of business."

Disgusted, I sighed. "Artificial intelligence."

"What?"

It was like almost any programing job I ever undertook. They never seem to correctly guess what is possible, and they hold you to their misguided standards. John knew I could program a computer, and he knew I majored in psychology, so naturally he thought I could develop AI that could replace a growing child's mind and excel. No team of the most brilliant software developers and psychologists could do that, but John knew they were trying. Why does every client assume that you can move mountains and still think you're a bumbling idiot? Fortunately, I never had a client who completely understood what he wanted.

"I can't teach your unit how to act like a boy," I told Eircheard, who looked deflated and relieved at the same time. "But I can write software to teach a brownie how to act like a boy."

"Well, you better be ready to pay a brownie enough to work 24/7 for the rest of his life because it's not coming out of my pay. I'll do my part, but don't blame me if the whole thing doesn't take. Can we get to the second order of business?"

I was afraid to ask, seeing that I only knew of two orders of business.

"We want you to sign this contract," he stated confidently. "It's an offer you can't refuse."

From out of his green coat jacket came a contract-looking stack of papers. It puzzled me why a leprechaun would reveal what I long suspected. Until the church brought its Latin alphabet, Gaelic had no written form. What language then would be on the paper? I would have hoped for Latin but expected ancient Greek. I was disappointed. The document was in modern English

Reading through it and looking for an offer, I found only

threats. I was to promise to introduce no male humans into these parts. The bulk of the document was what would happen to me if I chose not to comply by either not signing or breaking the "contract."

It was a chess match ambush, an attack for which I had not prepared. I'd need to find a solution over the board with time issues on the clock. I knew signing that contract was a confession of weakness, but I saw little advantage to add to my trouble a conflict with leprechauns. Furthermore, I was dressed in a ridiculous fashion, as if to say, "nothing important here, just a crazy old man all by himself who's so vulnerable that a troop of brownies forced him into playing a mythical deity."

Then I found an idea. I looked into his eyes as sternly as I could.

"You just made the naughty list, Eircheard. No present for you this Christmas!"

To that he said nothing, almost as if he didn't hear me. I needed to buy more time to think of a response while appearing unrushed and knowing. Act natural. Say something crazy.

"We are a triumvirate, Simotes, you and I.'

"Yes, much like the first," Eircheard replied, nodding. "We are an alliance of three powers, but in the end, there was only one emperor. Power always seeks more power. No one is willing to play second. Which of the three are you?"

"I think Simotes is Crassus." I pointed out.

The leprechaun looked like he wanted to disagree, but he nodded his concession.

"Yes," Eircheard agreed. "The man is flawed. He compels you, but he is unable to control himself. He will take himself out of power without either of us having to oppose him. That leave two pairs, oh Steward of Tara, Caesar and Pompey, You and I."

Did he just call me, "Steward of Tara?" Maybe I've been here before. Maybe he knows what the brownies have yet to learn. Or was it John Simons that told him what I would become?

"Maybe this is not like the first triumvirate, and you and I will stay allied."

"Has that ever happened before?"

" No," I admitted. "You can be Caesar if you want. Remember the Ides of Match. You can defeat me later, but I'll not be signing the document you gave me."

"Do you think that's wise? You are all alone right now. I have the leprechauns behind me, and you don't know our number."

"Not more than sixty," I told him, realizing that the girls were to be the wives/slaves of the leprechauns when they came of age. Less than sixty wives would bring conflict to the already fading race.

"Sixty against one," he challenged, though sounding less confident. One vampire can be a formidable foe. Still, he had a point. Why wasn't I scared? It wasn't because of an excess of confidence or even courage. Neither ever counted high in my short order of personal virtues.

Then I thought of the IRA. I was raised Catholic. That might be enough for the IRA to defend me, even though "now" was centuries before its existence, and I never had any affection for its methods. I couldn't lie, but I still could bluff. Fortunately, my dyslexic mis-speech did me one better.

"Ever heard of the IVA?" I heard myself say.

He just gave me a puzzled look. I said nothing, which might have seemed like a pause for dramatic effect, but I was trying to figure out what that could mean.

"Irish Vampires Association," I informed him the first moment I had it. "Don't feel ignorant if you've never heard of it, because it's the most secretive organization on the planet. The only reason I'm allowed to mention it is because I'm its spokesperson."

"And you're a member of this…"

"Oh, I didn't say that," I corrected quickly. "I can't divulge or even speculate about who's a member and who's not. The truth is, I don't even know myself…except of course, myself. I could be talking to the president of the IVA. I wouldn't know. I don't go talking about it. I only speak of it to people who need to know. Well, right now that's you. If you're a member, then you're the only one who knows that, and you need to know that I'm the spokesman because you don't want to go threatening one of your IVA brothers. If you're not a member, then you need to know it's not wise to threaten someone who is. That's all."

Eircheard snorted. "You well know I'm not a vampire. Why would I be a member?"

"You don't have to think you're a vampire to be in the IVA. You just have to believe you're Irish. If you're not a member but want to be one, I can tell you how."

"I'll decline…"

"No, no!' I interrupted as if I hadn't heard of his refusal. "Don't tell me if you're going to be a member. It will compromise our secrecy. It's quite simple. You can join at home. First, go to a room where you are completely alone and initiate yourself by pledging to do whatever you think the IVA wants you to do…which doesn't include threatening your IVA brother."

"And you expect me to believe…"

"No. Why would I? An association that doesn't know of its own members is crazy on the face of it. How could I know it exists? I'm just a crazy old vampire and all alone by the looks of it. I probably made the whole thing up. I don't know if I did or not. Let's not speak of it."

I didn't lie. Telling the truth to someone who thinks you're a liar is the best way to deceive.

"So if you're not going to sign this contract, maybe we can make another kind of deal and at least agree not to kill each other before the deliverables are exchanged."

"That's setting the bar pretty low," I told him. "What I want is a harder sell."

"Which is?"

"I want to buy your wife."

Eircheard's face turned red with rage. At least he took me seriously.

"You don't go selling a wife!" he finally articulated.

"Why not, you got her and the rest of the babies like any slaves being sold off a raider's ship, except the brownies didn't need a ship, did they? Did they promise to raise them before your De Danann friend and you take delivery? If you did anything else, it might feel like marrying your daughters."

"Because a wife is a slave that you can never sell." His grammar slipped, and his accent became thicker. "The point is, our wives are the De Danann's future. They well be brownie-raised and De Danann-educated. When they are of age, we will leave this bubble in time and transport to the future, buy up the land in some small, forgotten village, and repopulate the race with our younger wives. Look, this has all been worked out with your master, John Simotes. All that's to be done is the handshake, and I sealed the deal."

"What makes you think the girls wouldn't run off with some younger, taller men of the time and area, like your De Danann maidens did with the Milesians?"

I was guessing, but I seemed to have hit the bullseye.

"Milesians?" he snorted. "They were never more than a handful in number. You're all Fir Bolg to us. Besides, many of us are quite tall."

"The Milesians, or Celts as they are better known, never worried about their few numbers. Yet if you say 'Celt' in modern times, people assume you're talk about the Irish. As to your second point about being tall, do you know what we Fir Bolg call a tall leprechaun?"

"No."

"Shorty!"

The leprechaun was not amused. Still red-faced, he pulled a wallet sized photo of 42 from his plaid vest pocket. The picture showed a girl barely eighteen and completely naked. John must have gone into some future to get this picture. I blushed, trying to look away; the nudity of the child I had just made a deal with was…well, inappropriate. I do admit she was very attractive.

"So you don't want her for yourself?" Eircheard accused. "You're intending to sell her as a prostitute."

"Completely untrue. I intend to sell her as a sex slave."

"How is that better?"

"It makes me ruthless. Don't play innocent with me, Eircheard. You're buying sex slaves that you hope to keep placated by making sure they never lay eyes on a young man. If they never know better, they'll never want better. How many sunrises have you seen? Fifty years' worth?"

"Forty eight."

"So when you get to be sixty-two, you'll be ready to collect your eighteen-year-old bride!"

"What's wrong with that?"

I wasn't going to get anywhere this way. The trade I needed was a hard sell. The important thing about selling sex slaves is you have to be the biggest scoundrel in the room. No one should feel ashamed in front of his human trafficker.

"Nothing's wrong. Congratulations. I wish I had an

eighteen-year-old sex slave."

"Wife!"

His correction was harsh.

"Yes, wife," I agreed. "But I've got a better deal for you. I'll trade you your wife for a different female, one much more suited to your needs and tastes, perhaps."

"I'd need to see a picture first."

I did have a picture. I took it almost eight years ago for that brief period in her life when she became a professional dominatrix. Yes, I was going to sell my best friend, Trudy. How ruthless is that?

The picture was of a late forty-something heavyset woman in a leather catsuit holding a riding crop. She looked stern, yet somehow friendly. I wondered what a leprechaun that thinks a wife is a slave you cannot sell, thinks of a woman who dresses so.

"I'm sure this woman doesn't have many years of childbirth left." Eircheard scoffed.

"I don't know she has any."

I really didn't. She confided in me so many things. Would menopause be any different? One expects a childless woman to change over early.

"She hardly looks like much. You've seen my wife. Why would I even consider?"

"What would you rather have, a sex symbol or sex goddess? All those gold coins that the Milesians never found…I'm sure they paid for many a beauty, but did they ever grant you a sex goddess? Goddesses can be stolen, conquered, or even sold, but they cannot be rented."

Eircheard was not embarrassed.

"Well, this one looks like none of those are possible," he mused. "But what can she offer that would make a man forget a brownie-raised, leprechaun-educated, princess like this one?" He held the photo up to my face to make a point.

"She's a poet."

Eircheard knitted his eyebrows. He put his face very close to mine, so much so that I could smell the pipe on his breath.

"A real poet? You would traffic a poet? Why would you do that? Why would I go along? It doesn't sound to me like a fair trade."

"It's not. I'll need more than your wife."

"All the easier to walk away, I think." Eircheard started to do just that.

"I'm not even ready to fix a price," I yelled to his back. "How do you know you really want her if you've never had her? I'm not talking about renting her out, mind you."

Eircheard stopped in his tracks, though he didn't turn around.

"Free samples?"

"Seven years with her. You need to go to the year that she took this picture. If you're game, I'll take my answer tomorrow."

Now he turned. "Well…which is it, tomorrow or seven years from now?"

"That depends on if you buy her or not. If you're game, I'll send you to her seven years and a day back, from my perspective, which will be the future for you, but twenty-one years before the time you were going to settle with your child bride. After seven years in that future, I'll meet up with you in that future, which is one day away for me. If we don't have a deal, I'll send you back here tomorrow one day older than you are right now. If we do have a deal, you can continue your life with her in the future as if nothing happened. You wouldn't remember that anything did happen unless you write yourself a note. I recommend you don't do that as forgetting will be the best for you if you don't take this deal."

"You're expecting I'll fall in love with this lassie. You know full well, I'll be risking the Deep Time disease if I go to the future and come back again the day."

"I am, and I do."

"And you expect I'll pay everything I have for her, more like you'll kidnap me and you expecting all me gold for my freedom! We used to pay for your whores, we did, till they be getting the notion of taken all we could pay with!"

Eircheard's face was red. Steam seemed to blow out through his ears. Leprechaun lore has not endeared their race to the taller folk. Eircheard turned away. I blew it. Shouting again at his back, I said the only thing I could hope would save the deal.

"She might kidnap you, but you won't want to escape. It wouldn't be your gold she'd be after."

Eircheard sighed loudly before he turned to me. Anger had left him. There was no profit in resentment.

"With me," he said, shame in his face. "It has to be a certain way."

"Really," I tried to sound uninterested. Actually, I was uninterested. "I wouldn't worry about introducing your fetishes to her. Worry instead about being introduced to hers. Your child bride will learn to forgive your advanced age, find wisdom in all you say, and tolerate anything that will make you happy. Trudy will demand your manliness, find folly in every foolish thing you say, and the only way to shut her up will be to toss her on a lover's bed and pump her into carnal bliss."

He tried to seem uninterested, but the hunger in his eyes was unmistakable for any man that ever aspired to be the last man on earth.

"I'd love to try your deal, lad. But too many of us would rather have our wives and lives in this realm, in the time where the Fir Bolg forgot about us and the holy sight of Tara. They don't care about replenishing our numbers. If I go now, they'll never go into the future."

"I'll make sure that they do." I told him.

For a long time, he just looked back at me, measuring. I tried to look impressive, dressed in a Santa suit made for weather much colder than the mild Irish winter.

"Are you right-handed, lad?"

I nodded that I was, wondering where this was going.

"All the things you're saying," he decided. "They'll have to be in writing with the provision that I get both women if you try to cheat me."

"You draw up the papers and meet me back here in one hour. I'll sign the papers then. Be sure to BRING everything you can carry. I'll give you some money as reality doesn't accept maple leaves, and gold would just get you robbed. It might take some time before you can bed her, but you should find her behind a bar on a day when your clothes will fit the time."

"St. Patrick's Day," It was more of an exasperated statement. How could he know about a day honoring a man not born yet?

"New Year's Eve," I corrected. "December 31, 1999. Many Irish Americans will be wearing green. Your accent should adapt to the place, so your English will be without an Irish accent."

"And what do I say to this lassie to let her know she's supposed to pretend to fall in love with me?"

"Tell her she's supposed to fall in love with you, or the money you're paying for the drink has been wasted. After that, tell her that you think you might be able to have sex with her without paying for it, which is something you're not used to. Don't be too discouraged if you get your face slapped. She'll remember you, and you've set the bar pretty low for improving her opinion as you start frequenting the place where she serves. Smoke your pipe when you're with her and show her she can't drink you under the table."

"You tall folks never can." He started to walk away, then turned back. "Be the way, don't be having one of your pixies watching out when I come for the signing, like you did, expecting that I wouldn't notice her."

He had already scattered, but I traced where he pointed and saw her, which made my heart flutter.

For a human to spot a pixie is a very lucky thing, but approaching one is risky. If you're disrespectful or dismissive, you might become the subject of a pixie's natural love for mischief. There is safety in keeping distance. However, if a human of the opposite gender appeals to such a pixie, that pixie is likely to flirt. Pixies are quite attractive to other species and are known to offer much: games of seduction, romance, and adventure. Should a pixie wink at you, wink back, but don't approach it. Let the winged fairy come to you. You might blow a kiss to encourage this. A pixie might only bless your garden or farm and then fly away. But if it does approach you, expect kisses. But don't be too enthusiastic or aggressive about them. Better to match kiss for kiss. And don't be too chatty. Pixies detest nervous verbal advances. These creatures are quite promiscuous, and they regard human intimacy as too jealous and presumptuous. But if touching begins, it may lead to sexual adventure with a duration that matches a pixie's attention-span. The adventure may surpass a single night of passion but never long enough to produce an engagement ring.

She was not a pixie, however. Easy it was to confuse her, as they both have wings, but not all winged creatures are pixies. This was a little angel, the very one that is now both my lover and wife. If you be male and lay eyes on her, she may grace you with a wink, or even call you a "hon" or "cute." If the sight of you pleases her, she may even offer marriage in the same way her lover offers such. But do not seek a kiss from her nor a touch. In fact, keep your

GRUBBY HANDS OFF her. She is mine as I am hers. No other love shall be made by any other pair.

There were brownies occupying the ground between me and her. As I marched past them, I heard, "Fat human man can keep the suit." No doubt 42 had been doing her work, and my power seemed less meager to the troupe of them.

The kiss was hard, deep, and needful. She did not need to tell me that she had come from her future beyond her afterlife to guard me as I played "Santa." She always did, listening carefully to my interactions with the children that she might advise me latter on how to keep magic in the conversation. Now that she was past her lifetime, I saw plainly what I always suspected. Her angel wings were proof. I was careful not to harm them since the next kiss was a dance of passion, with her wings flapping expertly to keep her toes just beyond touching the grass.

"We can talk later," she whispered in my ear. "For your comfort, let's find a field where we can make love undisturbed."

I needed no encouragement.

We flew to such a field and discarded our clothes in a heap. During our lovemaking, I discovered that my concern about damaging her wings was unfounded as her wings only existed in the physical realm and only when she needed to use them. To enchant me, she put me on my back while using those wings for carnal motion. Afterward, she promised other tricks not possible while both of us lived, should another visit into space/time be allowed for her.

For a long time, we lay naked, me on my back and her wrapped around me with her head on my chest. With our eyes closed, anyone would have thought us sleeping, but we conversed with our thoughts as she and I could both hear each other.

"Please stake me," I pleaded, "that I might go with you."

A cloud passed over her thoughts.

I had always assumed that she had stolen my soul, so when I became a vampire, I had no soul left to suck out. This was the reason, I'd assumed, that John Simons failed to really compel me. Now, I was compelled to complete John-Peter because I loved the lad, although I knew better then to let John know either of these two facts. But then my lover, Nalla, this little angel, informed me something that she never told me in life.

"Souls can't be stolen the way artifacts are," she said. Rather, a soul can be "wired" to do the stealers bidding by influence; like tempting a remote-controlled car to drive forward. Your soul was already wired before I met you. Some mortal creature had placed the wiring within my soul but had yet to use it. So when I stole your soul, I merely added my own remote-control to the existing one, which kept you down the straight and narrow with my influence. No doubt the other soul stealer was a vampire, but until that vampire made its move by compelling you, we'll never know which vampire needs staking to free you of its influence so that you could perform the tasks required of you in my undead state, by the hosts of the divine."

"This doesn't make sense to me," I objected. "Common sense says that my best chance to escape damnation is to be staked before I do evil.

"Damnation is not on the table," she insisted. "Forgiveness can be granted for any acts you committed without free will. Rather, your actions could greatly reduce a need for forgiveness if you fulfill your part as an undead agent."

It was our first disagreement from beyond the grave. I was dead; why should I have more to do? Surely mortal men, be they undead or otherwise, had no jurisdiction in the dominion of the divine. Why not drive the stake and be done?

But this conversation showed me that the power had shifted in our relationship. Whereas my thinking would have carried the day in life, I now had to comply, as she had already passed to the beyond. Furthermore, I had to consider the life of John-Peter. If I were to die a real death before he was created, he would never be. The lad deserved better.

"Besides, my nature makes it impossible to take a life unless I'm willing to join with the fallen," she added.

Though unhappy, I had to agree. I disbelieved her, though, about damnation being off the table. I was on heaven's naughty list.

Maybe she did not want me to worry, but if I failed to find the soul-stealer and stake him or her, I would surely earn the damnation I believed I was destined to receive ever since I was a child.

"What is this place?" I spoke aloud, wishing to change the conversation. "And why are there no humans around, save the little girls from another time?"

"I'm sure you can guess. This place is a bubble on the surface of space/time. Though the sidhe exist independently, your imagination created this place as the leprechauns would have had it, as a further favor to them. They owe you." Then she added a warning: "Don't let them take advantage."

"What else did I do for them?"

"You have to find out for yourself. All I can tell you is that you have to be ruthless, or you'll never achieve what you're meant to achieve. If you fail to be ruthless, you may find yourself to be the king of all vampires."

"Well, what if I ruthlessly asked you what I did for them? Because I don't remember. They know that, and they're not going to tell me."

"If I told you, you'd never believe me. Find out!"

"I don't know how to find out. Neither do I know how to create John-Peter. I know I did it, but I also know that if I don't do it now, John-Peter will never walk the earth. I can't see this ending well. It's a matter of time before I fail at both."

"You can fail until you quit. You always say you're going to quit, but you never do."

That was true. I thought for a while, making the "to-do" list in my mind.

First, I have to build a boy, which involves writing the program for artificial intelligence that grows to become a prodigy, which is beyond anything I've ever done, and I've got to do that while being the village idiot that everyone expects me to be.

Second, I have to find the vampire that owns my soul and kill it.

Third, I have to master this realm so I can honor my promise to that little girl, setting up a conspiracy to kill me, by setting up a conspiracy to have myself slain, using, of course, the help of her prince.

Fourth, I'm to find out what I did for the leprechauns and

extract the proper payment. In the meantime, I have to run a newspaper delivery service up to the standards of a division manager who's trying to get rid of me.

Whatever will I do will all my free time?

"You missed one," Nalla said. "Five: you must keep your humanity the best you can."

She had been reading my thoughts.

"I know you're a vampire," she continued, "and you'll have to feed. I know your tastes, and I don't expect you'll just feed on animals, but you must not take any lives. You've always wanted to be feared. Try to remember when you're drinking the blood of some young hottie, that a corpse isn't going to remember much, and if you make another vampire... well, you'll know the mess you've made. Another thing: I don't mind you having other wives, but if you take another lover, I'll find it hard to forgive you. So keep it in your pants. I'll try to comfort you as often as I can, but you've got to stop coming to me during my natural life. I'm a widow now, and I've got to grieve and live out the rest of my life. I won't be able to do that if you lay beside me when I sleep."

"You get to move on," I whined. "But I have to stay faithful even though the rule is: till death do we part?"

"Sucks to be you."

But, of course, it never did suck. She always tolerated my perverted imagination the same way I tolerated hers.

"If it makes it easier, I do marry a lover again, many years after you stop your undead incursions into our bedroom. Don't feel sorry for me."

"That depends on the marriage."

"A Latin busboy near retirement age…short, heavy, a cutie who could barely speak English. I fell in love with him. He wanted a green card."

"That's terrible!"

"No. In a few years, he was so in love with me, he couldn't see straight. But that was during life, Edward. My afterlife lover is you."

I was still lying naked with a smile on my face when she disappeared. I lay there wishing I could stay here for the rest of my undead life…

That's when a troupe of brownies fell on me.

OK, they didn't really fall on me…more like surrounded me in a menacing way… or that's what it seemed, seeing I was naked, and they seemed very unhappy.

"Why Steward sleep?" one shouted at me. "Humans sleep at night! Steward has work to do."

"The Steward of Tara sleeps anytime he likes," I told them, trying to look formidable in my aged birthday suit. "Why do brownies disturb the Steward?"

That was the task that I forgot to list, yet somehow it was already finished. Did the lies of a little girl raise me from slave to commander in just a few hours?

"Glorna makes big trouble again," he answered respectfully.

Now, I wish I were the slave.

Glorna, a wood sprite, was always making problems by making his own rules and confronting everyone who abided by ancient protocol instead of Glorna logic. This time, he had insulted some banshee who was singing too loudly and out of tune, according Glorna's estimation. Feelings were frayed and needed smoothing out. I promised the banshee, whose voice was just fine, that I would chastise the wood sprite with a limerick he would never forget.

After the Glorna mess, I headed to the portal where Eircheard and I were to meet. I was several hours late, but Eircheard was even later than that. When he came, he was dragging several sacks filled with items he was hoping would have value in this unknown future that he was embarking on. I gave him all the money I could afford, which was hardly enough, but Eircheard was a capable business leprechaun who knew how to make a profit.

I gave him a map of Detroit, some tips on prices in modern times, and advice on the best places to sell his wares, which for the moment, were pawn shops. He wasn't interested. He wanted to know the quickest way to bed Trudy, which was, of course, to be patient and not too persistent. I reminded him several times he had nothing to lose if he didn't wind up keeping her. Instead, he'd be standing in this exact spot tomorrow with no memory of what happened or where he'd been, and he'd only know that he was one day older and there was no deal.

That's when he produced his contract.

I read it as carefully as my dyslexia allowed, which means, it took a very long time, and I learned nothing. I did expect it to be longer and worded cagily. He huffed several times as I went through it.

"Are you sure you're ready to sign this, lad? It's a half a page long, and I'm not ready to die of old age? What kind of trap were you expecting?"

"I don't know," I answered truthfully as I signed the document. "I expected to learn something I didn't already know."

"I learned something," he gloated as he pocketed the document. "It helps to know I have dealings with a liar. You should be putting yourself on your own naughty list."

I looked at him quizzically.

"You told me you were right-handed," He smirked and spoke to me for the last time in his thick Irish accent. "But you signed my papers with your left."

He was through the portal before I could say it. Just as well, I thought. It's good to have some lines on the board that your opponent doesn't know about.

I really am right-handed.

CHAPTER 9: HAPPY HUNTING

Something felt wrong about the building in every way that "wrong" could be applied. Moral corruption seemed to hang on the ivory that climbed the funeral parlor's two-storied red bricks. The main entrance face south towards the street, which denied the funeral procession parallel parking. To the east of the parking lot was a drive-thru window, no longer functional but it confirmed the building was unsuited for its somber purpose. Two businesses flanked it: a bar with a garden and a well-trafficked grocery store.

It was still early, but mourners had already begun to pile in. Most had a baffled look as if uncertain they'd found the right place. Already, Trudy took one of the few parking spots left in the parlor's lot.

The confrontation of the previous night seemed wrapped around the people that filed in, or was that her, regretting that she wasn't there to confront. Eddie was always too mild in defending himself, at least until his Irish temper flared. Then again, his temper never flared until the offender was no longer in front of him.

That's when she remembered the unloaded gun around her waist. Wishing she weren't here dressed as a cop, she unlocked the trunk of her bike with one hand and unbuckled with the other. Good! She had left Bathrobe's leather jacket in there the last time she rode, when the spring wind turned to summer heat. Now she could cover the badge and mark herself a mourner instead of police presence.

Nalla stood near the empty coffin. The reception line was long, for which Trudy was grateful, but when Nalla's eyes fell on her, she caught Trudy by surprise, charging forward and embracing her before she had a chance to think. The widow's tears wetted her cheek as her guilt rose with her suspicion. If roles were reversed, would she be hugging the woman that killed him?

"You were aiming for your own head and missed," Nalla had told her over the phone.

The hug held time at a standstill. Embraced as they were, Trudy imagined a choice of responses ranging from accusations to blackmail and accepted them all, but Nalla just kept hugging and weeping. Trudy was about to promise to turn herself in when Nalla finally spoke.

"There are some personal things that Ed always wanted you to have, should something happen. Stop by later; I've got to get back to the line."

With that, Trudy stood alone. Was she being forgiven?

The line was ridiculously long. Although he only had one son, and although Eddie's father was the last of thirteen and his mother the first of twelve, the great number of guests couldn't account for that. None of Eddie's five surviving brothers and two sisters were there, so Trudy couldn't find a single face she knew, but she could guess who belonged to whom. Uncles, aunts, and cousins all looked alike, and they clustered pale-faced and baffled next to the other mourners, who surely had gone to the wrong wake. Trudy saw ex-students and teachers from Nalla's school, including some who'd never met Eddie but had heard what happened and were there for the widow. Eddies co-workers were scattered around the state and spoke three different languages as they were all from the different facilities that he had worked at in his long newspaper distribution career.

"Who are these people, and are they safe to talk to?" a voice whispered behind her.

Trudy turned around. This was the younger sister, now a full woman, already twice divorced. The last time Trudy saw her was just as sad, back when Jane was no more than a teen. Eddie was the only sibling living on his own at the time.

Jane seemed to guess her thoughts, for she said softly., "It was the middle of the night. My big brother was just waking up for work when he got the call that Jammie had committed suicide. He made one call, and that was to you, Trudy. He thought he was going to finish the day before making the four-hour trip to where the rest of the family lived. But when he got there, you were waiting for him and that's the first time he realized that his younger brother was died. You drove and stayed with him that whole horrible day."

Both women hugged and wept.

"Jane, I've done something terrible." Trudy confessed.

"Let's share our regrets on another day," Jane sobbed. "Grief makes everything seem worse than it is. Here's my card. I'm not there anymore, but I'll write my personal cell on the back here. No, I don't do therapy anymore; it wasn't good for me or my marriage. I learned exactly what to tell people, but it didn't make me anything but a know-it-all in my own life."

That struck a chord with Trudy, who often worked as a financial advisor.

"There's seems to be two types of people here," Jane observed. "Family, which Ed wouldn't be able to name, and friends, which none of the family would recognize. Ed stayed away from any family functions. I don't think anyone beyond siblings and parents ever met his son."

"Blame that on Father Chokey."

"We didn't know any priests by that name, and we were related to three of them. Father George was our uncle who drank too much. They say he tried to molest the young girls with long hair in the family, but I don't think that's got anything to do with us. My hair was too short, and Molly was too smart."

"Do you really think that? How many times did Father George come to your house, uninvited, when he knew neither parent would be home? Do you really think he never got to your older sister after trying for so many years?"

Jane thought about that. Looking confused, she asked, "Then who was Father Chokey?"

"You weren't related to him. He started showing up after your father left. Remember him? He was the guy that gave your mother money and took Ed to play basketball, then brought him back an hour later."

"Father John? He gave us money because we were poor."

Trudy shook her head sadly. "Father John had a very poor

parish. Do you actually believe you were that poor? You lived in a house…"

"Wait! Are you saying my brother was molested some forty years ago and never said anything? And what would that have to do with family?"

"Do you remember the gold cross Molly and Ed used to wear all the time? Father George gave him that cross. Molly stopped wearing it, and your mother was fine with that, but do you remember how she reacted when Eddie stopped wearing it? Father John stopped coming around at the same time, didn't he? The cross marked him. What your mother never knew was that Father John got scared and didn't hurt him anymore after Eddie almost choked to death. Eddie's problem is he never thought of himself as a victim, he thought of himself as a prostitute; making money the easiest way a ten, eleven, and then twelve-year-old could possible do."

"Ed told you this? It can't be true!" But the expression on Jane's face showed she was putting the pieces together. "Anyway, why would Ed avoid us? Didn't he trust us?"

"Oh, Jane, no. He didn't trust himself. You were right earlier, this isn't the time, but I'm about to have a lot of time on my hands in the near future. I promise I'll write and tell you all I know. But come this way, I'll show you people that had less then you did who don't think they're poor at all."

Trudy walked. Jane followed, wanting more answers.

"But I know THIS guy," Trudy proclaimed loudly to a confused tall Mexican, not yet two years in the country."

"I'm sorry, I think you make a mistake…"

But Trudy already started to recite:

Tall Carlos from old Mexico
Is the kindest man you'll ever know.
But he's steel in the saddle
That just doesn't rattle
No matter how bad things may go.

"Did Ed write that?" a bewildered Jane asked.

"Jane, this is Carlos, one of Ed's coworkers. Carlos, this is Ed's younger sister Jane. No, Carlos, we've never met, but I know you from the limerick. I'm Trudy, Ed's best friend."

Carlos smiled widely and said he'd heard the limerick but did not understand the slang in it. Other coworkers explained, but all he got was that Ed had thought highly of him. Soon the two women were seated among a Spanish conversation, politely translated for the white and black people clustered in hearing range. In turn, English was translated to Spanish as the news carriers and paper handlers reminisced about Ed's time with them. As the volume grew, another group that knew Ed from a different distribution center made its way and introduced itself.

Trudy found herself at the center of a game that Ed would have loved. Can you guess who I am? Do you know my limerick? Do you know my nickname? In a very short time, coworkers became the loudest group in the crowded parlor.

"I know you, you're Grace." Then she told a blonde middle-aged tall man, "You're Pope Asshole the First."

People from the facility roared at her getting it right, while others looked sheepish at the blasphemy.

One of the co-workers explained it. In the time after one of the pope's deaths (no one remembered who) the papal election dominated the headlines, making "no pope yet" predictable and tiring so Ed "suggested" the distribution center elect their own pope. "Suggest" in this case meant thrusting a pen and paper at each handler or carrier until they wrote down a name. Dan, who was kind of Ed's sparring partner for gags, won the election, if Ed did indeed count the votes right. And so Pope Asshole the First was named. Every morning, (or night if you took one a.m. as such) Ed would genuflect in front of Dan who quipped, "I don't have a ring; you're going to have to kiss something else." After that Dan tried everything to give up his papal throne. Every morning, Dan made announcement that he was a converting to a new religion. Eventually he ran out of religions.

"If I told you that I was the first Queen of Christmas, would you know my name?" a youngish woman asked.

"Ah, a trick question." Trudy laughed as she recited:

Reasons to love her there's more than a dozen
She keeps the back room really buzzin.'
She's the first Q. O. C.
Call her Jill, call her Lee,

Just don't mess with her sister or cousin.

The women explained the reason for her limerick. Ed could never get her name right, and for some reason, called her Jill, when her name was Lee, but she was the unofficial spokeswoman for the "Lee" clan that had several family members working at the distribution center during Ed's time there. Ed had a white beard and a gut that made him the perfect Santa around Christmas time. One morning in December, he arrived with Christmas hats and tried to get everyone to sing carols. Later that season, he got it in his head that he was going to buy Christmas presents for everyone's kids. He decided to introduce a new position, "Queen of Christmas," to help him "make merry" during the season. He held an election, and Lee (Jill) won. As queen, Lee had to get the number, age, and gender of all the employees' children so Ed and Nalla could buy them presents. Ed moved from facility to facility through the years, but he always brought this tradition with him.

Talking about the Queen of Christmas brought to mind other traditions Ed introduced. For instance, one distribution center had a large Hispanic population, So Ed would made pinatas out of papier-mache, stuff them with chocolate, and bring them for breaking every May and September. As time went on, Ed kept adding to his list of self-imposed traditions. He grilled steaks on the Fourth of July, organized pallet jack races for Labor Day, and distributed small candy canes every day to every employee all through the Christmas season.

"Too many carriers are too busy to celebrate anything," Eddie once told her. "I tried to organize parties for the holidays outside work until I realized most didn't have time to show, and the ones that did show were more likely to be too tired or too drunk to work the next day. I realized that if there was going to be a celebration, it had to be at work."

But the wackiest holiday that Ed insisted on celebrating was his own birthday, located between the days of February 12 (Lincoln's birthday) and February 14 (Valentine's Day). Eddie joked that the purpose of his life was to do something that would make a three-day holiday that even news carriers could celebrate. "Calkins Day," as he called it, needed a parade and they would have one right in the warehouse. Ed would hop onto a pallet jack, and a carrier would pull Ed through the distribution center, while Ed waved to his constituents with one hand and tossed bite-sized, wrapped pieces of candies from the other one toward the workstations.

Trudy noticed the last group of coworkers and joined them. This group had a fair mix of Arabic workers speaking the language. Some of the women wore head scarfs. This facility was also no stranger to Eddie's strange way of celebrating nor his proposals of marriage.

It was good to hear of Eddie being remembered fondly, but Trudy was getting bored. Looking around, Trudy notice Jane had slipped out. Trudy took her example.

Before she could walk away, Trudy spotted a woman approaching the group. She could feel the energy; the woman seemed to be walking on springs. By the woman's black brimmed hat and black overcoat, Trudy realized this was the woman that Sheriff Matt feared. This freelance reporter was also a newspaper carrier. She had several routes, including one with Ed, and shared them with her family. Trudy got up from her seat and approached the hard-working reporter.

"You're the Goddess, are you not?"

The woman smiled and nodded energetically. "Yes, I am," she stated with a comical pride.

"So you, too, have a double mission." Trudy opened her jacket just enough for the Goddess to see her badge.

"Look, I know Beulah County is broke, but I'm hoping it doesn't keep a murderer free. I know it sounds crazy, but the killer isn't the guy you think it is. It's John!"

Was it the pills, or just a certain magic that happens when a journalist informs a poet? As the Goddess shared her explanation, Trudy went into trance, feeling the cool of the morning and smelling the sweat of the bagging coworkers, barely awake and apprehensive about an uninvited representative. The presence of a division manager at this time of the morning meant that Ed was in trouble…

"When I email you with a problem, I expect you to take care of it! If you want to be a clown, join the circus."

The tall, thin, aged man poked his finger painfully into Ed's chest.

If it were Trudy, or maybe anyone else, that man would need a new face, but Ed kept his hands on his hips and said in a steady voice, "That paper was delivered since the day it started three days ago."

Jake slapped his hand on a stuffing table and turned away in disgust. Then he sharply turned back toward Ed, putting his face in biting distance.

"There! See? Is everyone that worked for the Examiner as stupid as you? You want to be everyone's friend. You have cookouts and decorate, but the carriers lie to you because they don't want to put this paper on the porch!"

Eddie's ears were red before the word "lie" got thrown. Red ears meant that Ed was enraged. But now, his whole face was beet red. Ed was delivering that route himself. Barely containing his rage, he told Jake so. But Jake mocked Ed's voice, competence, and credibility. The bashing went on for fifteen minutes. Carriers said nothing but were clearly getting mad in Ed's defense…

"Look," the Goddess said to Trudy. "Do you see that man?"

The tall, slim man had finished bagging and was now watching the confrontation dispassionately. He had very long blond hair, almond-shaped blue eyes, and the merest hint of a mustache and beard. He also seemed to be waiting for something.

"On most days," the Goddess said, "John Simotes brings his cute young son to 'help.' The boy and Ed have a special connection. Before Jake got in, Ed questioned the boy's absence but got only reassurance that the boy was not ill.

"I'm checking that house this morning and if they don't have a paper, you don't get a paycheck, stupid!"

Ed had enough.

"I quit!" he shouted and walked toward the door.

"Good!" Jake shouted at his back. "Take all these losers you call 'carriers' with you!"

Jake must have realized it was dangerous for him to stay and slipped away before the shocked carriers had a change to react. Already one of them, a youngish Hispanic woman, ran to intercept

Ed, trying to calm him, lest he lose a job he needed.

But Ed had already started back. He couldn't quit because there was no one he could get in touch with to tell them he was no longer working. Jake could talk about withholding a paycheck until he was blue in the face, but Ed didn't work for Jake. Jake had no business even talking to Ed, because the newspaper that hired Jake, had a contract with Ed's boss, Robert, who never answered his phone before nine. Ed, who actually ran things, had no such contract.

"I need a digital camera," Ed muttered as he finished bagging the last of the unfilled route. His cellphone did not take pictures like some of the newer phones did. "Or better yet, let them fire me, I'd love to see who they'd replace me with."

"I'll take a picture," the young woman volunteered. "Just tell me the address."

"200 Tomas."

And she was off.

Not six seconds later, John Simotes left in a sudden hurry.

"Creepy, isn't it?" The Goddess asked. "And what's creepier is that Ed's van was found at the beginning of the route. He had only delivered it three or four times, and it had tricky turns, so he'd follow the route list. But when Rob went to get the papers, he only found the extras that Ed would take with him lest someone be short. Even more perplexing, that route should have generated a massive amount of complaints, but there was only one.

"200 Tomas. I take it that address is fairly close to the beginning of the route?"

"Exactly. Only two streets down. Just one person besides Ed knew that route well enough to get it done on time: John Simotes. He used to have that route but took a different, more difficult route that paid less. So, we have three people meeting in the area about the time that Ed was shot across from a park that's rumored to be haunted on a route too creepy for anyone to run. What I'd like to know: are any of those three people suspects?"

"We have a fourth suspect with more evidence," Trudy answered painfully. "But I'd like to hear your theory on what might have happened.

The Goddess looked visibly uncomfortable.

"It could be that Tomasa, the young woman who promised the picture, but was afraid of the area, took more than a camera with her. Maybe she saw Jake harassing Ed through his driver side window and shot at him but hit Ed. Jake didn't report it because he wasn't supposed to be confronting a contractor that the paper didn't contract. The pair of them left before Simons found the body and called the police."

Trudy picked up on the doubt in The Goddess' voice.

"But that doesn't explain how the route got done," Trudy said. " Please tell me what you really think happened…maybe what you fear happened, no matter how strange. We're not on the record."

"I don't think that either Jake or Tomasa went to 200 Tomas as they said, because the area IS haunted. Fog shows up from nowhere, and people hear women screaming at night. What I think…what I fear, but I've heard whispers before is….well, John Simotes is really John Simons."

"John Simons? Wasn't that the name of some nineteenth century musician?"

"Yes," The Goddess murmured. "And he's now a vampire."

Trudy couldn't believe what she was hearing.

"So you think that John Simons killed Eddie and made him a vampire? That would explain the route being finished. Eddie did it after he was killed, then returned with his truck to the spot he was shot."

The Goddess looked surprised and terrified that Trudy took her theory seriously.

"It also explains the lead ball found near the body," The Goddess said. "The weapon that fired it is at least a hundred years old. It also explains why the body was almost drained of blood and why the puddles on the truck floor weren't inches deep. Also, John Simons, who never missed a day, hasn't done his route since that night. His wife and boy have come into the center instead."

Trudy considered these words. Could someone else have killed Eddie? She remembered sadness, but no guilt, as she stumbled to Bathrobe's bed that morning after her shift. So had she gone back to the department to punch out before heading home? Trudy knew she could play sober no matter how drunk she got. Or was she so upset that she just drove directly to Bathrobe's house? No, wait, Bathrobe's gun was empty; she was certain of it. She also remembered that she shot Eddie and not with a 38 revolver, but maybe that was self-defense. Ed could have tried to bite her, or maybe she saw this Simons trying to bite Eddie. Maybe she shot at Simons and hit Eddie instead.

Trudy had a dreadful thought, and it pleased her. She could get away with this. She could actually get away with this. No jail. No way to ever really be sure she was guilty. Maybe she could just live in the doubt.

"There's something I can't tell you right now," Trudy finally told the waiting Goddess. "I know something else about the case, Beulah County, and the department, but I need time to mourn my friend. Give me five days, and I promise I'll tell you everything I know before I tell anyone else. Deal?"

The Goddess still was wearing that surprise and fear cocktail, along with just a trace of fatigue, born of doing routes, interviewing, writing, and now have to attend a wake, too. All of that surrendered to a smile as she nodded and shook Trudy's hand. "We have a deal."

As Trudy moved away, she had two thoughts.

Where did the Goddess get her energy?

Eddie, the vampire. Why did that not seem farfetched?

The wake was now packed, and she saw more of the people whose names she knew. Towards the entrance and working his way to Nalla, she caught a glimpse of Eddie's son and his son's wife but trying to get to him would mean pushing too impolitely.

What she really needed was the bathroom.

"Out the double door and down the hall," she was told, but getting there was going to take time and persistence.

Working to the end, she encountered Jane and a question.

"My friends in high school," Jane began. "Some of them were…"

"Your brother was never a pimp," Trudy told her plainly. "He was someone that a prostitute could talk to without being judged or played. Eddie was the awkward guy because he knew things he shouldn't, but it served him when someone needed to talk."

"But how did they get the idea? Is Ed why they are what they are?"

"Jane, they were already working before Eddie met them;

they just couldn't tell you. As far as what they are, they're wives and mothers now. Don't expect them to come here, though. Better to forget. I need the women's room now, Jane. I'll write to you if I don't see you."

It was no good. Jane was gone, accepting Trudy's sentence to explain a life. Trudy felt she had a poem somewhere in that thought, but she frantically needed the women's room and couldn't find it.

Suddenly, it was there. A crowd of this size always had a line to the women's room, but she was standing at the door of a restroom that was empty. Was it the good pills? New medication had its perils. For a second, she thought the luminated red sign read, "Vampires Abode."

Creepy.

The restroom was clean enough, as if none of the stalls had ever seen girls or women, but the decor seemed almost Victorian. "Relief and escape" was her mission that took her inside the nearest stall. What did she mean, "Victorian?" Not a single feature had that quality. "Relief" was achieved but "explore" seemed to conspire to replace "escape."

The mirrors across from the stalls were underscored with ivory sinks. Ivory or new medication? The lights dimmed to the level that candles produced. Trudy washed her hands and caught a flash in the mirror. Fearfully and slowly, she raised her head from the water to meet, not her eyes, but the unwavering eyes of Eddie the Confronter.

"Welcome to Happy Hunting Grounds," the image said coldly.

"What is this place?"

"It's a burial ground favored by vampires." Eddie showed his fangs. "But that's not your concern."

Trudy tried to never show fear, and she didn't show fear now. "What is then?"

"Are we telling secrets now that don't belong to us? Father Chokey paid good money for my silence as well as my service. My family needed that money. Secrets that are not mine belong in my coffin."

But Trudy wasn't taking the bait. "Why, Eddie? Tell me why I did it!"

Eddie's vampire image stayed silently on the mirror. Wait! Vampires don't cast a reflection!

He finally spoke as if he didn't hear her question or was too uncooperative to answer.

"It seems, Trudy, we have some unfinished business concerning what I did about winning the lottery."

"We do."

"Then maybe this town isn't big enough for the both of us."

"It's not," she heard herself answer.

Was that it? Was she still that mad at him after all these years? Why hadn't she told him? Why hadn't she told herself? Why hadn't he told her? But she felt it now. Damn the "why" chromosome! Eddie and all the guys like him deserve what they get and more. Why do we still love them? Why are we sorry when they finally get their just desserts?

"The playground where we first met is about two hundred yards from the street where I died. Do you remember the place?"

"I do."

"Then meet me there four days from now at four a.m. by your clock. We'll settle there. If you don't show, you've admitted that you were wrong."

Trudy looked straight into Eddies undead eyes. "If you're stupid enough to show, that will be the last time anyone ever sees you."

Her image replaced that of the bearded, white-haired vampire's. She remembered Wraith Park, named for William Wraith, one of Thornton's mayors back in the '40s. Mr. Wraith had bought the remote piece of property between Jenson and Thornton with the intention of expanding Thornton's borders; he solidified his intentions by installing a playground in his name. But corruption in his office thwarted Wraith's expansion plans. And someone thwarted Wraith. One morning some kids found him shot to death beneath the monkey bars. People stayed clear of the park ever since.

Except for Trudy. Except for Eddie.

And those who did come near it saw the mist, heard the whispers.

She was on the other side of Wraith Park on that fateful morning with her cruiser's passenger side window down and her arm almost out, holding a now empty pistol that pointed to a white van.

"I shot you there once, stupid ass!"

Regret, anger, love, with a garnish of fear was the cocktail of the evening, and Trudy had already drunk too much of it. Maybe that's what she needed. A drink. A drink at a bar where she could fill her part of the arrangement that she'd been neglecting with a man that never gave her cause to be angry. When was the last time she brought someone home? She could be the vampire again! How would that feel after almost a year?

"Not like it used to," she admitted out loud. These days, she hunted to satisfy someone else. It would feel tired.

She turned for the door.

But found a mirror.

CHAPTER 10: A GOVERNMENT OF, BY, AND FOR ED CALKINS

A desk and chair have no place in a women's restroom, but that was the image in front of Trudy as she hoped to leave not only the restroom, but the funeral parlor. Lights were off, but she could make out a computer monitor on the desk's surface. She didn't dare turn around to look at the reflection's source because that would mean placing her back to the full-length mirror. That might be Eddie's only chance to take her unawares.

"Mirrors and light": he had a theory about that. It wasn't an original theory. Plato's cave had been around far past its usefulness, but Eddie referred to it, back when he was still creating serious poetry. The theory compared the perception of reality to a pair of men standing backs to the entrance, looking on each other's shadows and thinking that they faced each other. He'd finally started leaving that idea alone, but then the evidence came in about the speed of light, which is constant. For example, when Eddie threw a newspaper from his truck, the newspaper added the speed of the truck to the power of the throw and went faster than Eddie could throw it. Conversely, the light from his headlights was not added to the speed of the beam, which went only at the same speed of light everywhere.

Eddie explained this in a novel, stubborn way, claiming that the true source of light does not move. Eddie claimed that his

125

headlights, like all light, were invisible until they reflected off some unmoving "dark matter mirror," which resided everywhere in the universe where "vision" is possible. One could see the mirror, not the light. This also changed the way he thought of time and space. Eddie used to infuriate everyone when he talked about space travel, saying that if people ever launched a probe at the nearest star, the star was just as likely to get further away the closer they approached it, just like objects reflected from a mirror get farther away as people approach the mirror.

Approach the mirror.

It made sense now. Trudy took a step.

Did the desk get closer or farther away?

It actually got closer.

The "mirror" was an entrance, like some hole in the fabric of reality. That or these new pills, while great for depression, were going to present some interesting challenges.

Trudy stepped out of reality and into the darkened office.

Just as she did, a light went on and a young, good-looking man opened the door, flicked on a switch, and stepped inside. Trudy was trying to think how to explain herself when she gasped in recognition.

But the boy apologized.

"Sorry Trudy," the boy said. "I'm not supposed to be here. I'll come back later; it's nothing I can't do at another time. Just please don't tell Ed Calkins you saw me here. I don't want to star in another limerick."

"Clint?"

"Ah, it's your first time," he replied as if he instantly knew everything she didn't. "Please call me Glorna from the other Tara of Ed Calkins' imagination, the one without humans. You know me because I've starred in your dreams. Actually, you're a queen in this realm, which is Tara with humans. A queen like you can call me anything you like. If I'm 'Clint' to you, well that's fine. I have been watching cowboy films, so I know everything about cowboys."

"Except how to raise cattle," Trudy quipped.

"What does cattle have to do with being a cowboy? My queen, you're confused. Herds of cattle are in Ireland. Cowboys live in the American west and have nothing to do with cows. It's just a name. Cowboys break laws, rob banks, kill outlaws for bounties....that sort of thing. No cowboy would be caught dead doing rancher's work. I know. I've watched all the movies."

Trudy didn't argue but looked back at the place she'd entered. Gone. The room was different, too.

Glorna pointed at the wall. "Don't worry. When you wish to leave, I'll open the portal. I'm a wood sprite from way back, so I'm omnipresent in this office. You probably want to know where you are right now, but I can't tell you. I've never been outside this building, you see, because I'm from the other Tara. I can tell you that we're more back in time rather than forward."

Pointing to the knives on either side of his belt, Glorna quipped, "I feel like I should have more advanced weapons."

Trudy felt the belt around her own waist. It was also a knife, but it should have been a...what?

"Don't expect to name anything that hasn't been invented yet. The only place that's allowed is the other Tara, and The Steward of Tara won't make that mistake again," Glorna explained. "Just please don't tell Ed Calkins I'm here. I'm supposed to be under house arrest...you know, for cowboy things."

"There was something on that table here."

"I'm sure there was. Are you ready to meet them?"

"Them?"

"Your subjects, my queen." Glorna bowed low and stayed bowed until Trudy passed. Then he rushed forward to open the gate.

The arched ceilings were twice as high as the hallway was wide. She was on a platform raised three steps above the stone floor. Looking outward was a single throne, jeweled with a splendor that she had seen previously but could not name where. Tapestries hung from the ceilings in green and red plaid, each slightly different than the rest. As she admired, the gate flew open. Six two-man war chariots rode abreast as width would allow. Behind them, the same, about nine or ten deep.

"What is the meaning?" Trudy asked.

Leather clad men disembarked bearing spears.

"We seek an audience with your Highness."

"Another time!" Trudy proclaimed, but the men were not asking.

Now she stood locked at neck, wrists, and ankles, with lengths of chains between each and a gray sack slit at the sides but covering her completely. From where she stood, she heard formal greetings in a tongue she could not name; yet, by some mystic power, she understood as if it were English in an Irish accent. One of the voices made her roll her unseen eyes.

"Greetings, young O'Murray, may the wind stay at your back. I, the humble Steward of Tara, stand at ready for your coronation. And might I say, my admiration of your skill in battle is only second to my praise of your generous nature."

"Rise, Steward," O'Murray answered. "I trust by your greeting that you understand my mandate to kill my rival and take my proper place as a king? Surely, you understand I did this for the island and not for any reasons selfish."

"That is the way I understand it now," hedged this "Steward," which sounded absurdly like Ed Calkins. "What I understand when the tale is composed is most dependent on the events that follow."

O'Murray paused seeming to hold his breath. "And were I to continue my campaign against the clan from the House of Brooks, would that also depend on events that follow."

"Oh, future king, that tale would be too momentous to hold my ghost composers back."

"Too inspiring?"

Eddie roared, laughing. "Too ridiculously, stupidly, cowardly, funny, I should think. Wouldn't King O'Murray find it such?"

"Yes, of course," the young future king tried to chuckle, but couldn't keep the disappointment out of his voice. "Such a campaign would be a shrine to farce. Perhaps one might not think the same of a campaign against East Fields?"

"Perhaps one might not, or perhaps one might," Eddie said, sounding thoughtful. "It would come down to who of the kings could be most devoted to the holy hill of Tara. But a humble Steward cannot be trusted to look so far into the future. What service might I be in helping you inspire the withholding of minstrels that might sing sadly of this historic day? Or, to phrase it directly, what have you brought me?"

"Maybe what I have for you is a sword to cut short your ruthless reign as well as the songs of your minstrels. Many a steward can be found that looks kindly on the house of O'Murray and many more that would strum and sing its praise, for a fee. None would miss this Ed Calkins if gold were in his place."

Trudy knew Eddie to be a coward, but not to threats like this one. She was not surprised when he answered in an unaffected voice.

"If there is a sword so foolish, young O'Murray, let the sword cut. But the songs that hold the legions back would also go silent. All the gold, no matter whose hands were chopped to get it, would find the pockets of the Roman Senate or the like. And what of the fairies? Can you silence their songs? Can you stop their misdeeds? What of the oaks and the bogs? Why the whole of Ireland would declare war on the Irish. And if none of this happened, how would you stop people from believing it will? This says nothing of the trial you've yet to complete with your chariot. Why do some would-be Kings find themselves unable to crash through Tara's scared stones? I believe the Oak House has better sense. I humbly ask again, what did you bring me?"

O'Murray sighed and then made some signal. Instantly, the grey sack was lifted from her body. Time had to stop for her to take it all in. The ancient phallic stone was the first sight she caught. The Stone of Destiny or 'Lia Fail' told her exactly where she was. Beyond she could see the Mound of Hostages, and was that the Rath of Synods to the north? Is that structure where Eddie lived now that he was dead?

Trudy then caught a glimpse of her follow prisoners. Each was a beautiful girl or woman, wearing a crown of flowers on hair of styled curls and a white silk tunic with a wide gold ribbon bow at the waist. Each was flanked by a pair of nearly naked, buff swordsmen, and they wore a tearful face of dread.

"I present you with a blood sacrifice of fifty plus one. Fifty of the most beautiful daughters and wives that we could capture from our hated enemy are yours for your ruthless pleasure. Please do not be offended by the one. She claims to be a queen who is unafraid of Ed Calkins or his like."

Eddie strolled to where Trudy was chained and lifted her chin to expose her neck. She glared at him.

"How brave is this queen!" the pompous "Steward" proclaimed. "Well done, young O'Murray. You have quite the eye to include one that less kingly men would have missed. Note the wisdom deep within those grey eyes and the care of self-adornment.

The age that has touched her face also has given her knowledge. She is the better half of fifty-one."

"And how fat she is," O'Murray gushed. "Clearly in this time of famine where crops have failed for four years, the queen is rich."

Eddie shot a cautionary glance at O'Murray. "One with deep grey eyes could be a poet. Her last words are sure to be remembered." Then, looking back at Trudy, he announced, "I will taste my sacrifice after the coronation's feast. Tie her to the stone, for now."

Eddie pointed to the Stone of Destiny.

The swordsmen looked confused and hesitant, but soon a key appeared and dropped the locks. Trudy longed to fight these muscled men to the last, but then remembered she was a queen. Once free, she proudly strolled to the stone's base without allowing the men to touch her. A length of rope appeared, and a discussion erupted over how to tie a queen to a rock. Trudy lost patience and told them to tie wrist to wrist behind her with the stone between.

But as soon as she was close enough to touch it, the stone screamed, loud enough to be heard for miles beyond the sacred hill. Then Trudy saw that Eddie was causing the noise. You see, the legend of the Stone of Destiny says it screams in delight whenever a worthy monarch stepped near it. She was to upstage O'Murray, perhaps as a lesson not to threaten the Steward.

O'Murray did not like it at all. He shouted to the Steward, "What of the other fifty wives and maidens? Don't you want any of them?"

"No!" the "Steward" shouted back. "They shall entertain us with their dancing." Then to a line of straighter darker trees, he ordered, "Hang them, if it pleases young O'Murray."

The future king shrugged.

Trudy shouted her objection, but the blasted "stone" screamed louder, Eddie's attendants rushed among the baffled swordsmen and quickly and efficiently prepared the women. The victims screamed and cried as they were unlocked from the chains only to have their hands bound behind them with rope. From a line of trees, green vines with pale pink flowers fell to shoulder height, tied into nooses. Any who saw would think Eddie controlled the row of oaks.

Some of the victims kicked and fought; others just wept. Within three minutes of Eddie's order, each were bounding and standing under a noose. Some had to be held to keep them upright. Others showed more dignity - or was it despair? Neither Trudy nor the stone had gone silent. Just the same, the noose went over each pretty crying, cursing head, hair brushed back or pulled aside, and with the crowns of flowers replaced if their struggles forced them off. Eddie himself inspected each noose, and he took his time doing it. Then he assumed his place near O'Murray and his men, who faced the forlorn females.

The Steward raised his right hand high and waited for effect, then dropped it emphatically. The trees pulled the vines upward, dangling the kicking victims not half a body length over the ground. Their faces reddened. The nooses would not break their slender necks; they would strangle.

"Eddie," Trudy shouted. "Stop! Don't you remember? This is exactly what Father Chokey did to you!"

Everyone ignored her, except one.

"Silence!" Eddie shouted. "I think the queen wishes to speak."

The stone went quiet, but O'Murray did not.

"Why should I let her speak? She's a prisoner…my prisoner, your sacrifice."

Eddie slowly turned to face the would-be king. Trudy watched in horror as the girls kicked and twitched. Some were losing their modesty to the delight of the swordsmen. Sweat poured on silk, as faces went red to purple. Trudy cried for the Steward's attention, but he held his hand in the fashion of a humble request for patience.

"Yes," Eddie laughed. "But she is a proven queen, as shown by the Stone of Destiny, while you will be king, if you pass all the trials. It would be very funny if a would-be king did not understand the differences in rank, would it not? That even a captive queen should be obeyed in every manner save her own fate is plainly obvious to even a simpleton. How funny would it be if a would-be king were less wise then a simpleton? Ha, Ha, Ha…."

O'Murray grumbled but admitted without sincerity, "Yes, it would be funny."

"Funny, yes. But you're not laughing. It is very funny. Perhaps you don't really get the joke. Would it please his Highness if I commissioned minstrels to make the ridiculousness plain?"

"No! Steward, I get it now! Ha Ha Ha....so funny... of course, we should let the queen speak."

By now, some of the girls' breasts had escaped their tunics.

"Cut them down!" Trudy yelled.

But Eddie stalled pretending not to understand. He kneeled before her and asked respectfully, "My queen, I sense that I have been given an order concerning the women now dangling from the nooses. Are you ordering me to cut the women after they have hanged, or are you forbidding me to let them strangle as they are by the vines the trees have provided?"

"I forbid you to hang them!"

The Steward turned to the trees.

"You heard the queen," he told them.

The vines disappeared, and the choking women fell to the ground, coughing and sweating.

"You're being an ass!" Trudy snarled at him in a whisper.

"Oh, I'm just getting started," he whispered back, then bowed and stated loudly, "My noble queen, if I am forbidden to suffocate the captives, what shall I do with them?"

"Return them to their villages, unharmed and unmolested."

"NO! NO! Anything but THAT!"

It was the captives screaming. Many fell to the ground begging mercy. O'Murray noticed her confusion, which seemed to confuse him.

One of the women made a run for it. Before the swordsmen reacted, she sprinted towards the Stone of Destiney and fell to her knees before Trudy. The queen noticed the thin leather bands above each of her biceps and took her for a shield maiden, which explained her courage.

"Wise queen, whom the Lia Fail has chosen, please give us mercy," the woman begged. "If we return to our villages unharmed, we would be taken for collaborators. We would be held as the reason our kingdom fell. Shame would fall not only on us but our children and their children four-fold. Please give us no better than our sisters, brothers, husbands, and fathers. If we shan't die in battle, or burn with our farms, have us raped and then put to the sword."

"But I would give you mercy!" Trudy protested.

That seemed to confuse everyone. Too baffled to speak,

everyone seemed to be waiting for someone else to suggest something. Why would a queen about to face her own death care about some peasant girls outside her lands? The pause was becoming unbearably unbecoming. Someone should know what to do.

"We could rape the women and forget the sword," a swordsman shrugged.

No one approved but the swordsmen. O'Murray shot a hostile glance. Mixing blood with a clan so hated would mar anything even Ed Calkins could do to his reputation.

Another bound woman spat on the ground and cried, "You could give the sword and skip the rape!"

"You could bury us after," a girl, barely thirteen, suggested hopefully when the queen did not seem pleased.

Eddie dropped to his knees again. "Wise and Noble Queen, I beg your mercy, too. Look upon the deep green grass that carpets this holy site. In a time of poor harvest, keeping the grounds is double-time work. The blood that would flow would ruin the lawn for a thousand paces in all direction. The brownies that help us are dreadfully overworked and understaffed. I beg that you forbid the sword as well."

"Set down rugs," a captive ventured.

"But the rugs would be as much trouble to clean as to bring them out and put them back."

Then what? Sell them to pirates? That might give scant mercy to the girls. However, if the pirates were caught before the "cargo" was sold, they'd stand before the new king all over again. Ransom them? That might have worked if O'Murray had left any young men alive to receive them. One girl reminded them that the Romans would crucify them. To that, Eddie, still on his knees, snarled that no one here was Roman.

He spoke to Trudy again.

"Wise and noble queen, I may have a solution that all might find pleasing. Allow me to summon the brownies to stand before us."

"Ooooh, I can't wait," Trudy said with a roll of her eyes.

But she granted permission, and horns sounded the summons. She overheard the whispered comments of the Steward's deputy.

"See how ruthless he is. He's got the victims purposing their own demise and making them wait for it as the debate stretches on."

The waiting seemed to be in slow motion. From the double spirals of the sacred hills, little dashes of brown emerged emerging from the deep green valley, like little ants beginning their climb. All the while, the captives despaired their unknown fate. Perhaps Eddie wanted them to die of old age.

When the brownies finally created a ring where the party stood, Trudy studied the leader of this mythical species. He was slight, brown, ugly, exhausted, clearly ill-humored. His name was Ramon, and he was pointing at the sacrificial captives but looking at the Steward.

"You slay pretty girls, you clean yourself!" he told the Steward

"And a good morning to you, Ramon, may the wind and rain profit you," Eddie said in a cheery fashion, which only increased the brownie's irritation. "I present to you Queen Trudy, tied to the Lia Fail, whose screams of delight you might have heard earlier. Also, O'Murray, who has come to this place, hoping to be King O'Murray, his swordsmen attendants, and their beautiful captives, still tied at the wrist as their hanging was interrupted."

"Get to point!" Ramon demanded.

"How impolite, my dear brownie. Have you been sleeping well? You look grumpy and overworked."

"Ramon is grumpy! Brownie work and work and work. Steward know why? Because brownies understaffed!"

"Understaffed?" Eddie faked confusion. "Why would that be? Don't you have enough females in your number. I would think that your baby stealing from human mothers, as you do every few generations, would keep your stock strong and numerous."

Ramon glared at him and stamped his little foot. "Brownies no steal babies anymore! Brownies no like getting laughed at!"

"Oh my, that would create a problem. Without human stock, brownies can become so ill-formed. But if the Queen," he gestured to Trudy, "and would-be King would allow me. I would like to present the brownies with a gift that might improve your mood, Ramon."

The brownies all looked suspicious as they crowded around them.

"What gift do brownies get?" Ramon demanded. "Cream, beer? Where is gift?"

"I would present you with the fifty wives and daughters of O'Murray's enemies as a gift from the would-be king."

"Breeders!" the brownies exclaimed, perking up. The gracious O'Murray waved his consent.

The captives exchanged skeptical glances.

Eddie looked toward Trudy as if waiting for her permission.

"I want to know more, Eddie! What would the lives of these women be like if I allow this?"

"Ramon, if you get these captives, would they be overworked or underfed?"

"Of course not. Nothing gets pretty girls uglier than too much work! Not enough food makes pretty girls too thin to have babies."

"Please, my queen," the shield maiden spoke. "We are peasants. Not being overworked or underfed is the best we can hope for, given that our village fell. The brownies can't be as ugly as the man I was promised to. Or at least," she gave them a quick look and down, "they don't smell as bad."

Ramon started to tap dance.

"And with so many pretty girls that brownies don't have to raise from babies, we'll have enough for each boy brownie to get at least one." Ramon spun around. "Oh, Steward, won't regret this. Brownies give fifty brownie points for each breeder."

"Ramon?" the Steward interrupted. "There are twenty-five male brownies…"

Ramon made a show of counting on his fingers.

"….and fifty breeders."

He was counting again on fingers and toes.

"…that doesn't mean each gets one and Ramon gets twenty-six.

"It does it mean that most get two, some get one and Ramon gets the rest?" the leader brownie tried.

"No, it means that every male brownie gets two breeders."

"Very well, brownies be back with chains and branding irons."

Trudy objected. "Branding irons? Is that really necessary?"

"My queen, humans all look alike," a brownie answered.

135

"How else could brownies tell which is whose?"

"Yes," the Steward decided. "But we have a king to crown. I trust that you brownies know how to obey royalty. She will decide who should brand whom. And if she decides that a breeder should get a different fate, you will obey her."

It was a job that broke Trudy heart, hearing the screams and smelling the searing of skin as the gleeful brownies burned their mark on the backs of their new slave breeders. But when the branding was done, Ramon got four girls as only 24 brownies were present when the girls were divided.

When all the branding and chaining was finished, the brownies left with their human captives, leaving Trudy alone to watch the sun set. A troupe of pixies flew mischievously toward the stone where she was tied and debated if there was humor in releasing her, since she was not bound in iron. Once they guessed her purpose as a sacrifice though, they decided to check the yonder hawthorn trees for gifts instead.

As the last rays fired and the night advanced, she could hear the cheering coming from the banquet hall below her. O'Murray must have passed his trials. She was bored and craved a drink.

When night came, so did the full of the moon. The cheering from the banquet hall had long since turned to drunken singing. She also heard goat-like sounds from the opposite direction. She tried to quell her rising fear. If evil was the standard, what was more menacing than a vampire coming to have her?

A second later, she had the dire answer.

It stood only as tall as a man, but had the head of a goat and red, intelligent eyes. It stood upright, with long nails at the end of its furry hands and hooves for feet. Despite her dread, something felt off. Was this the Father of Lies? And was he dressed in deep green trousers and matching shirt?

No! Wait! She still needed to confess to the murder, do the right thing, and serve her time in the most pious way she knew how to repent. If he took her now, where else would she go?

"In the name of...." she tried to pray but couldn't remember the name on whose behest she could ask from mercy.

"Fancy ya, I do," the goat head bleated lustfully. "Maybe we could have a turn 'fore we does business, we could. If it be bad boys ya crave, I be th' best baaaaad ya could find in a boy."

Oh, Trudy did love to play with bad boys, but not this one. Strange. He didn't even smell that goaty. He did have a decent-sized tent growing in his pants, but nothing that tempted her. Still, she flashed him an impish grin.

"Maybe I do," she purred.

"Once ya go goat, ya be kiss'n me hooves ta do me again."

"Perhaps, I should start with your lips." Trudy winked.

But when he came close, she kicked with a bullseye to his crotch.

The goat's louds bleats had more hurt in them than pain. Trudy felt a strange sense of guilt.

"Coulda' just said 'no', ya could," the devil grumbled.

It really was his feelings that she kicked.

"Sorry but being tied to a stone for sacrifice has made me a little jumpy."

"Less jumpy ya be if ya wore the right size shoe." His goat eyes fell to her feet. "Ya need a shoe least two sizes larger, lass."

"And you were saying something about doing business?" Trudy hedged, feeling a little more confident.

"Damn you I will if you don't dos me favor. Ed Calkins ya mus' promise ta kill." The goat head bleated again, sternly this time, to underscore the seriousness of his message.

"I already did."

"Of course ya did, saved all o' Ireland, too. Ya did, he did, she did, everybod' an' his brother are the ones what kills Ed Calkins. But I'll torment ya wif me demonic powers if ya don't promise ta do it again fer good. When ya does, I'll give ya back your soul."

He wiggled his long fingers as he said, "demonic powers." Where'd his hooves go? Something wasn't right.

"I would think that someone with demonic powers would be able to do it himself."

"Na, it be against the demonic rule o' ethics. No killin,' only soul snatchin.'"

"Assassins might need their souls back. Why don't you cut a deal with them?"

"Cut a deal, I tried. But assassins don't believe in souls; they believe in gold."

"And your gold turned to dust after you gave it to them, so the deal was off, right?"

He filled with demonic uncertainty, but he shook his head affirmatively, so Trudy went on.

"Why would the devil keep his word anyway?"

"Lassie, wif no written form o' the language, how's a demon supposed ta do business in Ireland if he don't keep his word?"

"And you do keep your word, but not as the devil."

"How 'bout ya hasta' kill Ed Calkins ifs ya can't say what I is?"

"You're a were-goat."

"Hmm, what does ya mean by were-goat? If ya mean sometimes I'm a goat and other times a man…"

"No, sometimes you're a goat, and other times you're a leprechaun."

"Ah, ya guessed me nature. Had ya goin' fer awhile, I did. Shoulda kept me mouth shut 'bout the shoes. Maybe we can cuta diffen' deal. How 'bout you kill Ed Calkins an' I'll get'im ta bite ya, fore ya kill'im a' course. I don't mean jus' bite ya, I mean drain ya blood 'n all so ya be a vampire jus' like me buddy Ed."

"If he's your buddy, why would you want him…" She was going to say "dead" but realized he was dead already. So instead she said, "…gone?"

"Ah, lassie, everybody got two natures. Me, I'm a goat sometimes and leprechaun others. You are a lioness when ya be doin' business an' bossin' people around, but when ya be makin' them poems, then ya be a drunk'n butterfly."

"How did you know…?"

"Not important. But what about me buddy Ed? Hmm? Kill him wif love, I would lest the pig eat the horse! Hurry up now, me buddy be almost done wif makin' a king an' all. Let me tells ya what ya gotta do. Ya hasta be where his askes be scatter jus a'ter a win that be twistin' gathers his pieces, it does. Getum wif a wooden stake an' a mallet. Drive the stake trough were the heart should be. I'd do it me self, were his ashes be scattered, I can't go. Ya be from there, so ya can."

"I don't want to be a vampire. No deal?"

"Ya don't want ta be a vampire?" The goat face was incredulous. "Don't ya be knowin' all th' things ya can do wif the power?"

"No deal," Trudy insisted.

"Maybe th' ropes be cuttin' inta ya senses." With that, the goat man chewed the ropes, unbinding her even while relishing the taste of the hemp. He spoke between bites. "Maybe we can cuta diffen' deal. Ya like gold, Lassie?"

"Not gold the turns to dust before it can be spent," Trudy scoffed.

"Silver? I gotta silver coin, I does…"

"That jumps back in your pocket as soon as I'm not looking."

"Know about that, ya does. Ah well, maybe ya could haf me goat skin canteen what be filled ta th' brim, it is." He showed it to her. It was there all along, green straps hanging across his shoulder, but she didn't see it till it moved away from his body.

"I'm not killing Eddie for a canteen of water."

"Ah, but its fulla mead!"

"No."

"How about soma me luck then?"

"How much luck can you have if you've been turned into a were-goat?"

That got him mad. He stuck out his forked tongue and turned to leave, then swerved back, as if reconsidering.

"The thin' about luck is, ya gotta know when it be knockin' at ya door, ya does. People don't treat it well 'cause th' don't see it fir what it is. I be tellin' ya Lassie, livin' in a places where the most dangerous critters don't want ta eat ya, that's lucky! Gold at th' end ofa rainbow, that's a start ofa ungrateful people what thinks they be unlucky 'cause they never find it! They be luck as sin they don't 'cause they don't 'ave the sense ta take some and lef' some fer the next one. Next one finds th' pot empty and curses, don't ya know. Ya can't 'ave me luck 'cause ya don't treat it right! Ya humans be too greedy fer a' own good, 'cept Ed Calkins what knows a good leprechaun when he sees one!"

Now he was gone, but she was free. She looked around for a place to run.

"Ahh, I firgot me manners I did." The goat-leprechaun appeared out of nowhere. "I should be taken ya ta a portal where ya ca fend fer yourself in yer own time. Follow me."

It was hard to do. The goat-leprechaun moved swiftly and passed frequently for her to catch up.

"Ya be faster if ya wore the right shoes," he berated more

than once.

Once in a while, he'd stop for a slug of his mead canteen. Always he'd pass the goat skin to her, and she drank from it gratefully. He led her down the hill, prancing all the way. They passed the Hall of Hostages and into a dark pathless forest where a small pond captured the moonlight.

"Gaze upon th' pond, lassie, but don't be starin' Keep gazin' till ya see someplace that ya know."

"Then what?"

"Then jump in. Don't mind ya if ya don't git wet an' wait till no folks 'round ta see ya."

Trudy saw a reflection of her face and the goat as she tried to gaze without staring. Nothing happened. She turned to remonstrate the were-goat, but he forced her face back to her reflection.

"Ya humans be all the same. No patience ya haf."

Then she saw it. Her likeness vanished, and she looked down on the women's restroom in the Happy Hunting Ground's funeral parlor.

"Jump!" he cried, giving her a hard push. Trudy landed lightly on her feet without getting wet.

An instant later, the were-goat leaped after her.

"Reconsider, did ya?" He asked.

Then she heard Glorna's voice behind her say, "My Queen." She whirled around. Glorna tipped his brim hat. "I see you've met Arkiens."

"I have, but I just want to go home. You realize you're both in a women's restroom? Do you know why it's called a 'women's restroom?' It's a place where women get a rest from men!"

"Sorry my Queen," Glorna tipped his hat again. "We shall leave, but you can't go home yet. Your destiny requires you to meet some who already know you."

Arkiens vanished. Trudy stared at Glorna, but he disappeared, too.

Unless it was he that held the door open.

CHAPTER 11: THE DIVINE REFERIGRATOR

Maybe someone else had a strange experience in the women's room. The mourners had thinned out and changed faces. The co-workers had all but left; they had busy days that started early and knew no weekends or holidays.

A small grouping of women chattered in low voices and stopped talking altogether when she approached them.

"Excuse me," Trudy said. "Did any of you notice anything strange about the bathrooms here?"

Of the five, three saw no lines, but wound up going across the street because of the creepy vibes they felt near the door. The other two had braved it. One felt as if a spy camera was watching her.

Trudy had a pretty good idea of the group's connection to Eddie. A veteran of self-help groups, Trudy felt sure she had found Eddie's. The groups unofficial leader was a thinning, white-haired woman who used a walker. She didn't talk much and looked annoyed at Trudy. The middle-aged, thirty-something, and twenty-something women were much more engaging.

"Trudy?" a male voice said.

She knew this couple right away. Carl and Kathy had come all the way from Texas to pay Eddie their last respects. They couldn't stay long. They came for the funeral, but with the missing body, could only stay for the wake. Carl was Eddie's roommate after college and part of the reason Eddie went back to newspapers.

Trudy hugged Carl and kissed him on the cheek before he walked away. Kathy was already walking away.

"That woman did not like you kissing her husband," a younger woman observed.

"More likely she was afraid I would kiss her."

"You're the poet-dominatrix," a short young woman blurted out, then blushed deeply, covering her mouth with both hands and letting her dark hair fall across her cheeks. She hadn't meant to "out" Trudy.

"It's not a big deal," Trudy said with a shrug. "But when you speak to me, you've got to be on your knees."

The broken ice now melted. They admitted being in Eddie's support group and knew she was his best friend. Taking turns, they introduced themselves by first name only, almost as if in a meeting.

"So, what else did Eddie say about my sex life?" she asked impishly after the introductions.

Dolly, the white-haired leader, spoke up.

"All we know about you is from your poetry. We never knew your name. He told us he had your permission and all of the poems he recited were topic-related."

Yeah, he did have permission. Eddie said he loved her poems, but Eddie liked a lot of things. He liked his wife's cooking and paintings. He liked the books his son read. More than that, he liked Trudy, which didn't make his opinion unbiased. But Trudy never hoped that her poems would ever have a following beyond him.

"The poem about you being a genie and making everyone love each other, that one gave you away," Lisa, the woman that had made the verbal blunder, said.

Trudy knew that poem and recited it:

I am the princess of both tease and denial,
The smarter the whip, the more hungry the smile.
Daddy, I don't miss your cold irony,
What I deny them, what you forced onto me
I differ with mother because it's all in the fee,

They give sums of money; I give some of me.
Dad's clout among suited, they're guarding the door.
They won't tell the tale of who and the whore.

If instead I was Genie and could make you love the wretched in
your life
Would that ever include me?
Mother?
Father?
Subjects of my credit card dungeon?

My name is too illicit for polite conversation
But some in my service are the toast of the nation
Queen mother denial met the king drunk of tease.
Came the parental union I just couldn't please
With a pen or my paddle, I give the best that I can
In both wanted and wanting, be woman or man
If you're smart as my whip, you must try the style
For I am the princess of tease and denial.

It wasn't her best work; she had tried couplets when she mostly wrote free form, but she liked it more now than she ever did, noticing the one of the women had tears in her eyes.

What she feared now were the questions. Eddie had pointed out there were two types of "vanilla": the carton in the fifty flavors ice cream store that some people liked over all others and the carton in the freezer that represented the only ice cream that existed. How do you explain "cuckold" to someone that never had the kind of relationship she had with Bathrobe? But she felt compelled to try.

"I'm no longer a 'professional' dominatrix,'" Trudy said. "Instead, I'm pursuing the 'lifestyle.' I know the boundaries between the two can seem blurred. But it means I'm presently in a kinky, non-professional relationship with a man that was not designed to be exclusive, but I'm not looking for anyone else. Does that make sense?"

They nodded.

"Is he a marriage prospect?" Shari, the heaviest of the group, asked.

Trudy regretfully shook her head. Other than that, they

seemed more interested in her poetry. The women talked about the support group as if Trudy were already part of it. The group was a self-help model for adults having problems that sprang from abusive or neglectful parents. When the group first formed, it had as many men in it as women. Both genders bonded, then clashed, then rebonded as groups like this tend to do. But when the clashing started, the men stopped coming, leaving Eddie the only one left.

As this happened, a split in the group grew, and some of the women decided that the program should exclude men as they were more apt to drop out. The women here tonight had taken the other side, which gave Eddie a meeting to attend. He never forgot his gratitude. Later, a workbook got published to address the same issues their group was working on. Still later, the self-help group revamped itsself to fit the structure of a different group addressing similar issues. It required that at least one woman and at least one man should be included so that gender issues could be addressed, which made everyone feel vindicated, except Eddie. He insisted that he would stay committed, but, from his perspective, this was a women's group.

Carma knew a guy from another program and recruited Bob, which worked out well.

"But now that Ed is gone, Bob might stop coming," Carma said.

The women seemed about to leave it at that, but Trudy needed to explain her best friend.

"You need to understand," Trudy said. "Eddie had something other men didn't, and that was my friendship at a younger age. Perhaps that made it easier for him to talk about difficult, personal things. He could be ruthlessly honest about his shame, fear, and guilt to the point of making other people uncomfortable. Exploring those things, along with other mysteries, was a lifelong mission to him, and he did improve. Despite his struggle with depression, Eddie was, maybe, the happiest person alive, but he never felt he understood manhood and other men."

"You're saying he was transgender?" Lisa asked.

Trudy shook her head again. "Eddie was not a transgender person, not the woman in a man's body. But to him, masculinity was not so much 'gender,' but more of a test where he got marked 'absent' when it was time to take the test. If you explore the layers of his extended family here at the wake, you'll see hints of why."

The conversation paused for a few moments as the women tried to piece together Trudy's information with the Ed they had known.

Finally white-haired Dolly half prayed, half muttered, "I hope he's hanging on the divine refrigerator."

That was another of Trudy's poems.

"Do you still know it?" Carma asked timidly.

Trudy did, so she began to recite:

A small open box has spinning a cardboard canvas into an uncertain circle.
Child's knees and feet surround it.
I pour my thoughts, emotions, hopes, and sins with colored tubes and frantic
Triumph and regret alternate into forever layers of spiral, my choices unrelenting and unaware.
I know of time, and it will stop and see my cardboard life for first and real.
I will likely grab it with youthful speed before the paint can dry.
My life is my creation for the Divine Creator,
I hope it will hang kindly on His refrigerator.

"You see," Trudy said. "Eddie had explained a theory to me, using the example of a toy that was popular in his childhood. It was a small plastic box with a motor inside that would rapidly turn small cardboard rectangles. The toy came with plastic bottles of primary colored paint, each with a nozzle that allowed drops. Eddie likened the spinning to time and the painted cardboard to one's life; the person pouring the paint was the soul. His point was that one could not truly see one's life until the 'spinning' stopped at the time of death. Only then did patterns become clear. His theory gave me hope, and I wrote the poem."

More silence followed. The silence made Trudy uncomfortable, and she hurried to fill it.

"Eddie used to write poetry, too," she said. "He never actually wrote anything down, but he recited. He had some talent but started more projects then he finished. It wasn't until he tried an epic poem he was going to call, 'The Masculine Conspiracy' that he really started getting discouraged. Some of the things he tried to include just upset him, and he didn't think anyone would understand it. The poem was difficult anyway because the 'conspiracy' was things left unsaid among boys and men, boys and boys, death and men, men and God, etc.... Trudy's voice trailed off and she became lost in her thoughts.

"Then what happened?" Lisa asked.

Trudy jolted back to the present.

"Maybe Eddie's courage failed," Trudy mused, "and the ruthless honesty was too much for him. Because that's when Ed started writing limericks, which I hated because I thought he could do better."

"May Ed's life hang on the divine refrigerator," Dolly said again, more definitely this time. The women nodded their heads.

After that, the group paused as if saying a private prayer. Carma was going to break the silence; Trudy saw it in her undecided face and dreaded it would be sexual

"I hope I'm not out of line," Carma said. "But was your friendship with Ed a friendship with benefits?"

"Never."

"OK."

"Maybe it could have been before Eddie got married, but I was mostly married or about to be," Trudy said. "Now we did have some uncommitted sex with each other, but it was rare and impulsive, at least on my part. In the whole time Eddie was single, we had sex once or twice, and I honestly can't say which. Once married, Eddie never cheated."

Those words visibly surprised the group. Then Dolly spoke.

"We all knew that Eddie's greatest regret was the way, in the first six years of his marriage, he made his wife insecure by his repeated proclamation that fidelity was a toxic mix of jealously and hypocrisy," Dolly said. "He told everyone they met that he believed in 'free love.' With that kind of talk, we just assumed... "

"No," Trudy said firmly. "Eddie might have been a dog at heart, but he was a loyal dog. Neither Eddie nor I saw that coming, while Nalla knew it all along."

"What about all Ed's wives?" Lisa asked.

Trudy laughed aloud.

"If you asked the question casually, you'd be surprised at the number of yeses," Trudy said. "Eddie was pocketing imaginary wives long before he married. But here's how Nalla's side of the family tells it. After Eddie and Nalla got engaged, her family threw her an engagement party. Eddie was told he was expected to ask her father for her hand, which unnerved him. Nalla's father was a stern, unsmiling type. Moreover, when it came time, all her uncles, just as stern and unsmiling, were sitting with him. Eddie's fear was very real when he did ask for permission, and he expected a lecture, at the very least. Instead, Nalla's father, John, called for her, and placed her hand in Eddie's, telling him to 'take her with my blessing.' Of course, Eddie has his own version."

"Which is?" Carma asked.

Trudy grinned. "Eddie said John leaned into him and whispered, 'I've got three daughters, you can have them all.'"

The other women smiled, too. Trudy saw that was the Ed they knew.

"That started the myth of Eddie's harem," Trudy said. "Eddie felt it was his right and responsibility as an Irishman to make myth. After the wedding, Eddie didn't vacation much, but when he did, it was always with his wife and two sisters-in-law, or as Eddie insisted, his three wives. The two sisters gave up on correcting him. As he got older, his wife and her sisters befriended more women that Ed met, and they became 'wives' in the same way the sisters were."

A young family walked in. Trudy recognized the father and felt a stab of guilt. She ought to have known him better, but her life got in the way. When she first met him, he was already a freshman in high school and living with Eddie full-time; now he appeared to be in his mid-30s. Rick, for that was the man's name, had a tight build, medium height, and thoughtful expressions - like his father had at that age. His dark beard was close to his face, and he had a confidence not in his father's toolbox. His wife was a super attractive redhead, too youthful to have the two sad-faced daughters, whose hands she held. The youngest looked like she was in preschool; tears ran down her face. The other was taller, about a couple years older and much more stoic but clearly downcast. This was not the time nor the place to meet Eddie's personal joy personified.

The other women followed her eyes.

"Eddie's son, daughter-in-law, and grandkids," Trudy

explained with a sudden urge to flee. An idea of where to go just hit her and she told the group. "The best way to bury an Irishman is at a bar. Let's find one."

Their smiles quickly turned to frowns.

"That's not an option for some of us," Dolly explained. "A better way to honor Ed might be a meeting. There's a coffee shop down the road. If we sit in the back and keep our voices down, I bet we could have one worthy of Ed's life."

The other women nodded and enthusiastically started putting on their coats.

"You should come, Trudy," Dolly said. "We don't want to pressure you, but your poems have come in your place for as long as we knew Ed. It would be fitting if you joined us, even if just to drink coffee and listen. And if you want to drink something stronger first, we'll wait."

Trudy declined. Still, each woman collected a hug from her in turn, writing their phone numbers on slips of paper in case she ever wanted to talk. Some of them referenced other poems that she had written and how they related to them.

Dolly was the last to hug her. "You know we love you," she whispered. "No matter who you are or what you've done, you're welcome in this group. Call me once in a while. Don't let your poetry go unread."

That's when Trudy heard it. The slam of some chair, someone calling someone else a bitch. The sound took her back to a time six years ago; her fragile life and madness flashed before her eyes. A man was being gently asked to leave over his loud protests. Trudy expected glass to shatter and gunshots to be fired as she sprinted to the confrontation. Eddie's son fell in behind her.

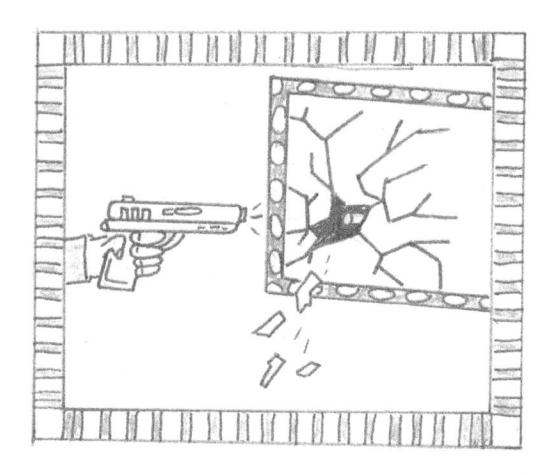

CHAPTER 12: SHOOT-OUT AT THE NOT OK CORRAL

She wasn't supposed to be there, and neither were they.

About six years ago, Trudy had a few free hours to put in some work. The Corral was not too far away from the restaurant where she had a lunch date with a man that had business in some fancy high-rise. The office, which was really her office, was down the hall from the bar, which was becoming more of a night club. It was nearby enough to finish payroll, purchase more stock, and balance the books before the evening rush hour made it impossible to get from downtown to her house on a loan in the big city. She was almost finished when she heard the clamor of a bar way too busy and loud for early afternoon. Inventory would wait. Trudy got off her seat and rushed off to play bartender.

The unexpected patrons were mostly from a local white boy gang that, after a confrontation and a payout, had pretty much behaved. Trudy had a deal with its president, Wild Bull, who put up a crazy, obey-no-rules front but proved to be rational. Today, however, that agreement was being tested. Trudy had warned him this was a bar, not a daycare center.

"You, you, you, and you, out now!" she demanded as she strode toward the entrance behind the long straight bar, which was nearly a quarter of a football field. They were minors and tried this before. The first problem was they all had drinks in front of them, and Trudy could guess it was more than soda. The other problem, a non-issue on any other day, was that she had liquid in her, and it was more than soda.

Three of the teens started to leave, but the oldest just gave her the finger. Trudy walked right up to the kid and pulled him off his chair by the collar. The kid raised a fist and then thought better of it and dropped it. Trudy looked every bit the part of a woman who'd been in a couple bar fights before, even though she was in her very late forties. Trudy knew there was no better way to lose street creed then fight an old woman and lose in a single punch. Besides that, she had gang members ready to back her up.

"Hands off me, bitch!" he cried in a high, squeaky voice.

Trudy let go but pointed firmly to the door.

He ran out with the other three. Smart boy.

Trudy wanted to get in the barmaids' faces about serving minors, but she knew they were young and afraid. There were four of them, and Trudy made five, and they had all they could do to keep up with the draining glasses and bottles of a louder, rowdier crowd than could be expected on a Tuesday afternoon. Trudy made some calls in between, trying to get some unscheduled help for the unexplained boom in business. The best she could do was get two from the evening shift to come in early.

Maybe if she had more time, she'd have made more of the chatter. Wild Bull wasn't president anymore. That's all she heard, but rumors around who controlled a gang always seemed liquid. As long as they kept their disputes out of the bar, Trudy had no opinion.

Three safe drops in less than an hour - this should make Boris very happy. Safe drops were important because of the agreement with Wild Bill. Every time five hundred dollars hit the register, a safe drop was made, which signaled the bar staff that the next round was on the house. If that seemed too generous, you'd have to understand Boris and his rise to prosperity. Boris was just a Russian guy who came to America with fifty thousand dollars in his pocket. From Trudy's point of view, he had no knowledge or business insight, all he had was some money and a little English when he sought to buy a piece of American action. Trudy was working at the bank when Boris walked in, expecting a loan for the restaurant he was going to buy, but that was nobody's business, the only business was how much they were going to loan him, because he had fifty thousand dollars. Trudy told him he needed a business plan. Boris told her to he wanted to talk to the man in charge, not some woman who was only fit to make change. Trudy marched him to the branch manager. The manager threw him out. The same thing must have happened when Boris went to the next bank down the street, and again on the next street, and still again in the next town, because Boris came back to Trudy's desk, not looking for a loan, but a date. Sensing that this was not compelled by any romantic intent, she agreed.

Over dinner, the man proved to be mostly what she expected; stubborn, arrogant, condescending, and clueless. Don't tell him about business; he had come to American with fifty thousand dollars. But wait, how did he have dollars and not rubles? The question impressed Boris. Yes, he had earned dollars trading on the Russian black market. Trudy understood now, Boris thought he was still in Russia. With her background as a real estate agent, Trudy talked Boris into buying a bar instead. She knew a bar for sale that he wouldn't need a loan to buy.

The bar, it was just a bar. Mostly old men came, drank, and left. At night, if it was the weekend, younger men came, drank, and left. It was hard to keep the place open past nine. The place barely made payroll. The place was tiny, but it was in the way of bigger development plans. Just as Trudy told him, a development company wanted this bar out of the way, and they were willing to pay big. Now Boris was just a guy with two hundred grand and a very big head. He sought Trudy out, offering to hire her as some kind of advisor, a role that would always be marred with undefined duties and compensation. Boris took out many loans and bought many properties, including the Corral.

Then, something he didn't expect happened; Boris got audited by the IRS. This was an outrage to him. Boris had already paid an accountant to adjust his books, so he wouldn't have to pay taxes. He had always insisted every problem could be solved with the right amount of money stuffed into the right pocket. When the auditor showed, Boris had a nice envelope for him. The auditor laughed, certain that the Russian was only joking. This spared Boris from prison.

It was, however, the first loud argument that Boris and Trudy had. The auditor warned Boris that paying lawyers to represent him would only cost him more money and prolong the audit. Boris agreed, planning instead to take this auditor out to wine and dine with expensive hookers in the mix. Trudy insisted that he should introduce this auditor to expensive, stubborn, lawyers that would fight the IRS every step of the way, no matter how much it cost.

Someone, or many some ones, must have talked some sense into Boris. Businessmen do go to prison in this country, and not every government employee is on the make. In the end, Boris' lawyers did a pretty good job of intimidating the IRS and reached a settlement of back taxes to the tone of sixty-three thousand with no prison time. Boris did not think that was a victory. He decided that the money should come from Trudy, who would work without pay until she matched that amount.

Trudy had a different idea. Not only did she not work for him, Trudy also never returned the car Boris had put in her name to hide the asset from the IRS. She was done with him for good.

For almost one year, Trudy's nonemployment seemed to hold. It's not that Boris ever forgave her, but he had a problem with the Corral, and no one seemed to know how to fix it. The place was busy; liquor disappeared; and the bar was losing lots of money. If she could change that, maybe they could have a new arrangement and try to act as if nothing happened.

Visiting a bar was not the worse assignment Trudy ever had. She was sure the barmaids were stealing, that was almost to be expected. Maybe they were stealing bottles as well. But when Trudy walked in, she spotted the problem immediately. The patrons were all wearing gang colors, and no one wearing those colors paid for any of the drinks.

At that instant, Trudy appointed herself the Corral's manager and loudly announced that anyone wearing gang colors wasn't allowed at the bar, and that no one got served without paying. To this, Wild Bull, who was sitting as all high-ranking gang members did, where he could watch the door, threw his glass at the bottles on the shelf. Within seconds, every member did the same, trying to break as many bottles as they could. Barmaids ducked for cover, but Trudy simply dialed the phone.

The bar was an empty sea of broken glass before she dialed the third number. Trudy never did call the police. The informal rule was a that a bar gets only so many police calls before it's deemed a nuisance, so a successful bar handled their own problems.

There was plenty of time to clean the glass. For the next two days, not a single drink was sold. On the third, a couple stumbled in for after-dinner drinks. Later three guys that could have been gang members ordered a drink, paid, and left. Trudy thought they were spying. By the end of the week things were looking dismal, with not fifty dollars rung on the register.

Up until then, that was the most money the bar ever took in. The week after that, a young woman walked in, maybe just old enough to serve. She wasn't thirsty but wanted to talk with the manager. She seemed nervous, and the bartender thought she was looking for a job.

"I have a message from Wild Bull," she told Trudy. "This is our bar. If you don't quit, he will kill you."

"Message received," Trudy said. "Tell Wild Bull I'm not going anywhere, but I'm willing to talk to him. He can find me right here anytime the bar is open."

If the girl was afraid before, she visibly shook now. "You don't understand, lady. You can't talk to Wild Bull. He's crazy. Save your life, it's not worth it."

"Are you afraid to tell him what I said?" Trudy asked.

The girl nodded.

"Then don't. I'll talk to him when he comes to kill me."

Business picked up that week. Customers that paid for drinks really changed profit margins. By Friday night, everything was as it had been with the same clientele not wearing colors. Then Wild Bull walked in.

"Where is she?" he roared.

"I'm right here," Trudy had already seen him walking in on the video feed. "Thanks for coming in."

You could have heard a pin drop.

"Let's not talk our business where everyone can hear," she broke the silence. "Come into my office, won't you?"

He looked in a mood to murder, but he followed her into the room. Once settled in a chair, he seemed to have a certain human intellect.

"Oh, sure, you can kill me," Trudy said in an even voice as she leaned over her desk. "That wouldn't be a problem if you don't mind everyone knowing. Can you trust everyone in the bar not to snitch? Besides," she added with a smile. "I have an offer for you, a face-saving agreement that doesn't mean the Corral is going out of

153

business."

Trudy and Wild Bull emerged from the office. At Trudy's instruction, the next round was free. Bull, whose name was Bill, didn't tell the gang about the check for three hundred dollars he'd get every week nor the "employee discount" he'd have on his drinks. All they knew was the free rounds every so often, but they'd have to follow some simple rules.

But now, as the Corral took in some unprecedented cash, afternoon faded to evening. Most of the gangsters hadn't left, and the Friday night regulars were having difficulty finding seating and getting drinks. The Corral's gangsters were usually surprisingly polite, but tonight the mood of the gang sifted from brooding to euphoric, and no one was willing to muscle their way around them.

Closing time found the staff relieved and exhausted. No fights and lots of tips had the tired barmaids grateful but dull-witted. Trudy was having hell trying to balance the registers. Two of the girls couldn't wait, telling Trudy to let them know if they were in trouble tomorrow. Four girls waited; each had rung up orders on the last register that still had a problem. Two of the girls had rides, a boyfriend of one and a couple, friends of the other. In all, seven souls were in the building that night.

As she counted the bills once again, Trudy knew she would always remember what she was thinking about. It was a long day, and none of the money she counted was hers, nor did she get a cut of any tip money. Was it worth it? If you looked at the check the Russian gave her, always with a lecture or insistence that she justify to him what she did to earn this money, no! The check was laughable. But when she looked at the perks, it was hard to deny them. Boris bought the mansion that she lived in, completely furnished it, and hired landscapers to keep up with the grounds. He even stocked the refrigerator and bar for her, while allowing her to pursue her "hobby" without interference. He frequently flipped mansions, so when he sold one, she'd live in another.

That's when she heard the knock on the barroom door. Probably another driver for one of the barmaids. Instead, when they opened the door, the four teenagers she'd kicked out earlier were now pointing four handguns at them.

"Everyone on the floor!"

Trudy was at the correct register. To the left and where no

one could find it was a loaded 22 revolver.

"Not you! Hands where I can see them."

Trudy complied. It wasn't worth the risk if the boys were just here to rob the place. If she had to shoot, she only had six bullets for four targets armed with better than her. Though she kept her back to their handguns, she could see everything through the mirror. It was installed deliberately so the bartender never turned blindside to the drinkers. The boys were cleaning out purses and wallets while roughly groping the barmaids.

Next, they would come for the registers, but wasn't that backwards? What was the end game anyway? Even if they didn't know about the video feeds, everyone here could ID these guys.

"Hey, bitch!"

The mirror could have saved her life, but from the way he held the gun before he fired it, he'd have missed. Trudy was supposed to turn around to face a bullet. Instead she grabbed the 22, dropped to the ground, and rolled with cover behind the bar.

The sound was deafening and stunned the boys into deadly inaction. Glass splattered everywhere but it was tardy, as if it missed its cue but compensated with volume. Trudy risked a rise for a shot in time to see all four guns trained on a spot bar level where she would have been if she just dropped. Five shots fired together; their bullets splattered bottles but went wide and high of where they pointed their barrels cowboy style. Hers downed a boy with a wound just below his side's arm pit. It would pierce his lung but miss his heart. As the boys pivoted, she risked another shot, dropping down again without knowing for sure that the shot was true.

Now, gunfire erupted everywhere, as if two guns needed no targets. Glass kept flying so intensely that Trudy had a hard time getting anywhere other than where she was, which was exactly what she had to do. She didn't know it yet, but a large piece of a mug had already pierced her upper thigh and she was ten minutes away from losing consciousness due to blood loss.

In the noise and the glass, Trudy did not know where she was or how she got four feet from one of the shooters back, but she aimed and fired. The image would haunt her till her dying day, for her bullet lodged into the small of his back, and he would never walk again.

Unknown to her, she exposed her back to the last gun still

firing. But when a bottle pulverized into glass dust, she corrected her position and returned fire at the still shooting boy, who must have gotten his firearm training watching Dirty Harry movies.

Trudy scanned the room, weapon ready, completely disbelieving that the fight was over. The floor was a sea of glass with blood and booze flowing among the lying bodies. She had no idea why she was the only one still able to shoot or why she was so dizzy.

"Drop it!"

But Trudy didn't, still unsure about the shot she never saw hit. Her eyes didn't focus anymore, but she saw the color blue blocking the city night air. Holding one hand out, she engaged the safety and dropped the 22 with two bullets still in the chambers. Seven unarmed people were in that bar at the time of the shooting. No one lost their lives and only two needed an ambulance.

Sixteen seconds ago, she was a bar manager. Now she was a hero.

It took the ambulance ride to tell her the police didn't see it that way. She was cuffed to her stretcher. She had a vague memory of being told she was going to surgery to remove some glass from her leg, and then feeling pain there for the first time.

Dazed and sleepy, she heard a TV news report about police engaging five gangbanger shooters in some bar and police subduing all of them without any civilians suffering more than superficial injuries. "Good job," she thought before losing wakefulness. The report never mentioned the bar's name was the 'Corral' and that Trudy was the fifth shooter.

Morning brought a clearer picture of the fresh hell she was burning in. Boris had been trying to call her through the night, but nurses, noticing the hostility in the man's voice, blocked the call to her room.

"What did you do to my bar?" he screamed at her. "I send you to fix it, and you tell me, 'problem with gangs.' You go to fix and now problem with gangs, problem with police, and no booze, no money, and too many repairs. You will pay for this. Whatever it cost comes out of what I pay you, Understand? If not, I sue you!"

A nurse came running in before Trudy could craft a reply. Her heart monitor went off like a fire alarm.

When the afternoon news came on, Trudy got a better sense

of her legal troubles, as the coverage was more in-depth. There was a shoot-up at the Corral last night, and police wouldn't say if the gunfight was between police and a gang; gang members themselves; or a heroic barmaid and four would-be robbers. What police would say is that the Corral was a gang-owned front for money laundering and part of an ongoing Vice Department investigation. Though they were still gathering evidence, the cash found in the building was more than what could be expected for a legitimate business and proof existed that the bar routinely served minors that were in the gang. As for the "heroic barmaid," she was a suspected prostitute and gang member, who would be questioned and charged as soon as she recovered. Charged with what? Police couldn't say just yet as it was an open investigation. When the reporter questioned, "Why was this a Vice matter given that shots were fired, and people hospitalized?" the spokesmen waffled.

Trudy knew exactly why.

The coverage continued with a short interview with one of the barmaids who was there during the shoot-out and told the story as it happened.

"Where's my purse?" Trudy asked the nurse.

"Why is that more important to you than your treatment options?" the nurse countered.

Well, Trudy, who was still handcuffed to her bed, wasn't going to tell the nurse that she had a handcuff key in her purse and the real thing that 'Vice' was looking for.

Actually, the nurses were under police orders, forbidding many things that made no sense concerning a middle-aged cut victim. Most were quite fed up with police acting like their good-natured patient was public enemy number one, or so one nurse told Trudy. When they did see the news report, they were all quite sure that Trudy was a hero, and the cops were being petty and jealous. The purse showed up at her bedside, but as she attempted to unlock the cuffs, a nurse walked in. It was then that Trudy showed the woman what police were so intent on finding in the Corral. She unlocked the cuff on her wrist.

"Wait just a minute," the nurse told Trudy. "I'll call a cab and take you down in a wheelchair."

It had been three years since Trudy had last spoken to Eddie, and she couldn't be sure that he was still married or living in the same house, but she could be sure of where he worked. Her loose plan was to get a ride to the distribution center and wait till the trucks were due. If Eddie wasn't working, then she'd find someone there that knew how to find him. Or, if she couldn't get a cab, she knew a number to the back room, the same phone that carriers used to call in sick. She could hide out somewhere and wait until he could pick her up and form a longer plan.

Yes, there were other people in her life that she could call, but none of them knew the back story, and Trudy wanted to keep it that way.

"Stop!"

The cab driver screeched to a stop. Trudy had just seen the man she had dated yesterday, before any of this had started. Maybe he really meant it when he said he wanted a relationship. Trudy hastily paid the baffled cabbie, keeping an eye on the short man and where he was headed. Nope, it wasn't a bar; it was a café. Almost running, she got within shouting range, but he wasn't paying attention.

Once inside, she feared an answer. Her former date was nearly arm-in-arm with a beautiful fashion model type, not a day over twenty-four. Then, to her relief, it was just a touchy feeling flirty type cocktail waitress sitting a regular at his favorite table. To her further relief, he was alone.

"Trudy?"

The man was a short heavy man with olive skin and thick hair chest peeking out of his casual V-neck shirt. His red hair was thinning, and he sported a pointed beard. Clearly, he'd finished his business trip in the city, and was stopping for a drink before the long ride back to Munsonville, a place they had in common. Trudy hoped they really did have something else.

"I know this is short notice, but it's really now or never," she told him after refusing a drink. "Did you mean what you said yesterday? Is that really something you'd want? And if so, do you want it with me?"

"Trudy, your timing is bad," he pleaded. "I can't stay in the city. I have to go home now. My business can't wait."

She looked directly at him, using her grey eyes to their full effect.

"I can't stay in the city either. I wish it weren't like this, but if you don't take me home with you, you'll likely never see me again. Are you sure you want the things we talked about? Are you sure you want them with me? Don't speak. Go to your car and think. You have your suitcase in the car, no? If your life is better without me, just drive away. A lot of men have fantasies; I understand. It's no shame, it just means you have an imagination. But if you want a lifestyle, you've got to put your skin in it."

"What do I have to do to prove I want this?"

"If you want this, go to your car and come back for me wearing just your bathrobe and nothing else."

The couple made it into a modest Ford Coup. She had the keys and a red-faced Bathrobe who was full of excitement and intrigue. Ten years ago, Trudy would have felt the same, but now she just felt cheap.

CHAPTER 13: MUCH TO DO ABOUT NOTHING OR WHAT TO DO ABOUT GLORNA

It's never a good thing when I'm suddenly sitting in my fourth-floor office that overlooks Filiocht Hill during a time where my Stewardship controls only the sidhe and not humans. My secretary is just outside the open door and if I needed to ask where I was and what I was supposed to be doing, the attractive blond merrow would answer without the slightest pause. She was older than most, but she hardly looked so. Never mind her true age. She had the looks of a teen, the mind of a thirty-something, and the wisdom of a sixty-something. She hid all of this under smiles and makeup...when she wanted to.

Actually, I know exactly why I'm here. Business has the 20-80 rule. Maybe you know it: 80 percent of all my problems come for 20 percent of my workers, customers, or locations...whatever the case. In newspaper delivery, which is where I should be, it's more like 10/90, and in ruthless business, well, it's the Glorna rule.

"So, Marci," I called to her. "I seem to have an unscheduled interview. Would I be right in assuming it's with a wood sprite?"

"Right you are," she called back cheerfully.

"And of the one hundred forty-seven wood sprites that work the trees, can I assume that I know this one by his first name as he is the only wood sprite whose first name I know?"

"For all the trouble that Glorna is, I'm surprised you keep

the wood sprites in existence."

It was a tempting thought. Maybe if the currency of the realm were other than maple leaves and oak leaves, I could tell all of them that I've stopped imagining they existed, forcing them to change their beliefs, which they'd never do, or disappear. As it is, I could never do that.

"What about inflation?" I shot back at Marci. "How could I regulate the economy here where money literally grows on trees! Without wood sprites, the sidhe would grab leaves from trees until there were no more to grab...the trees would die, and the economy would follow. I work very hard to make sure the right number of leaves get picked and that's why only I get to pick leaves."

Marci couldn't take it. She craned her neck through the doorway and looked at me with a wry expression.

"You pick leaves every time you want to spend," she accused.

I had to nod. That's what I like about Marci. Next Friday, I'll be picking two extra maples and one oak for her new raise.

The front door opened, and Marci shrieked, so I came out of the office and saw why: two male merrows flanked Glorna. While female merrows are as beautiful as mermaids with legs, male merrow are terrifying and resemble the monster in "The Creature from the Blackish Lagoon." Male and female merrows don't get along much and kind of have the same relationship that male and female leprechauns have: the females absolutely refuse to mate with the males. Family reunions are a big problem, but not as big as the one in front of me.

"Glorna kill woodsman!" one of them thundered. "Eat his flesh and drink his blood!"

"I was guarding my tree," Glorna smiled with a shrug, completely undisturbed by the hostiles bordering him or the Steward facing him, which could imagine him out of existence. If I only had such courage.

"In my office," I told Glorna. To the sea monster merrows, I dismissed them with, "You can go."

But they weren't ready.

"Big problems outside. Many angry. Leprechauns want Glorna punished. Wood sprites want Glorna released. They all come here to see Steward."

"I'll address them from my balcony later. Don't let anyone inside the building."

But it was too late. By the time I was back in my office, Marci was struggling to restore order among the petitioners, all wanting to "discuss" my handling of Glorna. Marci tried to hold the noise down to a low roar while assigning the numbers and noting the subject of their business with the Steward of Tara.

I could hear the shouts from the outside as well.

"If the Steward executes Glorna, we'll execute him!" an angry wood sprite declared. "Glorna was just doing his job!"

The threat was aimed at the leprechauns more than me. Believing that everything was a figment of my imagination, killing me would wipe everyone and everything into non-existence.

But the leprechauns didn't believe the same.

"Go ahead," they taunted. "We'll supply the rope."

Leprechauns and wood sprites have always had their differences. Wood sprites, without any solid evidence, always accuse leprechauns of lurking by oak trees for a chance to steal leaves when the wood sprites go to feed. The leprechauns always took afront to this slam on their honor.

With the leprechauns outnumbered one hundred forty-six to sixty-nine, one would think that they'd be less enthusiastic about a brawl. But two words describe a leprechaun's temper: short and stout. It would be the leprechauns throwing the first punches if I didn't do something.

The male merrows had called for backup in their attempts to push the warring side away from each other, but they were losing ground. Marci was having the same trouble keeping the petitioners from storming through the door.

The protests turned to scuffles outside my office. The leprechauns had the loudest voices, but the other sidhe had taken sides mostly against the wood sprites, claiming that wood sprites nip at the pixies, merrows, and brownies alike when no wrongdoing is done. What if they were merely climbing a tree, getting an apple, or just admiring the tree's beauty? Truth be told, that seemed unlikely. An oak leaf can be pretty tempting when you have thousands of trees and not nearly as many wood sprites.

The male merrows hadn't left yet, expecting some other orders from me and not looking happy (although they never look anything but angry) and not letting Glorna out of their hold.

"Keep order!" I told the merrows. They looked back at me as if keeping order might have something to do with tearing my limbs from my body. To Glorna I said, "Why don't you go watch TV for a while?"

I sent him to my bedroom where he would find DVDs of spaghetti western films. He flipped me off, saying spaghetti doesn't interest him. I spent another fifteen minutes trying to sell my plan to have him not be present to agitate the mobs. I told him about cowboys and how they were gunslingers that didn't play by the rules and took the law as well as their horses, fortunes, and lives into their own hands in the name of independent adventure. Glorna took the bait.

At the time, I considered it my good fortune that my goals aligned with his interests, but I would regret it later. Nonetheless, with him out of the way, I could now address the restless crowd of petitioners in my hallway, waiting for an audience.

Under my instructions, Marci left them in, one at a time. Each one gave me an earful, insisting on behalf of one side or the other. Some complained bitterly about wood sprite harassment, violence, and overreach. Others complained about how dangerous the job of a wood sprite is, especially when the Steward who imagined them wouldn't support their law enforcement efforts.

Outside, the noise kept getting louder. The leprechauns chanted, "Screw the wood sprites, save the Gauls! The Steward of Tara has no balls!" The wood sprites were less creative but promised full retaliation to "any drunken leprechaun foolish enough to be caught near a tree." A riot seemed in the making.

Then I heard something that terrified me. From the back of the hallway and talking insistently to Marci who was wrestling with the crowd, I heard the voice of a two-year-old girl. Yes, 42!

"I want an update on the prince he promised me months ago."

Well, I had no such update,

"The Steward would love to chat with you," Marci said breathlessly, but kindly, over the din. "But today is a bad day. Perhaps come back tomorrow when things are less complicated."

"Today's gonna get a lot worse for him if he doesn't talk to me today!"

The brownie slammed his fist on my desk, perhaps doubly unhappy that I wasn't giving his wise words their due attention. "Steward should do something!" He was now twice the size of the three feet he was when he walked in. "Wood sprites mean. Glorna bad!"

"Yes, let's see…that was wood sprites mean, Glorna bad… Did I get that right?"

I was pretending to take notes, but I don't think I fooled him with my pencil markings on a legal pad. If he weren't fooled, the leprechauns certainly wouldn't be either as brownies can't read.

"If that's all you have to say, I will certainly consider this very important point of view. I…"

But the brownie had left and was replaced by a six foot tall pixie, who was just as angry. Christ, they grow when they want to be heard. The parade of petitioners went on for hours with additional protests about how long they had to wait to yell at me. Marci did her best to sound firm, telling the complainers that if they didn't like the long lines, they should all come back tomorrow. More than one responded that, if they did come back tomorrow, it wouldn't be to talk…it would be to burn down the building and everyone in it.

Somewhere outside, a fire did start and sounds of muskets were the thunder to a perfect storm. I had to think of something, I just didn't know what.

"Call the Council of Scantily Clothed Merrows to an emergency hearing," I told Marci as she walked in to inform me about my next petitioner.

She looked daggers at me. That did it. I had offended the last person in the realm that didn't want to string me up. I realized, too late, that it was the right idea for the wrong Tara in time. When she did start talking, I realized the possibility of starting a sexual harassment riot in the midst of a police brutality riot, and all in a time when I had offended my personal guards.

"…and if you're going to imagine such a thing into existence," she promised me, "you're going to wish that you were the woodsman."

"Please, Marci…could you reject my apology another time?"

"Forty-two is here to see you," she informed me as she walked away.

"Tell her I'm not here."

But Marci wasn't listening. So, I did what I thought any ruthless dictator would do. I hid under my desk.

"Sure he's here," Marci told her gently, holding her hand when she walked her back into the room with the tenderness that a parent uses to show her that there was no monster underneath the bed. At that moment, I envied the little girl. My monsters were my parents. I could fool 42, but not Marci.

"Maybe he's just feeling shy today," she amended. "Just leave the office for a second, 42. I'll call you when I find him and make him not so shy."

The little girl did as she was told. As soon as 42 left, , Marci pulled the chair away and knelt to where I was crouching and shaking.

"What's wrong with you?" Her voice was almost the same one that she had just used with 42. "I've never seen you so scared. People should be scared of you. Don't you think they're afraid that you might not like them? You always insisted that they were. Why are you acting so differently today? Remember, you're a ruthless dictator that can enforce his will with the power of his limericks."

"I'm not that guy," I admitted. "I'm that guy before I became a ruthless dictator."

She understood me. I wasn't expecting that.

"Oh. You're from the past then? What are you doing here?"

"I've got a few things to wrap up before I face something terrible that I did before I became a vampire. I'm filling in for the Ed Calkins that you know in case that Ed Calkins doesn't make it here. Trust me, it could happen."

"Well, of course it could happen, but if you're filling in for your future self, you've got to act like your future self."

"You mean like a self-deluded fool?"

She gave me a cross look but nodded yes.

"Look," she told me. "You're being afraid over nothing. None of this exists except in your imagination. Glorna isn't real. Those leprechauns out there, they only exist because you imagined them. If you wanted to, you could image them as bunnies, elks, or donkeys...or worse."

I couldn't lie to her anymore. I confessed about imagining the whole time and place of Tara at a time when humans would have

165

abandoned its mythical powers, but I did not imagine the people here. They moved in before I could and brought their problems with them. It always happens in my imagination. I create the place and time, but other folks raid the place before I can get there myself. Also, I was very good at imagining, but I could never unimagine. I never learned that skill.

"But I can't imagine other people," I promised her. "They are created elsewhere. If I ever stopped existing, they would merely be pulled to the place they belonged in before."

"You were so confident that if anyone ever got out of line, you'd write an unflattering limerick that would shame them thousands of years after their time."

"Did it ever work?" I asked, still shivering in fear.

"Well, I wouldn't say it never worked."

"Does it work with the leprechauns?"

"Well, no, but…"

"Does it work with Glorna?"

"Of course not."

"Does it work with anyone? How about you?"

"Yes. Sure, It works with me," Marci lied. "I worry about you writing a negative limerick. That's the reason I do what you say."

"Is that what I need to do right now? Read limericks to the rioters?"

Cries to burn the Stewardship to the ground were coming loudly through the balcony windows. Flame torches were being lit. The merrow looked unnervingly at where the shouts were coming from. Then she looked at me.

"You need to give a speech that will put the fear of the Steward into them," she told me. "I'll go tell the crowd that you're going to set things right in a few minutes. But before I do, you should get a little confidence. Handle 42."

"I'll handle 42. You tell the rioters that I'm going to give a speech very soon."

"Right!"

"…after you write it for me."

Forty-two replaced Marci at the office threshold. Trying to look confident and adult-like, I sat up straight in my office chair as if I had been working on something very adult-like that would be

166

more important than anything a two-year-old girl could have to say.

"We had a deal," she told me, pulling off the very adult-like importance better than I did. I remembered the way she acted before she sat on my lap for what should have been her scolding for bad behavior all year. She didn't forget to negotiate just because her position was weak.

"Have a seat," I told her without looking up, pretending that the blank spot on my desk had some very important papers to read. She crossed her arms in a firm parental way that told me she wasn't settling for any nonsense.

"You wanted to be Steward of Tara; I wanted a boy. Now you are Steward of Tara. People here even believe that they are a figment of your imagination…"

"Not the leprechauns!"

"No, not the leprechauns or me. We're too smart for that. The point is, I have no boy."

"That's because I've been busy. Finding the right boy takes time. You wouldn't want me to get any boy I could find, would you?"

"You wouldn't want me to start lying again so everyone will know you're a silly old man and not a ruthless dictator, would you?"

Faint sounds came from my bedroom where Glorna was watching "The Good, the Bad, and the Ugly" and repeating one of the lines, "What a waste of so many good men." That gave me an idea.

"Look, 42. You've just started to be good. I don't owe you a boy until Christmas."

"Hey, that wasn't the deal. You…"

But I didn't let her finish.

"I found a prince that's perfect for you, but I've got to make him a boy again, because right now, he's a man. You wouldn't want him to be an old man by the time you grow up now, would you?"

"No." She still had her arms crossed, but her stern expression was failing her.

"Now, if you're going to be a good girl instead of threatening the Steward, I just might let you see him right now, but you've got to be quiet. He's brave, but shy."

"Ok."

"Come with me."

Together, we tiptoed to my bedroom door that was just beyond my office. With a crack of the door, we could both see him. He had taken the appearance of one of the movies actors, complete with gun belt and cowboy hat."

"There are two kinds of people in this world…" he recited. I knew it would work. She had seen enough. I gently closed the door.

"Well?" I demanded, sitting at my desk again.

She tried looking unimpressed. She failed.

"Does he have to wear that stupid hat?" was the only complaint she could voice.

"You can see him through the stream waters some time before Christmas. So, if there's nothing else for you to bother me with, I need to get back to ruthless business."

"He still has to kill that ruthless dictator like you promised me."

"He will. Now go. I've got a speech to give."

"Hear ye! Hear ye!" Marci announced from the office balcony to the rioters below, trying to sound authoritative. "His Ruthlessness will address ye commoners to decree his decision on the recent troubles!"

All eyes on the ground raised up to Marci the second she called for their attention. Before I made my dramatic entrance, I glanced at Marci's speech. It was a good one…logical, elegant, authoritative, and believable. Yeah, I wouldn't be reading this speech.

I stepped onto the balcony with my nose as high into the air as I could point it and still be looking down at the wretches who disturbed me. Invariably, this caused my eyes to cross, but I hoped from their vantage point, they would only see up my nose.

"It has come to my attention that many of you are concerned about the recent demise of two woodcutters who attempted to chop a tree down that my wood sprite, Glorna, was guarding. There has been much disagreement as to how this unimportant matter should be handled with only two common points from each side…that something must be done and that it must be done quickly. To both of these points, I can only conclude that my subjects have too much time on their hands, where I have not. By rights, I should be writing cruel limericks about each of you for pulling my attention on such trivial matters, but as I said, my time is short, and I must be on more important ruthless business."

"Wondering what to do about Glorna is much to do about nothing! Glorna is leaving the realm on his own behest from matters not concerning the recent troubles. He has…well, taken paternity leave…yes, that's it. As a new father, he needs to raise his child for the next eighteen years or so. We will deal with him then. For the immediate time, we will consider better policies regarding the guarding of trees. But before we do that, we must consider how to best wake the two corpses that used to be woodsmen. Such a wake shall last one full week, and all shall be required to attend. If we held that wake here, the local inns would require labor to keep the mourners feed, liquored, and bedded. I therefore declare a provincial holiday from this realm and shall open a portal from this time of Tara, to another time in its history when humans and sidhe lived together. You will find that your money is no good there, as humans will insist on paying your inn fees, be they food, drink, or leisure. I will keep this portal open during that week, so you can travel freely between realms but be advised: no human is to follow you to this realm, nor should you linger in the other beyond the week afforded. That is all."

They were cheering by the time I finished. No sidhe can resist a wake if it's a closed casket and open bar. As for the other side of the portal, which is the side my vacation property holds, humans have been disappointed that leprechauns and pixies are so shy in that realm. The inns there will joyfully pick up the tab for such guests, who will be just as interested to meet humans.

There was one flaw to the speech I gave.

"Not the speech I wrote for you," Marci told me.

"No, it wasn't. The speech you wrote was logical, elegant, authoritative, and believable. It was a really good speech."

"Then why didn't you use it?"

"I want to save it for when the stakes are higher."

She gave me a double-take, as if she might comment that the speech might not match another circumstance. Instead she gestured towards the office door.

"Some wood sprites are here to see you…all of them in fact."

"Send them in."

"One at a time?"

"No, all at once."

And so all at once my office was overcrowded with wood sprites who weren't buying the paternity leave idea that I snatched out of thin air. They were demanding (in many loud, differing voices) the truth. They wanted to see Glorna and have proof of my pledge that no harm would come to him.

Then, my Irish luck kicked in. Everyone fell quiet for a single moment, just long enough to hear something from my bedroom door. It sounded like a baby crying.

In the next moment, Glorna thundered into my office to confront his stunned counterparts.

"What the hell, guys?" Glorna complained. "I just got the kid to sleep."

Jaws fell open. In Glorna's arms was a newborn baby.

"Well, don't just stand there staring. The kid is hungry. Get a wet nurse to feed the fella. Come on guys, be quick about it. There has got to be a pair of unused nipples somewhere in this realm."

But nobody moved. It was as if they were too stunned. One of them asked where the mother was, which didn't appease Glorna's patience.

"Well, golly, folks," he mocked. "I've had so many human women I don't rightly know who the mother is! She died at birth, you morons!"

One of them could have left in search of a wet nurse. It wouldn't have been hard to find as brownies and pixies were plagued with still births at about three times the rate of human mothers. Instead, they all left. That left Glorna and I staring at each other.

"Did you use my bedroom mirror as a portal to another time?" I accused, thinking this realm had far too many portals. Then I remembered how I hoped to end this realm.

"What did you want me to do? The kid was hungry, and its mother's body was getting cold. The poor thing was calling to me. I had to rip him from the corpse's womb, or he would have died."

"Babies die when their mothers die before they can be born, Glorna. You can't go ripping babies out of corpses if it's going to change the past too much. I like my history the way it is, Glorna. I don't recall tales of Glorna the Midwife Ripper."

"Not every baby," Glorna protested. "Just this one. I could hear the poor thing's thoughts. What was I supposed to do?"

"How are you going to raise a human baby?"

I asked the question, but the answer was obvious. In a realm where there are brownies and pixies, too many babies is never a problem, especially if that baby is human. Then, I got another great idea!

"No!" he told me before I could float it. "You're not giving this baby to John Simons!"

"Yes! I am!"

"No, you're not! The baby doesn't want John Simons to be his father, and that's the end if it!"

"Why not?" But then my vampire nose started to work as did TAM's about the baby's mother. She was the wife of John Simons, the famed Bryony, but the baby's father was not her husband. Glorna was holding the last descendant of Henry Matthews, the famed author and vampire. John and Henry became vampires the day their love triangle exploded while Bryony died trying to give birth. Her death caused so much pain, neither of them thought to try and save the unborn baby. Henry Matthews killed John and hanged himself but they both respawned. So it was that the vampire duet was born of friendship, sex, lies, and hatred.

"You're right." I told Glorna. "Hold the fort. I have a ruthless journey to embark on. Marci! You and Glorna are in charge. I've got an errand to run…I don't know how long it will take, but it's for the baby."

"What are you getting?" they asked.

"An electronic womb!"

"What is that?" Marci asked.

"I have no idea." But I was gone.

Hot and feeling like hell, I lay face up. I was too weak to move and too dead to die. Even if a fleshy animal walked right over me, endured some open wound, and bled right into my mouth, I had not enough energy to digest it. I was a skeleton now with just enough rotting flesh to cover the white of my bones. I had made it this far, all the way from hell and back of barren molten rock to the lush greens of my imaginary Tara only to have the last of my energies fail as I tried to mount the hill to my palace. The double irony was that every time I imagined a place and time, people of some sort would settle there, with all their problems, mind you, and they would get there before I could, forcing me to immigrate into my own creation; but this time, I saw no one who could help me. Everyone was enjoying that free vacation that I provided them in the other realm of Tara, where Trudy was taken as sacrifice and Ramon ruled the brownies. There, food and drink were almost too plentiful, and the raiders that settled before I could accepted the vacationers as kings because even the worst at the game couldn't be as bad at 'king' as the native humans.

They would feast. I would starve.

Oh, I should quit whining. It's really not so bad. I don't have enough energy in my body to feel pain anymore, and at least nobody would disturb my thoughts. It's not like flies interrupted me, as I didn't have enough flesh for them to show interest. All my life I've craved alone time, a break from the constant fear of other people not approving…expecting more than I could do, of me thinking that things that were impossible for me should be easy for me to do while also thinking that the things I could do were too impossible for anyone to give me credit. Yes, a starving vampire could be grateful.

But I was lonely. Isn't that strange, literary genius who's reading this? Do you think there is some meaning to all of this, with me dying an undead life in a place deep within my own imagination? Do you have any thoughts you could share? Surely, you must give me a little credit for taking the burden of starving so lightly…

"Oh my God! What happened it you?" the merrow called in alarm.

Not now, Marci! I'm in the middle of being admired for my stoic nature by my fan base. Of course, I hadn't the energy to speak, and I was so light that she could drag me uphill to where my Stewardship abode lorded over the hill. Apparently, she hadn't figured out that I was incapable of answering her increasingly frantic inquires as to my skeleton state as she kept on repeating them. Funny it never occurred to her that I was a deceased decomposing corpse, but then, when I think of it, I realize that her own existence made the wrong of that obvious.

Marci is a pretty sharp merrow, and she never hesitated some indecision as what to do with me. The electronica generator I had could power my DVD set or a refrigerator, but not both, so I kept an icebox in my bedroom. With no ice houses or mountains near, I had to be careful to imagine ice replacing the melted water, lest the bags of blood stored in it would go bad. Marci barged into my bedroom to the protests of Glorna, who was trying to watch another Clint Eastwood film while the infant slept in his arms. The baby woke crying, and Glorna jumped on the bed at the sight of me.

"What!"

"The Steward," Marci explained. "He's starved and needs blood."

Carefully, she punctured a plastic bag with her long nails and let the contents slowly drip into my mouth. At first, I hadn't the energy to consume it, but gradually the cold blood...which by the way tastes much better when it's warm, started to take. I tried to speak.

"Eeeeeyyyyaaaa...eeeeeyyyyaaaa."

"He's trying say something," Glorna stated.

"Don't talk," Marci instructed. "Save your strength."

"Eeeeeyyyaaa."

"Quiet now," she cooed. "Whatever it is, it can wait."

"He wouldn't be trying to talk if it wasn't important," Glorna argued.

But the blood was working. My body grew its flesh back to my previous form, and I wiggled my fingers and toes. Still, I wanted more. Marci let the blood continue to drip till I had emptied six pints. I motioned for a seventh and then an eighth.

"Vampires were here looking for you," Glorna informed me.

"Can you be more specific?"

"Nope."

Quicker than she could had done it, I grabbed two more pints, ripped holes into the plastic, and gulped them down. Marci watched me. When I looked back at her, I saw her, for a split second, as delicious prey. Fear filled her eyes in the brief conversation between hunter and hunted, but I gripped my self-control, and the terror left her eyes as if it never had been there.

"You seem different from the Steward that just gave a speech," she told me. "Are you still an early Ed, seven seconds away from death, or are you a later version of yourself?"

I didn't know until I rattled my head. The bullet was still in there, so I was seven second Ed still. And I had a question for Marci.

"I ordered a week's vacation for all my subjects with free food, drink, and luxurious lodging. Glorna has a newborn to take care of, but I'm surprised to find my secretary here. Don't you like your vacation?"

Marci gave me a reproving look.

"I met the Consul of Scantily Clothed Merrows," she told me. "You are a pig!"

I admitted that I was. She admitted that the real reason she was here was to check on wet nurses for Glorna. Rumor had gotten out of Glorna's new appearance and female volunteers were too numerous for the mission of feeding an infant. Many of my female subject were all too willing to take time off from their vacation to be a wet nurse, but only if the new "father" would sit in the same room. Glorna needed a chaperone.

"And what were you trying to tell us earlier?" Glorna asked, rocking the infant as a gently swaying tree might.

"I remember nothing about my little trip except I got lost in time in a place before…or maybe after plants and animals exist. Now I have to go back."

The pair was more outraged then stunned and asked in unison, "Why?"

Oh, what I would have given for a clever answer! Other reasons, much cooler than the real one, would present themselves later. I would have liked to say, "I've been through the world's history and I have to go back and set it right." Or I could have said, "The world's future needs adjusting, and I must go there to correct it all." Instead, I had to go back because I forgot the one thing that I'd made the trip for in the first place.

I had forgotten to snatch the electronic womb.

This time, I took a cooler filled with all the blood I could get my hands on. I also took a legal pad with me so I could write down anything I might not remember about what happened/will happen on my trip through time. Thinking I was prepared for anything, I departed through the portal.

When I returned, my memory was blank, the cooler was empty, I had no legal pad, but I had in my hand, some kind of futuristic device. It was the size of a DVD player with a number pad on its side. Other than the number pad, the box was featureless.

Marci lost interest in the first five minutes of my investigation. She returned to her vacation; I like to think that she enjoyed hobnobbing with the Consul. But Glorna stuck around, holding the infant and making unhelpful comments.

Wishing I had also snatched some kind of manual, I did the only thing the device allowed and started keying in random sequences of numbers, in a manner as to not repeat any sequence that produced a very unsatisfying electronic chirper. It was two days before I got anything else, which was quite maddening. The password proved to be "1234567890."

Once in, however, the device grew to the size of a phone booth and sucked me inside as if I might lack the intelligence to open the zipper door. Once inside, the purpose of the device became clearer. It seemed to be a health care unit for anyone that was completely paralyzed. Some kind of tutor program explained that this model was made during the social media wars where millions of people went catatonic and were unable to perform basic functions or interact with any that might put them in their care.

The display screen was the size of a small TV with a touch screen keyboard on the bottom and a row of icons I did not understand. The screen informed me that it was scanning for internet and human connection. After a few seconds, the screen informed me that there was no detectible internet connection but that I could run a few basic games already in the system's cache. I played some of them. Once the game determined I was not paralyzed, blind, or deaf, it gave me a panoramic view of a world the game took place in. Whatever I did with my body, the character I controlled did as well, complete with the sounds and smells of the gaming world I was interacting with.

"Hey, Glorna, check this out," I shouted from inside the box. I did not hear the baby crying and Glorna cursing until both were inside with me.

But what I wanted to show him wasn't there anymore.

"Baby detected," the system announced. "Scanning for suitable parents. Two mythical creatures detected but neither is suitable for parental responsibility. Power source required as well as internet connection. Please comply with infant health care system's needs."

A tutorial video followed. It claimed that it could provide any and all of an infant's needs for the first eighteen years of a human life. All the device required was sunlight on its solar panel and a source of carbon to convert to food. Once these things where in place, all unsuitable mythical beings would be expelled lest their corrupting influence damage the child.

"I wonder if tree sap could fill that requirement," Glorna mused. "Then, I wouldn't have to chase down wet nurses."

"Get to work!" a mechanical voice commanded, startling both of us. Before we could react, a virtual crib floated down to the level of Glorna's arm, where he was holding the baby. The crib cradled the baby but, at the same time, pushed both Glorna and me out of the box and none too gently.

"Now what?" I looked at Glorna.

"Help me with this box. I'll take it to an oak tree that owes me a favor. It will know what to do."

"Aren't you afraid that the box won't take proper care of the little guy?"

"He's completely content right now. If there is a problem, I'll know about it."

We discussed the new development at length while we both carried the box and lifted it high into the branches of a well-meaning tree.

But what about human interaction? While Glorna was insisting that humans weren't all that interesting to "his" infant, I worried about a youth without any parental contact besides the likes of a rogue wood sprite. And education…while Glorna insisted that he could teach the child anything worth knowing, I didn't think he had the academic background to play professor.

"What about the internet? Don't you have it on that computer?"

"What computer?"

"In the office of that funeral parlor the vampire owns?"

For the next half hour, I tried to explain to Glorna the notion of connectivity.

"If the child were going to stay here," I explained, "in the safety of this time and space where troubles were few, unless you were in charge, he wouldn't have internet access as communication satellites hadn't been invented yet, let alone launched. I don't know much about satellites. Now I admit I could imagine a communication satellite orbiting the earth in the seventh century to the bafflement of any telescope that might caught is reflective light years later, but it would be a very lonely satellite with no others to talk to. Any communication satellite would need some meaningful signal to bounce off of it to some other satellite not only on the other side of the world, but also a decade or so into the future. Even that wouldn't matter if there weren't a whole line of such time traveling satellites bouncing signals back and forth from millions of miles, hundreds of years, and gigabits of data. Why, it would be dizzying to think of all the work, materials, and expertise to get a single internet connection this far back in time."

Then something strange happened in a realm where "strange" had a very high bar. My cellphone always laid helplessly in my pocket. It was hardly worth taking the chance of forgetting it somewhere, so I kept it always with me wherever I went or imagined I was going.

Now it rang.

First, it was someone informing me that my computer had expired. Not six seconds later, it was to inform me that the FBI was looking for me. Then it rang again with someone wanting to help with my erection problem....I shut the phone down cursing.

"Quick, something strange is happening!" Glorna shouted. "The baby program...we have to go into the box."

Just then, the box sucked us in. On a large display, about monitor size, the words "internet detected" stood where they could not be missed. But there was something else...some kind of progress bar was in motion, although I wasn't sure where, but it was clear that the program wasn't finished looking for something else. Then it stopped.

"Device detected" replaced the other message. All at once the panoramic view changed to what seemed to be a maternity ward.

"Commencing the expulsion of harmful influences...get out and stay out." The box kicked us out again.

It would take me a few more days to understand what had happened. I understood right away that the time traveling interactive satellites, which science would never invent, had been imagined into existence through my musing that they were impossible. What I hadn't figured out is what device did the electronic womb connected with? Only my Irish luck could make that the 360 oakwood unit that Eircheard would/had made as a changeling child.

"Oh, he likes this so much better." Glorna gushed.

He was content to leave the box in care of the oak tree and forget about it. But I had to wonder; how did it get internet? What

177

device did it connect to? Why was this easy thing of living in my imagination so hard? Why was fixing the real world with an imagination so easy?

CHAPTER 14: SOMEBODY ELSE'S DIRTY SECRET

"You have to leave." Nalla was pointing to a man that Trudy didn't recognize

By now, all eyes were on the heavy, tall, gray-haired man in the suit. The guy seemed like he wasn't going anywhere, until he looked at the new arrivals.

"You're a thief," he said, pointing to Rick, Eddie's son and the father of the family Trudy had seen him walk into the funeral home when she was sitting with the support group. "And you're a whore," he added as he pointed at Trudy.

Then he walked to the door. Trudy was relieved not to have to show her badge under her jacket.

"Do you know that guy?" Trudy asked Rick. "It might be my new medication, but I want to take the guy down."

"Yeah, he works for the paper and was trying to bust us for scrapping Shoppers," Rick said. "My father and I knew he was following us because he had it out for my father."

"Scrapping Shoppers?"

"The Shopper is a free newspaper filled with stuff people are selling or giving away," Rick said. "The problem is that people didn't want them, and we'd get in trouble if we didn't deliver them. So we'd take the Shoppers in two trips because with me in the van bagging, there was no room for the whole load. I think Mr. Noble learned pretty quickly that we delivered all of the first load. I would bag in the cargo bay of the van, while my dad had the newspapers in the front seat. By the time he finished with the down routes, and there always were down routes, I would have filled the laundry baskets with papers. It was a tight fit to be sure. Sometimes those baskets would fall on me and nearly crush the air out of me. But once my dad started throwing Shoppers, the surplus would disappear faster than my bagging could fill them. Sometimes, he'd have to help me, hanging a wicket of bags on his rearview mirror and bagging as he drove. I always thought that was crazy.

"In the early days, we'd drop at least seven hundred into the dumpster in a locked-out apartment complex within the Thornton city limits. Then maintenance workers stopped us from delivering there. They told us, 'Just throw what you'd throw by the doors in the trash. Your bosses won't know, our bosses don't care, and we won't have to call you in as trespassers to the police.' So we did and they didn't.

"The thing about that, while we were OK with the edict from maintenance, Mr. Noble wasn't. He followed us in once. We didn't see him because the complex was huge, but we were dumping a couple of bundles each garbage bin. When we realized that we hadn't got rid of our seven hundred quotas of Shoppers, we doubled back in time to see Mr. Noble being escorted off the property by security. He was trying to take pictures of the bundles in the trash, but security wouldn't let him.

"After that, it wasn't safe to use those bins anymore. And then a huge mobile trailer park joined the rank of 'don't come in here.' My dad's boss was very firm with Dad about getting rid of the papers and not getting caught. With so many Shoppers we had to 'lose,' it made sense to sell them to a recycling center. A lot of other carriers were already doing it. Dad knew it was just a matter of time before Noble would get pictures of him in the recycling center, but Dad died first and Noble never got to make his bust."

"Noble...do you mean Jake Noble?" Trudy asked.

"Could be." Rick allowed. "How do you know him? Client?"

Trudy frowned. "He looked much different then. I was out of the 'professional dominatrix' thing. The dungeons I affiliated with had dropped me for my problems with the bottle and depression. The community is very sensitive to that, even more so back then when the whole SM thing was coming out. It was trying to be as legitimate as homosexuality but having more of a problem. I was about the same age as you are then, so we're talking twenty years ago. Anyway, the internet had just found its way onto personal computers, and I found a way to be a lifestyle rather than a paid professional. But of course, city vice cops never bought that. I wasn't the only one living the dream that got harassed. I have a friend who knew some people."

"My dad?" Rick asked, surprised.

Trudy nodded. "One of Eddie's call girl buddies knew his face from the picture he sent me online. That was suspicious right there. Back then, you needed equipment that not everyone had."

"Noble?"

"Not yet. Listen. Eddie's friend got stopped on the way to a client that Vice was wiretapping for dealing coke. The cop, who was just a lieutenant then, offered to 'let her off' if she 'got him off.' She was smart enough to realize that playing dirty with this guy would be more trouble than its worth. Still, she had to change her number and start all over with her phone book. Care to guess who the cop is and what he wanted?"

"Shock me."

"Director Vito Vermon, head of vice in Detroit now, and he wanted to be spanked."

"The same guy that investigated the shootout?" Rick's jaw dropped. "What did you do to him? What do you have on him?"

Trudy couldn't help a wide smile as she reached in her purse and pulled out a badge. "Lieutenant Vito Vermon" was displayed above the badge number.

"Am I going to be a subject of investigation if I ask…"

Trudy, still smiling, launched into her story.

The mansion, Trudy said, belonged to her employer Boris, but she had a makeshift dungeon in the basement. There was no shortage of subbies at the time; some did garden work for the thrill of working in chains and not getting paid. She also had a middle-aged man in drag, talking in falsetto and dressing like an over-made maid. He called himself Cindy Slut.

In the living room, it wasn't hard to notice the concealed firearm on the rogue undercover lieutenant who was completely "working" on his own, but what galled Trudy was that he brought along a friend. Though from the very start this was an extortion rather than a sting, Vito was waiting to hear about money. Trudy had much better.

Using her seductive grey eyes, she got both men into the basement and onto her unseen tape recorder, catching every word they spoke. She took them through their range of options, which included anything a dominatrix might offer, except those that got her naked. The men didn't seem familiar with any of the options, and Trudy picked up on their awkwardness. Finally they spoke up. They wanted to be spanked. So they undressed, and Trudy tied them to two parallel spanking benches.

Gleefully, she grabbed a paddle and went to work reddening their screaming, begging butts. The results couldn't be more pleasing.

Vito, who was getting exactly what he always thought he wanted, was getting instead a lesson in difference between fantasy and reality. The other man was finding a new obsession as a pain puppy. Vito begged her to stop, confessed to his identity, admitted his intentions, and vowed to give everything in his wallet if she'd just let him loose. The other man just took it, fighting each smack with a tugging of the restraints and an erection threatening to burrow into the bench.

Trudy kept swinging. When her right arm was spent, she switched to her left and back to her right again until both arms were spent. Both men had blood blisters when she finally did stop. Next, she taunted Vito with the tape recorder, which she played back to him. Then she let them sweat it while she took their clothes and his gun to a safe place. Meanwhile the men, unaware that their restraints were on time release, struggled to free themselves.

When she came back, she was holding two spades and a pistol. With the same expression that she'd use for any pistol play (the gun was rubber, but they didn't know it), Trudy ordered them to take the spades to the backyard and start digging graves for themselves.

Camera surveillance had a different format back then, but Trudy found the video tape too entertaining to not upgrade later. It showed an identifiable Vito Vermon running nude, dropping a spade, and jumping a fence. Trudy watched everything through the window.

"Cindy Slut," she called disdainfully, giving the bad drag a stab of euphoria. "There's a naked man running around the neighborhood. Call the police."

If "Cindy" did or not was no concern. Trudy eventually found the other man. He was digging a hole the width of a grave in the back yard. He'd caught on to the game and wanted to play.

"You're not a cop," Trudy told him. "What do you do for a living?"

"Newspapers. I deliver newspaper."

"I've a friend that does that…not a lot of money, is it?"

"No. I can't afford you, although I wish I could."

"You can stay here from time to time if you pay for your own food."

And he did, for a year and three months – until Trudy found out he was married and owned the place where he worked.

"Wow," Rick struggled to take it all in. "What happened to the uniform, tape, and service weapon? Let me guess. They raided that mansion and got everything but the badge you're holding."

Trudy smiled coyly. "Yes, but they didn't take the copies of the video feed."

"And that's somewhere they'll never find?"

"Unless they look on YouTube with the right address."

"So the other man was Jake Noble? Did you find out that was the same guy stealing papers from my father's boss? When the Reporter pulled their contract from him and gave it to Robert, Jake had only the Post left in that area. So to retaliate he had his drivers pick up every Sunday Reporter they could find on the driveways, and Jake sold them at his newsstands. Of-course, the Reporter had a hard time believing the complaints we were getting until they investigated themselves. They 'marked' the papers my dad got and them made random purchases at Jake's outlets. Robert then got the police involved, but someone must have tipped Jake off because that Sunday, no one complained, and no marked papers were bought. Do you think…"

"Yes, I'm sure my friend Vito was the tipster. That happened maybe six months after I kicked Jake out. Your dad had lots of dirt on people, but he didn't rat people out, even the people he didn't like."

"So with all I know about you," Rick asked, "how'd you get to be a cop?"

183

"That's another dirty little secret about the underfunded county. With my past, I'm hardly qualified to be an auxiliary cop legally. I should have gotten more training, but the department didn't have enough money to hire a full-time police officer. So it was me or leaving Munsonville and other unincorporated areas unpatrolled. Sheriff Matt is an honest man, but they keep siphoning money out of the county office, and his job depends upon his silence. Rick, I told him everything: the bipolar depression, my drinking, my online presence as a dominatrix…he still hired me."

"Despite your run-in with Vermon in Detroit?"

"I think it's because of that incident in Detroit. He knows I've seen corruption and understand gangs. And I know how to handle a gun."

"I doubt Munsonville has a gang problem."

"No, but Munsonville is in Beulah County, and this county has its own dark secret. Too many teenage girls go missing around here. Most of them are probably runaways, but all of them are unsolved…"

Rick's youngest daughter ran up to him, crying and shyly grabbing his leg. She did not even peer at Trudy until he had safely scooped her up into his arms. Rick's wife and the other girl were heading over to him, too.

Suddenly Trudy felt as if someone small was inside her clothes, pushing around to get noticed, but too tiny to count.

Rick quickly introduced them to Trudy, so quickly Trudy didn't even catch their names, and then said shortly, "Why don't you take the kids home? I think they've had enough. Besides, I want to tell Ma about what I found out from the coroner, and I want to back Trudy up if anyone else wants to upset the wake."

And that was that. Three of Eddie's most valued girls turned their backs on Trudy and walked out of her life. Now, standing alone with his Eddie' son, Trudy longed to apologize. She shouldn't feel that way. The boy had met her maybe twice, but she was so much a part of Eddie's life that he knew all about her…and accepted her because she was part of his dad, and so a part of him. He had a way of saying all that in not a single word. When he did speak, it was all she wanted to hear.

"It's late and Ma won't leave until everyone else does," Rick said. "I need to talk. Do you know a bar around here?"

CHAPTER 15: SO A GIRL, A GUY, AND A BROWNIE WALK INTO A BAR

Trudy was already glowing with the fuzzy heat of another cold drink. Inside her clothes, she still felt something crawling upward from hip level towards her bra as she listened to Ed's son explain his father's missing body. The crawling didn't fluster her. Mix booze with pills not to be taken with alcohol. and you can expect any number of adventures from just sitting on a bar stool.

"The Beulah County morgue is so overworked that the coroner needed an extra day," Rick said with a sigh. "Somehow the message never traveled and with some confused mismatch, the undertaker rolled out an empty coffin that was supposed to have my dad in it. Ma shouldn't have to be dealing with this."

Trudy agreed. Then she felt something crawl up her boob.

"Hey!" she protested.

Rick gave a questioning look and started to talk, but Trudy motioned for his silence.

A small brownie jumped off her breast and onto the bar.

"My Queen," he proclaimed. "I love you." As he said this, he leaned sideways with folded hat over his heart.

"What?" Rick asked, following her gaze. "What are you staring at?"

"Do you believe in brownies?" she asked him without looking away from her new companion.

If he answered, she didn't hear, but the brownie vigorously nodded.

"Please, take me home, queen. I shall be your breeder. We shall make beautiful brownies together."

Trudy smile drunkenly. "To get me in bed, you've got to ply me with liquor first."

"I decline on grounds of my marriage," Rick said. "But if you get that drunk, I might have to carry you home."

"What is your name, little fella?"

"Uh, Rick."

"Anything," the brownie said. "I'm yours now."

"Not so fast," she warned, but Rick gave a short laugh and said, "You're the one trying to get me in bed."

"What shall I call you?"

"New Medication?"

Trudy caught the joke. "New Medication. Mr. Bar Keep, a vodka and tonic for the boy, a double Scotch neat for me, and a beer for the brownie named New Medication."

"New Medication is my name," the brownie agreed with another bow.

The barkeep was unimpressed but started preparing the drinks. Trudy gazed fondly on Eddie's only son. "All grown up and handsome," she mused.

Both answered at once.

"Thanks," New Medication declared, bowing.

"Thanks, but I'm already married," Rick said.

"Yeah, you are. And was that your redhead wife? Man, she's smoking hot! Eddie must have been so proud."

"Yes, but she's married too."

The drinks came. New Medication reacted as if he…well, won the lottery. In joyful splendor, he drove, literally dove, into his beer and drank hard and fast, as if his life depended on reaching the bottom of the glass, which it did, seeing he was drowning in his beer.

"Funny thing about that," Rick said, with a catch in his voice. "You're the only one who called him 'Eddie.' With everyone else, he was 'Ed', 'Edward,' 'Santa,' 'Dad,' 'Grandpa.' Or my stepmother's name for him: 'Man.' We've hardly met, but I know all about you. My dad loved you so much."

Once again, guilt stabbed her. Why, why, and why again?

Why was everything with love at its core so painful, so confrontational? In four days, she would kill Eddie the vampire like she had done to the man – that or he would kill her. Anger, love, and guilt were spinning in a blender of comfortable alcoholic bliss on a knife's edge. The mixture was radioactive and sad-sweet with a bitter garnish. The next morning promised punishment with no Bathrobe to ensure her comfort.

She decided to change the subject. "So what are they saying about your dad?"

Rick took a swig and then answered. "They're so messed up at the coroner's office. First, they said he was stabbed in the chest, now they're saying he was shot in the back of his head. They found a lead ball, like one shot from a musket on the scene, but now they say there's no trace of my father's DNA on it. Neither is there an exit wound on his skull, so they think the bullet is still in his brain. They wouldn't let me see the body, so I have to go on faith. Evidence is hard to piece together when the details change every time you look at the scene."

"Eddie believed you could change the past," she said absentmindedly, staring at the brownie in the beer and wondering how the little guy could breathe. "You can change the past, just not intentionally, if you change yourself. It's the only way to do it. It's the only way to change the future as well, but you can never be sure if or how you've changed it."

"He thought that, but he didn't believe it. If you could prove him wrong, he'd have changed his mind. Belief is much more powerful, or so he thought…er…believed."

"Hard to disagree when you're watching a brownie drink beer from the bottom of a glass," Trudy said with a huff.

Rick gave that remark a wry knowing smile. It was easy with this young man. Who she was and what she had done with her life seemed to embrace each other. The moments of silence in between the swirling of honesty and trust felt natural and approving. Comfort, closure, and quiet stirred gently and mixed with the look of his father; that's the way you make a Rick. How would you make that drink? Southern Comfort, that's whiskey against a background music of Janis Joplin. What is 'closure?' Bitters…a twist of lime? Maybe a shot of moonshine…that would close anything out. And quiet…if that isn't hot cocoa, who knows what is. All of that would have to come to a coffee color like Baileys Irish Cream. Why not toss a shot of that in?

Damn mirrors. Trudy's eye caught the back of the bar with the edge of her visor. She turned to face her reflection, half expecting to see Eddie's face in place of her own as she had in the funeral parlor a few hours - or a few seconds - before two thousand years ago.

See, Eddie, I made a drink of your son. So why did I kill you?

"Are you OK?" Rick broke the quiet with mild concern in his voice. He turned to inspect her, then turned away. "Of course, you're not OK. I miss him too."

Trudy only answered with tears, not looking away from the mirror.

"Eddie was hardly perfect, but he always meant well," she told him. "He was born here in America, but he always thought of himself as Irish."

On the forefinger not holding her Scotch, she felt pressure and glanced away from the mirror long enough to see the brownie had jumped from his beer and was hugging her finger in an effort to comfort her. It was strange that New Medication did not feel at all wet, considering he'd swum in his beer.

"Did you read my dad's poetry?"

Trudy wiped her eyes and answered bitterly. "I did, when he was still writing poetry, before he gave up on being a poet and started with those unfunny limericks."

"I never saw the humor in them either, but I never cared for poetry as he did. He told me about you and how the two of you memorized everything the other wrote."

"It's true. Even his limericks. It was strange the way I knew all the people Eddie worked with by the verse that he composed. That was Eddie hiding. You may not know this, but the bravest thing your father ever did was stay in your life while your natural mother tried so hard to drive him away. Your dad was a lovable coward. He hated conflict and did everything he could to keep haters happy. But when it came to you, he fought. But that fight spent the rest of his courage when your mother used Eddie's poems as testimony in court."

Trudy heard the splash of a brownie jumping back into his

beer but didn't look.

"A lot of people missed this, including my Dad, but he always stayed and fought. He had you to back him up. Later, he had Nalla."

Rick fell quiet. Trudy felt eyes on her from seven seats down: Rick, two empty chairs, a youthful couple that made her sick, then a chair and a man, in that order. Not interested. She tried to see him without looking at him. The man was very tall and large, too young to be as bald as he was. In theory, the suit fit him, but the girth of his chest wrinkled the spillage over his beltline.

"I'm going to prison," Trudy announced. "I did something terrible."

"Really? Does this spring from that shooting in Detroit? I'm betting a good lawyer could stop that. What are you charged with?"

"Nothing yet, but I'll be arrested in a couple days. I should have been in your life. I should have never introduced Eddie to your birth mother who was a hard case from the very start…"

Rick was unimpressed.

"False guilt," he said, dismissing her words. "If Dad never met my mother, I would not have existed, though my Dad would disagree. He always hypothesized that a person existed before he was born. Why don't you talk about what really makes you feel guilty?"

"I won't miss your father's metaphysics, but I feel I should have been in your life."

"And when would that have happened? Before my mother left, my dad had to fight to visit me. By the time that she gave me up, Dad was married to my stepmother, and you and my dad drifted apart when you moved to Detroit. These things were beyond your control."

"Control is hard to assess when you can't control yourself." She lifted her now empty Scotch. "The night before you were born, I took your dad out drinking. It was one of those rare times when he could get off of work, so we made the most of it, hopping from bar to bar. Eddie had a reputation for not being able to hold much liquor. He didn't try very hard, I think. Mostly when we did go out, he'd switch to ginger ale after two beers, but that night he drank more then I'd ever seen him. We closed the last bar talking about him becoming a father without ever learning how to be a son, let alone a man. I understood him; for a long time, I was the only one who did."

Rick took another swig. Trudy took a large gulp. New Medication kept steadily drinking.

"Anyway, I drove him home and helped him into his apartment in the wee hours when he would typically be working with those damn newspapers. After putting him to bed, I went back out again to some bars I knew stayed open after hours. I think I was as upset as he was about his impending fatherhood. That morning your mother went into labor, and his phones started ringing for the next four hours without him hearing it. When he finally woke to answer, he got the call that you had been born. The first call your dad made was to me, but I was out cold from the night before. He got there too late. You know the rest."

"I never blamed my father for that. I certainly don't blame you, Trudy."

She continued as if she hadn't heard.

"I was drunk the day your father died. I had started the pills I'm taking now but didn't want to feel any sharp edges. I felt depression coming on; the kind that always gets me fired for not being able to move. I blacked out somewhere at the start of my patrol. The only thing I remember is seeing your father's truck on Tomas Ave across Wraith Park. I don't remember why, but I do remember aiming. I rolled down the driver side window and I fired my pistol…"

"Wait! You don't think YOU killed him, do you?"

Trudy could only nod and cry.

"It's not possible. My father was shot in the back of his head, looking away from the park as if hunting for a street address."

"And…"

"If you were driving the towards him, he would have looked at you. Tomas is a narrow street."

"No, I was on Willow."

"…which is almost two football fields away from Tomas. You couldn't have seen him, let alone shoot him without a scope. I don't think your service pistol had a scope."

"All I can tell you is where I aim is where the bullet goes."

"Nobody's that good. How many bullets were left in your revolver?"

She told him about Bathrobe's pistol that she used, how all

the bullets were missing, and about how both Bathrobe and his pistol were missing. Bathrobe could be turning her in right now, along with the murder weapon. She told him that when she woke up that first morning, Bathrobe's gun was on the nightstand next to her, a place it didn't belong and that all the bullets were missing from the six chambers. She couldn't get herself out of bed to check the service 38 till this morning, when she found her uniform from two nights ago. The revolver was still in the hoister around the pants waist, but the bullets in the chambers, along with the reloadable six bullets around the belt, were all missing as well.

"Did you fire your service weapon, too?"

"I'm sure I didn't. Bathrobe must have taken it. Maybe he thought I'd go after him to keep him quite when he realized what happened. I might have even told him I did it."

"But this Bathrobe's gun was empty too. If you shot my father once, where did the other bullets go? Even if you emptied his gun shooting, where are the other five bullet holes?"

"I don't know what happened to the bullets," Trudy admitted.

"I do! Put the pieces together. You felt your depression coming on. You were taking meds from a new prescription, and you were drinking. You're the one that emptied both guns as a precaution for any thoughts of suicide. You hid the bullets from yourself."

Trudy shook her head.

"I don't remember unloading any weapons before I blacked out."

"But you've unloaded you guns before to prevent you from harming yourself."

It wasn't a question, but she nodded remorsefully.

"And you've put a barrel in your mouth before," Rick pressed. "Pulled the trigger, and only then remembered that you'd emptied the weapon and hid the bullets."

How did he know that? She never told anyone.

"Well? Did you?"

"Yes."

"Not only did you not murder my father, but you saved your own life."

"Rick, discharging a firearm takes a certain attention. It

191

requires the concentration of both voluntary and involuntary muscles. I remember doing that. I remember hitting my target and feeling that Eddie was finally at peace. As far as the other stuff, I don't know what happened, but I can't think of a better suspect given what I do remember."

"Trudy, I know how my father died. Poachers. The screams of women from the supposedly haunted forest; those are the screams of deer. I've heard them myself in the wee hours while bagging papers in the back of the van. Beulah County may have a vampire obsession, but it's got a real poaching problem. They're wasteful poachers, too. Both my dad and I have seen the corpses of deer and other wildlife lying around the woods that encase the township."

"Which could be vampires…"

"Or poachers interested in the fleshy parts of meat and no use for skin."

Trudy wasn't buying it.

"So you're going to tell me that a person aiming from two hundred yards away could not hit your father, but a poacher, missing his target hit your father from five hundred yards or more."

"I'm saying that a riffle will hit what an aimed pistol could not. Something is killing those animals, and I don't believe in vampires."

"Ah, but did you ever hear gunshots before?"

Rick admitted he hadn't. As Rick went on about silencers and the distance a stray bullet could travel, Trudy lost interest. Looking over to the beer glass, she saw her now drunk brownie trying to escape his prison that no longer held any beer. Trudy tipped the glass slideways and the floppy brownie staggered to freedom gesturing his distress.

The bartender looked over at them and noticed the empty beer glass on its side and the other two empty glasses, Trudy's and Rick's. He pointed at the glasses, silently asking the question.

Rick shook his head. "Just soda for me. I'm driving to my stepmother's house."

"Don't worry," Trudy said in a reassuring way. "I'll take you there on my motorcycle. You can leave your car where it is at the funeral parlor and get a ride with her in the morning."

Rick laughed.

"Let's make the right decision here. I could stop drinking or accept a ride on a cycle being driven by a woman who's drinking twice as much as me and seeing brownies. Well, given that the driver is the legendary Trudy, I'll have a gin and tonic, please. Your reputation for being able to drive impaired is well known to me."

Trudy looked down at the brownie sprawled on his back.

"I think New Medication has had enough, thank you," she told the bartender. "But I haven't. A double Scotch neat, please."

Rick stared into space as he waited for his drink. Trudy absently caressed her brownie with her finger. Finally Rick spoke.

"So your boyfriend and his gun are missing. It's a shame." He turned to her. "We could test for powder left from the discharge to prove it hadn't been fired."

"A police lab could do that. I'm guessing they have the gun now. But how could you test for powder?"

"My dog is my police lab. When you have friends like I do, you want to know if they've had drugs or fired a weapon before you let them into your house where your children are sleeping."

That was the son of Eddie. Broken people are drawn to them because they both understand the pain of breaking, and they don't judge. Now, Eddie is a vampire; an undead being without a soul. How unfair to end life of acceptance with another life of being the unacceptable.

For a long minute, they simply looked at each other.

"Look," Rick said, holding her gaze. "If the bullet they dig out of my dad's brain comes from a pistol, I'll go with you to the station where you can tell your story. If it comes from a rifle, let the story die there. But please give yourself a fair trial."

All this time, New Medication had been struggling to his feet. Now that he was on them, he said in a small, slurred voice, "Where can I wet without causing offense?"

Trudy gently scooped him up and put him in her purse.

"I'm sorry, Rick, but I've got to get this brownie into a restroom before his swims in my purse."

"I'm relieved you didn't ask me to take him to the men's room," Rick joked.

She spotted the women's restroom and hurried to it. Would she be back in a few minutes or a few hundred years? She pushed the door open. The room was empty, which normally was a good thing. She rushed into a stall and shut the door before she could notice the mirrors. She held the little guy over the bowl with both hands and then shut her eyes in respect. The sound and length of it was rather disturbing. How did a little body hold triple the volume…never mind. Some questions need never be answered.

Once out of the stall, she caught the mirrors staring at her, but they only showed the refection of a murderess and her brownie. There would be no trips to the distant past this time.

Instead, she found her past when she returned to the bar. In fact, he was sitting in her chair.

That tall heavy bald man with a nice suit that didn't really fit him was engaging Rick with philosophical theory. The liquor clearly was hitting him because he was passionately explaining Plato's Cave.

"…the idea is that we're all in an entrance to a cave with the sunlight at our backs and what we're seeing is just the shadows," the ugly man explained.

"Yes! But that was in the golden age of Greece before the Greeks discovered bankruptcy and the rest of us string theory. Now, they might use the projector analogy with rapidly moving projections of light mimicking motion while the actual projector is stationary."

"The actual analogy was flawed from the start. The way I remember it, two men who stood abreast of each other would think they were standing face to face. Wouldn't they know they weren't by seeing their own shadow?"

"Or," Trudy interrupted, "If those two men were shooting at each other, wouldn't they be shooting at their shadows and never actually drop the other?"

"Trudy!" The ugly man stood up to hug her. She endured it and then claimed her chair and lowered her much more comfortable brownie on to the bar.

"Don't you remember me?" the man seemed shocked. "I was just talking to your son here…"

"He's not my son," Trudy told him. "I think you've mistaken me for someone else."

"Trudy," Rick said. "This is Malcolm, a friend of my father's from his teenage years. You knew him better than my father did. When he read that about his death, he flew in from Seattle to pay his respects…"

"Actually, I came hoping to see you," Malcolm confessed, turning away from Rick to Trudy. "I just always assumed that Eddie and you would marry."

"I can understand that. You and Eddie used to play chess together."

"Actually; we only played once, but yes. I am Bobby Fisher, as you used to call me. Of course, I never got that good. But I did become a master in my twenties, hung on to it in my thirties. I'm not a master anymore, but I'm still very good. What about Eddie?"

"Wow," Trudy realized. "I don't think he ever played again after his junior year of high school. The whole 'chess' thing ended badly for him, but he moved on. Rick, do you have a match?"

Malcolm shuffled from one foot to the other. Clearly Malcolm was uncomfortable with standing, but Trudy really didn't want him standing, or sitting, next to her.

"Rick, clear a chair for Malcolm and buy him a drink. There's a chair next to you, right? Do you have a match?"

Rick pulled out the chair on his right, the one that left Rick between Malcolm and Trudy. Malcolm accepted the chair but refused the drink.

"So, Trudy," Malcolm said, ignoring Rick. "Catch me up on your life."

Trudy gave him the resume pitch that touched on her husbands, residences, and jobs that seemed not to touch the reality of who she was. The three of those things had changed enough over the years as to sound like a full life story.

"Wow, girl, you've had an interesting life," Malcolm said.

It was too interesting. The poems, the lovers, the depressions and mania, the pills against them, the shoot outs, and the bars...all of that was stricken from the record like the ridiculous understated obituary the papers published about Eddie.

Trudy fished out a small bobby pin out of her purse. "Rick? That match?"

New Medication had dropped his pants and was bending over, naked butt ready for what needed to be done.

Rick didn't have a match, but Malcolm produced a lighter. Trudy took it without looking at him and carefully heated the pointy end of the pin.

"What are you doing?" Rick asked, incredulously.

"I'm branding my brownie."

Once again, Trudy smelled burning skin, but this branding seemed so much tamer than it did in the bathroom 1,200 years ago or this afternoon. If New Medication felt anything, he didn't complain.

"I make lots of money." Malcolm said, oblivious to the tension. "I became a software developer in Detroit before graduating to the big time in Seattle where I met his first wife. There I got a big house with a big car and a big portfolio. After a few years, my wife met a surgeon who got her big boobs. After that, she got a big lawyer and divorced me, taking the big house, car, portfolio, boobs, and lawyer with her. That happened two more times to me."

"Any kids?" Trudy asked as she set the bobby pin on the bar. New Medication shook his head and hiked up his pants.

"I always thought that I should have taken a wife here, before I moved to Detroit," Malcolm reflected with a glance at Trudy. "I am sorry to hear about Eddie. I always expected him to do better than I did. I heard he learned to write computer programs but couldn't navigate the corporate culture to get good job. To tell the truth, I thought that maybe it would be different if you and I had gotten together."

Rick just rubbed his forehead. Trudy felt sorry for him. A guy was coming on to a girl, and he was sitting between them. All Rick wanted to do was talk about Plato's Cave. She looked down at New Medication who was lying on his back with a tiny tent in his brown trousers and a lusty drunken smile on his face. Trudy stroked the tent with her pinkie and said, "Malcolm, I have a boyfriend, and I'm going to prison."

"Trudy, I'll wait," he promised earnestly "It's the way love works. Everyone gets a turn with everyone that doesn't work until the pieces fit, and life is finally worth living. This time, I won't make the mistake of leaving the prize. I can get a hair transplant and lose the weight. I can be anything you want me to be."

"Go back to Seattle, Malcolm," she told him firmly, without interrupting her attentions of the joyful brownie, "If it never happened with Eddie, it certainly will never ever happen with you. He would have never come to your funeral just to hit on your wife. You're too much trouble, while this guy I have now is no trouble at all."

"No, I'm not leaving." Malcolm insisted.

But Rick was already out of his chair.

"You heard the lady," Rick told him.

Confused and hurt, Malcolm slunk off. Just then, she felt the wetness on her pinkie and the tiny brown pants. No, this one was no trouble at all.

"I wasn't going to fight him," Rick reassured her. "If needed, I'd have called the police."

Now that she'd relieved the little man of his discomfort, she carefully gathered New Medication, who was now sleeping on the bar, and stuffed him into her bra.

"Letting him sleep in paradise," she told Rick's questioning face. He didn't see the brownie, but did he see the wet spot? Guys never did. "You wanted to say something about Plato's cave when a past crush intruded?"

As Rick talked, reinvigorated by a subject more to his liking (or maybe it was just the second drink), complex physics and philosophy danced in Trudy's understanding without the tedious exasperation the bar room academics typically produce. The boy knew his stuff and expressed it better than his father could.

Rick pointed out that the original platonic analogy had a narrow point that had been repeated in many ancient cultures. Simply put, there was more to the physical reality than one could perceive. To make Eddie's point, one had to start with his theory of time, with its paradigm divided into two parts: the finite past/future and the infinite present, all of which is counterintuitive to our animalistic perception, he said.

It's natural to see time as two opposite, infinite vectors sharing a common point with the point being the present and the direction being the past and present, respectively. But the point or present seems to be moving down along the future. The present, as a point, has no duration and thus we get the same ancient paradox about standing before a moving arrow; since there are an infinite number of points between the arrow and you, the arrow should never hit; yet the distance is finite and the arrow will strike. In Eddie's view, an animal trapped in space-time never experiences the present. The closest anyone comes to realizing the present is when he is experiencing an event from the very recent past; say as his nerve endings report an arrow hitting his body. Then that person feels the pain and the impending, inevitable future. Ed hypothesized that space-time is future and past, but the present, which living beings can't see; is here-now where nothing moves, and everything happens at once.

But here's the part about Plato's Cave. Ed hypothesized that everything is space-time is reflected…or better, projected from here-now and what Plato's Cave describes is a triple reflection of two individuals with the light and the projects coming from the here-now present materializing at the caves mouth. The cave is space-time. The shadow casting objects are the two people standing shoulder to shoulder as they actually are in space-time, which is not as limited as the shadows, which represent what our senses can detect.

Here is the rub, which is the whole point. One man does not perceive both shadows the same way. While one can see, hear, taste, and touch another's shadow, one can do all that and more with his own. For example, he can feel his shadow's pain in a way that convinces people that they ARE their shadows even though they are not. Shadows are just like the characters people control in video games. While they're comfortably seated on easy chairs in here-now, they move their character through the perils of space-time.

Trudy listened and followed without boredom. Liquor was a wonderful when dealing with pseudo-intellectualism. Part of her wanted to make the whole thing work.

"Do you want me to rip holes in that hypothesis?" Trudy offered.

"No!"

They both chuckled, then laughed and then broke into loud, uncontrollable guffaws. Maybe the joke was more that neither could keep from laughing even in a tragic setting. Or maybe there were no more tears to cry. If there was one thing Trudy wanted to avoid, it was the thought process of the tragedy.

"A part of the here-now hypothesis does need answering," she told Rick, when they finally caught their breaths. "In the case of one man shooting another: is it the shadow or shadow-caster holding the weapon?"

"The shadow-caster," Rich answered without pause. "The shadow-caster with the gun, shoots the other's shadow. The shadow-caster without the gun feels the shot, believes himself to be dead, and reports to the soul, which is sitting on the couch in the here-now, that the game is over. That soul then shuts the game off and goes back to living in the heaven or hell of here-now based on what happened in the video game. You might have to be a gamer to understand that."

"Rick, this is actually important. I know you don't believe in vampires, but if Eddie did, how would he explain being one?"

He started to wave her away. But he must have seen the intensity in deep, grey eyes because he slumped and then thought about it.

"Any undead thing is a problem in this theory," he mused. "Plato wouldn't agree that any such thing is possible, but my dad…well. He would say that the only way to be undead is to disbelieve that you died. In that case, one of the nature mirrors would be broken. The apparent shadow would be you looking not at the cave wall but the cave's mouth with the light too bright to see, and the vampire's body a reverse halo. We're talking about vampires?"

"Yes. Your father."

"Well, if he's a vampire, you didn't kill him, right?"

"Work with me here. I shot your father. I don't know why. He came to me a few hours ago in the mirror and challenged me to a duel. Take what I say as fact and explain it."

"Ok, I'll try, but is he seeking revenge, or does he just want to feed? Some versions of the myth have vampires becoming vampires without being bitten by other vampires. But most of those guys are already infected with some score to settle. I suppose if you'd shot him, he'd be unhappy with you. Did he say why he's gunning for you?"

"Yes, but it wasn't for shooting him. He pointed to a problem we had years ago but never really resolved. Also, he's unhappy about some things I said today. Rick, if I explained it all, it would only create further offense. I did ask him why I shot him, but he didn't seem to hear me."

"Do you want me to go with you? To show you there are no monsters under the bed?"

"I would. But this duel doesn't happen till three days and a few hours from now. I doubt you'll be willing to interrupt your life to investigate a story you're certain isn't true."

"A good night's sleep and none of this will be real, Trudy."

"What I need is a weapon… a gun that shoots vampires."

Rick was a gamer. With a drink in front of him and speculation that interested him, she might get something useful…something to save her life and face her prison term.

It worked. Rick took a sip of his drink and thought. After a few seconds he went through a list of roleplaying vendors and what they assumed of vampires in the rules they offered. In most cases, any weapon would stop a vampire. A shot from a pistol, for example, would cause the vampire to fall, bleed, and resemble any corpse. But the next night, the vampire would reanimate unless a wooden stake was driven into his heart before he attempted it or at the moment of reanimation, depending on the vendor.

For Trudy's purpose, that wasn't good enough. Waiting in prison for retaliation wasn't the closure she needed. Eddie's body was to be cremated, so staking him in his coffin wasn't an option. Rick rejected her plea to break into the morgue and stake him there. Besides, that would be a forfeit of the duel and an admission that she was wrong. She needed a weapon that would kill the vampire on the spot. The suggestion of a crossbow with a wooden bolt had two objections. If the bolt, even a wooden one, was not taken as a stake the result might be the same as a gun with a bullet. Also, hitting the heart and the low speed of a bolt might be difficult in that the flesh pierced would likely move the organ rather than pierce it. The surest way would be to hold a wooden stake in one hand, mallet in the other, and drive it home at personal range. But no vampire worth his fangs is going to wait for that. Some kind of gun that shoots stakes was possible, but difficult. The barrel would need to be long and its width would have to be the same shape as the stake because the tendency for the stake is to spin like a frisbee. The stake could be behind a modified bullet, but it would need some metal bracket the size of the stake's base or the bullet will beat the stake to its target.

"Ya know," he said as he thought about it. "I'm going to build this stake shooting, vampire killing gun for you. It would give me street creed as a roleplaying nerd."

"I'm no better than Malcolm." Trudy blurted out as the new drink lifted some border beyond drunk but this side of passing out.

"Why do you say that?"

"I always thought I could be with Nalla," she admitted. "She would stabilize me the way she stabilized him. I've had female lovers, but she's the only one I could have as a partner. If I'd shared a home and bank account with her, I wouldn't be going home to somebody else's house alone.

"Wait, Bathrobe left you?"

"Without even a goodbye. Does that make sense? Shouldn't he toss me out? He's turning me in right now."

"You don't want Nalla," Rick insisted.

"Why not?"

"I can see you sharing a house and bank account with her, but I can't see you in the same bed. You'd be great together as roommates, but I can't see anything else coming of it, and you know I'm right. She's too straight and too vanilla."

"Of all the women I've slept with, do you know how many of them first turned me away because they were too straight? How do you know Nalla's vanilla?"

"Ok, I don't know if my stepmother is vanilla or not, and I don't want to know. But if she wasn't too straight, you'd have gotten to her before my father did."

He was right, she knew.

Trudy downed three more drinks before Rick finished his last, just as the bar was closing.

"Hey," Rick said as if the idea just occurred to him. "Would you write a poem for the funeral?"

"That's only two days away."

"That's not enough time?"

He promised the gun; she promised a poem; and they both agreed to work on neither tonight.

The ride to Eddie's condo was cool, dark, and silent. Rick clung awkwardly to her, not knowing to lean with the bike, but Trudy's balance trumped. A couple lines popped into her head as she drove down the empty street.

Eddie my Eddie
You talk like spaghetti,
And wondered a thousand whys.
Of your theory's defense
Well, it never made sense
But the truth burned bright blue in your eyes.

Something? Maybe. It wasn't all she was feeling, but how do you miss someone you're hoping you can kill? Still, the sad loss of a friend was there, but so was the day he won the lottery. Poor Nalla would need a shoulder, but Trudy was better than Malcolm or at least willing to believe the woman was completely straight. In the coming years of prison, Trudy would try to be a better friend to her.

They were outside the condo, with Rick fumbling for his key that he kept…somewhere. He was drunker now than when they'd left the bar. Trudy felt like she should be carrying him in, then putting him to bed like she did on the first day she met him when he was only four. A year after that, Eddie married Nalla, who quickly became all the mother Rick ever needed.

There was a poem somewhere in the landscape that would never find words. Rick was going back through the doors he grew up opening as a child. Back then, Nalla filled the shortage of just father and son. Now, it was son that would bring the masculine to the widow…and Trudy was the one out in the chilled night looking in. Alone! And doubly alone. They had a father and husband that wasn't coming back, but Trudy had a dead man that wouldn't die with no one to believe her, let alone help her.

Trudy's hands felt cold, and she shoved them in her pockets. Ah, yes, the piece of paper with the phone number on it…Dolly, the old woman that so warmly invited her a way to work through so many problems. Maybe, besides depression and boozes, there was room enough for that group to cope with vampires. Wow, a self-help for vampires and the women that love/hate them…

Maybe she could find another bottle at Bathrobe's house. Maybe she wouldn't wake up and have to face all those problems. Maybe the next bottle of Scotch wouldn't be so chatty.

CHAPTER 16: THE GAME OF MY LIFE

Even as a ruthless vampire is unable to remember who, where, and why, I can never forget the game of my life.

Time was running out as I scanned the opposition's defenses. Sweat from my eyes dribbled down my face. With a little more than a minute left on the clock, I tried to keep my poise. Before the game started, a loss of this type seemed unthinkable, but there it was, with only seconds separating winner from loser, and the rest of my life in the balance. It was all on me to find an eligible man deep and uncovered, but I still had to deliver victory. No other options were present. I was tactically overmatched, and time pressure forbade any other chance for a win. Sure, many other fifteen-year old boys must have felt this same pressure, except this game really was the one to set the tone for the rest of my life. There would be no second chance, no redemption, no forgetting.

I made my move. Out of the corner of my eye, I saw what I dreaded. A red flag rose. I knew if it fell, I'd wonder for the rest of my life what might have been if I'd only done this game differently. A strange thought came to me. Fighting the daze of fatigue, I reached within my soul to put out better than I ever was.

Why was I doing this? What was it that made this game so important?

Remember now, I was fifteen, so there really was only one possible answer. Why does any teenage boy give his all? Teenage girls! I was no different, except I was willing to work for it. I knew that an average effort towards football wouldn't get me noticed. Two hundred other boys tried out for freshman football, and nearly all of them were faster, stronger, and heavier than I was. I knew my efforts had to be superhuman. Before the first tryouts, I had already put myself into training. Every morning before my paper route, I'd wake up an hour early and do pushups till I could do them no more. Then I'd do sit ups, pull ups, and jumping jacks, same way. After the route, I'd put away my bike and run until – you guessed it – until I could run no more.

Tryouts could have gotten me discouraged. By the way, since coaches knew the better candidates by name, I understood that many of the boys felt they'd already decided who'd made the team. In this private, Catholic school, many of the chosen had been given a full ride, saving $500 per year on tuition. I had to work part-time to earn even that, as my single parent home couldn't afford the expense, nor were my grades sufficient enough to earn such a ride. I did have a "poor boy" scholarship, which I suspected Fr. John Chokey had arranged, but that only cut the tuition in half. I had to earn the rest or attend an inferior public school.

"Winners never quit, and quitters never win!"

I heard that and other inspirational messages at least ten times during each tryout/practice. Every day for a month, fewer and fewer boys came out. Then school started and even fewer boys came out, with even fewer placed on the team roster. But football games aren't won by sitting on the bench. I fought hard, worked with uncomplaining relentlessness, and stayed committed to getting a spot as a starter. By midseason, it was clear that, despite my devotion, I was too slow, weak, and small to actually play for the school. My freshman season ended without me on the playing field for a single snap.

I was also having problems with grades. That was nothing new to me. I struggled all through my schooling career, although I'd managed to qualify for a top high school and even a top college. Nobody really understood dyslexia then, and I wasn't diagnosed till my last year in college. I tried hard, or I didn't try at all, depending on perspective of teacher or student. Still, my grades left me eligible to try out for varsity my sophomore year. So I threw myself into spring training with a vigor that was viewed as comical, even by some of the less sensitive coaches.

"Let them laugh," I told myself. "I'll find a leadership role on this team and pull us all to victory."

I had plenty to be discouraged about my sophomore year. The team did well, but once again I never got on the playing field; in fact, I never dressed for the game. While they had sixty complete football gear for practices, they only had fifty-five game jerseys, and I was one of the five who was on the team every day but game day. Still I hung tough and didn't quit. Of that five, I was the only one that tried out again as a junior.

My junior year was a breakout year for the name "Calkins." Though the season ended with a playoff loss, the best offense center in the league was Calkins, but not Ed Calkins. My cousin Larry held that honor for that season and the next. He would go on to win a full ride to an ivy league university. I don't mean to dismiss my contributions to the team for I had found a role for myself. You might have heard of the joke: "I play guard, tackle, and end…coach told me to sit at the end of the bench, guard the water bucket, and tackle anyone that comes near it." Heard that one? No, I wasn't even good enough for the bench. As in the previous the year, I was only on the team during practice where I found my true calling… blocking dummy.

Though I was only one hundred and forty pounds in a downpour, I was the right height to give real football players a surface to practice hitting. Better than that, I never quit, which was quite annoying to blockers, thus fueling a better effort. And, too, my obligatory grunts were so high pitched, they irritated the blockers' ears and, thus, inspired greater force.

So football never got me noticed, expect for ridicule, even though I gave football everything I ever had. My athletic career, like my academic career, was something I survived, and I'm proud of that much, but it never gave me a sense of manliness or a well-paying job. It did, however, teach me lessons of value. On the football field, I learned that everyone, no matter how small or physically flawed, is tougher than me so if I didn't want to look foolish, I'd better act respectful lest I get my butt kicked by a midget - or even a girl. School taught me that no matter how much I learned, how much I studied, or how much I knew, anyone who listened to me or read anything that I wrote would assume they were smarter than me. So I learned to get the thing I wanted out of life by acting stupid.

I also did learn to take pleasure in doing hard work. Because of that alone, I am luckier than most.

During my high school years, other important things were going on in the world. In Vietnam, the United States was losing its first war, which was unthinkable a decade earlier. Hippies still refused to cut their hair, and Catholics started living in sin, rather than getting married. With all this corruption, coupled with a president resigning and the sexual revolution breaking out of bedrooms everywhere, someone, mainly Catholic teenage boys, had to fight back. We heard one message everywhere we went. It was our moral responsibility to never believe the crazy notion the times were changing and that all was right with God and the USA.

We were told long hair on boys was unnatural, disgusting, immoral, and made young men cowards. They felt only short-haired boys too young to get drafted would lie about their age for God and country. Corruption? Forget about Watergate. The real corruption was easy to spot in any man's hairline that didn't reveal ears. Hair that covered ears, that's where the devil speaks...and the woman with him? She's probably on the pill instead of making babies like she's supposed to. Together, they were the reason people had to pay taxes, not to kill Charlie, but to support marijuana farms in crazy sex-filled commie communes where nobody married anybody.

Then there was the sexual revolution. Now, I've heard of the double standard that might have existed around the country, if not the world, but in our all-male Catholic high school, we were lectured daily on the perils of damnation for having sex before marriage. Not that we were encouraged to get married. Marriage was a bad thing, but it was survivable if you prayed a lot and worked hard. After all, not every man had the stuff to become a priest. But if you're going to be weak and go for marriage, avoid the eternal fires and get some priest to marry you. At least that way, your suffering will come to an end when you die.

One of the Dominican brothers that taught was more vulgar than most in his lectures.

"Remember that every date with your girlfriend is a fight for your soul," he told us. "You know in your head that anything you could do with her isn't worth burning forever in hell, but your little head (yes, he'd actually point to his crotch) doesn't. It's a battle between the big head and the little head. Yes, if you go down that way, you can be forgiven, but you're much more likely to blow off salvation altogether. How many of those hippies do you think go to confession? Remember that. Unfortunately, some of you will only remember that in hell."

Of course, I was a nerd, so damnation by the traditional "date with girlfriend" route was kind of slim. My plan to win damnation was as simple as it was ruthless, with a touch of elegance that bordered on genius, even though the objects of my affection swore it would never work. My method for carnal knowledge? Being the last man on earth. No, I wasn't going to play mad scientist and kill every other man on the planet; that idea lacked elegance. I was going to wait for some less nerdier nerds to have the same thought and start killing the other guys while I hid, waiting for the numbers to go down. Then I'd spring out and kill the last surviving killer. The plan might seem extreme to you, but having every woman or girl on earth seemed like fair compensation to me. I also envisioned less extreme versions of the plan; I could be the last man in the state, zip code, or village. That would work, although it would create an American postal bride wave. Or I could be the last single man in the world, country, state, zip code, or village. Maybe I'd have to settle for being the last man that some bad girl never had. I might have to settle for that. But in either case, it involved a lot of waiting things out.

Then there was the biggest conflict of all. The commies. Yes, the Cold War was in full swing, and, although my age group was just a little too young for the draft, we still had to fight the bigger picture. With a remorseful apology to Vietnam vets, I have to admit that my age group was told that "Nam" was a little war compared to what we'd see if we didn't stem the flow of communism. That's how truly evil communism was. Sin could take us to hell when we died, but commies would make sure we didn't have to wait.

On that front, we didn't have lot of good news, but we did have Bobby Fischer. Except for a few nerds, everyone knew that chess was a commie game that no real American would bother to learn. Some even felt the game itself was a communist plot. Nevertheless, the year 1972 saw the greatest chess players in the world square off with Fischer representing the Free World and Spassky representing the Godless communists. This time Godly won, crushing the way for this ill-charmed contentious man to be the media sweetheart of the free world.

Quite suddenly, everyone in America started playing chess. In bars and hangouts where the incoherent used to argue politics, religion, and philosophy, they now argued chess theories and, in some cases, even played the game.

My remarkable opportunity came with an unlikely invitation to a teenage party. I should note that this might not be as unlikely as it seemed, as the party was sponsored by an adult group, which marked it as a party for the unattractive or socially inept. Parties that cool kids went to were mostly "goodbye" parties for parents leaving for somewhere, usually vacations, trusting their teenage children would behave sanely and not do anything rash, like throw a party. Parents of that era were experts at misplaced trust.

Misplaced trust could have been the buzz phase to describe the 70s, as pedophiles seemed to lurk around every trusted institution where children or underaged teens were served. The abuse of Churches is well-known today, but back then a child could find molestation by pediatricians, nurses, child psychiatrists or psychologists, carnival workers, juvenile case workers, crossing guards, daycare workers, teen club moderators, and parents. Anywhere children were, so were pedophiles, and no one ever seemed to catch on.

We didn't know it then; it wasn't a party talking point even for the socially awkward, but everyone in this teen club was molested by someone from the above occupations at some earlier time. Though a different definition was assigned to this club, Trudy, a girl my age whom I met at Wraith Park, suggested that I, coming from a single parent home, qualified as a member and could attend the party as one of her guests.

Luck favored me. Among broken teens, I was less likely to stand out. By now, it was the September of 1973 and I arrived late to the party as I had football practice, a fact I hoped to use to impress some gullible girl. I never got the chance to mention that. In fact, I never got a chance to introduce myself as the party was dominated by a chess board, where Trudy was proving her intellectual superiority over her new twenty-something boyfriend by beating him.

Knowledge of chess was mostly required of nerds back then

in that there was no Klingon language to learn yet, and "Dungeons and Dragons" had yet to spawn. True, there was Star Trek and the "Trekkies" that worshiped it, but Star Wars had yet to debut; so true nerds had only chess, philosophy, or homework to replace our lack of companionship.

"Do you know how to play?" Trudy asked, seeing me sitting there, looking out of place. I could play winner, if I wanted, but there were three others before me. I waited. It wasn't like me to keep my mouth shut, but I already realized that anything that came out of my mouth would make me less attractive to the girls, who were in equal number with the boys. So I endured the running uninformed commentaries of the next three games, hoping for my chance.

Yes, I played chess. Before high school, I was the best player I knew. My dad taught me the game because he was bored with the other "family" games he felt required to play with my siblings and me as proof that he did more than drink all the time. Monopoly was too long, checkers too boring, and we kids didn't have enough money for poker. In a couple years, I excelled in the game and could beat my dad, so he quit playing, claiming it was the game that drove him to drink. With no one to play against, I played myself, turning the board after every move.

It was after football practice finished late one evening, and I discovered I needed a book from my school locker, that I heard chess pieces moving in one of the classrooms. Investigating, I discovered that my high school had a chess team I could try out for. Of course, this was out of the question, as all the matches coincided with freshman football, but there was also a club, and anyone could play. I played three games on the spot with team candidates, losing each one. Still, I was evenly matched enough to get instruction on how to improve and how to read chess notation so I could review that games I played.

By the time of this party, I had gotten better, sometimes beating the players that had made the team. Because I could only play after football practice, I was playing only the players that practiced the hardest, or at least the longest.

When it came to my turn at the party, Trudy still held the board, having beaten the other three players. I knew by then that I could easily take her apart and did just that with a "Scholar's Mate" in three moves. After that, I found myself still playing Trudy, but really the whole party, as kibitzing replaced any conversation.

By the fourth game, I was really feeling good. While the games could have bored me to tears, I was the focus of a party and not through ridicule!

I was being set up for a knockdown.

"He's really good," Trudy remarked as her loyal followers marveled. "But I don't think he could beat Malcolm." Then looking at me she asked. "How many players in your school can say they never lost a game…ever?

I knew I wasn't a very good liar, so I admitted that I didn't know anyone who never lost. Unable to keep silent, I admitted that I lost about one third of my games against chess team members and drew still another third. Surely, this Malcolm didn't win every game he played; draws were the most common results in high level play. But no, Trudy claimed he won every game he ever played.

Not everyone agreed with Trudy. One of the girls pointed out that I had beaten her quicker than Malcolm had. Apparently, he liked to play with his food, removing pieces one by one like pulling the wings and legs off a fly. I always went for the kill, checkmating where I could with all the pieces on the board.

"Maybe I could play him," I suggested. "That way we could know."

That way, too, I'd get invited to another party with girls in it.

But I was not invited to the next party. I found out because my mother had joined the adult club that had spawned the teen club. She was having trouble meeting single men who properly justified her loathing for the gender. This club was perfect for her. My exclusion was explained by the host's parents not knowing me and the fact that it fell on one of the teen's birthdays.

The next party was different. Trudy called me herself, informing me that Malcolm was coming and bringing his chess clock. I'd never played with a chess clock, but I had a week to prepare. The high school chess team did use chess clocks, and after explaining the importance of the game to be played, the boys were willing to coach me.

Now Trudy was not a beautiful girl, but she had a directness that fed into her charismatic sex appeal. At a time when teenage girls were divided into the ones that did and the ones that did not, having

210

a girlfriend was no guarantee of more than a peck on the cheek lest boys not respect her. There were good girls and easy girls, with none wanting to be the latter. Trudy broke the mold. No teenage boy could call her easy, because to teenage boys, she was completely unavailable. Neither was she a good girl; she was the prototype of the selectively promiscuous attitude that would come to her peers a decade later. I was expecting to score not with her but with the boy-crazy girls that orbited around her because they were unable to navigate the slut/princess mentality of the day. I didn't have to explain all of that to the chess club. They understood perfectly when I told them there were girls at the party.

The week passed quickly, and I went to the address ready to play chess, but there was a change of plans. The party was in the basement. That alone wasn't enough to change anything, but the teen club moderator was upstairs drinking with the host's mom.

"Not now." Trudy said to Malcolm, pointing to his chess clock. "We may never get a chance like this, so this is a make out party."

Everyone liked the sound of that, but no one except Trudy seemed to know what a make out party was. Simple! Pair up, shut off lights, and make out. Trudy's boyfriend wasn't present, so she pointed at a guy and then at a couch. Something like, "You! There." Each of the remaining girls were to do the same thing. Giggling or blushing, each girl complied. But of course, there were three more guys than girls, so Malcolm, I, and someone else went unselected and bore the duty of lookout.

What could we do? It was too dark to play chess, and we didn't want to sound rude. Someday there would be both a make out party and enough girls to go around. What else could we talk about? Only three things interested me; girls, football, and chess. I didn't know much about girls, and Malcolm didn't care about football. For the first three minutes, we waited for the third guy to start us off. It took us that long to realize he had left.

So we discussed the Fischer-Spassky match down to some of the chess notated moves, which might have convinced Malcolm that I would be worth beating. He felt that Spassky was the better player, but Fischer had gotten in his head. I felt that Fischer had gotten in his own head but was the better player.

While listening to the soundtrack of teenagers making out,

chess wasn't going to carry the party. Malcolm admitted he was hurt, but not surprised, that he was not chosen, while I admitted to being only frustrated. Which girl did we want? Both would have been happy with any, but Trudy was our first choice, as it was sure with her that there would be some running of bases...even if she did the running. The fact was, neither of us had ever kissed a girl, but Malcolm was confident that future make out parties might have enough, or more, girls than boys. He figured if he just stuck around longer and was better known, he would be better liked and not last all the time. We seemed to share a mild version that of "last man alive" plan.

He wasn't there the day that the conditions for such a party included one extra girl, so Trudy offered to share her choice with the unpaired girl. The lucky guy didn't say much, partly because as Trudy's boyfriend he was neither a teen nor a virgin, but it's rumored all bases were skipped, and the party of three went oral.

In my time as a teen, to get close to that far with a girl, you had to have a car. None of the teens in the club had a car, but we had Trudy.

The party ended quickly with a smashing bottle and some yelling from upstairs. The parents, who were supposed to be chaperoning the party, were also having an affair, but now they were fighting. Kids took their cue and ditched the place through the basement door, even the daughter of the mother hosting the party.

Trudy apologized to both of us once we were outside. If there were only one of us, she'd have let us share her, but four boys and one girl was too hard to do, and boys tended to get all inhibited with having to share anyway.

The next three parties were not nearly as enticing, but by then my mother had joined the club, so I became a member of the teen club and not just a guest. Her joining was predictable even though I had the good sense not to tell her about the club. She, while looking for a husband, loathed men in general. She cited them as morally weak and repeatedly found those men who could support her theory. Most of the male parents kept very loose or no contacts with their own kids and thus were free to screw up somebody else's.

Still, teen parties were scheduled monthly, and each one seemed an opportunity to make out or play chess against the undefeated Malcolm. But fall had turned to winter, and winter to spring; thus like the melting snow, interest in chess waned. No longer was chess a center of activity. That gave way to listening to four guys practice their "air" instruments to the radio. We were to believe they were a band, though none of them had musical instruments, let alone ability to play them.

The game wasn't going to happen at any party, but it was definitely going to happen. Though chess lost its relevance, the debate on who was smarter continued. While Trudy and her followers stuck by Malcolm, some of the boys, who must have viewed me as less of a rival for the girls in the club, sided with me. The way the guys were acting, it almost confirmed what I suspected. Even though this group was a collection of the socially undesired, there was a pecking order which allowed for only one smart kid. As far as academic achievement, the collection already had an "A" student, Debbie, so the "brain" slot was taken. Two chess geniuses would have to narrow to one.

On the fourth party, Trudy had enough. The talk had to stop and the knowable had to be made known. The Malcolm and Eddie match would be held at her house on a Sunday afternoon, as it wouldn't affect my football practice or Malcolm's marching band. The date and time were set. Wagers were made and anyone who wished to watch the game was invited.

At some point that day, Malcolm and I made a wager…one we'd never admit to anyone. The stakes were already as high as they could get, but with this wager…Malcolm must have been confident of victory. I had little to lose except this chance.

I got there on time, but I could have believed I was early. Outside of Malcolm sitting in front of a set-up board and his chess clock aside, no one was there but Trudy and her curious mother, who disbelieved that her daughter was hosting a game of chess that she was going to watch.

I felt the blood rushing through my veins, but I tried to act confident with the obvious question and its heavy pull. Which seat was mine…that is: would I play the black pieces or the white? White had an advantage.

Malcolm was fair. Solemnly, he grabbed a white pawn in one hand and a black pawn in the other, then placed the hands behind his back where he could mix them, then held both closed fists out.

"Pick one."

I picked black, not a true disaster. If I were able to pull out a draw, Trudy might suspect me as the better player or at least declare another game with me as white. Malcolm set the clocks. A chess clock is a simple thing: two faces, one for each player, with an hour and minute hand and a button above each face. When a player made his move, he would press the button above his own, stopping his clock and starting the other. The most intimidating feature was the two red flaps, or flags, situated to the minute hand, which would lift the flap up at one minute to midnight. If that flag dropped before a win or draw was achieved, that player simply lost.

I was sweating a little…I always sweated as I had overdeveloped underarms. But so was Malcolm. Trudy's mother noticed the seriousness we players were radiating. She had to ask.

"You're not playing for money, are you?"

Both of our hearts must have skipped a beat. If she knew what we were actually playing for…

Malcolm recovered with a joke.

"No, we're playing for your daughter's hand.'

Trudy's mother laughed and then monologued about how she would be proud to have either one of us as Trudy's husband or boyfriend. Her continuing praise of our collective upstanding virtues was "parent speak" that we were too nerdy to score any sexual advances with her daughter. The game began while she was still talking. Malcolm started his clock, made his move, started mine, and scribbled its notation on the paper beside him as we were both recording this game. Trudy wanted to crawl under the table.

Now, if you're not a chess nut, there's probably nothing more boring than watching to guys go into deep thought over a chess game. We each had forty minutes on our clock, the high school chess matches' norm, so although we'd have to conserve our mulling over potential moves, we had plenty of time to bore any bystanders. Worse than that, we played a textbook opening called the "giuoco piano," which means "peaceful game" in Italian, but boring, boring, boring to casual chess observers.

Trudy's mom left when she realized no one was listening to her. Trudy tried to stay interested, but she expected to keep appraised of who was winning by the value of the pieces captured. She couldn't take it either and disappeared into her room.

Almost as soon as she left, pieces started flying of the board.

I know that it's a bad idea to write about the moves in the game, but I've been studying this one game all my life. I wouldn't be the nerd I am if I didn't want to give you each chess notated move, complete with analysis and commentary. While I can skip that, I simply must get off my chest what happened on the board in the biggest game of my life.

As if reading for a textbook, the predictable pieces left the board without any real advantage to either. Two center pawns apiece, black squared bishops, knight for knight, exchange evenly giving me hope that if I could keep exchange, it would end in a draw. Later, an exchange of my knight for his bishop but doubled my Queen's bishop's pawn gave him a slight strategic advantage and me a slight tactical one. With our centers squares vacated, we both castled king side.

Then came the move. It was the only conversation in the game. While this game had no master strokes or obvious blunders, it did have a defining move, and this was it. I would never make the same move in the hundreds of recorded games that I would play before leaving high school. Still, on this day I would chew up nearly ten minutes of my clock trying to talk myself out of it. The move I was contemplating was both elegant and tragic with a sense of romanticized melancholy. Then, with a dramatic flair, my red bishop took his unprotected queen's rook's pawn.

Shocked, hurt, and maybe outraged at my boldness, he looked up at me but responded first, completely reasonably, with pawn to queen's knight three, effectively sealing off my bishop from play.

"Did you forget?" he asked me gently.

I shook my head. I hadn't forgotten. No. I made my move as deliberately as the statement I was making by it, a sad statement, though bold.

You see, the move I made under, as far as we could tell, almost identical positions, was the same move that Fischer made in that first game vs Spassky. Everyone concluded, including Malcolm and I, that move was the blunder that cost America that first game against the Russian world campion. What was I saying here? Was I trying to get into Malcolm's head? Was I trying to undermine his confidence? Or was I in my own head and just being sad?

There was some logic to my move. Malcolm was about to

mount an attack on my king side, using all his major pieces and threating checkmate. My bishop, though out of play, would cost him two precious moves to claim my bishop for two pawns, diverting at least a rook away from his attack and give me a chance to improve my defense.

But Malcolm would have none of it. He ignored a bishop that would never see play. With brute force, he doubled his queen and rook, while advancing his knight, keeping me in constant peril of making a fatal mistake. I was able to trade queens, then rooks, but that knight kept checking me, trying to fork my pawns. I'm not sure if he saw this right away, or later when I did, but he had to keep checking me, lest I advance my doubled pawn, forcing an exchange that would free my bishop.

Trying to dance with his knight, I committed my last rook to my king's defense, which forced a hard decision for my opponent. He could trade our last rooks and take a two-pawn advantage, but I'd get my bishop back if he left me two free moves. The exchange happened.

Realizing that I was unable to defend my king, I raced my king to the toward the center of the board. With my red bishop still on the board, the game was now a chase, him up in pieces, but one move short of queening a pawn first. If there was any way for Malcolm to reverse the game or get a draw at this point, he never found it, nor did I upon many replaying and reliving this victory. My twenty-fifth move would be my last.

Malcolm toppled his king.

For what he lost that day, Malcolm was a true gentleman. He didn't swipe the pieces of the board, cry "foul" in some way, or try to make excuses as I might have done in my immaturity. I, for my part, managed to mask my elation. I offered my hand, telling him that it was a good game and that he'd played it well. He shook my hand, though he must have been dying inside. Still, he had to leave right away. He had just remembered he was supposed to do something.

Trudy must have heard the rustling of coats. Who was leaving without even saying goodbye?

Running down the stairs, she caught him at the door with coat on and chess clock under his arm.

Confused, she asked the obvious question. "Who won?"

"He did," Malcolm admitted, waiting for a comment.

I've found in life that just because somebody lost, it doesn't mean his rival won. That would have been the case only if Trudy had looked at him sideways. Such a look would mean, "I thought you were good. How could you have never lost a game if the first guy I put on you beat you?" But Trudy didn't do that. Instead she gave me that sideways glance. With nothing to explain, Malcolm left. I don't doubt it was to cry in his pillow as I would had done.

"Why didn't you tell me you're that smart?' she challenged me the moment Malcolm was not among us.

I saw the gambit. I could have explained that my high school had an extremely proficient chess team and that my being able to handle them on equal terms qualified me as a future grandmaster. Maybe she'd never know otherwise. Maybe I could believe the same and convince myself that I was the next Bobby Fischer. But I would have to defend that lie.

The truth is often a buzz-kill, but it's the most powerful piece of anyone's mind, if you develop it. I told her what I had just finished telling Malcolm with my bishop takes queen's rook's pawn. I wasn't that smart, and neither was Malcolm. We were just two guys with nothing more enjoyable to do then study chess after our homework was done. Neither one of us would ever be grandmaster no matter how hard we played, studied, and practiced. We were good, maybe better than a hundred random teens who knew the game. Maybe, if we kept playing and tried really hard, we'd be better than a random thousand, but to ever get national notice, we'd need to be better than millions. There were too many guys like us that couldn't get girlfriends. One in a hundred thousand was bound to have a photographic memory and never have to study a losing position a second time.

She resisted at first, pointing out the things the Malcolm could do in chess, like playing and winning without seeing the board or playing several games at once and winning them all. I could do those things as well. A lot of boys could if they played on a team.

The board was still as it was when the white king fell. I offered to replay the game for her, complete with my analyses. She declined, disappointing me, but not surprising. She told me to leave; that she wanted to be alone. All I could think was that I somehow blew it with a girl again, and I gathered my coat. The exit out was not three yards from the table where the game was played. Trudy sat in Malcolm's seat and touched the downed white king.

She started getting teary-eyed.

I was wondering how much she bet on the game, but of course, I was on the wrong track. Looking back at me, she explained with anger in her voice.

"We're a bunch of oddballs in this group, all for different reasons. We're a group of outcasts that no other group with take, but I always hoped for some kind of justice...like maybe someone would prove to be so good at something that everyone else that ignored or mocked us would be forced to turn around and take notice."

Yeah! That was it! Every nerd that ever lived must have felt that way. Wait till that ray gun gets invented that kills all the cool guys.

"There's always football."

"You're too small, too slow, and too weak. Guys that lift nothing more than beer cans are stronger than you," she responded coldly. "You'd have a better chance getting noticed for chess."

"Did I get noticed by you?"

It was the question I had as I walked out the door. I don't remember if I actually asked her, but she did answer the next day when she called me for the first time just to talk. Mostly, she apologized for taking her disappointment out on me. Yes, she did lose a bet, and someone was going to get head this month.

I'm quite sure that I haven't explained it yet, why winning that game was so important and how it changed the course of my teenage years. Maybe, I'm making too much of it, or the grandeur of defeating Malcolm grows in my mind with its retelling. I really don't think so.

Let me explain it this way, though I think it's something more. Maybe winning that game and having this small group know about it gave me just a little more confidence and Malcolm the reverse. Maybe all the stupid or inappropriate things I said were now taken with that "He beat Malcolm in chess" grain of salt. I started to feel like I belonged to this group. While Malcolm still came to teen club functions, he faded somewhat.

Trudy was out of my league and would stay so well into my twenties, but we did become friends. Trudy wasn't just the first girl that was nice to me; she was the first friend that was nice to me. I won the right to hang around and that worked the way I hoped it would, getting chance after chance with the girls that clung to her.

There were other make out parties…five in all before the teen club's demise. At that point there were eight core members, five guys and three girls. I sat out again for three of those parties but the last two…well, that's when I kissed my first girl.

The teen club was doomed, however, and would only last ten more months. At the start of my sophomore year, a mystery was solved about Tammy. She was quite attractive if she didn't pick her nose, but she never spoke. Strangely, she was always the first to be picked up and the last to be dropped off during teen club functions. It turns out the teen club moderator, the same guy having an affair with Debbie's mother, was doing her. The resulting scandal was enough to call the adult members into action. Being the rational parents of the 70s, they defined the problem and got rid of the teen club. How else were the forty-somethings going to compete for the men in the group if the fourteen-year old sluts were there to take all the men away?

The result was that fewer teens met more often, and I made the cut. By that time, I wasn't just Trudy's friend, I was her best friend. Although that wasn't getting me in Trudy's pants, it was giving me contact with other girls who were less desirable but far better than nothing. Dates were few, and none led to anything, but it did give me just a little more confidence. By the time I hit twenty-one, I lived with a girl that Trudy hand-picked for me. I lost my virginity and became an expectant father on the same night, and it seemed to me that my life was going exactly as my detractors expected it would.

It turns out, we were wrong.

I stayed with the mother until she found another less nerdy guy, but I kept support and contact with my son. The relationship lasted just long enough for me to learn about being a boyfriend and father, which almost had me scrapping the "last man on earth" plan. Winning that game was the only thing the big head ever did for the little head. Or maybe it's the reverse.

Then I met my lover for life. At first, it seemed to me that, although I was physically attracted to her, she was on track to "friend zone" me, which is a great phase to describe so many relationships

I had but the term didn't exist back then. Maybe again, it was that little extra confidence that let me slightly push for something more…slightly being the operative word that might be replaceable by nerdy.

I realize that if I end this tale here, I would leave out three important elements unexplained: what was with the beginning about the red flag dropping, why did I refer to chess notation but didn't use it, and what was the bet that me and Malcolm had.

As to the first, look, I'm writing about chess. It would have been hard for me to draw you in without as much drama as possible. It's not that the game didn't happen, just that it wasn't as important. That game would happen two years later, when I was a much better player. As a junior, I would be co-captain of the chess team that played the last round in the state tournament. All other game were finished back then, and the opposition had just locked in first place. Our team would finish second if I won, third if I drew, and fourth if I lost.

I lost.

With not enough time on the clock, I made too many mistakes on the board and toppled my king before the red flag fell. I was too inexperienced compared to my opponent and had to find over the board answers to positions he had previously encountered.

I still had a lot to be proud of. Not playing throughout the chess season because it conflicted with football made my making the tournament very unlikely. Further still, the chess team was under .500 in the regular matches, so qualifying against the teams that had beaten the team that didn't include me made me feel impressive. Of five games in the semi-finals, I won three, lost one, and drew one. In the eight game finals, I won four, lost two, and drew two. Impressive as it was, it didn't seem as important as the one game match with Malcolm.

Once back home, I learned just how unimportant the downstate tournament was. Though the fourth-place finish did make the opening announcements, no one from outside the chess club ever congratulated us. More the that, when I was reunited with my father, who I hadn't seen for six years, I excitedly told him about the downstate showdown. He thought for a moment then answered, "I guess that's O.K., as long as it doesn't take any of your attention away from football."

It was then I realized that girls were not the reason for either game, I was trying to impress my father. My senior year would be the worst year of my life, which my former coach kept pointing out. He claimed that I'd become a quitter. I didn't go to the same school or play football or chess. Looking back, I'm surprised I didn't take my own life, but I had Trudy. I didn't need chess anymore; she and I had discovered poetry. Both from reading and writing, we learned a lot about triumph, despair, loss, love, and how not to seduce women.

From that bad year comes a simple fact that makes me think I'm the luckiest man in the world. I don't have to kill every other male, because since then, every year of my life has been a little better than the last, without exception.

So, who's the loser now, coach?

Which brings us to the chess notation thing. If I know chess notation, why did I write "Bishop takes queen's rook's pawn" instead of "bishop to H2" or the like. If you didn't play chess back in the 70's, you might not know that chess notation used to be like that. Since then (not sure when), the Chess Federation simplified it. Before, each move was described by the file of the major piece that was there in setting up the board, and the rank from the perspective of the mover. I found that very easy. Now, the files are described by the alphabetic order, left to right by white's perspective, and the ranks are also by white's perspective, no matter who moves.

I'm incapable of learning the new way. I could master the ranks, but I never learn the alphabet. While I know all the letters, I could never place them in order. I know what you're going to say. Learn the song. It doesn't help. I know the melody, but like any songs I sing, I keep mixing up the lyrics. If there's only the first three as in "abc," I can do that. I also know "xyz," but anything in the middle is a problem for me. All my life, I've lived in fear of going to a job interview and being asked to recite the alphabet.

Now comes the last question, one I thought I might be too ashamed to answer as it plays into that, "last man on earth" mentality. Before the game, I went to Malcolm's house to compose a letter with him to Trudy. In that letter, we explained that Trudy's life would never be complete until she married either Malcolm or Eddie. Rather the duel to the death, we both agreed that the groom should be the winner of the first match between the both of us. We typed the letter, and both signed it, then we typed another copy and signed again. The plan was to wait until Trudy had slept with every guy she knew except the both of us. Malcolm told Trudy's mother the truth. We were playing for her daughter's hand - only Trudy didn't know.

Bishop takes queen's rook's pawn is a waiting move both bold and humble. I'd never get carnal knowledge of every woman on the planet that way, but I did find something that merely being the last man alive wouldn't get me: love. While other nerds won their brides by wearing them down, that bishop taught me how to wait them out. Just stay there on the board until someone notices that you haven't gone away and believes that, if you're with her, you never will. My lifetime lover would become my wife, mother to my son, and, in time, grandmother to my granddaughters. Each step of that was a greater joy than the last one. I still get depressed, but it's always about the past when I was younger than nineteen. Yes, I quit playing football and chess, but sometimes I can't quit being that nerdy, lonely kid that wanted every other man on the planet dead. Just as true, I can't seem to quit being husband, dad, and grandpa. If you ever meet me, you might call me happy-go-lucky, as many people have. You might catch me smiling in a quiet moment for no apparent reason and wonder about my mental health. You might worry what I've been up to or why I keep so happy where other men doing better see themselves as failures.

Why? Bishop takes queen's rook's pawn.

Try not to be afraid. I threw away my plans for being the last man alive before I threw away the letter making Trudy my wife, lest someone find it and either rat me out to the authorities or Trudy or use those plans themselves.

So if you're wondering how I expect to survive as a psychotic vampire, remember bishop takes quean's rook's pawn from the other side of the board. Will the would-be prime evil know enough to let his bishop sit? Will he/she/it have the patience to play the peaceful game and not reveal the true prime of its evil intent?

Whether in undead or living life, I count my luck in every situation. Luck isn't a passive thing. It's the recognition, post-mortem, of how well you've lived by the luck you've been granted. The bishop will move, and I'll be ready, if only by strange unlikely coincidence.

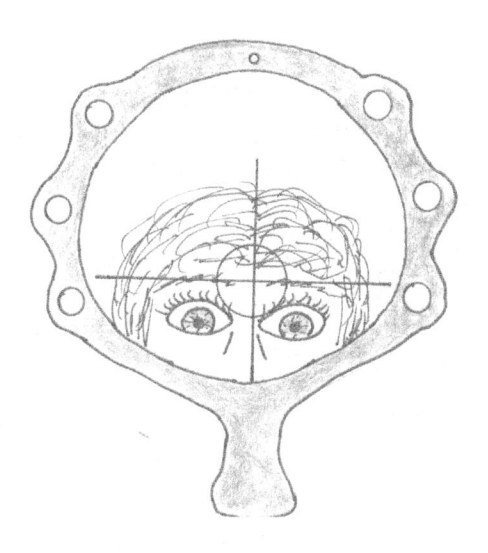

CHAPTER 17: MARY STEWARD, I DO NOT BELIEVE IN YOU

"Say 'you don't believe' into the mirror," she told herself. But the mirror could never tell the truth anymore. As vampire, she had become the mistress of information, but the mirror, or even a simple photograph, could never capture her image.

It was a ransacked ruin of an ancient one room wooden shack on the east bank of the Mississippi that no being, living or undead, would choose to occupy, yet the mirror frame was there, placed just to the right with the fallen roof still giving it shelter from rain and snow. But the mirror frame had no mirror in it.

The last lights were fading, and Mary Steward lit a candle to study her image. When she'd been fourteen, a young artist took her here with the intention of painting her nude.

"You're only going to be as beautiful as you are for another ten years," he told her foolishly.

Fool!

He believed it was his seduction that made her follow him so far from New Orleans, but she did undress and stand before him while he painted, hoping that he would create something of worth. Double fool he was when he couldn't reproduce her stunning beauty. Maybe he intended to make love to her. That would have made him a fool again because Mary had no more use for him. So she slayed him with a painter's knife while he slept, making him the fourth man she murdered. Now she needed to find a man who'd provide for her.

The river was untamed back then, and any human traffic would be very rare. Nonetheless, a two-man canoe surprised her by paddling down river with a single oarsman. Disembarking, this French-Canadian told her that he had lost his partner and needed companionship. He described himself as a fur trapper but forgot to mention he was a vampire until he bit her and sucked out her soul.

With a vampire master controlling her, she was more imprisoned than if she'd been in any stockade or jail house as she was clearly too beautiful to hang. He compelled her to stay in current times and not wander beyond fifty paces from the painter's shack. Like a dog tied to a tree, this prevented her from feeding on anything more satisfying than the small animals that strayed into the range of her leash. For him, it was different. Getting human blood was just a matter of stepping back into time, as tribes of natives used the river for fishing and trading. Still, he must have gotten lost. For one day he left and never returned.

She knew he wasn't destroyed. She sensed his ability to compel her like a collar of chains. But her restrictions lost some of their potency, and she could move through space/time to hunt. For the first hundred years, she was careful to be seen only by her victims. She feared a stake to her chest or, worse, the return of her vampire master.

She heard faint whisperings about the revolutions of the various colonies from their European sovereignties but saw no change in her diet. Only once in that time did she see another vampire. She had sneaked into the camping grounds of caravan of homesteaders. She isolated him and went to bite, but he showed his fangs, hissing. She retreated, and he never pursued her. It would be another hundred years when the same vampire returned to invite her to a party for vampires and their hosts, set back in a Victorian mansion on the New England coast eighty years into the past. By then, her caution was tempered with boredom and loneliness, so she agreed.

It was at that party that she saw the fullness if the undead life on display. Vampires had sub-societies and hierarchies that favorited older and more experienced vampires. This fit her perfectly for she was both. She decided to use her feminine charm to infiltrate the highest, deepest associations of vampire life for clandestine information that she could use against her vampire master if he ever came back.

She could also feed. Steamboats now trafficked the grand river with impunity. Many a captain ran his charge up and back, profiting with each trip, and sought to build his estate and family along the famed river's banks. Mary was not interested in children but had much to gain as a mistress to several wealthy men, each completely in the dark about the other. It was a game she had played since coming of age. Soon, she was rich in her own right, which marked her as an heiress rather than a common girl.

But you can't drink money, and riverboat captains tended to be aged. No matter, young men made easier prey, as if hunting the living could be any easier. She relaxed her caution, as no lawman in his right mind would suspect that young, beautiful heiress was the cause of the alarmingly large number of bloodless bodies found in every corner of the river's banks. Still, she did not go into the future.

Then war broke out. War always broke, of course, but this one was different. The number of violent deaths increased exponentially, making living men a rarity and new male vampires very common. Such vampires were mostly clueless, but they understood new technologies that gave them a concerning leg up on the older ones. Most of these vampires stayed aligned to the armies for which they had died and continued their war beyond the grave.

Hoping to mitigate this, she bit two young soldiers from opposing sides, sucked out their souls, and compelled them as cruelly as her master had once compelled her. She was hoping to use their knowledge of modern machinery to her own advantage, but they proved to be more trouble than they were worth. They constantly plotted to be free of her, which should have been easy enough for her to foil. But between the two of them, she spent more time in their minds spoiling their mischief than getting into her own. Eventually, she got fed up and staked them both.

She had learned much from that era, and began feeding on women, finding them less trouble and just as satisfying. She resolved never to take another soul, as it was just too troubling. The better idea was to get a host; one that had knowledge of modern technology and would willingly let herself/himself be bitten repeatedly. True, it required restraint, but the hosts she took were so in love with her that they needed no compelling. Moreover, they never plotted against her, unless they found out about her other hosts.

All of this changed with the opening of 1900s, when advancements moved at a furious pace. What might change in a century now took only a decade. Horses used for the last six thousand years became obsolete to strange, motorized vehicles. Two wars were fought on battlefields around the globe, and between that came a worldwide economic depression. New vampires came in roaring. First a world war brought soldiers, sailors, and aviators, hungry for blood, revenge, and winning the war. Then came prohibition, and, with that, the syndicate hungry for blood, revenge, and "a piece of the action," which meant, of course, all the action. Then came the Depression. Stockbrokers who had advanced into the economically elite by cornering the markets took their own lives when the market crashed. These vampires were hungry for blood, revenge, and "cornering the market."

Of course, none of this concerned the older vampires, who couldn't imagine why anything other than blood and revenge was important. It was true that this group was more organized than other waves of new vampires ever were. But those vampires never went after each other as these did. Axis and Allies continued their war, syndicate families "wacked" each other while trying to organize crime, and stockbroking vampires cornered the market, killing any vampire that got in their way. Humans that weren't part of the undead that changed into bats flew in the skies at frightening speeds. Keeping up with all of this was work. Mary didn't like work.

She had been a vampire now for at least three hundred years, and it was getting tiresome. Rich beyond her imagination, she could not imagine what happiness the money might bring her. Everything that once thrilled her now bored her. She'd been warned this would happen.

"Get an ambition," some ancient who'd lived since the dark ages had told her.

She did have one ambition, and she had one fear. Ambition-wise, she wanted to find an artist that could paint her former beauty. But every new "artist" failed to put the passion in her lovely eyes. If only she could only gaze upon her adorable perfection the way any other sighted being could, it would be heaven to her. Instead, she wound up slaying the artists.

Also, she had not forgotten her master vampire, whose dominance wrapped around her neck like a cold heavy chain. If he returned, he'd constrain her again. He must be eliminated.

It was at a party during this time that she first met "Daddy Don." Of course, nobody called him that but her as he was a chieftain of a crime syndicate that controlled any illegal businesses, including booze, gambling, prostitution, and loan sharking. It was cute, in a creepy way, that he and his underlings still thought that stuff was important, but she never let on that it wasn't. For her, Daddy Don might be an ally if her master ever returned. She made it clear to him that if that happened, her master could compel her not to see him again and that would be "bad for business" if he had to find a different "dolly."

The living world was still just getting over the Great Depression when war came again to every country on the globe with twice the force the last one had. More vampires streamed into the ranks of the undead, and it looked like the number of vampires less then forty years undead would triple the number of older vampires, changing fashion and styles that had become so comfortable. An atomic bomb created an explosion even vampires couldn't survive, and for the first time in history, the undead had reason to fear war. World War II led to the Cold War, where nuclear missiles were feared to be the weapon of choice, and the uncertainty that followed put the Kingdom of the Damned in unfamiliar territory. The unspoken boredom at vampire parties was replaced with unspoken fear, even for Mary. In despair, she seduced a Mayan magus to predict the future for her.

A trip so far in the past was a new thing for her, but she had to know. She met him one evening while he was alone, watching the nighttime sky in the early part of the fourteenth century. She told him her concerns, and he reassured her that the world wasn't coming to an end…not until the fall of 2014. She told him that she wasn't worried about the world. She was worried about what might happen to her.

The magi dropped his gaze and faced the beautiful vampire for the first time. Of course, he fell in love with her.

"To tell you what the future holds for you," he told her. "I would need to see the sky in your time."

The magi became her host, offering his blood to this strange goddess from the future, which was not all that extraordinary given his era.

Once he arrived in her time, the magi began his reading on the first clear night. For the living, he hadn't much to tell. Death, destruction, war, pestilence, poverty, starvation, and a host of naturally occurring catastrophes were pretty standard in this type of predictions. What was interesting was the coming of a vampire king that, if things went well, would bring peace and harmony to the vampire population. But there were a few caveats. For one, this future king didn't want peace or harmony. Nor did he want to be king, but he would control the vampire victim home delivery market for lazy vampires wanting a meal without leaving the comfort of their own home.

"That sounds wonderful," Mary gushed. "How does he do that?"

"He develops computer software over a dedicated network," Magi told her before he had to admit that he had no idea what "computer," "software" or "network" meant. What he did know was that it wasn't so wonderful. Ordering victims this way killed the vampire more often than the victim. He would manage to keep that a secret from his vampire customers.

Mary took note.

"So, how does he become king without wanting it?"

Magi studied the sky again and for a very long time, he said nothing.

"Evil spirits," he muttered, shaking his head. "Evil never gets along with other evils...kind of like my mothers-in-law. One always wants to be in charge. He allies with some vampires he finds that got lost in time, and he brings them back."

Magi explained that the plot had been hatched by a great evil spirit before vampires roamed the earth. A tribe of zombie minions had laid out a trap to grab some schmuck, make him evil, make him crazy, give him power, make him a vampire, and make him crazier. That much should have been easy. Then these zombie minions, which might be vampires by a different name, would narrow themselves down to one, lest they turn on each other before making this would-be king disillusioned and thus willing to bring peace and harmony by ruling with an iron fist and a judgmental demeanor. The plan had one flaw.

"Which was?"

"The schmuck they picked was Irish."

"Great," Mary said irritably. "All I have to do is single out the one vampire that's Irish! Do you have any other insightful observations on how I might find this schmuck?"

Magi studied the sky again as Mary impatiently watched. Finally, he spoke.

"Stars say that the one who would be vampire king will be the longest existing vampire in history within minutes of his becoming undead. Such will make him crazy but very hard to kill."

"How is that possible, you imbecile?"

"Take it up with the stars," he told her evenly. "He does have one hidden weakness that the evil spirits plan to exploit. He cares about his living granddaughters. The spirits plan to use that computer thingy against him to have them both killed. If they do that, he won't care about anyone living enough not to become king."

"Does he have any other secrets?"

"Yes, he has two. You must beware of his limericks. If you displease him, he will compose one that will discredit you and hurt your feelings."

"Oh, no! Not my feelings," Mary snarled sarcastically. "What's his other secret?"

"I don't know. It's a secret."

Mary had enough. She ripped the life out of him and drank the blood, not knowing or caring that she just killed the Mayan who would have discovered that the long calendar was more than a hundred years off.

Over the next fifty years, Mary searched for Irish vampires to seduce. If one were to be king, why not her as queen? By now, her fear of nuclear war had faded, and her boredom was replaced with obsession. Find an Irish vampire and try to rule him out.

She knew just where to start. The Irish vampire she would want would be the only one alive.

"Hey, Don Daddy," she purred in his ear while lounging strategical on his lap and searching for something stiff to stroke beneath his silk suit pants and large belly. "I think Irish vampires might prove bad for business."

"Why's that, Doll Face?"

"I'm told that they are irresistibly cute…the men I mean."

"Can't have my dolly falling for some other guy."

Daddy Don took the bait, never suspecting that the number of "some other guys" was already nine or ten on any given day. Still, his "family" specialized in loan sharking and had an uncommon ability for finding people, both dead and living, who didn't want to be found. Before the turn of the century, the laws had changed legalizing all the "crime" the syndicate had been trying to organize. Still, the "families" ran the operations as if they were illegal, replacing speakeasies with bars, gambling parlors with casinos, and houses of ill repute with sex dating websites. The easiest change was loan sharking, now replaced with paycheck loan shops.

Nonetheless, the families had learned computing and could search the internet for Irish vampires. Search as they might, they never found a single one, which amused Daddy Don to no end.

Then something wonderful happened in the fall of 2006. She was at some annual Victorian ball when a crazy old vampire walked in, wearing a green kilt and matching cap. The only thing missing was a button proclaiming, "Kiss me, I'm Irish."

It didn't end well, so she left early to find Daddy Don.

"What's woe, Doll Face?"

The beefy chieftain used his pocket napkin to wipe Mary's tears.

She told him more than she intended, but her feelings were very hurt. Worst of all was that stupid limerick the old fool had to recite to the servants working the party, who couldn't seem to withhold their chuckling.

With your beautiful body so glam
I would guess you're seducing a scam.
And the way that you wooed
Well I hate to be crude
But I'd rather lay down with a lamb.

She also told him about her master vampire. She hadn't felt his control this strong since he'd disappeared into the perilous future four hundred years earlier. Now, she was hearing whispers about a secret vampire society that carefully guarded its privacy; even members didn't know who the other members were. It sounded foolish, but so did the warnings about his limericks.

"Not to worry, Doll Face. You're my girl now. If your old guy shows up…whack…a stake through his heart."

"But what about that secret vampire club?"

"It won't be secret anymore. We're going to pay a visit to this new vampire. I have a feeling he'll be in a talkative mood. We'll make him an offer he can't refuse."

"But if he's as powerful as the magi says…"

"Aaaah, Dolly, don't worry about me. Even if he is, I'll send three patsies; nobody knows they are on my payroll…because they're not. But they owe me money, so they do what I say. If they get whacked, no one will know I sent them. If not, Ed Calkins will have a lot to tell them about this vampire club…what's it called? The I.V.A. After that, he'll sleep with the fishes. How's that, Doll Face?"

"I love it, Daddy," Mary gushed. "Toss him in the water, clothes and all."

"Sure, Dolly," Don laughed.

The next day, Don got wacked. Everyone knew who "done it" but the mob didn't seem to care. Worse than that, she couldn't replace him with any other mobster chieftain as they all seemed to think she was marked.

Now, eleven years later, she was still among the living, frantically searching for Ed Calkins and trying to learn his one true weakness…besides being insane. At first, she hoped to find Ed Calkins himself, maybe flatter him more than seduce him. After a few drinks, perhaps the old fool would start boasting about his granddaughters the way granddaddies always seemed to do. She would actually be interested, which would be a welcome change for him. But she couldn't find him. He didn't go to parties, and he seemed to feed in the distant past. Some vampires mentioned him as spending a lot of time in his imagination, where he thought he was the Steward of Tara. Why would a king do janitorial work?

One day, she finally located him. He was in Munsonville, doing media work in the middle of the night, seven day a week. His grandchildren were right there…not hidden at all, just on the other side of the reality split that happens with the undead.

"Mary Steward, I do not believe in you," she told the object she wished was a mirror.

The locals along this stretch of the river believed if they viewed a mirror by candle and proclaimed their disbelief in Mary Steward three times, her image would show instead of their own. It was a little-known legend used as a dare for ghost story fright. Her new host knew of it, but so did her father.

But standing in the middle of the ramshackle shack, she couldn't see much by candlelight. At this point, she owned several mansions staffed with servants, but she was spending more and more time here. Her grave was out back, but no one would ever find it. Vampires knew the importance of keeping the location of their burial remains a secret. Exposing that knowledge made them vulnerable to vampire slayers.

So why did she keep coming back? The mirror.

She kept returning to stand before the mirror frame that housed the nude painting of her when she was still alive. Mary loosened her white mink robe, hoping to reveal her body in the state of nudity that the painting portrayed. It was still no good, of course. Her legs, mound, torso, and breasts...she could see those for herself. Those were not the flaws of the painting.

Somewhere, she heard a fly buzzing her. She snatched its wing with vampire speed and held it over the candle. The fly saw her beautiful face; she could not. At least she could feel jealous rage as the fly slowly incinerated.

She would have gladly suffered the fly's pain just to see her alluring eyes again.

Mary came later that night for another visit, but this time her victim would be awake. The neck that she had tasted promised a feast for years to come. The blood of a teenage girl was sweet and full of intrigue, but what tasted best was the revenge it would impose on that foolish vampire who crossed her. His tasteless rejection was bad enough, but he'd continued the insult with a limerick she couldn't forget.

Getting into the house was typically no problem, except this time the father was awake. She heard his breathing and felt his vigilant thoughts. A father protecting his daughter through her adolescence was as cliché as it was ineffective. He might have his own rules and lay down the law, but these had no jurisdiction in the discovering mind of a child coming of age. Inside her mind are thoughts she cannot share, darkly mysterious possibilities of what form love and indulgence might claim.

She had little fear he'd stop her, although an interruption of her encounter would prove disappointing. So she waited for the sleep he fought back to claim his eyelids and change his shallow breaths to slumber.

Now she sang to her victim in a voice so high and sweet that only the youth could hear it, and just barely.

Mary had a little lamb, little lamb, little lamb
Mary had a little lamb with blood as red as rose
And every time she bit her neck, bit her neck, bit her neck
Every time she bit her neck the bond that held her grows.

She cast her shadow on the bedroom door but waited. Best keep the agitated beauty mindful, wondering, and waiting. Once Mary had her, she would parade her around parties and the like, showing off her host to the envious souls of the damned while the host followed Mary like a love-struck puppy. That fat old vampire would know, yet wouldn't be able to break the bond. Would he beg for her life, would he try to snap her out with lectures that she'd rebuke, or would he just brood at her inevitable fate? It didn't matter. He would take every chance to be at the gatherings where Mary and her lamb attended. And at every chance, she'd offer the same deal. He would spill information till he said enough to keep this little lamb alive for another day. One day, when he was king and ruled the vampire world, she would still rule him.

Mary knew she was in the girl's head. The granddaughter of Ed Calkins was having disturbing dreams about Mary Steward every night since the first visit. Those dreams were too explicit to share with any living agent that could help her, and that was good; not because the living could stop her, but the hint hitting the ear of the rumored IVA might mean that Mary was not the only vampire in the house. Mary had sources of her own, and they had been watching carefully for any movement in the darkest haunts of the undead. Nothing. Maybe the IVA was only one crazy vampire and three letters.

Now.

The door didn't have to open, but it gave theater to her entrance. The girl lay facing the door, her long legs unconsciously uncovered by the turning of a night without sleep. No surprise hit her face when the opened door showed no face. She merely turned her back to the door and stared towards the window.

Smart girl. Their eyes locked...victim and seductress. A strange thought hit the girl's head...something like "I hope Dad got this right."

"I'm your daddy now, my lamb."

Mary used her most enticing purr.

Something wasn't right. A naïve baton pushed past her breasts and then she saw it. Something beautiful and frightening that she hadn't seen since the day she died centuries ago. She wasn't staring into the eyes of her victim; she was staring into her own.

"How?"

But that was all she would say.

The bang was loud. Already, dad was on his feet, his weapon in hand, sprinting to his daughter's bedroom. Too late, he found her, still in bed, her back to the door. There was no corpse of a person just killed, that would be almost as bad. A stake still burning at the blunt end lay amidst the ashes of what was a troubled woman.

"Tomorrow," Michaela mewed, rolling over almost asleep.

Dad nodded. The girl hadn't slept in days since the bite marks and erotic dreams marred her tranquility. He would sweep the ashes into a trash bag. The following morning, or even the next, the two of them would drive six or seven hundred miles to where Mary Steward's tomb stone lay and scatter her ashes with as much sorrow as could be generated by the passing of a woman who died before the country was a nation.

Michaela slept without a troubled thought. The gun had worked the way dad said it would, and it would work again. How many of her friends would have found themselves hosts to an undead monster if the same had happened to them? All of them, she was sure. She had made a mistake that she wouldn't make a second time. She hesitated before firing. A mistake like that could have killed her, had not the vampire thought of her as a frightened, lovestruck, little girl. The next vampire wasn't going to take her so lightly, and Grandpa certainly would know what she's made of. One vampire down, two to go.

"I'm coming for you, Grandpa. Don't worry, I will not hesitate, and I will not miss."

CHAPTER 18: KINGDOM OF THE DAMNED, PART I

I have no idea why I'm here.

Once again, I find myself in a strange place that I don't remember going to, dressed in a way I cannot explain. I'm at a Victorian-era party of some kind, with music, dancing, and much to consume. I'm dressed lavishly in a kilt and matching cap, adorned with gold and bronze pieces at my wrists. I was clothed quite inappropriately for the Annual Harrington Ball, but no one seemed alarmed. If I had been here before, from a different perspective, of course, I'm sure I made an impression that allowed me to violate dress codes. A sudden TAM comes to me. This ball is popular with vampires, but I can't stay too long. I have to work this morning at one a.m. on the fifth day beyond my natural life and three days before the duel with Trudy.

For a time, nobody talks to me. I just walked around, nodded to the people within my field of vision, and tried not to look lost, bored, or terrified. I wish I could hide among the servants working the ball. I would very much like to attend to the horses and the carriages they pull, while the arriving guests dismount the cabs to begin their night of music and folly.

Gossip hits my ears. I keep forgetting I'm a vampire now, and my hearing, like most of the guests, is superhuman and just primed for spying. Somewhere far south and over my shoulder, I hear three youngish maidens giggling about Simons and his new child bride Bryony. Married slightly more than a year, and she was already his best friend's mistress. One claimed she saw the dubious pair disappearing in the closet, for a quick bite no doubt.

I see her. She makes sure of it, but I'm trying to keep up with the conversation around me while feeling like the house is closing in on me, as if I was playing the French Defense against a player that knew it well and used my every move to narrow my options.

She was dark-haired and wore a red, corseted, low cut dress. Her hair and vampy eyes screamed what she was and the danger she posed. Why are the dangerous ones so alluring?

"You've new here," she told me, practically purring. "You must be recently bitten."

"Yes, very recently," I responded, tying to look past her. "I'd say I was bitten about one hundred and fifty years from now."

I couldn't look away far enough to not notice her disapproving, calculated pout. Thank darkness, I learned well about women like her before, but this one was a vampire. Meaning asking her in a disgusted voice to just tell me what she wanted would not produce the closure I needed.

"Vampire protocol dictates you answer how long ago you were bitten by your own reckoning," she informed me. "What time period you are from is a different question that needs only the vaguest of answers. To that question, say only that you're a futuristic vampire. I ask again. How long were you bitten?"

"Days," I tried to be dismissive, but unwillingly, I met her hungry eyes and could not break away.

"Like what you see?" she demanded. "Would you like to be bitten again?"

Her eyes promised devotion to bliss. Another vampire, even one my age, would have fallen for her promise, but I had the advantage of being bought by old men as a youth. I knew how old men smelled to youthful noses. That disgust revisited itself when I became the old man doing the smelling.

"Do you like fossils, Miss Vampy? I knew a girl like you with a fetish for such and an appetite she couldn't control. Naturally, she was barred from every museum in the city. Perhaps you should think of an alternative payment method for whatever it is that you want from me."

She nodded, more impressed than insulted.

"Bold," she conceded. "For a vampire of only days, you know your way around women of the damned. I'll tell you what I want. I want you. You don't have to be an old man with a pot belly anymore. You can be as young and handsome as I require, and with the properly sized anatomy as might please me. Why if you're so inclined, you could be my vixen."

That gave me an idea.

"And you could then change into a form that I'd be more…well, interested in…in the carnal sense, I mean."

Contempt was in her, which somehow made her more desirable.

"What, you want blond hair? Or do you prefer young boys?"

"I'll pass on the blond hair. Could you do white and curly hair that covers your whole body and with four legs instead of two. I'll also pass on the young boys. I prefer sheep. I'm Irish country at heart. Could you stand about four feet tall and make a sound like this when I …you know. Baaaaah."

The next instant, she was not standing before me, but rather transported to the other side of the room in a huff.

"And you wonder why no one invites you to parties," a deep menacing voice said in my ear.

I whirled around, alarmed. "John!"

"Shouldn't you be working on something?"

"Shouldn't you have no knowledge that I should be?"

I meant it as a real question. A TAM had come to me. From John's perspective, this was years before John's attempts to regain his soul began to fail.

"I require a favor," he told me in an odd voice that I believe he believed would compel me. "I require you to keep the young woman with me occupied while I conduct some 'business.'"

"How will I know her?"

"She'll be the girl at my side when the messenger comes for me."

"I hear and obey."

John gave me a strange look but what was I to say? Without further comment, he was gone. I was hoping my mission would not keep me here too late. Besides feeling bored and out of place, I had a down route to run in the morning.

I continued to wander form room to room, pretending to seek

conversation and drain the contents of glasses handed to me, lest I offend the host. The true was that not a drop of liquor hit my system as I was wary. I finally found a coat man willing to imbibe my share, despite the chance it would create the impression that I had things of value in my outer garments and not the trust that they would be left when I departed.

I saw her first, and it did not please me.

John's young woman was not Bryony. She was someone else who was pretending to be his child bride, but she did not have to pretend to be a child. Morals were different in this time, I knew, but that seemed too self-serving for an adult man wishing to exploit adolescent trust. John was not a man, but a vampire. Still, I played along.

"John! I don't believe I've met your bride." I told him, playing along but with a hint of disapproval and sarcasm.

Melissa almost dropped her glass. Did she know me? This woman who was playing the role of John's wife Bryony in the Victorian era was, in my time, John's bride and mother to John-Peter, but now she was still in high school. She stood before me, too innocent to know of her violation, as if asleep and tied to railroad tracks, while the storm of nefarious vampires rode the on-coming train, dividing the helpless prey.

He introduced her as "Bryony," and I pretended not to know her by any other name nor did she give me any impression that she knew me.

John's cue came, and I acted, compelled to keep her in place. I asked her to marry me of course, but it didn't help, as she changed the subject. I might have grabbed her, tossed her over my shoulder and ran for all I was worth, but what of John-Peter? And what of me? Would my motives remain pure with so much temptation and no soul to hold me to compassion?

I tried to charm her, which meant boring her with ancient lore and hints of my deliberate self-delusion. I told her of my mythical seduction of my lover, whom I likened to the famed Colpa. I expounded my virtues as a ruthless poet, whose exploits drove the De Dananns into such fear that they took to the underground and changed into leprechauns. Through all of this, she politely listened, but I don't think she learned much.

Poor girl...how does one change the fate of a child that

doesn't accept a POMBEC? What did I mean by that? What is a POMBEC? Do you know?

I retreated when John finally came back. Who was more relieved, Melissa or me?

My plan was to call it a night, but I was unable to direct myself to claim my coat and be done with it. However, there was a glass in my hand. Perhaps the coat man needed refreshment.

"You are an odd bird."

I spun around and nearly collided into a dashing young man holding his top hat and overcoat.

"Do you know what a POMBEC is?" The words flew out of my mouth without my mind to filter them.

"Of course," he replied. "It's a narrowly used acronym for 'Proposal Of Marriage By Ed Calkins. You do know who Ed Calkins is, don't you?"

"I'm not sure."

"First you come in, wearing a dress. Then you refuse an offer of sex but replace it with an offer of marriage. One might think you play for the other side."

As he said this, he placed two fingers on my shoulder and slowly walked them towards my neck. Smiling, I pushed his fingers away. By his voice and his manner, this dandy boy was advertising.

"Pay to play." I answered. "I was a boy whore many years ago. Bet I've had more old men than you've had in a lifetime."

"So direct with a complete stranger," he teased. "Pity I didn't bring more money. It might be fun to play with a newly bitten vampire. Less than a week, correct?"

"Play with me, indeed. I'm betting we've met before, from your perspective. I suspect we know each other quite well, or you wouldn't be acting so…"

"Fabulous?"

"OK. Tell me, are we close friends?"

"Friends," he reflected theatrically. "Let me see. I find your company laborious, your delusion of grandeur unentertaining, your poetry insufferable, and your thinking misguided - at best.

"So, we are friends." I concluded.

"Allies," he corrected. "We are allies with a similar purpose on something important to me. I knew you'd be here less than a week of your new life as a vampire, so…"

He paused, smiled softly and then added, "…why not give you a leg up? All vampires, well, any vampires that matter, can't resist attending a Harrington ball. John has his reasons, and I have mine, which is to cause pain to the other one."

"John? You're friends with John Simons?"

"Yes, John and I are 'friends,' too, if a man who cheats with the other's wife, stabs him to death, and then kills himself can be called 'friends.' Of course, we're friends. We hate each other, and we became vampires together. And another thing," he leaned quite close. "Stop resisting the urge to feed. The more you deny yourself, the sooner you'll be compelled to commit atrocities."

"Compelled?" I clung to the one word that interested me.

"Yes." He held out his hand. "Henry Matthews. Charmed to meet you, too, Ed Calkins."

"I only asked about the compelled part because it seems to me that I've been compelled to be here, quite against my will."

"Hmm, that sounds serious. Against your will, you say? That can only be the work of another vampire." Henry looked around. "We should talk but not here. Someplace less visible. Follow me."

I followed him out of the room and down the hall to a table just big enough for its four chairs. It was so close to the kitchen that I took it for the place where the house chef and his senior staff had their meals. With such a party, it seemed unlikely that they would dine while the demands of the ball required so much labor.

"Kellen Wechsler," Henry said once we were seated and set his outerwear down. "Do you know him?"

"John's manager, but I never met him."

"That is unlikely an accident. When John Simons plays for vampires, all eyes turn to Kellen Wechsler."

"I didn't mean to say you didn't see him, I meant I wasn't introduced," I defended.

Henry grinned. "You mean you might have seen him, but you wouldn't know, because you couldn't match a face to the name. I think you didn't see him. If you had, you'd know him by another name and, thus, know of your peril."

"A lot to assume, seeing this is my first time meeting vampires other than John Simons."

"Oh, my dear Steward, quickly toss your sanity aside, or you'll never achieve your destiny. The world depends on it."

I laughed until I realized he wasn't joking. For a while, he just peered at me with a troubled expression. Then he sighed, stood up, and walked away. I just sat there, wondering if he'd taken offense. But he soon returned, carrying what appeared to be a wine bottle and two goblets. He uncorked the bottle and released the mouthwatering taste of blood. He poured two glasses and handed one to me.

"Welcome to the Kingdom of the Damned," Henry said as he settled back into his chair. "Do you know the two ways to become a vampire? Live a corrupt life that ends in violence or become a vampire's victim. In the first case, like mine, you're free from any master other than your own evil appetite. In the second case, yours, the vampire that drained your blood has mastery over you and compels you as he or she pleases."

He took a sip and waited for my reaction. I had none. So he continued.

"Now vampires have been around since the beginning of man, and it's always been as I said, until the case of you and John. I killed John before I killed myself. Therefore, John should have no one compelling him. Yet Kellen has a hold on him that can't be explained any other way than how I'm about to explain it. Even before his death, Kellen 'compelled' John to let the woman he loved die while giving birth. Kellen is a careful, calculating vampire. Vampires kill their masters or mistresses to achieve freedom, so Kellen is careful to hide his mastery of John, and makes John believe that, what he does at Kellen's mandate, he does of his own free will. He has to be far more careful with you because you're watching for him. You believe you can escape damnation if you free your soul from the deity that stole it. You're motivated in ways he can't predict and dangerous because of your own insanity. Do you know what Deep Time Psychosis is?"

I found it strange that I did.

"Not strange at all," Henry insisted. "You are the first vampire to contract it. You're also the first vampire to coin the term and try to treat it. It's how I know John Simons is not compelling you. I asked you to do something for me, which involved you going into the future. If John compelled you, he wouldn't have let you go."

"Henry, I'm confused by your relationship with John," I confessed. "This might be a sore subject, in that it ended in a murder/suicide, but I take it you and he were lovers."

He sighed again, took another sip, and leaned back. "We were indeed 'lovers,' but that didn't create our animosity. We were drifting apart before John started becoming famous for his music, and Kellen dominated his life. We stopped being lovers without ever...well, breaking it off. But then John met Bryony, and everything changed. I fell in love with her from the first moment I saw her, but I never pursued her."

"Why not?"

Henry stared hard at me for a long moment.

"Inappropriate," he finally said. "Inappropriate at the time. But John eventually fell in love with her and then married her, quite against Kellen's wishes. But although John went against his manager in courtship and marriage, he obeyed Kellen like a dutiful boy whore throughout that marriage, which meant he neglected the only person John would ever love. Because he spent so little time with her, John recruited me as her chaperone, thinking he knew all about my 'preferences.' Bryony was so young, sad, lonely, and beautiful, that despite my other tastes, I could not resist her. Even so, I could have played understudy to him, but he was never around, being compelled like a monkey on a leash. When even Bryony realized that her husband's relationship with his manager was more than just business, she was heartbroken and turned to me for comfort. Bryony's pregnancy was unlikely to be the cause of his scant attentions, but our denials off set his suspicion. Bryony died giving birth. She would have survived if John had called for her doctor sooner. We didn't know at the time that her infant survived. That seemed unlikely with an infant corpse beside the mother's body...an early oakwood model unit, you told me later. You claim your wood sprite tore the child from the womb and replaced it with a decoy he had stolen from a leprechaun. Furthermore, you had a sample of that child's DNA tested, and I came up as the father. I begged you before, and I'm begging you now: protect that infant from John, especially considering that, for a short time, John will be my son's adopted father. Melissa, whom you recognize as the mother, the child who, in extreme irony, is playing the part of Bryony, will be my son's stepmother, so I need you to protect her, too. You had to go into the deep future to get a device called an electronic womb that will let my son have a normal childhood by living his life remotely. When you did this, you got lost."

"Hmmm, a love for a young woman and an interest in another…one might think that you are playing for the other team," I teased.

"Melissa is my student in 1975!" he snapped quite unexpectedly.

I apologized, knowing the code of honor teachers have for their students. Then, trying to distract him, I asked, "So what are the perils of this mission that puts you so in my debt?"

He took another sip and smiled, but I couldn't tell if it was a friendly smile or a seething smile.

"To understand the Kingdom of the Damned, you'll need to know how to kill a vampire. Before your little invention, most living humans only knew one way to do it: discover the vampire's coffin, lie in wait for that vampire to start reanimating, and then drive a wooden stake through its chest."

"That's the only way?"

"In theory, other methods exist, but the practice is tricky. A silver knife or bullet may disable a vampire. Here's the problem. If a vampire bleeds and falls, the mortal may foolishly believe he extinguished the unholy threat. But in reality, the vampire will reanimate in the place it was put to rest. Only a decomposing corpse confirms that the undead has been destroyed. A beheaded vampire will expire the same as staked vampire, but most of the living lack that strength to accomplish it. Crosses, garlic, direct sunlight, or holy water are myths that serve the undead well."

"Such myths have a vampire origin?"

"Yes." He gave me strange look. "But don't just fear being killed. There are many diseases that are fatal to vampires. Perhaps keep a thermometer with you."

"You mentioned getting lost."

"Yes. You see, my dear Calkins, the Kingdom of the Damned is a small community. You need only a party like this one to keep up with who's been staked, removed by another vampire, or perished from disease. In vampire history, many simply went missing. Most were Deep Time traveling vampires, much like yourself. In the vast years, some of the missing turned up again. Some were just depressed and sealed themselves from all company…until they had to feed. Others turned up as victims of some unlikely adventure, such as the vampire that was frozen in a glacier in the height of the last ice age. He found himself in a museum. Most comical."

"Except for the vampire."

"Well, yes. My point is, even with these plausible explanations, too many vampires disappear. We only have one source to explain it."

"Is that source credible?"

A strange look appeared once again on his face.

"No. Any credible vampire would stay completely away from Deep Time. When we visit the past, we're careful not to enter the past as it was, but the past as it exists in our differing perspectives of 'now.' If, by some mistake or intention, we change the past, we've only changed events or happenstance that does not change humanity. The same with the future. Years go by, and any paradoxes are resolved by forgetfulness or misinterpretation."

Henry's countenance darkened, and he took another, more thoughtful, sip. "Deep Time is different. If you go back in time to change your present, no problem. Eventually you will perish and no harm, or good, will result from your incursion. Not so when you go back to the future to change the course of human existence, even if the change seems trivial. That sort of incursion will drive you insane."

"What is this not credible source claiming?"

"Deep Time travel involves going through portals where you don't know the space or time on the other end, but it's a continuum. Think of it as a train ride with changing directions. You travel very rapidly but can only get off when a train reaches a station. Since you've never taken this train, you can only assume the next stop is the place you want. According to rumor, our 'source' fell asleep while riding this time train. When he did get off, he encountered a time and place where no life existed. Molten metals shot up from the burning, melting, hell-scape. Maybe it was the distant past, maybe the distant future, it's impossible to tell. Some claim he'd entered hell itself."

"Why didn't this source just get back on the train?"

"Rumor says he did…millions of times for as many years, but the other side of every portal looked the same as the last. He couldn't determine which direction; past, future, or maybe something sideways, was the way back to where plants and animals existed. But the source did find other vampires. Apparently, they couldn't be starved out of existence, but they were too weak to move. Liken them to someone walking the tracks in the way that we walk along the 'tracks' of our future, one day at a time. Except in that case, they know they're heading to their future. Many of these vampires were clumped together, as if they'd wandered and found each other, one by one, while they still had the strength to change their position. This 'source' kept getting weaker and weaker as he was unable to feed."

"Until he jumped into the right portal?"

"Yes – and most likely with help from a supernatural deity. Some say Satan helped him. Or perhaps it was some other fallen agent. In either case, this supernatural being found it difficult to provide help and spent a great deal of effort giving it. The deity was omni-present and had no need for space/time. It could not direct the source because it didn't know the victim's origin, except from its perspective of 'here/now.' So to direct this source, the deity reanimated a Mayan Magi and transmitted the location of the stars. This took many attempts as the source was a poor and inaccurate communicator. After much effort, and with this source barely able to wiggle for lack of sustenance, the source finally went through a portal that allowed him to feed. Once within the timeline of existing life, the source navigated his way back to his own space/time."

"And so he lived to tell the tale," I concluded.

"He did, but he didn't. I haven't finished the story. Something more needed to be done, though I doubt any sane vampire would have attempted it. The other starved vampires, given that 'forever' allows all things possible, would eventually find their way back to their own times and want revenge for being abandoned in hell. Instead of learning his lesson, this source reversed course and returned to the space/time of that hellish landscape. But what he found there, what he brought with him to use on the other vampires, and if he needed the same supernatural help to get in and out the portal, is unknown. We should assume he brought a wooden stake and mallet, ending any threat, but this is a crazy vampire. If he brought blood with him, he might have brought those vampires back. They would be in debt to him, and vampires do not like to be in debt. One might say this crazy vampire painted a very large target on his back…a back he should watch."

"I would think that any vampire who has the favor of a supernatural deity would be too dangerous to mess with."

Henry snickered. "Well, there's the rub. Not everyone agrees that a supernatural deity fueled his escape. They think he was simply Irish."

"The luck of the Irish," I mused…until realizing I'm the only known Irish vampire. "Wait. Am I the unreliable source?"

"You never said you were."

"Then what are you saying?" I asked impatiently.

"No. I said YOU never said that…any of it. If you had, anyone could easily dismiss it." Henry leaned close and dropped his voice. "John Simons is a powerful vampire and since you became one, he's kept a close eye on you. But one day, for a few hours, he was frantic to find you. The link between a master vampire and his slave is such that he'd know if you'd been staked. And if that wasn't enough, Kellen Wechsler was even more than frantic. He was actually n a rage, screaming to all around him that no one gets away from his power. During that hour, or two, it was very clear that you were missing and that the pair had plans, opposing plans, with you being critical to those plans. For his part, Kellen organized a vampire search party from every time in every part of the globe. If you were on the earth during the time of men, they'd have found you, but they didn't."

"So what happened next?"

"Nothing. It was as if everyone simply forgot anything that happened and that hour or two became the smallest part of a second. I forgot, too but since I'm a writer, I keep a journal. Imagine my surprise when I read about your disappearance and Kellen's rage regarding it. As I was reading it, the same thing happened a second time. Ed Calkins was missing, and every vampire with any connection to Kellen had to search or else. In much less than an hour, which became less than a second, the entire incident was forgotten again. Of course, I knew about it because of my journal, but I'm not the only vampire who keeps one. That is our first clue. Our second clue came with invitations to some wild parties from vampires no one knew. Do you know what the IVA is?"

"Irish Republican Army…the Catholic resistance through the Trouble."

"No. The I.V.A. stands for Irish Vampire Association. You're considered to be the only known member, except you've never admitted it. You've told people how to join. You've told me how to join. Most of us just think you're just crazy, except these vampires no one seems to know, but you, crash our parties, one at a time. Always inexplicably, his name winds up on the guest list. The unknown vampire always introduces himself with, "Hi, good to finally meet you...I don't know how we've never met before...strange, huh?' Always, the stranger appeared to know us, but only one vampire seemed to know the stranger...you. Furthermore, none of these new vampires are ever seen together. Then after every unknown vampire was introduced, they invited us to rather extreme events thrown in their honor. One was the dedication to an Aztec temple, complete with the sacrifices of fifty warriors, each having their living hearts torn out of their chests. Or the day at a Roman colosseum where the vampire's guests were seated with the Emperor. Every blood sacrifice you can imagine, these new vampires hosted."

"How is it thought that these new vampires relate to me?"

"The rumor is that you, 'the source,' took two items back with you: stakes and blood in gallon containers. You forced each vampire to swear alliance to you, the Irish Empire, and the IVA before you let them drink. You never implied a direction back to modern time, but you have all kinds of ridiculous stories about Neanderthal men and the ancient times. You even implied once that you were in Portugal, trying to make it to India, and that you hitched a ride with Christopher Columbus on his famous voyage. Although no one believes you or finds your pathetic attempt at humor charming, no one completely discounts what's not told directly. For example, how many vampires did you encounter on your ride to the present?"

"You don't believe any of this, do you? It certainly seems unlikely."

He grabbed me by the collar with frightening speed. Henry's expression was a mix of fear, rage, and desperation.

"Fall apart, man! Quit being rational! Your enemies can read your mind! You must scatter your wits and believe the unbelievable or..."

"Or what?"

"... or you'll never survive!"

I shook with fright and tried to compose myself.

"Not surviving hardly worries me," I told him as calmly as I could. "I'm already dead."

He stared at me long and hard and then released his grip.

"Maybe this will unhinge you," Henry said as he reached into his pocket. "You gave me this gift with one condition: that upon my passing, I would leave it to one of your living family."

He held out a strange black rock. Funny, but when I say "black" and "strange," I mean like a small piece of reality that had become a black hole...a missing piece of the natural world. The rock was flat in dimension and heavier than it should have been for how thin it was, which was perhaps slightly thicker than paper.

"Open your hand," Henry said.

I did, and Henry placed the rock on my palm.

"It's a mirror," he said, watching my reaction intently. "It's made from a substance not found in the time of life."

I pointed the rock at other objects. Nothing changed in its blackness.

"It reflects reality the way non-living things see it. If you had a powerful enough microscope, you might see the unchanging particles in random motion the way they were since the beginning of creations. What you'll never see is life or the living."

I looked at him, bewildered. "It's just a dark, flat, rock."

"Gaze into it and see."

I did and saw something I had not seen since I'd become undead. My reflection! It was as clear as the day before my death when I could see myself in a mirror!

"Do you believe you now?" Henry sneered. "This was my last chance to convince you to take yourself with a dose of pompous grandeur. A sane vampire can't do what you must. A sane vampire will never kill Kellen to save Melissa, create a normal life for my unborn son, or make a three-day holiday, complete with a parade, to commemorate his birthday."

"Calkins Day," I brightened. "I like the ring to that...celebrated on the thirteenth of February...right between Lincoln's birthday and Valentine's day. There could be a big parade with candy, balloons, and leprechauns. It seems meant to be."

Henry smiled softly and raised his glass. "Ah, there's my

delusional fool."

"AHEM!"

My smile was short lived. Glorna was behind me, and he wanted me to know it. Of course, he was under house arrest right now, which meant I told him not to go anywhere, which meant he found it imperative to go anywhere but where I told him. That he was standing in front of me only could mean bad news.

"Henry, could you give us a moment?"

"Us?"

I heard the confusion in his voice. Couldn't he see the small wood sprite standing in the room? Then he understood.

"Ah, your imagination requires your attention. No worry. Tend to your ruthless business, and I'll see you in another time."

Glorna stood before me, staring at me like John Simons had done. He had killed a woodsman by drinking his blood and eating his bloodied meat. Could he be a vampire? At that moment, I had to know.

He spoke to me in a strangely authoritarian voice, gazing directly into my eyes, which made me dizzy, sleepy… Glorna spoke. His voice sounded powerful and…disembodied.

"From this day forward, you will do whatever I say you will do. You will hear and obey."

After a short and strange conversation with Glorna, I made my way to the nearest exit, unsure how to get back to my own time; and just as unsure as to what that time was. It was then that I realized I hadn't said goodbye to Henry, which was important as, from his perspective, this was the last time we would see each other. Of course, I couldn't tell him that, but he would soon meet his end, his final end, at the hands of the man he killed so many years ago.

I wanted to say something or maybe use a famous Irish blessing; "May ye be in heaven a half hour before the devil knows you're dead." How would he take that? I though on it so hard, I didn't know where I was.

That's when I saw him, praying that he didn't see me.

Father Chokey.

CHAPTER 18: KINGDOM OF THE DAMNED, PART II

"Not every confusing memory involving time travel can be considered Deep Time Psychosis or DTP. Quit coming to me about the time you came on to your mother. That's not DTP, it's just disgusting. Nor is it DTP if your perception of who, what, and when differs from any other person that might recall the same experience. One must expect disagreement on what is in the future or past; that's only commonsense. Consider that every venture beyond one's own time has three question each having the same two properties. Who are you, where are you, and what are you doing? Each of those questions must be answered in terms of when and where. For example, let's pretend I'm sane. In that case, I'm Ed Calkins in Detroit in 2013, but I'm talking to all of you in from my balcony in Tara, sometime in the 700s, and I'm lecturing on a problem I discovered somewhere on this planet sometime before or after life existed. My ability to say these things is contrary to DTP. DTP happens when I cannot tell the difference between who, where, and what I am. DTP happens when my own perspective disagrees with itself."

Lecture by Ed Calkins on DTP to the Knights of the Red Branch

His feet felt very small.

It was late evening, a time when, even on a weekday, the youthful would be worshipping the freedom from work or school, but his victims lived a different life. He had been following them for months, the cause of all his problems and the fool that managed them. Finding the apartment parking lot was the easy part. Now he had to find the correct car.

It seemed so senseless, what he would do. Sometimes one had to play dirty, and no one knew the newspaper distribution business as well as he did. To be respected, you had to be feared.

Yes, this looked like the car he had followed. He spied around him. No witnesses. Good. Bending to his knees, he pulled his pocket-knife out and cut, wishing it were throats instead of tires.

I don't remember leaving the party, but I had some office work to do before getting a nap and leaving for work. Homelessness is actually a very big problem for new vampires. No one plans to be a vampire. So after it happens, it's hard to imagine vampires with their families because simply going home means spouse and children could become the first meals. I'm on the fence about creating a homeless shelter for new vampires. Here's my rationale.

The population is known for biting, and that's bad, but if a vampire is going to bite, maybe they shouldn't start with the other homeless living, who are more likely to be addicted to drugs or have HIV. Picture this. A vampire bites someone on heroin and gets high off the blood. Now he's interested in making as many heroin addicts as possible to insure a reliable source. Also HIV can be spread from vampire to victim or victim to vampire, meaning that an infected vampire is going to spread the disease even if he or she is not inclined to kill their victims. A homeless shelter could help with these problems, but maybe sympathy for homeless vampires is a little misplaced. After burial, vampires without a home can always sleep in their coffins or, if alternate arrangements are made, they can sleep at their own time of death. But the luck of the Irish seems to follow me, for I have an apartment that I must have secured shortly after dying. This apartment gives me access to the internet and an industrial printer that allows me to print route lists for the carriers. Most vampires don't have that foresight after undergoing the trauma of dying, reanimating as vampires, and wanting desperately to drink the blood of the living. Finding a place to live is seldom the first order of business.

Speaking of first order of business, mine is answering emails, which is the most stressful part of my day. Like some evil charm, my blood pressure rises at the task of explaining eleven of the seventeen costumer complaints we got the following day. In most cases, I really don't, and never will, know why the subscriber didn't get a paper, but I'm expected to promise to investigate, kick the carrier in the butt, verify delivery for the next couple of days, and swear that it will never happen again. Emails are never kindly worded, but my response has to satisfy Jake Noble, or I'll be faced with another email about the same incident tomorrow.

The next part involves a lot of paper. I'll go through more than 500 sheets on a weekday and almost double that on Sunday, but once the process is started, my mind is free to wander.

"I can't come to the phone right now, as I am not convinced that I exist, but if you could leave my name, address, telephone number, and a short message explaining where I should be and what I'm supposed to be doing there, I would be grateful for the insight. Also include the time of this call. Be sure to include the date, month, and year. Also, if you have any proof of my existence, sharing it with me might be the only way of ensuring a return phone call."

That was the message on my answering machine. Always, people comment on it before they express their reasons for calling, but they never comply with the request of the message. Most calls are not related to work, so the requested information is valuable as my land line phone still rings when I'm skipping through surface or Deep Time. Work-related calls are different. I've got some three hundred pages printing right now, and each one of them has the date of delivery, along with the addresses that need to be delivered. While none of this proves I exist to me, it does prove I have work to do regardless of my existence status.

Great! The caller is Matt, one of my carriers. He's sick and won't be in tonight, which means the tomorrow morning that starts in four hours. I have to do his route along with the down route. The irony isn't lost on me. A carrier gets sick, and a dead one takes his place. Maybe I should commandeer some brownies to help me, just in case the morning gets worse.

I'm almost done printing, and I can't forget what Henry Mathews told me about feeding. I might have left that part out earlier because it doesn't reflect well on me, and I want you to like me. He told me that no matter how humane I try to be, the "lust for blood" will get the better of me. I can live on animal blood, but that will only satisfy my "hunger." The sweetest blood is the blood from a willing neck, like John Simons gets from his young host, Melissa. That's not an option for me as my Nalla would regard such as cheating.

What is more disturbing is the way the evening ended. Do you understand it? Glorna came. Didn't I have him under house arrest, pending…what? It's hard for me to keep track of all the points in time. In any case, he specifically requested an audience in private, which is so unlike him as he likes as many people as possible to see him being defiant. The conversation was as short as it was strange. I don't think I got a word in. Do you remember what he said? I could have sworn he was lecturing me about not being a hypocrite.

Is that what he said? I'm asking you, the spy …er reader, because you understand this better than anyone, right? You could call me at this number, then I could go back in time, just far enough to listen to your message…or wait, I'd go forward in time. I suppose that's not our relationship, though. I'm supposed to write the greatest novel ever written, but one that only you can truly understand. We're still going with that, right? I'm a great novelist, and you are the only literary genius that can understand its greatness, even if I cannot. I'm trying to believe that still…trying to believe in both of us, but that means you can't advise me, and I can't let your insight change the plot as that would be cheating. Right? I'll assume it is.

My nap was a dream of blood and vixens long dead or far into the unseen future. I tried to calm myself as I did when I was living not five days and four deaths ago, but every time I imagined a serene place and time, people packed with suitcase full of problems settle there before I can enjoy the peace, bringing their conflicts to me as if I owned, or at least governed, the place I imagined. First marched in the leprechauns - an old, unmarried, dying race - expecting that I would somehow save them. "A wife is a slave you cannot sell," Eircheard had told me. I can guess why their women jumped through some future portal to find better companionship. Anywhere, they would have found it. Then came the brownies looking for work, the pixies, looking for trouble, and the merrows looking to escape their sea monster husbands. All of them thought that they were only figments of my imagination, but they thought the space and time was real. That must be a symptom of Deep Time Psychosis. Everyone thinks what you imagine is real. If I could imagine other people, everyone would think they were real, too. Is that what really happened in that hellish landscape before or after life? Did I imagine it all, expect vampires moved in?

I tried not to think…to shut down my undead brain and nap but the hellish torments haunted me. Fire and hunger sizzled on the edges of my mindscape, but that wasn't the worst of it…loneliness was. Being so alone that even a vampire that would kill you as easy as look at you: that was better than just nothing, than just no one.

Then there was the pleasure of a willing neck like the one Melissa offered Simons. How I craved that compliance! What I would do to own a willing host that I could feed from, and if I could restrain myself, maybe become living again. If not…well, that was even better. But getting a willing neck would not endear me to the little angel that stole my soul…or would steal it when I found the right vampire chest.

I would have to feed on the terrified.

I would become a monster.

What was the alternative? I was the vampire six days now from my death, or was I the vampire somewhere seven seconds between dead and dying that would last about ten years so that I could create John-Peter so Simons could have a son? The later could be visiting the former, or was I just alternating perpetually between time-scapes like a leaf in a hurricane?

It's better just to do. I don't need to exist that way; I only need to act in any way that supports existence by the virtue of things getting done. The name, shape, time, and occupied space becomes incidental. Do the job I see. Or I could reverse the idea and only be singular, only I would be important. Where I am or what I was doing would fade against the splendor of an identity more real than anyone anywhere at any time.

I woke before my alarm to a quote, yet I could not name the speaker.

"Just because it's impossible doesn't mean it's not required."

I had called in ten brownies from my imagined Tara with people to come into this modern time and assist with bagging the papers as I had my first undead workday. This time, I called in only ten, which included Ramon. Five would have been more than enough, but brownies love their brownie points, and they always find work to do beyond the newspapers. I walked through the graveyard to where my white van sat.

This time it was me waiting for them.

I was already on the road when the phone calls started, which I put on speaker as to keep my hands free. The first was Matt. He wanted to be sure I believed he was really sick, as he knew I already had an unfilled route to throw. He offered to deliver today's papers with tomorrow's.

"Matt," I told him. "It doesn't work that way. Newspapers have dates on them."

"Come on, Ed. You can't do both routes. You'll be out there till noon."

"I may be, Matt, but I'm going to keep delivering until every paper in our account has been delivered."

No sooner than I hung up with Matt came another call about four slashed tires and who would do such a thing. That meant three routes were down. The phone call after that one introduced the same "all four tires" slashed narrative, but after some begging on my part, the carrier offered to use his sister's car.

Simons was the fourth call, and he was shouting.

"I KNOW who slashed my tires," he bellowed. "Jack Noble, our own division manager took a knife to all four of them. If you don't do something, I'm simply going to kill him. I went back a few hours in time to see it with my own eyes."

"John, please don't do that…just give me a chance to handle it"

"Then **HANDLE IT**…and don't expect me to run my route on rims!"

I shuddered as he slammed the phone.

The last phone call was unexpectedly hostile given that it came from the Goddess. Her voice had none of the rage of the previous call, but it was far more menacing.

"Listen, vampire, I'll find you and stake you both if you don't stay away from my family, my property, or me. I've covered Munsonville for years, and I know of every vampire story and any vampire trick that…"

"What makes you think I'm a vampire?"

"I was at your wake last night."

"Really? Were there many people there?"

255

"Focus, Ed."

"I didn't slash your tires, Goddess." I still called her that even while she was threatening me. Did I even remember her actual name?

"Then how did you know they were slashed?"

I told her about the other phone calls, how it couldn't have been John who slashed them because he was at a vampire party with me, and that she shouldn't try staking me by herself.

"Get Trudy or my granddaughter to do it," I told her. "My son is building a weapon that should make it easier. But you need to wait. Right now, I have five routes to do, and I've got to make John-Peter, even though he was born years ago. In addition, I have to kill some other vampire connected with John Simons, and I have to do it right now, three days ago, and fourteen years into the future; all of this has to be done before I answer to a crime I committed several years ago and three days from now. You should have me staked sometime after that, but before I completely lose my humanity and cause more harm than good. I trust you."

"Oh," was all she said, sounding like she would listen as I tried to explain things that I didn't understand myself. I told her about how John saw me dying and drained my blood so that I could make a changeling from software, psychology, and a leprechaun's trick, which I know I did, but I didn't know how I was going to do it. I told her about my role as Steward of Tara in two different times that was all built with my imagination except people, human and sidhe, settled there. I told her about the party last night, which was at least one hundred years ago, seeing Henry Matthews (the author turned vampire) and what he told me about my soul and my Deep Time Psychosis. All while I talked, she just listened without skepticism.

After I finished speaking, she told me that, for some reason, she was immune from the time healing paradox that vampirism creates. She accepted all I told her.

"Other people that were at your wake will not be surprised to see you passing out papers this morning," she told me. "To them, you never died. Others that are here this morning will be replaced by people you remember as always being there. I don't know why it's different for me. What you must not do is go home to your wife…er…lover. Stay away from your family, or you'll find yourself feeding on them. I will have you and John staked when its time."

"Wow. You know all this? You should write a book."

"It would take at least five volumes that no one would believe is more than wild fiction," she said.

Then she told me about my wake: how my wife, son, and grandkids fared, my mother's fit, Trudy meeting my support group, Jake getting thrown out, and some of the local vampires that lurked before me as if she were making light conversation.

"Goddess, what am I going to do about John-Peter?"

"Whatever it is, you're going to do it. He seems like a happy boy with parents that love him."

"You wouldn't have to worry about John," I told her. "He's doomed as his cure for vampirism has failed. There is a chance you don't have to worry about me either. I've got a duel to the death Three days and three hours from now and losing could be well… career ending, if 'vampire' is a career. And as much as I wish I was getting staked today… I've got to go. I've got five routes to handle and a division manager trying to get me fired."

"You should quit. I don't understand why you haven't already."

"Lest the pig eat the horse," I told her.

That she didn't understand.

"You should quit now," she insisted.

"I know but who would I quit to? Robert is in Florida."

"Nothing personal…I mean about staking you."

"I know that, too."

The brownies had been muffling laughter all during the speaker phone conversations, but now they let their giggles go.

"Stupid lady try to kill Steward," Ramon chuckled. "Steward can't die. Steward too fat."

The giggles changed to fits of belly-clenching laughter. Though I saw no humor in his joke, I wish I had his comical touch.

Despite the nightmare I was driving to, the brownies love their ride to the "newspaper barn." Ramon even asked to drive. I declined, of course, guessing that he had no interest in the posted speed limit and would assume that his company with "the Steward" would keep him above any petty laws about how to drive the "wheel box."

257

I did catch a small break. The papers were early…all of them. I made the most of that as the brownies took their customary nap in the white wheel box. With no one to bother me, I made short work of counting out the carriers' papers and setting them up on the bagging benches.

Now I needed to do what I dreaded most. I had to make two phone calls. My first call was to Robert, or rather Robert's answering machine, a message he might not hear before trouble calls him. It wouldn't be the first time Jake woke him (before he had a chance to hear my message and two hours after the work should be done) to tell him how badly I was running his business.

The next call was to Jake Noble.

How do I explain this call? You're thinking I'm going to yell at him; put him on the defensive by saying my current problem was all of his fault and none of mine. Instead, I took a lecture about my own incompetence. I heard how I was too trusting, too nice, and to much of a big clown with my stupid traditions that celebrate various holidays. It might be embarrassing if the brownies could hear my getting dressed down from the man that I knew was the fault of my trouble. I took it all, feeling like it truly was my fault as well as my problem.

"You call those fool carriers of yours and tell them they're fired if they don't come to work! Slashed tires, my eye! They just all know how naïve you are."

"It's not my call. I don't fire or hire; Robert does," I told him, though he already knew. "And by the way, it's not my job to fire myself either. That job belongs to somebody else."

"Well, Robert is in big trouble, and it's your fault. You better have all those papers delivered today, and they better all be delivered on time."

Of course, that was impossible.

"I'll deliver every paper," I lied and was rewarded with the slam of a phone. Seething with impotent anger, I cut my phone and wheeled the unbagged papers toward the parking lot.

"Hey, you've got to deliver those!" she shouted.

It was Becky from a different account. Officially, she was a carrier, but everyone knew her for something different…more like you. She was a spy…er…that is she would be like you if she had extremely developed tastes in novels. Sorry. I'm still trying to believe in us both.

Anyway, she spies for Jake Noble. I can hear her calling him on her cell as I walk away without answering her. She tells him I'm not going to deliver.

"I'm going to deliver every paper!" I yelled out, lying again. "I'm going to bag everything as I go."

The lie was pointless, but my comments made both caller and receiver unravel a bit.

Once in the van, I woke the brownies; they went to work bagging.

Always the rule of thumb is you do the route you know best first when it's the darkest, but with the vision that vampirism has given me, I can do any route and see addresses as well as I could in the day. John's route is closer but more spread out. I debated with myself on which would save the most subscriber complaints and resigned to doing his first. Vampirism does not help me read any better, so I do something I would never advise anyone else. I do John's route by memory, even though it's been weeks since I did it last. I would miss a few houses, but the time it would save would justify it. Whereas I have a good memory, I'm horrible at reading numbers. I think you know that by now.

Why did I ever build a career with newspaper distribution?

John's route went no quicker than it did before my death. There were few papers that required "porching," so the van covered the vast distance no faster as it was not undead. Still, I finished in record time and flew into the unfilled route that I was keeping down to offset the cost of my own salary. On that route, being a vampire helped as my personal speed was frightening. Where the paper needed the porch, I was out of the van and back again before the driver side door could slam shut. While my speed was accelerated by being undead, my stamina faltered and was no better than my fifty plus years of life.

I was out of breath and halfway through the open route when the brownies were finished bagging and ready to deploy as cleaning aids to the sleeping elderly. This would cost some time, as I would have to double back to pick them up, but their enthusiasm prompted my generosity. Brownies are a strange a lot, but very sympathetic to those of advanced age. One might call them downright charitable if it wasn't for their nasty habit of stealing newborn babies.

Ramon, who insisted on being last, reminded me that he needed to return to the old lady he visited last time as he did all the talking and forgot to listen. I wouldn't have remembered the house, but brownies always seem to know where people feeble with age live. I was alone by the time I finished that route. The next one would take several hours, and I would need to read the list.

On the way to the third route, I had time to think about time and the word salad it made when I tried to explain my situation to the Goddess. I got a chill when I realized I was being truthful when I told her that I had to finish everything in three days, lest Trudy take my undead life while I still had work on my plate. Who was I? Ed Calkins, but Ed Calkins from what time and place? True, I had traveled to Tara in two different ancient times, the very distant past or future if Henry could be believed, and I'd traveled to a time in the not so distant future where I stole that crazy electronic womb, but what time was I in when I did the traveling? There were only two possibilities. Either I was the Ed Calkins the vampire three days beyond my death, or I was Ed Calkins the vampire who would give Melissa an object essential to John-Peter in the seven seconds that remained of my life. Do you see how I can be confused? Only the annoying feel of a bullet rattling in my head told me. I could be traveling to my own past to finish up what I failed to finish, or I could have traveled from dying to the early days beyond my death. As I've already said, I'm too responsible to go to a dual with unfinished work.

I was halfway done with my third route when I could wait no longer to pick up the brownies. It was already 8 a.m. which made me an hour and a half late, but the brownies must have been waiting for nearly an hour. Great, more anger would be directed at me.

Ramon was first. I saw him sitting on the porch but not with the expression I expected. Ramon was crying. I wish I hadn't noticed, but the view (or his tearfulness) looked as if two miniature water sprayers had replaced his eyebrows. It almost made me laugh. He did not run to the white wheel box when I pulled up, so I went to him and sat beside him to hear of his woes.

"Old lady wait for Ramon," he sobbed. "Old lady wait and wait and wait.

As he said this, he pounded his fists on the wooden porch in frustration. I looked around for clues and saw three days of papers still on the porch. Oh no - but it happens. The old lady died alone and wouldn't be found until someone noticed the smell coming from the untended house.

"Poor old lady," Ramon lamented with deep grief that made me feel selfish and ashamed. "Ramon never tell you how interesting you are. Ramon talk and talk and talk but didn't come to listen."

Then I made a mistake born of a desperate need to say something of comfort.

"Maybe you can tell her that when you go to heaven," I told him.

"Ramon no go to heaven! Steward imagine Ramon! Why Steward imagine Ramon being so sad!"

There was the anger I expected. I had to come up with an answer.

"When the Steward dies, do you think that Ramon will just disappear? I'll imagine the brownies in heaven, and I'll need to imagine their leader. Then you can tell the old lady how interesting she is."

Ramon looked at me as if I lost my mind.

"But Steward go to other place," he told me, pointing down. "Ruthless dictators go to hell."

"Yes, but even in hell, I can imagine Ramon in heaven with pools of cold beer and where Ramon's job is to jump in and drink till the pool gets filled again. I can image Ramon in heaven with his brownie friends and lots of beautiful breeders to be nice to Ramon."

Ramon had closed his eyes imagining that. A smile took his lips.

"But that's if I still like Ramon. If I don't like Ramon, I can imagine him in the other place, shoveling hot coal with burning feet and a large devil to whip Ramon if he doesn't work fast enough."

Now Ramon shuddered. Thinking, he said to me, "Maybe Steward not so fat. Maybe nice Steward is just right for old human."

Thanks, Ramon. I always wanted to be just fat enough to be old. Still, I knew the brownie's reference point. Brownie's stomachs swell only after a big meal that returns to normal long before they are ready to eat again. Even humans in Ramon's time are more likely to be underfed than to have a pot belly like mine. When I play Santa in my time, I need padding to fit in the suit. In Ramon's time, only the very rich could ever be that fat.

It was very late for the brownies and, with no more work that they could help me with, I had to send them back to their time. It was another delay, but I was quickly coming to the time when delivering wouldn't do any more good. People would give up calling for their paper around one p.m. and wouldn't look for it till the next morning. Still, this was Robert's call, and I hope he would do so before I gave up.

The nearest portal for the brownies was still the Happy Hunting Grounds funeral parlor in Thornton. I had already dropped them off and was heading back to the route when Robert did call. Jake had called first, but my boss hadn't talked to him.

"What happened!" Robert demanded.

"Four sets of slashed tires and a sickie."

"Impossible!"

"Witnesses say otherwise." I did not want to defend my carriers, who were the victims here, but if I "called out" Jake Noble, I'd be that much less believable.

"Some people are going to lose their jobs if they don't stop jerking us around. If there were slashed tires, where's the police reports?"

"Where are their…do you realize just one cop covers this whole area? One."

"I'm not buying it. Everyone not at work tomorrow is getting fired…"

"Start with me."

"…and what's this I hear about you dumping all the papers?"

"Another lie. Betty told Jake I was leaving with unbagged papers. That was true. I was so far behind, so I bagged as I went. Don't let them tell you differently. I've finished the down route and John's, but I'm bogging down on Matt's…if you can find someone to do better…"

"Now don't get your panties in a bunch. You've got to get to the bottom of this. How much do you have done?"

"More than half, but I'm losing steam."

"It's already nine-thirty, but wait, you're an hour behind us here. Work till noon. After that, I'll cover for you, but you've got to get a handle on this, or we're out of business."

He hung up.

Thanks for "covering" for me, Robert, considering it's your

business I'm trying to keep together. I hope you haven't had too much sunshine and you didn't have to wait too long for breakfast.

The rest of the third route was a lot of backing in and out of shared townhouse driveways. My neck ached, and I was hungry. My mood and time did not improve as the traffic didn't seem to believe in my existence. Pulling in, backing out, braking, and enduring dirty looks as I had no right to be on the road. Before I finished, John called wanting to know what I was doing about his tires.

"John, I'm a little busy now," I hissed through my teeth.

"You said you would handle it!"

That was the trigger that fired off my temper.

"I have enough of your mandates, vampire! I've got five routes to do that I've got to finish three hours ago! I've got a child to create with no idea how that's even possible, and now you want me to play detective while I'm doing all of those things!"

"Remember, I don't need the route. If you won't handle Jake Noble, you can run my route for good!"

"Yeah? You'll know I've got too much to do when your boy resembles a piano bench leg! Do you think I can't find a way out of this task? How well will your prospective fatherhood take to me if I drive a stake through my own heart! I'm about ready to do it!"

"Relax," John said. "You've already created John-Peter with my blood, and he's fine. Killing yourself will not change that. If your short on time, take that seven seconds and stretch the middle of it an extra year or so. And take care of my tir…"

"Keep thinking so, John. If it were true, I wouldn't be breaking down right now about finishing an impossible task…"

"Ed don't fall apart on me. I'm commanding you to….don't hang up on me! I'm warning you…"

But I did. Nor did I take his calls when he kept calling back. For the next four minutes, the phone rang and rang and rang. I threw the phone in the glove compartment, but I could still hear the ringing. It was then that I got brilliant.

The phone has an off switch.

About an hour after I shut down the phone, I reached the last block of the last subdivision and noticed a Buick. The car seemed to follow me, and the driver looked crazy. I feared it was a mad-as-hell subscriber, that, with my being so late with his paper, had jumped in his car ready to play "Dirty Harry" with his puck-like carrier. Well,

263

it wouldn't be the first time.

But when I pulled into a narrow driveway, this short, stooped man with heavy, thick-rimmed black glasses and artificially dark hair slicked back blocked my path. I tried the horn, but he wasn't budging.

"What the hell," I asked.

"Mr. Calkins, I hope? I'd feel stupid if I trapped the wrong van."

"What do you want?"

"Well, I don't want to have this conversation in a stranger's driveway."

"Who are you?"

"I'm Dr. Abner Rothgard, and we really need to talk. Please get in your van and turn your phone back on."

I was confused, but he sounded so sure and patient….like a man used to dealing with crazy people. I drove away first, checking my rear view to make sure he wasn't following me. At the light, I on turned the phone on, and it rang immediately.

"Hello, again, this is Dr. Rothgard, a specialist in vampire health issues. You ought to schedule a check-up as I'm the only one of my kind. However, I'm not qualified to treat your insanity."

"Do you often box people in to acquire new patients you refuse to treat? I suggest advertising instead."

I realized the folly of that as the words left my mouth.

"Fascinating," the doctor told me. "I'm a big fan of your work. Someday, I'd like to pick your brain about a mutual client and how you did what you did. Of course, that conversation must wait until you know what it is that you did."

"Is being fascinating an urgent medical condition?"

" Actually, I have a question. Your honest answer is imperative. Do you sometimes get a very sharp, but momentary, pain that doesn't return for days?"

I did get such a pain. But the place and the sensation changed. I might feel like a knife to my belly, a bullet to my skull, a dual cut on my neck or a piercing of my rib cage. All these pains were about a day apart and never lasted. All at once, I understood Dr. Rothgard's concern.

"I'm the seven second Ed Calkins." I realized aloud. I knew this not by the pain, but the rattling bullet.

"I'm afraid so," Dr. Rothgard said. "My other patient is linked to your…functionality. You went back into time to make a changeling baby at the behest of another patient of mine."

"John Simons."

"Correct. But very wrong. You went back in time, but then went into your own future without finishing the seven seconds it takes to die. In short, you're living the first few days of your undead life while you're actually still dying. That's why you're crazy. You'll get even crazier if you ever meet yourself. You must stay away for anywhere you've been during the time you were there and don't do anything you've already done at the time you did it. If you don't stay functional that changeling baby, whose medical mysteries are already beyond my skill sets, although he seems to be adapting, that little boy could turn into an oak piano leg if you don't keep it together."

But I only heard one thing. "Is there someone you could recommend that treats crazy vampires?"

"There is, but you won't listen to him."

"John Simons?" It was my best guess.

"No, you. Maybe not you now, but you in the future."

"I don't think I'd be very helpful to myself."

"I'm inclined to agree."

"Then why did you hunt me down like this?"

"Two reasons. One, I can give you a clue. Baby John-Peter ate an incredible amount of food; maybe seven or eight times what a normal child consumes. You gave his mother a miniature leprechaun and the consumption decreased to double or triple. Two, I'm passing your phone number to someone that contacted me. She's a psychologist in your future, and she's making an appointment that she claims you need to keep. Try not to make her crazy, too."

"Does this psychologist have a name?"

"None that she'd give me. Call me in a couple days to make an appointment for your checkup."

The phone went dead.

By the time I got to the beginning of the fourth route, it was eleven-fifteen and I was too tired to throw a temper tantrum. I delivered. All the while though, I had my eye on the clock. This route was mostly the driveways of urban sprawl, straight with uniform addresses. I still had to read and drive, but I wasn't having to back up or turn around much, so I made time.

Again, the phone rang.

"Ed, this is the Goddess. Are you still out there?"

"Yes, for another forty-five minutes. If Robert hadn't called, I'd be quitting around one, but he said noon, so I'm not going to argue with him about that. He wants police reports."

"Don't worry about it. I just got off the phone with John Simons, and we agreed that you have too much going on right now. We'll get our money's worth, so don't worry. Everyone will be at work tomorrow if we have to rent cars to do it. We'll be getting reimbursed."

A load fell from my shoulders. I told her as much.

"Try not to worry," the Goddess reassured me.

I resisted asking her if she'd reconsider meeting me with a stake and mallet in her hand. Instead, I told her that I was going to speak to a psychologist about my problem. She, thinking I was joking, responded with a polite laugh.

I was fifteen minutes on when the phone rang again.

"Mr. Calkins," a feminine voice said with an accusing tone. "This is Dr. Roslyn, a therapist, calling from the year 2020. You have an appointment with me tomorrow, at one o'clock from my perspective or twelve years and two months and a week or two from yours. I'm calling because you really need to keep that appointment or refund the money. If you fail to be there, it might well be the things you do in the days to follow…again from your perspective. I understand you're losing it right now. Is that true?"

"I am going through a hard time…"

"I could care less. Are you going to kill yourself? If you are, you can't because you have to be there as I don't think you can leave me the money you owe in your will. Oh, does my communication lack empathy? Let me rephrase. I hope you're miserable. I hope you're overloaded will unresolved issues causing pain and guilt, but you realized that as much as you want to stake yourself. Yet you can't because you owe a therapist money for the work she did."

"Wow, I thought I'd be a terrible therapist."

"You'd be the worst."

"Do we…"

"…know each other? Trudy's dream. I cross-examined you

on the witness stand."

"But that wasn't real."

"Of course it wasn't real. You're crazy. Half the things you do aren't real, the other half is just plain stupid. It amazes me anyone could stand you enough to bite you and make you a vampire. That's why I'm calling. Don't do anything stupid, or you'll be a deadbeat as well as an asshole."

"What are you suggesting I do to be less stupid, crazy, or less of an asshole?"

"If you followed your own advice, you'd take lysergic acid diethylamide"

"LSD? I'm not taking that again!"

"Of course, you're not," she retorted, then balked. "Wait, you've had it before?"

"Yes. Once when I was young, to impress a girl. I'm never going near the stuff again."

"Bad trip? Not that I care."

"No, loved it. If I ever did it again…I'm afraid I would do it all the time."

"Well, you prescribe it all the time in limerick form…

> *A psychotic is never pain free.*
> *And that's why you have come to see me.*
> *Please excuse all my candor*
> *But you need delusions of grandeur*
> *And for that I prescribe LSD."*

"I wrote that?"

"What other nut case would write a prescription like that? In fact, you wrote your whole thesis of DTP in a series of limericks."

Something wasn't adding up. Was I not listening to her, or was I not understanding her? I asked a different question and wished I didn't.

"How would LSD help me now?"

"Let's see you answer your own question. When you took LSD last, how did you feel?"

"Wise! Very wise…as if everything were clear to me. Nothing confused me. Almost as if I'd been whacked on the head with that 'clarity wand' that the Goddess presented, and you objected to in Trudy's dream."

"And what do you think would happen if you took this LSD all the time?"

"I would lose touch with reality...I see things that weren't there...believe things that are not true...I'd....OK, I see your point. I'm already a psychotic, why not feel better about it? The thing is, I don't need LSD for delusions of grandeur; I only need my imagination. But, if I prescribed LSD for myself, why do I need to see you?"

"You idiot! I'm not your therapist, I'm your patient!"

"I'm hardly qualified to do therapy. I've barely a bachelor's degree from a no-name college.

"Isn't that funny?" Her voice was full of irony. "I've got PHDs in four subjects from Yale, but I don't have a penis, nor do I have a license or clientele."

"Yes, but didn't you go to jail for violating the trust invested in that license when you had it?"

"Men get away with it all the time."

As she continued talking, she filled me in in with the backstory of this unlikely conversation. Trudy sought therapy from Dr. Roslyn after Dr. Roslyn got out of prison for her relationship with a different underage patient, but Trudy never paid the agreed amount. If fact, she never paid at all, which, in my opinion, was what the therapy was worth. Somehow, that was partly my fault. In addition, Dr. Roslyn got into trouble again with another underaged girl that she had no license to treat. That was the fault of society, but it was mainly the fault of men. With the prospect of going to jail, she found a network application that I wrote that connects vampires with victims and became a vampire with DTP, which stands for Deep Time Psychosis, as she contracted it trying to kill the two girls before they got Dr. Roslyn two prison terms. I was clearly at fault for that.

"So, you have to treat me," she insisted. "First of all, you owe me since your friend never paid me for my services. Secondly, you're the only vampire that treats vampire mental health issues. You did promise me you would."

"God help us all!" I gasped. Then I wondered. "Does it help?"

"The LSD or the therapy?"

"Well both…or either. Does it help at all?"

"No, you bonehead. I'm just calling fourteen years in my past to waste a little time on a moron! Yes, it helps. No, I don't want to admit it. And yes, I want you to win at the duel you're going to have with Trudy twelve years ago, but if you don't win, use your dying breath to tell her she's gotta pay up."

The phone hung up as if it never rang.

By now, it was closer to one then noon, but I was still delivering. At first, I just assumed that it was me not being willing to leave a route I started unfinished, but when I did finish, I found myself starting the last route. I was being compelled against my will again! Why? Why would anyone but me care if the last route got done or not? Even the subscribers didn't care at this point.

I tried to stop, but I couldn't. All trying did was slow me down. Damn, was every day going to be like this one? I don't need a stake to go to hell.

It was after 4 p.m. when I threw the last paper. I was tired, hungry, and still had more work to do. I wouldn't be able to nap until I reassured myself that I was making progress on John Simon's little mandate. But as I sat my butt on the computer chair to check for recent documents, I started to reflect. The reflection felt like it wanted to become a dream.

CHAPTER 18: KINGDOM OF THE DAMNED, PART III

I started learning how to write computer programs years ago because I thought it would make me feel smart. That's really all I ever wanted. The irony is, though I quickly found I had an ability for writing useful programs that were faster and cheaper than my competitors made me feel very stupid. My customers and competitors all agreed with me. If I wasn't an idiot, why wasn't I charging more? How many times would I pay for what I learned? Now, John Simons just assumed that, because I could program, I could program artificial intelligence beyond what would be possible for several centuries at best. Why didn't I just stick to newspapers? Now, twelve years from today, I'd be a therapist and all my patients would agree with me; I'm stupid. Crazy, but stupid.

"Be ruthless! You've got to be ruthless."

Nalla was saying that, but her voice sounded like a doorbell.

"Be ruthless! Don't be toothless. You can't be too stupid if you're just too ruthless."

"Nalla, I heard you the first time," I told her.

"Then why haven't you answered the doorbell?"

Nalla wasn't there. It really was the doorbell.

The lobby doorbells of the studio apartments were on the first floor lobby, I could see who was disturbing me from my apartment on the fourth floor. I buzzed without asking who was coming to visit. The whys and hows were always too complicated.

I'm not a very social vampire.

They were at my door as soon as I opened it to meet them in the lobby. Three men wearing brimmed hats and fine silk suits stood humorlessly before me. One held a stake and mallet. Another noticed my staring at these implements and said, "We're here to kill you." The trio looked like a stereotypical mafia hit squad. Somehow, I knew that they were also vampires. Maybe they'd understand.

"Can you come back in three days, I'm really too busy right now?"

They shook their heads, so with a shrug I invited them in.

As if they had done this so many times before, one of them grabbed a chair, the other produced a rope, and the biggest of them invited me to sit.

"Don't you want to know what this is about?" asked the most personable of the group.

I really didn't but I had to hold up my end of the conversation by asking.

"Seems you were at a party last night and offended a dame."

"Yeah, I did."

A smile took my face as I thought of that insult. They returned my smile for the slightest of their own for the briefest of a second before replacing it with a mobster type look of being offended. Mobster faces are so hard to describe. It's like the serious face you'd use to tell someone their grandmother died if you were trying not to laugh about it, and very good at not laughing.

"So, before we kill you, we want to know about your friends in the IVA. We want to know all about them, and we have ways to make you quite chatty."

"I'm guessing you boys owe her a favor, or is it now the other way around?" I asked.

"Let's just say she's good for business."

I wondered what business that was.

The other two men were tying me to the chair, so I thought about my duties as a host. "Can I offer you a beverage?"

One of the men, the one who'd just finished the tying, asked with surprise, "You know we're going to torture you before we kill you, right?"

"But it's nothing personal, right? It's just that I'm bad for business. I saw 'The Godfather' you know…come to think of it, I didn't see the movie, but I read the book."

"Yeah, we're supposed to say that, but I really don't like you," the other admitted.

"Maybe you'd like me better if I offered you a beverage. It will make this whole mafia hit feel more professional."

The third sounded defeated. "Whatdagot?"

Wow! What do mobsters drink? Did I have beer in the refrigerator? I realized with some surprise that it didn't matter what I had a second ago. I had whatever I imagined and right now I needed to imagine big. I remembered the bottle my wife and I had at my twentieth wedding anniversary. The French wine was old when we bought it together when we were just dating. My son tried to convince me before that anniversary. He'd been on the internet, looking at the value of wines from the region that had been aged in the bottle as long as this one. He told me that selling it could net me thousands and that no drinking experience was worth that kind of money. My son is wise, but this time he was wrong. True, the bottle didn't last the evening, whereas the money could be sitting in some savings bond earning more than a hundred dollars every year. But tasting a wine of forty years is an unforgettable memory. Given the choice, I was wise to choose the latter.

"There's a bottle under the cabinet in the bathroom. Bring it out. It hasn't seen the daylight in many years. You'll find a corkscrew on the shelf above the sink."

"That's a lot of trouble for the bottle as cheap as this one can afford." The one not holding the stake and mallet and not retrieving the bottle spat that from the corner of his lips.

"Holy hell!" shouted the guy who went for the bottle. "This wine is fifty years old. How does a guy living in a studio apartment get a hold of something like this?"

"He's a vampire, you moron. Probably stole it from some hundred dollar a plate joint around here!" the guy with the stake shouted back.

I'm was tired of thinking of these guys by where they stood and what they were holding.

"So, my name is Ed Calkins," I started as the guy holding the bottle walked to stand next to the other guy who can now be identified as the guy holding the bottle. "We haven't been introduced."

"What's it to you," said the guy holding nothing. "Are you writing a book?"

I nodded that I was. "Get four wine glasses from the closet."

"You're not going to be drinking with us," the bottle-holding guy told me.

But then the stake and mallet guy got a different idea. "No, he needs to drink first!"

The bottle guy was having trouble with the cork, the same way it happened the first time. When the cork finally came off, the aroma of aged perfection took the air.

"I said drink!" He held the bottle to my lips.

"No!"

"He's trying to poison us!"

"What? Are we barbarians? Let the bottle breath first! And then, pour it in a glass like we have some appreciation for the finer things in life. Are you ever going to introduce yourselves? It's really hard to write a book if you have to describe three almost identical Italians."

"Sicilians!" they corrected in unison.

"I'm Tommie Gun Tony." (the bottle guy)

"They call me Tommie the Tooth." (the wine glasses guy)

Tommie Gun Tony and Tommie the Tooth both looked at the other unnamed Sicilian, waiting for him to amend that.

"I'm Hank," he finally told me. I kept looking at him expecting a nickname.

His brothers seemed to enjoy his discomfort, almost smiling in sadist pleasure.

"My brother doesn't like his nickname," Tommie the Tooth explained. "They call him, Hank the Lobster."

"I think the bottle's had enough air," Hank the Lobster said with a dismissive wave of his clawed hand. "Make him drink."

They did not have to force me. The wine tasted…I really don't know how the wine tasted, because I was really scared even though I'm trying to write like I'm not. But I'm sure it tasted as good as the first time on that twentieth year of being wed. Actually, I was trying to get drunk so as to better endure the torture when it started, which I was going to use every trick to delay.

"More, please. I have to prove that I didn't contaminate the wine with low doses of poison that would only take effect when the proper threshold is reached."

Lobster nodded.

"More but not too much. We don't want our friend here drunk when the conversation starts."

Actually, he was already too late. Though a lifelong beer drinker, I never had much ability to hold it well. I hadn't eaten at all, and I was tired. This compounded with the age of the wine that had elevated the alcohol content exponentially, which was something I hoped they wouldn't realize and get drunk as well.

"Guys! That's fifty-year-old wine!" I complained "Sip and savor. Tell me that's not the best wine you've ever had."

"Hardly fair to say that to prohibition mafia," Tooth shot back. "We died in a gun fight with those other punk guys for Chicago."

"Capone?"

"You got it," Lobster said. We don't like other guys breaking in our action. Now that liquor is legal, we have to stick to other things these days like gambling, prostitution, and loan sharking. Hell, in most states, that stuff is legal, too, but we still control it."

"State casinos and racetracks?"

"We run them." (Tommie Gun)

"Online adult dating?"

"Ours." (Tooth)

"Payday loans."

"Yours truly." (Lobster)

"ABwow. You guys had to reinvent yourselves. Do you ever get to whack anyone like the good old days?"

"Only vampires and other Sicilians," Lobster admitted with something close to sadness.

"Well, I imagine you don't let other vampires in your casinos as time travel makes that an unfair advantage."

"Oh no," Tooth proclaimed. "Vampires are always welcome at our casinos and racetracks, as long as they don't win. Winners are never welcome anywhere. It's not just guys like us. You know, when the stock market crashed in 1929, the number of suicides from the big market players had long lines by high windows, waiting for their turn to jump. A lot of those market players became market playing vampires, and they don't like other vampires winning either."

"Well, all of this was very interesting," Lobster commented.

"But now that we've all had our wine, I think it's time to talk about something else, like why they call him Tommie the Tooth. Give it to him."

"Before we ask any questions?" Tooth sounded surprised. He must have been a little drunk already because he sounded more surprised than almost surprised.

"Why bother waiting?" Tommie Gun Tony asked. "Guys never start talking until the pain starts."

"But haven't I been perfectly cooperative thus far? Give me a chance."

"Ok," Tommie Gun Tony agreed, sounding like he didn't believe I'd cooperate much longer. Producing a pad and pencil from his Italian silk suit pocket, he got in a writing position. "What are the names of your friends in the IVA?"

"Now be patient, please, because in order to answer, I have to ask a question. I know, because I've seen the movies, that you're going to tell me that you ask the questions. Still, I need to be clear. Are you asking me who the other members are of the Irish Vampires Association?"

"Get the pliers." Tony decided.

"And also, tell me that you assume I'm a member of the IVA?"

"Of course you're a member!" Lobster shouted. "Why would we be here if you weren't a member?"

"So, your answer is 'yes'm You believe me to be a member because you've reasoned that I must be, correct?"

"Get the pliers!" (Lobster this time.)

"Why are you in such a hurry to get blood on your expensive suit? I'm going to give you names, but I've got to do the same thing you're doing. I can't be sure who is a member, but I can be sure some people are not. Do you follow?"

"Whatta waiting for, Tony? Start pulling his teeth." (Lobster again.)

Tony's face turned red.

"I forgot the pliers."

Lobster groaned.

"And I don't want to get blood on my suit. Christ, Hank, I haven't got the thing paid off yet...it'll take me three more months. Can I at least keep the new suit smell until its paid for?"

275

"I have pliers," I told him. "But I don't have expensive suits."

I didn't have pliers and wouldn't unless I imagined them. That always is a problem, though. Try not to think of pears. If you remember what not to think of, you're thinking it. If I remember what not to imagine…"

"He does have an expensive suit," Tony the Tooth was already in my closet. It's hard to hide anything you're trying not to imagine in a studio apartment.

"Did you find the pliers?" I called back to him.

"No!"

"Top draw left side of the dresser."

"How the hell does this guy afford a suit that fits me and not him?" the Tooth cried in frustration. "Aren't we the ones that are supposed to live the high life?"

"He doesn't have an expensive house, car, boat, or gun." Lobster shouted back. "Find the damn pliers before he dies of old age."

"I'll tell you something else I don't have that you have, Hank the Lobster. I don't have debt."

"What-do-ya mean you don't have debt? Everybody has debt. What about your van? I mean, you had to have a house before you died. What about your loans on the house? Didn't you ever go out to eat? What about that? Clothes, food, tools…they all cost money. How do you buy those things without borrowing money?" Tommie was incredulous.

"Everything was paid."

"Hey, nobody has so much money that they don't owe anything expect the big bosses that loan you money." Lobster insisted.

"I found the pliers!" Tooth called.

"Good!" the three of us shouted in unison.

"But it's the wrong kind!"

"What kind do you need?" I called. "Needle nose pliers?"

"Yeah!"

"Same dresser, one drawer lower."

"I can't find it….wait. Got it!"

"Why do you borrow so much money?" I asked Lobster.

Tommie started laughing. The wine had done its work.

"They don't call my little brother 'lobster' for nothing. The guy has it with every meal. Hank is always spending more than he could ever make. Every couple of days, he's gotta go get another payday loan from the boss to pay the last loan."

"I get really good rates," Lobster proclaimed defensively. "I get the employee discount and the family discount. I only pay two percent."

"Wow, that is good. When I had a mortgage, I paid nine percent annually."

"Yeah, we don't care about your sex life." Tommie gun fired.

"No, I mean I paid nine percent interest every year, compounded quarterly. What did you mean?"

"Wow, why do you even work?" Hank marveled. "My loans are two percent daily, compounded daily. It's a good thing I'm never gonna have to pay because I'll never make the kind of money I owe. Good thing I'm in the mafia. It only forecloses if you screw up."

Tommie Gun looked depressed. "Seems like the boss upstairs got us working till we get whacked. I'd love to quit, but I can't afford it....that's everyone, right?"

"I got it!" Tooth announced, holding up the pliers.

"I got it, too." I told them. "Check this out.

A spending Mafia hitman name Hank
Whose plush lifestyle's too rich for a bank
Said his loan sharking mobsters
Hank will sleep with those lobsters
If ever his earnings should tank.

"Very funny," Lobster said, making clear it wasn't. "Pull the wise guy's teeth."

"But I'm going to give you names…"

"How will we know they're the real names?" (Lobster again).

"You'll know better than anyone if they're real or not. Once you start pulling teeth, I might not be able to enunciate."

I was running out of time and answers. Tommie the Tooth lunged forward to do his work. I think he was about to tell me to open wide, but someone caught his attention.

Glorna! He was holding a pistol in each hand.

"I know what you're thinking. Did he fire six shots or only five? Well do ya, punk?"

It wasn't a bad imitation of Dirty Harry, just to the wrong spectators. It didn't help that he muffed the lines either.

"Oh, how cute!" said Tommie Gun Tony with thinly forced fondness. "He's got a cap gun, and he wants to play cops and robbers."

The Lobster was impatient.

"Scram, wood sprite! We're too busy to play!"

How did they see Glorna when Henry Mathews could not? I had a theory that drew on my prejudice against Irish Americans. Maybe I could use it…if I could just count on Glorna to be Glorna.

"Put the guns down," I told him. "I need you to work, not play. Start answering Jake Noble's emails for me. After that, you can print the route lists."

To my anguish, Glorna did something he never had done before. I could see he wasn't happy about it, but he did it anyway. I'd have been dumbstruck trying to understand why if I hadn't been so mortified and scared.

He did what I told him to do.

I told him to put the guns down because I wanted him to do anything but that. It never failed before.

Glorna was already on the computer reading my passwords from the paper taped to the screen when Tommie the Tooth picked the pistols up where a deflated Glorna had left them.

"Cap guns!" he cried. "I'd give them to my kids if I weren't a vampire."

"44s you moron!" Tommie Gun Tony admonished as he opened the chamber. "Look, silver bullets. The wood sprite had the jump on us. He could have been a problem if the genius over here hadn't told the little guy to put them away."

Through all of this, Tommie Gun Tony hadn't put his notebook or pencil away. It laid near his now empty wine glass. I nodded towards it.

"You better write this down now because I can't talk when I'm getting my teeth pulled. There are five very important ways to tell who's not an IVA member."

Hank the Lobster didn't like it.

"Just pull the old man's teeth out already. He can talk when you're done."

"And your fine suit will be full of blood." I told Tommie the Tooth.

"Give it a minute." The Tooth told the Lobster.

"Jesus!" Lobster moaned. "Getting you to pull teeth is like pulling teeth."

Tommie Gun picked up his pad. "Start talking. Five ways…"

"Yes, first anyone can join the IVA even if they don't think they're a vampire. They just have to think they're Irish, which isn't helpful here. Second, every IVA member is also an office holder, holding whatever office he or she thinks should belong to him or her. The budget for that office is the same as the members' dues, which also isn't helpful. Third, the member must initiate him or herself and tell no one about it or that he or she is a member. If someone should say something, he is immediately expelled, which is helpful because anyone who says he is a member, isn't. Fourth, a member must never hurt or kill anyone he suspects might be another IVA member. The Irish Vampires Association loves whacking a vampire as much as any other vampire association, but we have so few targets since anyone could be a member."

"What's the fifth thing?" Tooth asked.

Actually, I couldn't remember. Instead I told him that I had to save something of importance for when the torture started. Somewhere north of me, I could hear the printer popping out the route lists that I told Glorna to start.

Glorna, please do something disruptive like you always do.

"Based on those four things, I think we can start the tooth pulling," Tommie Gun concluded. "Open wide, crazy old man!"

"Maybe we should ask for names first." (Tooth)

"As I so patiently explained, I can't tell you for sure who is a member. I can only tell you for sure who is not a member. Or I could tell you three names of who I strongly suspect are members…but I really don't want to do that."

The Lobster jumped on that. "Tell us or else!"

"Or else what?" Tommie gun questioned. "We already told the guy we're going to pull his teeth before killing him. Actually, he seems too drunk to feel much pain anyway. Maybe we should come back when he's hung over."

The Lobster agreed. "Yeah, maybe we'll do that if he tells us the names he doesn't want to say."

I didn't believe him, nor did I really think that I was so drunk I wouldn't feel my teeth getting pulled. The only thing left to do was pull their leg.

"Names!" Tooth shouted.

"OK, OK…get ready to write this down…but please don't ask me to spell anything…."

"Names! Now!"

I don't know who said that.

"Tommie the Tooth, Tommie Gun Tony, and Hank the Lobster."

"Wise guy! Pull his teeth Tommie!"

"Why don't you do it this time, Tony? I don't want to get blood on my suit."

I tried to sound confident, but I doubt my voice didn't squeak a little as I tried to lay out a case as to how all the evidence pointed to the three of them being members of the Irish Vampires Association. I pointed out that Tooth forgot his pliers and though they had already been here almost an hour, none of them harmed me. In fact, it seemed to me that they were waiting for each other to start, so they could know which one wasn't an IVA member and whom to whack. I also pointed out that Glorna was about to kill them, but I stopped him because I thought they all belonged to the IVA.

"There's a flaw in your logic, wise guy." Lobster broke in. "We are family, my brothers and I. Family members don't whack family."

"Except for Joey," Tony admitted.

"Yeah, expect for Joey…but Joey was a fink and a tattletale." (Lobster)

"Which is how you knew he wasn't an IVA member," I pointed out. "IVA members have to be able to keep a secret. For all I know, each one of you is initiating yourself right now and the president of the IVA might be in this very room…or not. We'll never know."

"There's another problem for you, wise guy." Tommie the Tooth had one of those half smiles that vanished before it froze on his face. "Me and the boys don't think we're Irish, we know we're

Sicilians. There are two kinds of people in the world…"

"Those with a gun, and those who dig!" Glorna shouted.

I was hoping for a better disruption than that.

"No! Those who are Sicilian and those who wish they were Sicilian." Tommie Gun Tony finished proudly.

"Actually," I interjected mildly. "There's only one kind of people in the world; those that are a wee bit Irish."

"Bull! Our mother was Sicilian, and our father was Sicilian…one hundred percent, end of story." Tooth looked to Tommie Gun for confirmation. "Right?"

"Of course right. Hank?"

But as Tommie Gun was asking, Lobster had picked up the two pistols on the table, pointing one at each brother.

"Papa and Mama were both Sicilians, but the milkman was Irish," he told them.

"Oh, get off it, Hank. That doesn't prove anything. Mama wasn't that kind of girl." (Tooth)

"Really? Papa had so many dollies. Do you think he had time for Mama?"

Tommie Gun added, "Remember when Papa died? Mama cried for three months."

Hank gave that half vanishing smile. "Do you remember when the milkman retired?"

"She didn't cry at all."

"But she started buying cucumbers that she never cooked with."

They both did a verse of screaming and covering their ears. They didn't want to hear that, but Lobster still had a gun turned on each of them.

"Careful, Hank," I warned him. "There are a lot of Irish milkmen throughout the long parade of time."

"Get of it, wise guy," Tommie gun insisted. "You're just trying to save your skin."

"Actually, I'm trying to save yours. All three of you guys saw Glorna the wood sprite. Do Sicilians believe in wood sprites? I know the Irish do."

The three of them thought for a long time. Glorna was finished with printing the route lists.

"Can I go now?"

Of course, he could.

"So what happens now that we seem to all be members of the...."

I lifted a finger in caution.

"Might be members."

"Yeah, might be members that just initiated ourselves without telling each other about it and standing in front of someone we couldn't kill because he is probably part of the IVA. If that were true, what would we probably do?"

Does it matter which one said that? I hope not because I was too scared or drunk, if not too crazy, to know. I pointed out that the three of them could be sure that the boss who put them up to the hit was not a member of the IVA and therefore fair game. So also the dame, whose name I learned was Mary Steward, was not a member if she paid for the hit. If that were the case and I was a member, I would likely want to deal with her myself. As far as the boss upstairs, who held all their debt, they would want to do him themselves, assuming of course they were members. Either way, nobody would be so brave as to avenge that boss because if three Sicilian brothers could be IVA members, anyone could.

I must have fallen asleep.

When I awakened, I was still in the chair, but I wasn't tied to it. There were pliers on the table, but no bottle, glasses, or guns. The route lists were printed, but the emails were answered with less than polite words. I had all my teeth, but I didn't feel drunk.

Maybe the Irish-Sicilian brothers were too polite to wake me, but they untied me, tidied up, and took the 44s with silver bullets to finish a different job. Maybe the whole thing never happened, and I printed the lists in a half sleep, answering emails with harsh honesty that I'm always careful not to show.

Maybe it didn't matter.

CHAPTER 19: THE ROAD TRIP CONTINUES

Trudy's last wakeful moments held a foggy dull wonder as to why the paralyzing depressive cloud failed to descend on her as it promised. Bathrobe was still among the missing, as was his 44 and the bullets for that and her service revolver, but then again, there was too much of a fog to test Rick's theory that it was she who hid both from herself.

Fog thickened like some demonic curse around the bed Bathrobe shared with her when he allowed it. That bed began to spin in proportion to the thick fog's acceleration like a muscle car that lost its traction. Spinning, spinning, spinning…waiting for someone or something to hit while the air around her was too thick to see or breath, yet she was calm.

Suddenly, the spinning stopped without the car. Not so with the fog. That gently reduced, granting sparse glimpses of yellow and bright. The convertible she drove found freedom and needed no words to explain itself. The straight narrow road invented an independence born of hot empty skies too sunny to be blue and all, but black road was yellow sand down a flat horizon. All road, no questions.

Then, without reason, the car started to slow. By the time it stopped, she knew it was right for the lone sign to the road's right. "Tavern" it read, but there was writing under it that she could not yet read. There was no need to pull to the side of the road. First there was no road, then no convertible.

Standing under the sign, she could now read the words that looked handwritten and misplaced.

"Courthouse what awards for the killin' a Ed Calkins. The honorable goat an judge Arkiens presiding."

She knew where she was and felt ready. She was younger today, maybe in her early twenties, but dressed in that same waist-pinching western costume she had worn the last time she was here. Her colt 45 was holstered at her hip and, somehow, she was sure it was loaded.

She busted in, doors swinging behind her. The bar and patrons were the same, save the high energy of the place. Old men were hooting and hollering as if they were watching a burlesque show some thirty years before now. Glorna, who looked still like Clint, only more like a young man then a boy, was already at the bar drinking. Was that whiskey? What a difference a day makes.

Trudy took a seat next to him. Without breaking his gaze, he pointed to where the mirrors had been. Now they were one hole in three walls and a ceiling. In the open air was a modern courtroom complete with fourteen or fifteen lawyers snapping at each other while pleading their case to the ancient man seated at the judge's bench.

"Trial," Glorna told her. "Yours, mine, and some others."

The bar crowd cheered at every thinly veiled insult. Other than that, no one seemed to understand anything the attorneys were saying, and that included the man on the bench.

"Your Honor, I beg you to call order," said a bailiff-looking fella above the lawyers' shouting match. In the chaos of this court, only the loud voices could be heard over the other interruptions. Someone threw a high heeled shoe.

"I'm not an honor. I just took this open seat because it was close to the action," the one man said shrugging. The smile did not leave his face.

Glorna continued. "The other defendants are John Simons…"

A tall forbidding figure dressed in a fine Victorian suit appeared as Glorna pointed him out. The man looked every bit a vampire. He peered around the barroom as if owned it and expected someone to serve him a drink.

"…Jake Noble…"

Trudy turned to see a modern suit with Jake stuffed into it. He was glaring at her, not breaking eye contact even as he downed a shot.

"Some unnamed poacher…"

A short, Latin man with a thin beard sat straight at the bar, drank nothing, and talked to no one.

"And you and me," Glorna finished.

Then, a terrifying sight silenced lawyer and spectator alike as a black robe glided into the courtroom. Inside that robe was a goat face with malicious red eyes. Trudy was about to reassure Glorna that the judge wasn't the devil, but Glorna whispered first about who he was and what a were-goat is.

The old man sitting on the judge's bench shivered, too fearful to move. He seemed to disappear as the honorable Arkiens mounted the bench.

"Court will come to order!" the bailiff-looking fellow sang, but it already had; the stunned lawyers were too scared to speak.

Arkiens gave the courtroom a once over, as if trying to get his bearings. Once he had, he addressed the startled court and the barroom beyond.

"This is not a criminal trial," he told the lawyers. "This courtroom, what isn't supposed to be in the western states before they be states, is only here cause a Trudy's dream. The court is supposed ta decide if some soul gets the prize for killin me buddy, Ed Calkins, so ya doesn't need all the fancy talk an dress ta try defendin' your criminals cause they be contestants, but I thank ya fer your effort. I be the judge what needs ta decide if they be 'nough proof what says they killed Ed Calkins an deserve the prize…"

Arkiens reached below his beach and held a noose out for all to see. "…ta be hung as a hero fer killing me buddy, Ed Calkins."

No one moved, spoke, or otherwise reacted.

"I be sorry fer my appearance," Arkiens continued. "But it's Trudy's dream, not mine, and she dreams a full moon what changes me into a goat, which means I doesn't read till I be a leprechaun again. I thank ya fer your briefs, I found em very tasty. I don't haf the belly ta finish all of em, but I'll be sure ta finish the lot as soon as the moon comes up full again."

His eyes fell on the sixteen lawyers that sat four to a table, each for the four defendants that Arkiens referred to as contestant.

"Not a Irishman among ya. Does ya know the Stateside joke about why there be no Irish lawyers in the U.S.? Does ya?"

No one answered.

"Can't pass th' bar, they can't."

Arkiens giggled by himself. He seemed to notice that once he stopped giggling.

"In my courtroom, when th' judge tells a joke, the lawyers laugh."

Arkiens waved his hand, and all the lawyers disappeared. With another wave, each of the "contestants" were sitting on the first seat of a different table. With a third wave, each had another at their table.

"I don't much like lawyers," Arkiens explained. "But I think what each person wif a claim in me courtroom should has a advocate… what means a buddy ta speak fer them so th' truth comes out, ya know."

Arkiens went on to introduce each advocate as he pointed left to right, from his perspective.

"Advocatin fer John Simons be his lovely wife, Melissa, what failed ta marry me buddy but got bitten by th' same vampire that mighta bitten Ed Calkins, he mighta. If Melissa can prove it, John Simons wins th' prize, he does."

"Advocatin' fer Jake Noble, his good buddy what causes a whole bunch o' trouble as a' important fancy police guy, Vito Vermon, what likes ta be spanked. Jake been known ta cause trouble wif his knife an it be a fact that he was there around th' time what Ed Calkins died. If Vito can prove that it be Jake what puts the knife in Ed Calkins' belly, then Jake wins the prize."

Jake snarled. Vito blushed.

"Advocatin fer Glorna th' wood spite be his good pixie buddy, Aodhan what loves a good adventure an claims that Glorna be the one what puts the knife in Ed Calkins' belly, but doesn't remember cause he be 'compelled' by Ed Calkins himself, what be the vampire what bites him. Seems a lot to prove ta me, but Aodhan is a pixie what loves a challenge, he does."

"Advocatin' fer Trudy, what the judge fancies but she refused, is Dr. Roslyn, who is not a doctor anymore, but she be a lesbian, what used ta mean she be what lives on th' island a Lesbos, but now it means she like women an girls instead of fellas. She fancies Trudy, too, but she gots her where the judge got kicked in th' jewels what Dr. Roslyn doesn't has. She claims that Trudy shot Ed Calkins with a pistol from more than five hundred steps by me goat's feet what the judge doubts, but if the doctor can prove it, Trudy wins th prize. The judge notes that Trudy was there at the time, but she can't remember a reason what would explain wantin ta kill Ed Calkins, what was her best buddy, he was.

"An finally, advocatin' fer the unnamed hunter, what is too poor fer a name an comes from an unknown country is Ed Calkins own son, Ricky, what has a different last name. Rick claims that his hunter friend was shootin fer some deer meat, but missed an shot his father. If Rick can prove that, he still has ta argue why his hunter should get the prize when killin' might not mean if ya shoot someone what ya doesn't mean ta. I'll keep an open mind, I will.

"Now, doesn't ya advocates think ya be callin all kind a witnesses. The judge has no patience fer long an borin questions what doesn't prove anythin' except advocates like ta hear themselves talk. This be Trudy's dream an th' judge hasta has a decision by th time she wakes, he does, so I be calling th only witness I be needing ta hear from an I be askin the most important questions fer ya. I call Ed Calkins to the stand, I does."

With the wave of his hand, Ed Calkins appeared in the witness box, unnerved and dressed in a kilt. He scratched his white hair and stroked his white beard, which was reduced from the "Santa" beard length he wore around Christmas.

"Bailiff lookin fella, swear th witness in," the judge commanded. "An remember he speaks what language that be mixin' the letters an words…"

"Dyslexic?" he suggested.

"That be th one."

"Do I swear to tell the truth, the whole truth, and nothing but the truth, so help you dog?" the bailiff-looking fella asked.

"You do."

But Eddie didn't look so sure. He looked less sure when the judge reminded him that he could be charged with perjury if he told a lie, which means he could never do business in Ireland again unless it was after English was spoken there. He seemed more confident when Arkiens asked him to describe what happen to him on April 5th, 2007 at four a.m. on Tomas Street in unincorporated Beulah

County.

Eddie responded that he couldn't be sure as he was having a very bad day. First, he was stabbed by someone, then he was shot, and after that, he was drained of his blood…all of that happened after he was dead. Eddie admitted that it was very likely that he got the order of things mixed up, including any number of years, but he did remember being dead and still being very upset about a paper he delivered mistakenly. Eddie started in about the paper, the wrong address, and how mad at himself he was that he couldn't get a simple thing right.

"That be all very upsettin,'" Arkiens told him. "But we doesn't care about a paper. We cares bout the shootin and stabben and bitin. Does ya know who bites ya?"

"I don't know that anyone bit me. I do remember John Simons saying everything was going to be OK. I was already dead though. That's the how I remember it."

"Does ya know who stabbed ya?"

"No. I only know I was stabbed. I think my wallet was taken. The joke's on the bloke that got no more than a dead man's driver's license."

"Does ya know who shot ya?"

"I do not, but I would swear I was dead before any of those things happened. I must have reanimated every time. I was having a bad day."

"Does ya think any a the contestants has a reason ta kills ya?"

"No."

"Well," Arkiens concluded. "Can ya tell us anythin' that might get one a our contestants th' prize?"

"No."

Arkiens was satisfied.

"I be settin ta dismiss the claim to the prize based a what th witness ha been saying. Any objections?"

The judge looked to Melissa first, who shook her head. Vito also declined as did Rick. Arkiens waved his hand and the declining advocates along with their clients disappeared. Only Aodhan and Dr. Roslyn wanted to question the witness further.

Aodhan was given the first go at Eddie and go he did. A pixie, like a spite or brownie, can be any size he or she chooses at the moment, but mostly they chose the size of a wasp or bee when humans are around. It makes it easier to hide and, in the case of a winged pixie, they can be mistaken for something else. When near human size, whether male or female, they're considered attractive by almost all species of people that prefer the pixie's gender. Trudy knew, though wasn't sure how, the importance of not swatting at winged creatures when passing through an enchanted prairie. While pixies love to annoy others, they are quick to take offense to disrespect. One does not want to offend a pixie. They retaliate; that's true enough; moreover it's really about the fun that might have you if you don't offend them, and they commodore you into an adventure.

But Aodhan wanted to stare Eddie down and did so as might a Marine drill sergeant, that is, a Marine the size of a hummingbird with fairylike wings that fluttered as delicately as his near falsetto voice. Nonetheless, he pronounced his contempt, putting his nose and hostile stare within an inch of Eddie's.

The judge would have none of it.

"Th' advocate what tries ta be a pain will quit it!" Arkiens proclaimed with a pound of his gavel. "Keep respectful distance fer th witness what ya tries to intimidate."

The pixie did fly backward but kept his hostile gaze and spoke in a voice that a bad actor might use to call out a villain.

"Isn't it true, oh Steward of Tara, that you are known throughout the realm as a vampire and liar?"

Eddie was taken back.

"I am a vampire," he admitted.

"But you haven't answered my question," Aodhan turned to the barroom audience as he made his theatrical protests. "The court is not interested in your personal observations. You should answer the question asked. Are you known throughout the realm as a vampire and a liar? It's a simple question. Yes, you are or no, you are not?"

"I am known by some to be a vampire. I am known by none to be a liar." Eddie tried to sound certain.

"May I remind you that you are under oath. If you lie on the stand, none in the Irish realm will ever do business with you again. Are you going to change your answer?"

"No!"

"One would expect a vampire of your high standing to

realize that if part of the statement if false the whole statement is untrue. Is your sworn testimony no and no again?"

"No...er yes." Eddie stammered as his ears reddened. Any that knew him also knew that Eddie was a hair trigger away from rage when his ears reddened.

"I've asked three questions of you, but you've given me five answers. Please stop trying to be difficult, and this time answer all three question honestly. The first question: 'Are you known throughout the realm as a vampire and liar?' What is your answer?"

"No!"

"Then you're changing your answer?"

Eddie jumped to his feet.

"I have not changed my answer! Anyone with ears and a mind knows this!"

"Really? Does 'I am a vampire' sound like another word for 'no'? What if I asked you if you'd like some tea? Does 'I am a vampire' tell me whether to brew a cup or not?"

The gavel slammed!

"Pur seed wif ya case!" the judge demanded. "An th witless should sit down. I will not haf tomfoolery in me courtroom as I doesn't care 'bout fancy words trippin me buddy all crazy like."

Eddie seemed to understand that "witless" meant "witness" and did sit down but his ears were now bright red.

Aodhan deeply bowed in midair.

"Forgive me, your Honor. I know that time and the dignity of the court are wasted on this disreputable witness who has already lied under oath, so I'll get to my point."

Then turning to Eddie, he asked in a recriminating voice, "Why did you bite my client?"

"I didn't bite Glorna!"

"Did I ask if you bit my client? I did not. I asked you why you bit my client as you appear to lie every time you speak! I'm not going to waste the court's time with your perjury! Why did you bite Glorna? Surely a wood sprite's blood isn't all that tasty to a human vampire. Why did you bite my client?"

Eddie didn't answer, but Trudy could see the wheels in his head spinning. It was a warning that should prepare all for a scathing limerick.

"Well?"

Aodhan is an insolate pixie,
Whose court antics are whistling dixie
He makes people mad....

The gavel sounded, shattering the room.
"No limericks in me court!"
Eddie seemed to calm a little. Actually, he looked relieved.
"Sorry, your honor…and thanks. That would have been the worst ever, and I wouldn't want to do my worst in the presence of a true poet." Eddie nodded at Trudy without easing the frost between them. She understood that the duel was still on. "But I must object. The advocate is begging the question."
"Witnesses can't object!" Aodhan objected. "Besides, begging questions isn't against any laws."
All eyes went to the judge, awaiting his ruling. The court found silence as Arkiens seemed to reach a breaking point. A full minute passed before his eyes fell on Trudy.
"Hard ta believe a dream wif you in it would be a nightmare, it is. Did ya haf ta dream a full moon, did ya? I be haf as smart in goat form an I can't follow the fancy words an objections a th' court.
The judge sighed and looked to Aodhan, almost pleading. "Can ya explain yer case wif out askin me buddy any more questions, I wonder? I don't want ta grow old waitin fer a point."
Aodhan was happy to comply.
"My theory is simple. Ed Calkins bit his client so he could compel him to do his bidding. Evidence of that was the fact that Glorna agreed to be imprisoned in a leprechaun oak wood late model unit impersonating a human boy for as long as that boy lived. What wood sprite in his right mind would agree to live inside a robot? Glorna, who has a proven record of honesty, claims he murdered Ed Calkins for being too ruthless, but he doesn't remember more than that. Why he doesn't is explained by the vampire that compelled him. Ed Calkins, however, proved he's a liar when he testified under oath that he couldn't think of a reason why any of the contestants would want to kill him, which is obviously false for a vampire that imagined several entire races of people, let alone a time in Tara with no humans. He should be able to imagine just about anything. He further perjured himself when he claimed that no one knew him as a liar, when the advocate himself did."

"Well then, if ya be finished, Aodhan , I'll be thinkin it over. Ya make a compelin' case, ya does. Is th' doctor what isn't really a doctor ready ta question the witless ….er witness?"

Dr. Roslyn stood up, masking her anger at her introduction.

"Ready, your honor."

Trudy knew how much she resented having to suck up to legal authority.

"Mr. Calkins," she began. "How long have you been a pervert?"

Eddie's ears got red again. He paused a minute then tried to answer calmly. "About a decade after you."

"Yes, Mr. Calkins, but this isn't about me, this is about you. You're the one my client killed, and she should be getting a medal for it, shouldn't she? You, and guys like you, are the reason for not just her alcoholism and depression. Guys like you pretend to be her friend and then at the first vulnerable moment, you strike. You bed her and then leave her without ever looking back at the pain you caused. So I ask again, how long have you been a pervert?"

Eddie threw his hands up.

"I don't know how to answer. What makes me a pervert - wanting to have sex with your client?"

"In part," Dr Roslyn asserted.

The gavel sounded.

"Wait jus a minute, doctor what isn't a doctor. If wantin sex wif th contestant is perversion… well it seem ta me that be everyone what is here in me courtroom. Ya gotta go wif a different line, ya does."

Dr. Roslyn was clearly annoyed. With great effort, she gathered herself and redirected.

"Mr. Calkins, would you describe yourself as a friend of my client?"

"Yes!"

"Just a friend, not a lover?'

"No, we are not lovers."

"Mr. Calkins, how many times have you had sex with my client?"

"Objection!" Trudy had enough.

"Lassie," Arkiens informed her gently. "Ya can dream anythin' ya does, but ya can't be objectin ta yer own advocate.

Objection overruled, what mean th advocate can pro seed. Answer th' question, me buddy."

"Once or twice," Eddie admitted.

"Well, which is it? Was it once or twice?"

Eddie sighed. "Both times we were pretty drunk and not alone. Things got hot and heavy with a small group, like a small Roman orgy. Her story is that it was twice. I disagree. In that the second time, by her reckoning, I had already gone to work by the time the clothes started to peal."

"But you're not known as much of a drinker, are you, Mr. Calkins."

"No."

"But the first time, you did drink, didn't you? You drank so she would drink. You were trying to get my client drunk so you could have her!"

Dr. Roslyn slammed her fist on her table to underscore her point.

"No."

"And the second time, you let her drink so much, hoping that she wouldn't remember. YOU RAPED HER, Mr. Calkins, didn't you?"

"Of COURSE not!"

The gavel sounded hard.

"Please, me ears. Ya doesn't haf ta shout, I be six goat feet away from ya. Bof a ya calm down. Ya can pro seed wif a different line when ya can ask a question in normal conversational volume, not like ya be shoutin a war cry from the bottom of a jug."

"Very well," Dr. Roslyn allowed, though clearly, she didn't want to. With a visible effort to compose herself, she looked again on her witless witness.

"Mr. Calkins, is your 'friend' Trudy a good shot?"

"Yes."

"And given that she was there the same time you were shot, would you be willing to admit that even though she was five hundred feet away, she could have pumped a bullet in your head, just the way that someone obviously had?"

"I'll admit she could have. I'm just insisting she had no reason to do so!"

"Mr. Calkins, could you please tell the court what happened

293

the day you won the lottery?"

Trudy was on her feet ready to object in a number of ways, but the bailiff looking fella was on her before she could disrupt the proceedings.

"I plead the fifth on grounds I may incriminate myself." Eddie said unhappily.

Dr. Roslyn, looking pleased with herself, informed Eddie that he couldn't plead the fifth because he wasn't on trial. Arkiens told him the same thing after rebuking Dr. Roslyn that this was his courtroom, and he made the rules.

"Th witless will answer th' question," Arkiens decided with a bang of his gavel. "Tell th' court what happened th day what you won th' lottery."

Eddie looked like he wanted the ground to swallow him. "I will not."

"But ya hasta. Th' judge what rules ya did can charge ya wif contempt of court if ya doesn't."

"Charge away," Eddie told him.

Arkiens was about to bang his gavel. He must have seen the swing tavern door as someone, or something, ran from the back of the bar to the front of the courtroom. Whispers could be heard. The Goddess had come to these parts.

Dressed in her black brimmed hat and matching black coat, she carried a briefcase and addressed the court.

"Sorry I'm late, your Honor. I got here as quickly as I could."

"Who be ya an what be yer business in me courtroom."

"I am the Goddess. I'm here to advocate for Ed Calkins. You were about to charge, convict, and hang him for contempt of court, were you not?"

"I was," Arkiens admitted. "The witless be givin me no choice. He hasta tell me what he did th' day he won the lottery, he does. If he won't, he hangs. Its th' only sentence I be knownin what ta give."

The Goddess looked at Eddie for confirmation.

"I'd rather hang," he told her.

"That is your ruling, your Honor," Dr. Roslyn insisted. "You have to do it to keep the rule of law in your courtroom. If he refuses to testify, everyone will. How can you judge a contest if the witnesses only answer the question that please them?"

Arkiens looked to the Goddess. Clearly, he accepted her as his advocate.

"Your Honor, this question, 'What happened the day you won the lottery?' is begging the question all over again. It's never been established that Ed Calkins did win the lottery, giving my client no truthful way to answer the question if he never won the lottery. If someone is going to claim he did, those lottery winners are easy to trace. I ask that you rule on this the way you did in the past. Let Dr. Roslyn just tell you what she thinks happened, then let her prove that Ed Calkins did win the lottery, because that's going to be my challenge to anything she asserts."

Dr. Roslyn didn't like that suggestion and countered with her own.

"Why don't we just ask Mr. Calkins, under oath, if he won the lottery. Then this problem of 'begging the question' will go away."

Arkiens looked annoyed and thought it over. Trudy guessed that he wished he wasn't in goat form. As a leprechaun, he would have much better management of the laws and facts. He simply wasn't ready to make all these complicated rulings.

"Does ya ever win th' lottery?" he finally asked, looking resigned at Eddie who seemed now, much more relaxed.

"I thought I did," he admitted. "I don't know if anyone other than Trudy or me would come to that conclusion as I never purchased a winning ticket."

"Objection, your Honor! The witness is being evasive. If he won't answer my question, why don't we just string him up and be done with it? It's the easiest way. You'd be doing the world a favor."

"Instead, I be doin what me did th last time," he proclaimed, banging his gavel. "Th' doctor what isn't a doctor will tell us what she be thinkin happen on th' day what Ed Calkins be winnin th' lottery. After that, the Goddess be gettin her chance, she will."

"I will do nothing of the kind," Dr. Roslyn shot back.

"Then ya be charged wif contempt!"

"No, I won't," she spat back, then changed her tone. "What I mean is, I can't. I have no idea what happened the day Mr. Calkins won the lottery. I only know it upset her greatly. She would never talk about it. I also know that whatever occurred within that week, Mr. Calkins had not a dime left to reimburse the expenses of my mental health services."

"Well this be goin nowhere…"

"Your Honor," the Goddess interrupted. "I may have a solution. I have in my briefcase here…"

All eyes fell on the Goddess as she rummaged through her briefcase. The rummaging seemed melodramatic as the case contained only one slim item. She grasped the baton, holding it up for all to see.

"…the wand of clarity. You see, both contestants think they may have killed my client, but, for different reasons, they do not remember why…"

Both advocates were on their feet objecting before she could finish. Arkiens slammed the gavel.

"Why a be bof objectin," Arkiens whined. "It be th' easiest way fer the judge ta tell if th' contestants win th' prize."

Aodhan went first, real concern showing on his face. His voice made his argument more of a plea.

"Your Honor, my client doesn't exist. He's a figment of someone's imagination. If the wand forces him to face the truth, then he may simply disappear, and I'll lose my best friend."

The judge nodded sympathetically before banging his gavel.

"Th' contestant Glorna doesn't hafta get bopped wif th' wand."

Dr Roslyn was about to argue, but Trudy didn't care. She lunged toward the Goddess hoping to use that wand on herself. The bailiff looking fella restrained her, but the judge did not lose the sympathy in his eyes.

"A course, a poet be wantin th' wand. What possible reason does th' doctor what isn't a doctor wantin keep her client from th truth?"

"Your Honor, my client had been drinking very heavily the night she shot Mr. Calkins, and she also had taken a dangerous number of pills. Having that combination of pills and alcohol is the only way she'll ever recover the memory and what her motive was when she fired that pistol. But that dose was nearly fatal that night. I fear that the same wand that gives her clarity might re-create that fatal combination."

"Goddess, can ya guarantee th court that that won't be happin, can ya?"

The Goddess stood straight up. "I cannot."

"Then th' contestant doesn't get ta be bopped wif th wand." Arkiens slammed the gavel and continued. "Th' court be goin on too long wif out a rulin, I be thinkin. Trudy what dreams all this might wake up any time b'fore I gets ta finish eatin the rest a th' briefs. So th' witless an his buddy th' Goddess can go an so can th' other advocates, ya can."

With the wave of his hand, everyone he dismissed verbally disappeared.

Arkiens looked over the two members still inside his courtroom. There was a sad sincerity in his voice, and a heavy burden in his eyes.

"I thank th' bof of ya fer bein in me courtroom today. Glorna, ya look so nice dressed like one a those movies what I watch wif me buddy Ed Calkins when we was drinkin mead tagether, we were. An Trudy, I do fancy ya an don't hold it again ya that ya kicked me in the nuts. I fact, I fin it kinda endearin, I does. Bof of ya make some really good reason why I should be awardin ya the prize fer killing Ed Calkins. But as a humble servant a th' truth, I can't be swayed be personal affection or fancy arguments that doesn't prove. Glorna, ya be a brave wood sprite want stands up ta Ed Calkins an I'm sure ya be a good cowboy, but ya doesn't win the prize fer killing th' Steward a Tara. I get that if Ed Calkins be bitin ya, he coulda compelled ya to stab him wif a knife. I be knowin why he might want ya to do that. Still, ya never proved it."

"Trudy, th' poet what put her foot into me privates, I'd luv ta give ya an award fer th' contestant what the judge fancies most, but I don't have the jurisdiction. As far as shootin from so far away, well, me crotch tells me how accurate ya can be. Now, I understand ya doesn't want ta talk about it, but I can guess ya getting mad about Ed Calkins winnin a whole bunch a money an not havin any ta share two days later. He mighta go drinkin an whorin until all the money be spent an you not getting a penny ta pay th' doctor what isn't a doctor. But all a that be none of me business cause I gotta go by the testimony in me court, I does. Ya doesn't get the prize either."

"But just because ya doesn't get ta hang as heroes doesn't mean ya go empty handed. Forks here haf been waitin a long time fer a hangin, they haf an so instead a hangin ya as heroes, ya has to hang as common horse thieves. We doesn't has th' time to call in a

297

new hangman, so Trudy, ya has ta do th' job yer self, ya does. There be some rope, two horses an a tree so get busy. I want th' business done before th' sun gets too warm, I does."

Arkiens banged his gavel one last time, and the courtroom vanished a spilt second before the pair teleported to the courtyard.

Now the pair found themselves on saddled horses. Trudy worked the ropes, tying them into nooses, while Glorna helped, standing high on his stirrups to get the ropes over the low branches of the sandy courtyard's only tree.

The bar patrons and others watched on from the bar with a large transparent barrier, which gave the bar a skybox feeling in a crowded stadium. In that way, Trudy and Glorna were alone in front of a large fan base. They couldn't be called mourners. They were more like fans, cheering the two condemned to their glorious death. Trudy noticed many young women blowing kisses at Glorna, which made her wonder if he had been 'particular' with any of them.

The nooses were ready. A startling roar of approval rose from the skybox. Glorna adjusted the ropes' length, so the nooses hung just shy of neck's height for both of them. He shot a questioning look at Trudy, as if to ask if he should put his neck through. Trudy shook her head, so Glorna guided his horse to stand alongside hers.

"These hangings need some drama," Trudy explained. "Let the crowd wait for the binding and noosing. Let them wonder what the holdup is. We'll just sit here for a while and take it all in."

Glorna nodded, playing the strong and silent type that to fit the actor he resembled. The quiet matched the desert that seemed to stretch on for miles. To the west, one could see mountain peaks like an azure king in the kingdom of high and clear. Sky and mountain peaks so close, like Glorna and her, in a timeless trance of kinship and grace.

"Mighty fine horses," Glorna finally broke the silent veil. "You dream very well, I'd say."

Trudy hunted for sarcasm in his voice but couldn't find it. It was the truth he spoke. The only thing she wanted to know for sure took her voice. "Do you suppose this whole thing is real?"

Glorna nodded his head disapprovingly and then spat out, almost under his breath, "humans."

"Ah that's right," Trudy spoke with a hint of skepticism.

"You're a wood spite. I take it you've got something against human beings."

"Nay, just find them peculiar, that's all. Humans don't seem to believe in much compared to other folks. But against all the evidence, they seem to always believe they really exist. Leprechauns are the same way, except they believe other folks exist as much as they believe they do."

"What evidence?"

Glorna looked at her in mild surprise.

"This is your dream, right? It will all disappear when you wake up. It's got in it you, other people, the sky, sun, and wind. It's got sounds, smells, actions, and time just like the life you live when you're awake."

"...and?"

"What's to say you're not a part of someone else's dream when you wake up?"

"Is that what you believe?"

"Theory's as good as the other. I don't know that I believe it, but it seems the most likely one to me."

Trudy was incredulous.

"Do you believe you're a figment of Eddie's imagination?"

Glorna chuckled. "That's what Aodhan thinks about himself, only he'd say 'indispensable substance' in place of 'figment.' Got to admire that pixie, speaking truth to power with his creator. Not many with that courage. Me? I'm beginning to think I'm a figment of your imagination. I don't think I'd look the way I do if it were Ed Calkins. Maybe I'm the figment of both your imaginations combined. Don't rightly know, I guess. Don't really want to know."

Trudy drank that thought like bitter beer. She was still pondering when the skybox audience started banging on the window.

"I reckon there's enough drama," Glorna quipped.

"Yes. Here, let me tie your hands behind you."

"Won't much like that. Makes me look pathetic in front of the ladies."

"Not as pathetic as you trying to grip the rope once your horse disappears from under you. The drop isn't high enough to break your neck, so you're going to be kicking for at least a minute.

Here. I'll put this poncho over you, and no one will see your hand are tied. Trust me, the ladies will love it. Good. Now I'm going to ask you to help tie mine. I'll make the knot; all you have to do is pull."

The horses started forward towards the dangling nooses. From the skybox came a cheer, not a malicious cheer, more like a general statement of approval. The ladies were blowing kisses at Glorna, and the goat faced Arkiens was blowing something at her.

"Mighty fine horses." Glorna repeated.

They stopped when the riders were in reach of the nooses.

"Watch what I do," Trudy told him. "It's important that the noose goes around your neck right, with the eye on your jugular. If you don't do that, you'll slowly suffocate, which will be...undignified."

With an awkward twist of the head and torso, Trudy got it right. Glorna followed. A questioning look went to Trudy. She shook her head. He was ready to put the spur into his mount.

"Drama," he realized out loud.

"Let's just talk for a moment. Tell me what life as a wood sprite is like."

"OK. There's a tree that you live in and protect. You eat grubs and nasties that might hurt the wood. You stand guard against woodsmen, human or otherwise. My tree was an oak."

"But you don't live there now. What happened?"

"Well, I guess you could say I ran afoul of the Steward of Tara. A woodsman tried to cut down my oak, so I ate him...drank all his blood, chewed on the fleshy parts of the meat. Ed Calkins couldn't have that, so he let this leprechaun put me into this oakwood unit, which is kind of a robot designed to fool a young mother into thinking that her baby hadn't been stolen. Wouldn't have needed me for that, but, for some reason, this leprechaun and Ed Calkins conspired to deceive a vampire and his wife for eighteen years. I was supposed to run the robot from inside."

"Doesn't sound like much fun."

"Actually, it wouldn't have been that bad if I'd known anything about being a growing boy. Ed Calkins was supposed to write some fancy instructions for the robot that would have taught me how to be a normal boy."

"But Eddie doesn't know how to do that either."

"Exactly. It would have been a real problem if I hadn't snatched a baby."

"I didn't take you for a cannibal and baby thief."

"I'm not a cannibal, if you believe in wood spites, and the baby I snatched was still inside his dead mother. I had some kind of connection to the little guy...could tell what he was thinking. I heard him crying because he was suffocating. So I jumped through the time portal and ripped him out of his dead mother's womb."

"If you had a real baby, why would you need this late model oakwood unit?"

"I don't know. It was something about the way the kid smelled that wouldn't be OK with the father. So he gave me to the leprechaun for his oakwood unit and put the kid in some kind of mechanical womb where he could see, hear, and feel as if he was the robot. I was supposed to do everything the kid would. As it turned out, I didn't have to. The interfaces that the Steward thought wouldn't work, did and the kid controls the robot without me. I just hang around in case anything ever goes wrong. It's almost as fun as caretaking for an oak tree, minus the gratitude.

"Why not put the baby in the unit?"

"Wouldn't fit."

It was time now. The skybox was in a fevered pitch, waiting for something truly entertaining to happen.

"Mighty fine horses," Glorna said again.

"You already said that."

"These horses are too good for a hanging. They're really fine. Are you scared?"

No. If anything, I'm annoyed."

"Like we're part of some bad joke...something from an old western movie that the Steward made me watch with him. I get it now. Ready?

"Ready!"

Both put their spurs to their mounts. A glimpse of a pot-bellied man in the follow through of a throw flanked her. As if perfectly timed, just as the ropes went taunt, two bagged newspapers flew into the air, struck the ropes, and caused them to disappear along with the ropes that bound their wrists. Figures. Eddie, stealing thunder. Free hands grabbing reigns, they charged off with the skybox erupting in delight.

The horses galloped like thoroughbreds down a straight cinder road like they knew where to go. Glorna had the slightest of grins.

"Mighty fine horses, ma'am," was all he said.

Trudy drank in the beauty of the mountain king in the vast distance. Now her field of vision became a telescope, and she could see a bald eagle perched on a mountain's peak. The poem flooded her memory; one of Eddie's favorites of the ones she didn't write. Alfred, Lord Tennyson wrote it almost two hundred years ago.

> "He clasps the crag with crooked hands.
> Close to the sun in lonely lands,
> Ringed with the azure world, he stands.
>
> The wrinkled sea beneath him crawls.
> He watches from his mountain walls,
> And like a thunderbolt he falls."

When they talked about it, which was more often than anyone would have guessed, Eddie liked that Olympian lack of distinction between "falling" and "driving." The king of a mountaintop should own every event in his kingdom, be it intended or tragic. She was the queen of her dream, and this was her mountaintop. From her speeding horse, she was the Zeus of her own plunge. With eagle eyes and crooked hands, she would drive on the fish that was her own heart and tear it till loneliness reigned her on her empty mountain throne. Eddie, why won't you die like a man? Why do I blame you? Why do I blame me?

When the vision left her, the horses had changed into Harley motorcycles, with more power on an easy chair than she'd ever ridden. The road was blacktop again, but straight, flat, and as endless as it had been on the way to the courtroom. Glorna lost his brimmed hat and poncho to a leather jacket and motorcycle helmet. "The bucket disease," she could have told him, but didn't want to hurt his machismo. Her hair flew free in the cool typhoon of speed on a hot, windless, yellow desert day. Nothing moved but the very fast. She was the queen of motion. She was the thunderbolt from the mountaintop.

Now, only she drove her bike. Glorna tightly spooned her,

riding double.

"Lean with me on the turns," she shouted, but her voice was as necessary as it was audible. Glorna knew that. He just would. Besides, there was no way to stay on the road and turn. Moreover, there was no desire to leave a perfect road.

Why did he stop crafting poems? Eddie, be the thunderbolt, Believe that you can! Don't sit behind the drunken mess of a helmetless poet roaring on a collision course disguised as the straight and narrow. But he was dead, and she had murdered him.

Glorna was no longer there. Had he fallen or simply vanished? She hoped the latter, feared the former, but could not care enough to stop and look. Or was that her cowardice that kept her pointing forward as ferocious speed for fear of the damage chasing her from times and places past.

Then it happened. The thing she feared forced her feet to pavement running forward like a child dismounting a swinging swing. The motorcycle had vanished. Yes, of course it did. Why wouldn't it? His did - and so did he. She should have turned around at the first change for horses to bikes. Back at the courtroom, there was a bar and cheering patrons that would be buying their drinks now. She should turn back now. On foot, it would be long and miserable, but she would make it.

Oh, but what if Glorna had fallen, instead of disappearing. He wouldn't like it, Glorna nor his ghost. Best to keep walking forward. She walked and wished, wished and walked. Why wasn't there wine, at least for the heroes who hang? She should have drunk her fill before she took flight. But the court, and the case, and the clash of the hammer, that slimmest slight chance that contempt earns the slammer...

Eddie! Those were Eddie's lines, maybe to a limerick or some other humorous poems. He was better than that. No, not good, just better. Stop it! Stop rhyming! Stop making the reality fit to a word that has the same ending. Walk quickly straight. Don't be late. Stop it!

The black road had disappeared. The rising yellow's what she feared. Stop it! I swear to dog I will shoot me if I don't stop rhyming! God, this is a nightmare. It's like dying white hair. I swear to God, Eddie, I'll kill you if you don't leave my witless mind! Give me my mind back. Rhymes all this hit points stack. Clarity is the main attack. Drunkenness is what I lack. Eddie's words, I all give back.

STOP IT!

Then it did.

They were at her childhood house, at the table where a family once had their meals. She was a teenager, or maybe it just felt that way, for this is where everyone sat back when the teen club met, and mother wasn't around. This is where she held court back then. Wine, yes, apple wine was in her glass and on her breath. It was terrible stuff, but it was what teenagers could get their hands on.

Beside her on the right side was a grown up Rick, Eddie's son. He wouldn't touch his glass as it was the cheapest wine he'd ever tasted, maybe three dollars too cheap to be called "drinkable." He tried to be polite at first, but...

Glorna was to her left, which made her feel guilty. He wasn't talking. Discreetly, she glanced at him, searching for evidence of a motorcycle fall.

"I hear you," he whispered, being just as discreet. "I can feel your guilt. Can you forgive yourself for not being the only existing person in the realm?"

What did he mean? But then he whispered, "Don't worry about it."

The fourth person was a familiar man she'd never met. He was short and studious, reading books through reading glasses and smoking a pipe. Who did he remind her of?

"Arkiens," Glorna told her. That wasn't it. The red-bearded, middle-aged man looked up from his book as if he'd been called on.

"Trudy, this is Arkiens in his leprechaun form." Rick told her. "You've stopped dreaming that the moon is full."

"And I thank you for it." said the leprechaun that looked all too human. "These rules and this game would be far too complicated for me to officiate with the mind of a goat. Give me a minute, and I'll be ready to start."

In front of the familiar man were books that looked like workbooks for grade school, note pads for each of them, pens, and "dice," which weren't exactly dice. Each had a different number of symmetrical sides. There must have been thirty pairs.

Then, Trudy knew.

"We're here to play a role playing game," she said, finally

realizing it.

"Most games take months, but we cannot leave until you, the players, solve the mystery. If you don't, it will have dire consequences to the Irish folks of all types." Arkiens instructed. "We're going to take an adventure through the mind of the great Steward of Tara."

"Cool," piped Rick.

God, would this nightmare never end?

CHAPTER 20: TURNING STATE'S EVIDENCE

She was high and circling her kingdom of the azure sky. The wrinkled, crawling sea floated the toy boat beneath her, but gave no food. Desert. Blue of shade and splendor, but desert when it came to feasting. Her teammates Rick (an orc named Hagger), his hot wife (Dark Elf), and Glorna (a cowboy named Cowboy, although it wasn't in the rules), along with herself (an eagle) were playing a complicated roleplaying game under the direction of the honorable Arkiens in leprechaun form.

It was the feast she feared. Captain Windfree, a non-player character or NPC, had a nasty habit when it came to filling his belly, and the party of adventuring passengers would soon be sitting inside cooking pots if she didn't soon find something more conventional for dinner. She could certainly do it. She had a vision of 58 which, even from this height, could detect a meal two feet under the sea's blue. Her talons had an unusual strength for her character of 28, which was due to extremely lucky dice rolling or a dungeon master that was sweet on her. She could lift a cow if one were in the water.

Her party was trying to get to Rome to gather evidence in their quest to uncover what and how Eddie had done to make the leprechauns indebted to him. Hagger was never known for patience and guessed that Eddie had saved the world from Irish domination by introducing alcohol to the island. That guess was so offensive it cost another guess, which narrowed them to one. Ironically, now they were on such a trip where a captain with a bad sense of direction had traded his cargo of perfume for Egyptian beer and was headed back to his Irish homeland.

The plan was to divert him to Rome first, where they could investigate a range of theories that might win the game. Dark Elf, who was sitting next to her, had suggested that a long trip filled with peril, might increase their experience points, which would ultimately aid them in their quest for enlightenment, so that took a portal that landed them on the banks of the Nile.

Eagle looked to the east and the fifty-sided die rolled. Thirty-eight, nothing for as far as she could see, which was two miles and some feet. She tried again at east by northeast. Twenty-four. That was worst. Then she tried northeast. Forty-eight! Surely that was a meal!

"You see nothing for two miles in that direction." Arkiens said.

Why was the leprechaun dungeon master, who openly fancied her, being such a jerk?

There was a reason, and it was a good one. Trudy dove her eagle character to the decks of the tiny, battered ship without exhausting her search for fish.

"What?" Cowboy asked.

"Her stamina is only 6." Dark Elf pointed out.

Had Trudy been younger and six psychiatric prescriptions earlier, this evening would have had an erotic sexual intrigue that she would keep to herself, yet still enjoy. That was years ago. Now, the only adventure was the quest, which she was enjoying more than she thought she would.

Trudy looked at no one but the unhappy leprechaun with deep sympathetic eyes.

"I realize now," she told him, "that a well thought-out campaign is like a well-written poem, requiring thought, taste, flare, and a well-arranged range of actions and results...."

"The player is flirting with the DM," Hagger objected. "That's against the rules."

Dark Elf tried to quiet him and whispered, "If it gets us a meal…"

But the DM ruled.

"I'll allow it." Only his eyes were smiling. "Please go on, Eagle. What is your point?"

"But the hardest poem to write happens when the reader will not follow the train of thought, or, in this case, the plot line." Looking away to her fellow players, she asked, "What was our mission?"

"Yours was to get us a meal," Cowboy reminded her.

"How is a fish going to help us guess what Eddie did for the leprechauns and how he did it?"

"The experience point," Dark Elf broke in.

"And if our quest was to build experience points, we'd be on the right track. Why are we trying to get to Rome?"

"To investigate a theory about this having to do something with Roman domination, which was what was going on in the world around the time-frame that my Dad saved the leprechauns."

"Sure, Rick...er...Hagger, but do we need to be in Rome to know what the Romans are up to? Can't we try and complete our mission here? We have to guess what your dad did for the leprechauns. For that, we have all three guesses. Then we have to guess how he did it. The first guess on that was so bad, it cost us an extra guess, so now we only have one."

"A portal opens out of nowhere," the DM proclaimed. He tossed a large book on the table. "A book falls through it with some kind of cosmic sign that reads. 'Look in here for the answers.'"

Rick...er Hagger examined the volume's title.

"'History of the World Before Ed Calkins Fixed Everything,'" he read, groaning. Clearly, he did not like the campaign's turn.

"Please, tell me the author isn't Ed Calkins," Cowboy complained.

Trudy flipped the cover.

"It's worse. He wrote the whole thing in limericks." Looking at Arkiens, she begged, "Please don't make us read through the entire volume."

"Another portal opens, and a pamphlet falls out." Arkiens tossed a small notepad on the table. "It's titled, 'History of the World Before Ed Calkins Fixed Everything: Cliff's Notes.'"

There was no title at all on "Cliff's Notes." One sentence inside caught Eagle's eye: "The only important limerick starts at 'Limerick 1342' through 'Limerick 1348.' Everything else is without merit, meaning, or content."

Eagle flipped through the pages, found Limerick 1342, and read it aloud.

> The aged son of Tiberius Caesar
> Had a young wife and wanted to please her.
> The nation I'll lift
> I give you this gift
> An island you can rule at your leisure.

"That doesn't sound like Tiberius," Hagger complained. "It was Claudius with the young wife, but she wanted to rule Rome."

> So the scores of legions they piled in
> From Wessex to the north of the highland.
> And so all Great Britain
> Turned from lion to kitten
> And is now known as Empress Island.

"Definitely Claudius," Hagger insisted. "He came the closest to conquering all of England."

"Aged son might be a clue." Dark Elf suggested.

"Still points to Claudius. Not many Roman emperors lived very long, and none of them gave land to their wives to rule."

"Maybe this one did," Cowboy pointed out. "Remember this was history before Ed Calkins changed it."

Eagle read on.

> With legionnaires stretched for a mile
> The emperor thought with a smile,
> For myself, the best
> I'll take what is west
> I will conquer the Emerald Isle.

> It was only a few hours by water,
> The invaders were taller and broader.
> The resistance of sort
> Fought by brave men too short
> You could say the whole war was a slaughter.

> So the emperor called his senators over

*To rename the land after his dog Rover.
And of those caught wearing green
We shall treat them quite mean
You shall see no short fairies or green clover.*

*Now historians, don't have a cow.
It's past the way it was not that way now
Was it force or persuasion,
That stopped the invasion?
I know I did it I just don't know how.*

"My dad always pointed out that, although China is bigger in every sense, you're more likely to see a statue of a leprechaun than that of a dragon," Hagger remarked sadly.

"But even with a pair of six shooters, how does one man stop an invasion?" Cowboy asked.

"I do think it's safe to guess then that what Ed Calkins did for the leprechauns is stopped Rome from invading Ireland," Dark Elf said.

"Right!" Cowboy agreed. "I guess that Ed Calkins stopped a Roman invasion of Ireland, which ensured the survival of the leprechauns."

But Arkiens wasn't counting the guess just yet. "It could be argued that Rome DID conquer Ireland. Be clearer about when the invasion was stopped."

"It's hard to date something that never happened," Eagle complained. "Can we date this as sometime during the Imperial Rome, after the republic but before the fall?"

"Close enough," DM allowed.

A four-sided die fell from the shelf and rolled onto the board. The DM matched the number to his book of results just to be formal.

"Correct!" he announced. "You have finished half your mission."

Hagger frowned an orcish frown. "That was the easy part."

"Wait, don't you modern types have cell phones that can look things up?" Cowboy asked.

"Worth a try. Google, 'How did Ed Calkins stop the Roman invasion of Ireland?'"

Eagle, Dark Elf, and Haggar all tried and got the same

message: No one knows, not even Ed Calkins. No one can find out because it never happened. The only way to know is to win the knowledge in a role-playing game with a real leprechaun as a DM.

"This dream has gone on too long without any liquor," Eagle complained. "How about a drink? I'll check the refrigerator and see if I've got anything with alcohol in it."

The other players frowned. Role-playing campaigns and booze did not mix.

"I'm surprised you lasted this long," Haggar said.

"Apple wine, very cheap," Eagle whined. "This is what I could afford back then. Oh well, any port in a storm...though I'd rather have port. Does anyone else want a glass?"

Nobody did. The three other players wanted to get back to the game. Arkiens only drank mead and only in goat form, which surprised Trudy. Because no one else was drinking, she drank from the bottle and asked the DM this question: "If Eddie is such a good friend of yours, why do you want everyone to kill him?"

"A fair question..." the DM started.

"No! It's not fair," Haggar challenged. "Asking the DM personal questions in order to flirt is against the rules of the game. If we're going to chat, that's one thing, and my Dark Elf and I are outa here, but if we're playing a game, play!"

"I'll rephrase the argument then. I look up to the sky at the sun god. I shout to the sky, 'Why does the leprechaun god want everyone to kill Ed Calkins when he's his friend?'"

Again, only Arkiens' eyes smiled.

"A portal opens," he said. "Six brownies and five pixies pop out. One of the pixies asks in a real annoying voice, 'Will you solve our problems? We used to live in Ed Calkins' imagination, but since someone killed him without destroying him, that place he imagined doesn't exist anymore, so we can't go to him for all our troubles, and we sure have lots of troubles. Please help us. We will badger you mercilessly until you solve all our troubles for us. Do you want to hear our troubles? We will tell you all about our troubles so you can solve them.'"

"Cowboy, quick! Use your disbelief spell to get rid of them," Dark Elf cried.

"I disbelieve in brownies and pixies."

A forty-sided die fell onto the table. The number was high

311

enough and the mythical creatures disappeared but not before a ghost moaned out that when Ed Calkins dies in an imaginary realm, that realm disappears for all who believe that Ed Calkins died there, including Ed Calkins. The ghost explained that imaginary realms imagined by Ed Calkins were bubbles in space-time, valued by raiders, sidhe, and human genotypes with superior brains because they were imagined to be ideas.

"The ghost is talking too long," Hagger complained.

"Well, Trudy had a question," the DM said. "When I answered that question without the use of ghosts, portals, or other plot devices that roleplaying games include in their rules, the rules forbade the use of flirting with the DM to gain advantage in a campaign."

"Genotypes with superior brains?" Haggar continued, ignoring him. "You wouldn't mean 'leprechauns' by that, would you? You don't consider leprechauns as part of the sidhe even though Irish lore places them as such. If leprechauns are not fairies, what are they?"

"Humans." Arkiens answered sadly. "Humans that became shorter and smarter than the Fir Bolg that took over the surface of the real world. But we are humans without our women, so we are doomed for extinction unless we find women to mate with."

"What happened to your women?" Dark Elf asked, which annoyed Haggar, who was trying to play the game.

"They left us for better treatment. Some found mates among the Fir Bolg of their time. Others used portals into your time when your kind treated them as equals. At first, we leprechauns felt the loss was good riddance, as we had plenty of gold to bed nearly any women of beauty. Now, we regret it. Trudy, have you yet figured out why I fancy you so much?"

"No one here is named 'Trudy,'" Haggar argued.

Still, the person who wasn't there, or was there but as an Eagle, was not a woman to be fancied by a plot-master, campaign designing, DM who should be sticking to the rules, not trying to use his powers to bed a character. So Trudy shook her head.

Arkiens seemed mildly surprised.

"You are a leprechaun," he told her.

For a moment, everyone seemed stunned. Even Haggar didn't complain that the game had no character sheet for leprechauns.

"I'm not that short, and I'm certainly not Irish," Trudy objected.

"Leprechauns were not always short, and we never were Irish. Some of us did live in Ireland at one time. It was the safest place to show yourself to the 'Fir Bolg,' the name we have for every human who is not a 'leprechaun.' Irish people were the only ones to pay attention to us when they weren't trying to steal our gold. Leprechauns live in every part of the world. The most foolish of us allow themselves to be seen above ground. In Ireland, that wasn't so foolish."

"But if you're not sidhe and live in the real world, what are you doing in the imagination of Ed Calkins?"

"As I said, it was a safe place, the two instances of 'Tara' that Ed Calkins imagined. In an effort to survive, we've split up and travel time through portals, making mirrors that we've crafted. The problem is, we can make the portal from the time we're in, but someone has to make the other portal to the place we go to. Ed Calkins is not just a vampire, he's a psychotic vampire who can imagine space/time into existence as little bubbles in the cosmos. His problem is he can never get to those imagined places without also imagining a portal. When he did, we beat him there. And when he gets there, it's as a refugee, not a leader. He has to win over the leprechauns, raiding humans, or sidhe, to be allowed to stay. It's like he has to stand in line and pay the cover charge to get into his own imagination."

"Not the way I found him when we met," Eagle said. "He was only the Steward of Tara, but he seemed to use that office to enforce his will as might any ruthless dictator willing to hang fifty maidens that he didn't know what to do with. How can you be friends with a vampire so cruel? I was hoping you were going to tell me that you were friends with the man, but now he's a vampire without a soul, and he has to be stopped. That's true in my case. I'm going to kill this vampire in two days."

Haggar looked at his watch. "One day. It's past four a.m."

Arkiens' smiling eyes seemed to glow. Were they really smiling like the song said, or was it some magical power at work? If so, was that power good, neutral, or evil?

"The Ed Calkins you encountered when you traveled

through that portal in the women's room at the Happy Hunting Grounds funeral parlor was an Ed Calkins four years into the future, by your perspective. He's different from the Ed Calkins you're going to duel with. That Ed Calkins is less crazy and a lot less confident, so he's not nearly as dangerous. Just the same, he's more than you can handle. That Ed Calkins knows who he is by rattling the bullet still in his head. If he means to harm you, which he doesn't, he'll almost kill you, bite you, or even marry you as a way to subdue you. He won't write a limerick that dooms your good image for as long as the age of humans. Remember, Ed Calkins doesn't like violence, no matter what the age. In Tara, even though he was expected to have the blood of those maidens, he found a way to grant them the most mercy he could find and left it to you to think of something better. But you mustn't think that he has a soul, let alone a kind one. Push him, and he'd do the thing you fear most, think badly of you in a way that would make others think the same. Yes, that is crazy, but it's a crazy that he's deliberately imposed on himself as he is dying, to make himself as harmless as any insatiable human blood-craving predator without a conscience can be. That is how I know you won't be destroying him in the next twenty-four hours. It's also how I know he won't harm you. You shouldn't judge him, but you have to fear him...or at least, take him seriously."

Trudy had almost finished the bottle of apple wine, and she was getting tired of the games, especially since she wasn't sure there was another bottle in the refrigerator in her dream. She knew, too, that Haggar was getting impatient with the game he so loved to play. Trying as much as he could to see the stern and bow of a wooden sail ship tossed by waves and the smell of sea water in every direction, he was being forced to see a circular wooden table with a woman, his wife, and a leprechaun making small talk in every direction. The only character he could believe was Cowboy, as the wood sprite really did look and talk like a western movie.

"If, as you say, he had to stand in line and pay the cover to get into his own imagination, he must've had a method to get everyone to then think that he was the owner of the place," Eagle insisted. "He must've had some way to persuade everyone, or only gullible people, go into his imagination."

"Gullible people," Haggar mused. "That doesn't describe Romans."

"Vampires have hypnotic powers," Cowboy reminded him.

That launched a conversation on vampires and hypnotism and debates on how that might work and if the legends were correct.

The DM leaned into Trudy and whispered, "Google it."

Haggar noticed, but Trudy was already on it, reading out loud what the google in her dreams knew about Ed Calkins the vampire.

"The Steward of Tara, and only known Irish vampire of note, is not particularly skilled at hypnosis the way many lesser vampires excel in the deed. Reasons for this are highly speculative and include the notion that he's too proficient in human psychology to believe in the results, or he views himself as too ruthless require pseudoscience to mingle with his own mythology. Many have theorized that the threat of being laughed at supersedes any other method of imposing the will of Ed Calkins on lesser creatures which lack his own ruthless qualities..."

"Did my dad blog this?" Haggar interrupted. "I don't think it's helpful."

"...and so the fear that a limerick might stain the reputation of any would-be hero that might defy him makes the idea of vampiric hypnosis obsolete to the ruthless exploitation of fear; unless, of course, the simple option is available of telling someone that what they wanted to believe is true."

"I stand corrected," Haggar admitted. "Since we know that the Romans wouldn't give a fig about being thought of badly."

Cowboy disagreed.

"I don't care what Google said," Cowboy said, pushing back his hat. "Ed Calkins hypnotized me, and I'm not one to be easily manipulated. I make a point not to obey anyone; yet, since he had a private talk with me at a party, I do whatever he says, even if I really don't want to do it. I was never like that before."

Arkiens had that same eye twinkle again. It wasn't a smile. It was something else. Whatever it was, it was full of wisdom that never touched his mouth. Leprechauns can be so....poetic when they don't look like goats.

"Really, Glorna?" the DM said. "Think about it. You've been disobeying the Steward since you came to the other Tara. Do you really believe that if he could have hypnotized you then, he wouldn't have? Ed Calkins isn't the only vampire with any power.

Here's another question: why did you travel into his lifetime as a mortal and kill him? I know I asked you to do it, but you don't do things you're told to do. You didn't even know an Ed Calkins when you did it. I'd say another vampire got to you…one that's very good at hypnosis."

Frowning, Cowboy pondered on Arkiens' words, clearly not liking the chance that it was true.

"I was doing what cowboys do," he decided. "I was paid to kill some outlaw that was being too ruthless, and that's what I did."

"But you did it before you even knew what a cowboy was." Trudy pointed out. "In fact, you still don't know what a cowboy is. I know you've watched all the movies, but when did that start?"

Haggar tried to groan an orcish groan, but he was too disgusted. This wasn't helping the campaign any. If the crazy vampire didn't stop the Romans by thinking badly of them, he must have stopped them by telling them something they wanted to believe.

Then Dark Elf saw the light…er…darkness.

"If Ed Calkins could make people believe, I'm guessing he made the Romans believe that Ed Calkins was the Roman emperor."

Everyone gasped. The choice of words made this an official final guess. The four-sided die fell to the table. Two! An unexplained hourglass turned upside down. Were they defeated? The leprechaun looked it up.

"Wrong, but close enough to get an additional guess. This additional guess expires in five minutes and some odd seconds when the sand runs out. Since this is you last guess, you have that much time to win the game."

"Close? Close in what way?" Haggar demanded.

"In such a way that Ed Calkins might have taken the answer you've given as the correct answer that was missing some detail. You might consider how he would have contacted people in Rome."

"Portals," Trudy answered. "That's how I got to Tara and back."

"I shouldn't ask this because it will help you, but at this point, I'm more of a player then I am a DM as I'm invested in finding the truth. What did those portals have in common? Some were mirrors, were they not?"

"Yes, mirrors. Instead of reflecting, they showed another

reality." Then she got it. "The others were reflective streams or bodies of water. Each should have reflected but instead projected an entrance. With that, Eddie could have visited anyone in Rome with another mirror, right?"

"Vampires' reflections do not show on a mirror," Dark Elf reminded her.

But Cowboy knew.

"That's true," Cowboy said. "The steward often complained that he had to wear a beard because he couldn't see his face to shave."

Ideas were being tossed left and right but time was running out. Trudy was thinking hard.

"The aged son of Tiberius Caesar. Who would that be, Rick, er, Hagger?"

"Well Tiberius's successor did not live long, but that family had a history of brothers, fathers, and sons killing each other and adopting to have desirable heirs, so it could be anyone that survived their own youth."

Time was running out.

"Quick, who seceded Tiberius?"

She sounded so sharp that Rick stumbled on his answer.

"Gaius...but he was known by another name: Caligula. Couldn't be him though, he died..."

"No time! I guess that Eddie made the Roman Emperor believe that he was Ed Calkins."

The die didn't roll.

"Quick, explain how that stopped an invasion."

"The Emperor believed that, as Ed Calkins, he could act as Ed Calkins and the Romans would take him seriously, but he couldn't. So when he tried...."

But the die had enough and fell on the table. Arkiens didn't need to look at his manual to understand the result.

"One! We win!" the leprechaun smiled all the way to his lips.

"Hey, way to go!" Rick praised and shook her.

The cowboy shook her, too. "Good job, ma'am. If I ever need a sidekick, I'd reckon you're the one."

They kept shaking her. Shaking and shaking and shaking. "There's the knocking on the door!" someone said in a voice too high. The shaking didn't stop. Somebody had started banging on the table. This celebration had gotten too entirely loud and physical. The banging got louder; the shaking got harder.

"What?"

Darkness. She was in a soft bed, but not comfortable.

New Medication was doing the shaking. The brownie had grown to nearly human size, and the pounding on the door got more forceful. The fearful brownie pointed downstairs to where late night callers had never heard of a doorbell. In one easy motion, New Medication shrank to pocket size and jumped in one as Trudy flew the covers off and charged towards the intrusion.

"Matt!"

He stood there flanked by two no-nonsense-looking plain clothes detectives, which meant they were in expensive suits and ties. It was clear the party was here to arrest her.

"You need to come with us, Ma'am."

Ma'am?

There was no conversation in the back seat of the cruiser. Matt, who drove, seemed as if he didn't know her as anyone other than another suspect in a murder that didn't directly affect his department. He didn't seem like someone worried that, if she were charged, he'd be the only cop left in said department. They hadn't cuffed her or asked for her gun and badge, which was a good thing because she didn't have either. Somehow, she was dressed in a jeans suit and leather jacket, as if she were going for an evening ride on her bike.

The ride from Munsonville seemed like a haze of cheap apple wine. Screams could be heard but not identified as human or other. They passed through the forests flanking the two-lane highway. Lake Munson was covered in mist that the scant light from white clouds seemed to reflect back in a dull glow, as if its wet beaches hosted the ghosts of waves from winds and waters long expired. That mist rolled out from its beach, past the prairie and through the forests on to the curving road, where headlights might, for a nanosecond, reveal horror, and then disappear before one could be sure of anything but the peril of the solid yellow lines and hardened tree trunks. It was just another patrol through Beulah County.

Now she was seated on the wrong chair of the department interrogation room. Matt, still not seeming to know her, was the only person present. He was polite, but firm and confident in a way that told her he had all the answers to the questions, complete with photographs and lab results, needing only her inconsistencies in how she explained them.

New Medication popped out of her pocket, fists up ready to defend her, but Matt didn't believe in brownies. With the first hostile question, the brownie landed a punch right on Matt's chin, but the boxing move had no effect. Only Trudy knew that Matt was being beaten to a pulp…if a pulp could look like Matt unblemished and pain-free in every sense.

First, there was a photo of Bathrobe. Who was he? What was she doing sleeping in his bed when he hadn't been there in days? And if he'd simply gone missing, why hadn't she reported it? Then he showed her Bathrobe's 44. It had her fingerprints on it, but not Bathrobe's. The pistol had been fired, and the bullet matched the one taken from the brain of the victim. And then there was the cruiser she had driven the night of the murder. When the body was discovered, she had radioed that she was nowhere near the crime scene, which was verifiable, but the call came two hours after the time of death, and she was two hours away from that position. In fact, tire marks on the dirt shoulder put her cruiser facing the victim and two hundred yards apart from where the van would be found. Between her cruiser and the victim was the clearing of Wraith Park that gave her a clear shot, and her marksmanship was completely on record.

"How do you explain it, Trudy!"

He used her name for the first time, but it was too late. She was going to confess willingly, but, now, Matt had her backed into a corner and stole her honor.

"I want a lawyer."

"Wrong answer!" He slammed his fist into the table between them with a bang that sounded like the shot that killed Eddie.

Trudy shook awake. It was a dream. She still had time to do the right thing.

The bed was as comfortable as her night clothes. Between her breasts, she heard and felt the heat and snoring of a tiny brownie still sleeping in heaven. What a prison companion he will make!

The sun was taking the sky and peering like a peeper through the bedroom window when morning allowed a phone call. For a time, she listened to the rhythm as if it were a songbird praising the clear sky sunrise.

The obligation to answer took over.

It was Matt.

"Trudy, I'm in trouble today. I've got some officers for the State that are going to be riding with me all day today. They're coming to help of course, but I'm getting 'oversight' feelings about the whole thing. Someone is making a stink about the murder even though the case is less than a week old, and we stilled haven't heard the official cause of death from the coroner, even though the body has a bullet hole in its skull." He sighed heavily.

"How can I help?"

"I need you to work today. Some people are reporting that their tires got slashed overnight, and they want a police report."

"Matt, I've been drinking…."

"Mouthwash and a black coffee," he ordered. "You clean up well. I know you."

Really?

"Trudy, take the car with the broken radio and take your time out there. I don't want you to be available to answer questions you can't."

"Am I a suspect?"

"You know you are. Let's make you the last lead they investigate. You are not the prime suspect, but I'm hoping to close this before the whole thing blowsup in my face."

"Matt, I have to make a report of my own. My boyfriend is missing. He hasn't come home since the night before the funeral."

Silence. It lasted for a full seven seconds. Trudy just let him think. She knew the procedure and awkward questions where forthcoming.

His mercy surprised her.

"Trudy, I don't want to know more about your personal life, and I really don't want anyone else to know that doesn't have to. Are we talking 'boyfriend' or client?"

It was strange how much that hurt. Even though she could honestly say he was a boyfriend, she'd have to admit that she didn't know his real name, where he worked, or even if he had family, possibly a wife, somewhere unknown to her. Matt didn't press for details. She told him that she lived in his house and used his money, but he didn't pay her, and it wasn't a spousal situation, but she did care and was really worried.

She didn't realize how worried until she started crying.

Were they fighting? No, they weren't, but Trudy drank a lot and so did Bathrobe. There's no telling what was going through his head when he left without telling her.

"Don't worry, Trudy," Matt aid. "Maybe he realized that he had business in the city and forgot to tell you. Or maybe he did tell you, and you forgot."

Trudy digested that. Bathrobe did leave for business on occasion.

"I'll make a report later - when you can fill in more details. OK?"

"OK."

"In the meantime, I'll look out for him using the description you provided."

"OK."

Great. How many short, fat, middle aged, balding, hairy-chested men could there be in the world?

It was late in the lunch rush at Sue's Diner. Sheriff Matt was sitting near the counter of the lakefront venue having a quick burger, and several parties had finally had enough coffee to order their top of the mid-day meal. Ruthie seated the two suited men. Although they weren't really regulars, she already knew they were barely ten percent tippers. Today was slow, and half the wait staff had gone home, which meant one waitress called it a day and the hostess/manager was now the one waitress covering all the tables. This included Matt, the two cheap suits, and the party of five that had all gone to the restroom at the same time, a strange thing for them to do because Sue's Diner only had a single restroom.

As Ruthie filled coffee cups, she heard her "favorite husband" mentioned as a target for removal. She moved slowly, not because she was nosy but because the coffee pot was hot, and she needed to be careful, she told herself. She heard the cheap guy tell the less cheap guy that Ed Calkins had "dumped the down routes."

"Tell me more, Jake," Less Cheap said.

"You gotta let Ed and Robert go," Jake Noble insisted. "OK, maybe Robert can stay, but only if he gets Ed. He's the bad apple that's ruining the bunch! I'll show you."

Less Cheap nodded and patted his pocket. "Good. Because I have something to show you, too."

Less Cheap was Jake's boss, and he was enjoying himself as Jake was actually on the bubble himself. The numbers in Jake's district were bad but not as damning as the photo in Less Cheap's pocket. Still, Less Cheap intended to keep an open mind. If this bad apple was really the problem, Jake had a job, along with a brownie point for spotting the bad apple. Moreover, if the story Less Cheap had received about Jake from another source proved to be unprovable, Less Cheap would assume it was because some of Jake's underlings didn't like him. If that were the case, Jake was promotion material.

Jake pulled out a wide computer paper printout listing the subscriber complains of the following day. That printout was several pages long. He had taken a yellow marker to all of the same subscribers that kept calling back.

"See?"

"I see a few calls, maybe six out of seven hundred, that could be explained as a misunderstanding between customer and customer service. Let's stick to what we can prove. Like this picture I got in my inbox this morning."

Ruthie saw Less Cheap hand Jake a photo of Jake crouched by a car tire with a pocketknife in his hand.

"Photoshop!" Jake replied immediately. "If this was an actual photo, why don't the police have it?"

"Actually, I got a photo too," Matt said, turning around. "Does yours have a guy who looks like you, bending down to slash a tire?"

Let's see if the slasher can talk himself out of this one, Less Cheap thought happily. If he could, he was Post material, thinking outside the box and stopping at nothing to get ahead. The paper could use that kind of thinking. If he didn't talk his way out, he was just a criminal element with no place among the prestige that the Post was known for.

"But you didn't make an arrest because you know the photo is a fake, right?' Jake challenged.

"I don't know if it's a fake, but it doesn't show a crime being committed," Matt said. " It just shows a guy with a knife next to a tire. My department doesn't have time for that kind of thing. If it's an incident, let a small claims court handle it. It's a civil matter as far as I'm concerned."

"But you don't believe the photo is real, right?"

"I don't care if the photo is real. Like I said, it's a civil matter. You seem to know the people involved better than I do. I'd take your word for it."

Less Cheap was impressed. Why didn't he deal with difficult employees the same way? "Better do what Less Cheap wants, or you'll be buying new tires, kid." Actual, Less Cheap didn't have that kind of nerve, but with Jake Noble on his team, he didn't have to.

The meal went quickly. Less Cheap wanted to get back to the office to review a list of agents that he had fired, and excitement was mounting. If it was fun calling someone and telling them they were no longer needed, it was even more fun to call someone that you fired. Offer them a harder job at half the pay and have them obliged to thank you, promising to do much better next time.

"Anything else?" Ruthie asked.

"We're good," Less Cheap said.

Ruthie tallied up the check, ripped it from her pad, and set it in the middle of the table. Less Cheap saw the total: five thousand six hundred ten dollars and seventeen cents. What? He picked it up. The check was carefully itemized. It included two coffees, one chef's special, one scrambled with bacon, twenty tires, four care rentals and an extra "service charge" for putting up with a jerk.

Less Cheap was not amused and motioned for the waitress/hostess/manager, but she didn't notice as she was standing by the entrance door, which was also the exit door, with a key in her hand. At that exact moment, three men holding baseball bats emerged from the restroom.

"Locking up early?" a cheerful sheriff asked Ruthie who nodded just as cheerily.

"Officer!" Less Cheap pointed fearfully at the men holding bats.

The sheriff tipped his hat. "Like I said, it's a civil matter. I'm sure you'll work it out."

Ruthie locked the door behind him as he left.

A woman wearing a black overcoat and matching brimmed hat appeared and held out her hand.

"I'm the Goddess," she told Less Cheap. "I'm one of the

carriers that got her tires slashed by your division manager. I'm also a reporter of the Examiner, a paper with which the Post has a contract to distribute our papers in a fair, competitive way."

When neither man rose to shake her hand, the Goddess tossed a stack of photos showing Jake Noble slashing the tires of different cars.

"What's this." Jake demanded.

"Photos taken from apartment surveillance cameras."

"That's a lie! There were no surveillance cameras in any of those parking lots!"

Before Jake could try run back his statement, a second woman appeared and said, "I'm the Examiner's video tech. Wanna hear this?"

She had Jake's confession on live feed.

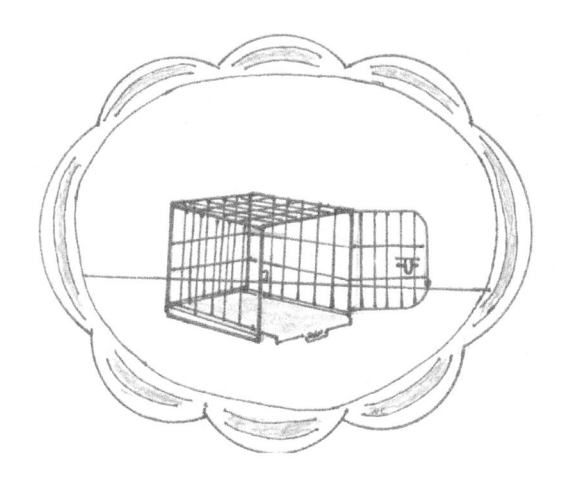

CHAPTER 21: KISS, KILL, OR MARRY

Depression again! I'm rapidly running out of seven seconds to die in, and I only have this day of the ten years that the seconds stretched to. After that, I'll have just enough time to confront the wrong I committed on the day of my natural life when I won the lottery. Every muscle or nerve in my dying body wants to do nothing more than die, but I'm compelled to finish filling in for myself in the future. If I weren't so depressed, I might be alarmed at what, or who, was compelling me, but that would take energy I just don't have. I can't concentrate, and my limbs hurt as if after a varsity workout. Without self-worth or purpose, I drag what is left of me to the ending of my dying.

    I try to remind myself that I must do what the future requires of me now in case I'm not there to do it when the year matches my years. I have three different missions before nightfall on my last day of life as a mortal man. First, I must go to Tara in a year that called itself 815 without running into myself who's now fourteen years a vampire and vacationing there. Because he is me, I know he's just as willing to avoid me as I him, but I can't count on him (me) remembering. I must meet 42, so I can field her complaints about my way of filling her order of "a boy." Then, I need to have that awkward conversation about payment. After that, it's a trip to the funeral parlor owned by my archenemy Kellen Wechsler, who had stolen my soul. There the space/time is Thornton, October 12, 1995, but the host I'll be entertaining could be from anywhere. Whoever that is, he or she will have used my program's interface vial a dial in modem, which is extremal rare in that time, to be selected as a vampire's meal. That vampire would have used a different interface to select that meal while having an idea that the "victim" was also paying me for the opportunity to kill that said vampire, whose name happens to be Father Chokey to me, and Kellen Wechsler to the rest of the world. Last, I must deliver on a promise and give my component to a changeling infant boy. Unfortunately, the only visible component I have is Glorna, and I'm afraid John Simons will reject my contribution as too minimal. The space/time for this transaction is the backyard of Eircheard's Emporium in Jenson (a half hour west of Munsonville, remember?) in the months before the September attack on the world trade center in New York. In addition to John's potential displeasure, Eircheard might also be dissatisfied with a different arrangement concerning me.

It's always the same for me. Give someone exactly what they've asked for at a bargain price, and they'll complain that they are being cheated.

Oh, well. Time to get yelled at.

I appear before her clandestine love interest; John-Peter's back has disappeared from her view. It's the wee hours when brownies work on human farms but Angela, as she has now been named, is as jumpy as she is frustrated. All charades of innocence drain in an angry fatigue from her youthful, beautiful face. The girl is now a woman of considerable intellectual merit, but she's still a spoiled child. That's not fair. Being brownie-raised and leprechaun-educated, it's not possible she was spoiled, at least not by modern standards. What can be said is she expected more out of life than her other human sisters.

She lets me know she's unhappy about everything. I promised her a boy that would be a brave prince who recuses her as his princess and slays the ruthless dictator who holds her captive. I never told her that I was that ruthless dictator and wouldn't mind being slain. Moreover, I never told her that, in recusing her, he would destroy the whole realm, which is a dealbreaker for her. She wasn't going to tell me why. Also, she didn't like him. There just wasn't that attraction. He was supposed to be brave, but they had just finished making out, and he hadn't tried anything. How did I expect that I could demand from her a fee for my service? She had earned more from me than I was paying when she made me the Steward of Tara.

I shook my head, agreeing all the time, because I knew what was really bothering her. When she finally lost patience with my agreeable manner, she quieted herself enough to listen. That's when I informed her that, despite his habit now, of appearing as a youthful human boy, she had been making out with a wood sprite.

Immediately, she began cursing and spitting out the grubs and tree pests that wood sprites are rumored to eat. Through that cursing, I reminded her that Glorna hadn't suddenly changed from a handsome prince into a creature of the tree; he had always been that way, but he had deceived her based on appearances. Did she see why I was not too concerned about her lack of interest in the boy I was going to provide her? Did she think she gained any credibility when she got pregnant by that pixie boy she played with?

At the mention of that, she seemed to waver just an instant before going on the offense.

"What? I'm damaged merchandise now that I'm not a virgin?"

Maybe she expected that I would deny that she was being sold, but I voiced her true objection born of guilt. The boy that she birthed was half human, half pixie and would not be brownie-raised or leprechaun-educated. When Glorna and his four human conspirators assassinated me, the whole realm created by my imagination would collapse. The other conspirators had good reason to kill me. I enslaved them, forced them to write limericks, and then took the credit for writing the limericks. Truth be told, they were moderate poets at best. I enslaved them knowing that they would aid Glorna, who was still being co-opted by Jean-Pierre Mathews to run the being known as John-Peter Simotes. At this point, Glorna and Jean-Pierre forgot they were different people. Angela's real objection to "John-Peter's plan was that it didn't ensure the survival of the other sidhe, which included pixies and her son. I could have assured her that, as merchandise, she had not lost any value by proving she was fertile. Instead, I assured her that her son would be sucked into the realm that the pixies inhabited before they invaded my imagination and that they would have no memory of their time in this realm. The same would be for her and the other girls, whom her "prince" had agreed to rescue. Without such a memory, the lack of a mother/child bond would be recreated without pain.

"Look, 42," I told a much more attentive girl than I first confronted. "If you really don't like the prince that I've chosen for you, pick another. John-Peter's actions will put you in a life with your choice of elite young men, just as you have become an elite young woman."

"Elite young merchandise," she corrected me bitterly.

"Yes, but don't take it that your choice of elite young men will come without a price to you. You see, if I were selling slaves I'd only get paid once. Matchmaking comes at twice the profit."

"A wife is a slave you cannot sell," she quoted. There was no chance I didn't know where that was first said.

"And who would pay to be a slave?" I asked stupidly. I had forgotten about Trudy's clients. "No, where you are going, wives are the equal of their husbands. You may demand a full refund if that isn't the case. In any case, I never need my customers' cooperation in taking payment."

She stood up, almost as a challenge, and stared me in the eye.

"So now it comes down to price." she told me, trying to sound fearless.

I didn't need to be a vampire to know her thoughts. She, like so many young women I had known, was used to bargaining with aged lecherous men and used the mask of jaded courage to increase profit. What else would a vampire do? Standing there, she even tossed her blond hair to expose her jugular vein.

I could taste her fear. I can no longer feel guilt, but I still feel shame. It came to me when, for a second, I desired what she was offering, even knowing the role that I must play with her.

"I can't stop you, so what are you waiting for?" she told me.

Just in time, I thought about Nalla and how much I missed her. I hadn't a conscience anymore, but that didn't dull my sense of cost.

"Yes, payment! The first part of it has already been granted. Here in Tara, you called me 'Steward' and treated me like your king. In your next life, you will call me 'uncle' and treat me like a father-in-law."

I didn't bite her. Was she disappointed or relieved? She seemed not to know, except she felt her weakness and somehow had to cover whatever it was with something disrespectful and cocky.

"In your dreams, old man. I'll never call you 'uncle.'"

But she would.

A portal took me into a well-traveled place and time. It was where the creature known as John-Peter Simotes would visit in the last day of his conscious life. He would, unremorsefully, see the lifeless body of his step-father in the basement of his own funeral parlor with a young, beautiful French girl holding the murder weapon and sounding as someone completely unable to explain herself to law enforcement. That event was carved in stone long before I monkeyed with it.

My part in this was the software.

Kellen Wechsler thought he had installed a copy of it on his office computer. The program was quite diabolical, perfect for the lazy vampire who wanted a live, fearful, struggling, meal, but didn't want to go off hunting for one that might agree with his or her appetite. Graphic pictures of the vampires' potential choices could be browsed through for existing stock and selected for either blood sampling that allowed the victim's reuse, fatal attacking, or the ordered victim could be made a vampire that the customer could compel.

On this day, Kellen would select a young French woman to be his fatal meal, She, locked in a cage just larger than what a large dog might be imprisoned in, would be discreetly delivered from a van into the very basement office from which the computer logged the sale.

There was a lot I hoped he didn't know.

I hoped that he hadn't known that the server filling his order was on the computer of his upper office desk, a place he seldom visited and the classified location of most of my programing efforts as well as the stockroom where I resupplied. Far more classified was how I stocked. For that, I selected from paying customers who desired one of three types of interaction with vampires, which, basically could be described as kiss, kill, or marry. Why would anyone willingly interact with vampires? The three basic reasons fell into the three choices.

One selecting the "kiss" option might be bored with one's marital situation and wish for something…different. Getting bit by a vampire not looking to kill might hold a certain intrigue for the discerning customer with enough money to pay. Of course, I'd guarantee that customer's safety but if something should happen…well it's unlikely there'd be a subject alive to sue.

Another case that isn't as profitable, but costs all the customer's worldly goods, is the "marry" option. Such are largely people in a great deal of trouble. Most are going to prison for life, but some are wanted by mobsters, dictators, or other types of enforcers that don't easy forgive or forget but don't usually put much effort in holding corpses responsible. Being bitten by the vampire of one's choice is quite an alternative even though that selected vampire will dominate you for the rest of your undead life.

The last option was designed especially with Kellen in mind.

As I jumped through the portal, I was very surprised to see Glorna already there.

"Need some help?" he offered. "I thought you might want an extra set of ears and eyes."

I was relieved to see him, not because I needed him now, but this way I would not have to hunt him down going four years into the past or eighteen years from where we were.

"Sure. We should have a match any second now," I told him.

Just as quickly, the screen showed the Wechsler account, a selection of victims to be drained of blood in a grisly murder. By the stated terms, we, the Vampire Vending Corp. was required to remove the victim's remains before any discovery was possible and placed in a less incriminating place and time. What he didn't know was that a different arrangement made this option more palatable to the other customer.

"Selection confirmed," the screen assured me.

I was so proud of the software I designed. It seemed so innocent. I was less happy when I saw the selection.

"Michaela?"

I was mortified.

"Hey, Grandpa, you seem different? You're not biting vegans again, are you?" She spoke to me with a casual confidence that would make any grandfather proud had I not known what she was selected for. She pointed at Glorna. "Who's the cowboy?"

"No! I forbid it!"

"Don't worry, Grandpa. I'm not here to kill you yet. I'm here for that Kellen guy…what's his last name?"

"You're not going to see him! Glorna, get another selection."

330

"But he chose me!" Michaela insisted. "Grandma told me he would. She was very clear that I had to do this before I could come to kill you… Maybe I shouldn't have told you that."

"Michaela, when you come to kill me, I'm not going to fight you. This vampire will, and he's very powerful."

"That's why it has to be me!" She was losing patience. "Grandpa, I've been practicing my whole life for this. Dad built a special weapon, and I know how to use it better than any person alive. We've been through simulation after simulation. I've already got one vampire. I'm the only person alive who can get this one, and I promised Grandma I would."

"That's the problem. You can't use that weapon. You have to use the silver sword we put in the cage, or the weapon your father built you might not be there when you need to use it. Even if it doesn't disappear, using it will change the timeline in a way we can't be sure of."

"Grandpa! This guy has your soul! If he's not killed, Grandma can't steal it back from him, and she died three years ago, so she can't kill him herself. You'll never see her again, Grandpa! And I'll still be the one that has to kill you. The whole thing will be so much easier on me if I know that, when I do kill you, you'll be with Grandma."

That was touching.

"You believe that now?"

"I have to. It's the only way I can…"

She was fighting tears, and never finished. She could see my mind had changed. I wondered if it would have if I still had a conscience.

It was very simple. There were three cages that looked the same but served differently. The Kimberly cage for the "kiss" option had a mirror for its bottom covered by a small carpet that could disintegrate if the person that was transported in it became distressed. In that case, even if the "victim" was out of the cage, the mirror would become a portal and suck the person through.

The Mary cage was for the "marry" option and had nothing special in it at all. In that option, the agreement of both the victim and vampire was ironclad as soon as both selected the matching option.

The Kilroy cage was for the "kill" option, and it had

everything the Kimberly cage had and more. Any vampire that chose a victim to kill would find a victim armed with an invisible silver sword that would only lose visibility when it sunk into vampire flesh. Also with it was a Maple 136 model unit of leprechaun construction. I must admit I would have preferred a younger Michaela that might not have guessed the model's purpose when it wasn't being used to kill vampires.

"It's a leprechaun sex doll!" Michaela laughed as I showed her how to activate it. There were "magical" runes on the activation dial.

"Leprechauns prefer to call it a love doll."

"Disgusting….I'm afraid to ask…" And she didn't.

"This one is 'fearful'," I told her. "Make sure to activate this one or John-Peter might get an education he's too young for."

"Disgusting," she told me again.

I had to agree. It would fool mental health workers for the duration of the unit's life, which would be long enough to be convincing but short enough not to be suspicious when the unit didn't age. I can imagine coroners debating for ages on the cause of death when the unit finally starts to rot.

"And the sword?"

"Don't try to grab it; you'll cut your hand. It will appear in your right hand when you see the time is right to use it. I'm assuming that you know how not to miss when you swing it?"

"Of course, Grandpa. I got this."

"And when you see the vampire's eyes?"

"I'll know he's at my back. Grandpa, I've done this before."

"Not with a sword. He'll respawn if we don't stake him in his coffin. I've got that part coved though. Just stab him and get back. He'll never kill again."

"And you'll get your soul back."

I helped her into the cage, even though she didn't want help.

"It's very comfortable in here," she told me, surprised.

"Yes, it used to belong to a dominatrix with a lot of aged clients that were locked in it overnight. It had to be comfortable."

I locked the cage with a padlock that Kellen thought only he had the key to.

"I'm sorry about killing you," she spoke with mild regret. "It's nothing personal. I really miss Grandma."

My eyes started to water.

A brownie took the cage downstairs. The cage would wait another five minutes before it would be opened, and the night would play out as if it were carved in stone. Wait! When was that ever the case with time travel?

"Look at this!" Glorna cried in alarm.

"What?"

It wasn't there before. I'm sure of it. Almost, it seemed a taunt by another time traveler that wanted to show he was two steps ahead of our plans. Yet there it was, and we both had seen it before in one of Trudy's dreams. The Goddess held it when she was defending me. She would have used it if the judge, Arkiens, had allowed it.

The Wand of Clarity.

"Do you think we've been played?" Glorna asked.

"No, it can't be," I insisted. By what means could it not be? Was that my denial that I was now to face, only to discover that the bishop had moved, and I was in checkmate? "You go first."

Glorna hesitated but hit himself on the head with the wand. For a time he went into a deep trance. When he came to, he was panicking.

"I thought you hypnotized me, but it was another vampire! One that was very powerful and evil! He hypnotized me…or bit me, I'm not sure. Anyway, he compelled me to hypnotize you to do whatever I tell you to."

"Glorna, that doesn't make sense. You haven't told me to do anything I didn't want to do. When do you think you hypnotized me?"

"At that ball. Remember? You were talking to a vampire, and I interrupted you, then I hypnotized you to do whatever I tell you to…and yet I thought you had hypnotized me because I started doing everything you told me to do. Do you remember?"

"Yes, except differently. You got very strange. You lectured me about not being a hypocrite and that I should do what I say I should do."

"No, I said 'Do what I tell you to do.' I'm sure of it."

"Ok, I've got that one figured out. How did you hypnotize me? Was it your voice?"

"No…no, it was my eyes. I looked into your eyes and told

333

you what to do."

"Give me the wand."

I struck myself….went into a trance…and came out laughing so hard I could not stop and might had died trying to catch my breath, but of course, I was already dead and didn't really need to breathe.

It was very evil, that deadly sin that just never got the respect it deserved. Pride and lust that got the top two, but the sin of enabling never made the top seven. The other sins all laughed at it because it acted like a virtue, but that wasn't where it belonged. The corrupted creature that embodied it committed sin after sin, pouring gold into the hats of undeserving beggars that lined the path to hell, but got no condemnation for its atrocities. Damned souls just weren't giving it credit. It was feeding the lazy, crediting the stupid, sexting the unattractive, and otherwise getting others to fund the sinfulness of sinners, and it still wasn't getting recognition for the hosts of hell.

Very well! It would teach hell a lesson and steal the souls from its fires to face eternity in a fate far worse than even the fury of a woman's scorn.

But how to do it?

What if all of humanity became undead? And still further, what if the notion that a vampire could be destroyed to meet its hellish fate became obsolete? How would those corrupt souls find their righteous damnation if they never finished being undead? Most vampires didn't like each other, and the few vampires that did like each other, also hated each other, so it wasn't hard to destroy a vampire, just enable another vampire to do it. But want if "enable" refused? What if vampires all became pacifists like those hippies, vegans, and democrats that it had been corrupting? The first thing that would happen is a lot less vampires would be dying off. The next thing would be the reputation of vampires. They would become more benign at first and then, over the years, they might get darn right attractive. A mother raising brawling kids might quip, "Why can't you guys be little vampires?" Soon, being a vampire would be a mark of honor. The U.N. would insist on vampires being the only type of ambassadors accepted on the floor. Parents everywhere would try to get their son or daughter to find a nice, rich vampire to bite them, so they never get old enough to tap into Medicare and Social Security. With so many people asking to be bitten, it wouldn't take long for all of humanity to become undead. That's when the fun would start. With no undead people, vampires would have to feed on animals. Even if, somehow, animals never became completely extinct while the earth could support them, what would happen when the sun went supernova? Vampires can't burn without respawning, and neither can they starve out of existence. With no food left, they would get too weak to move and lay where the dying planet used to orbit until time itself ends. What if time doesn't end until everyone is dead? All those souls would never visit the mercy of hell, and it would all be because of the deadliest of sins: enabling.

Now, how was this demented plan supposed to work? I could say I don't remember, and that would be true, but maybe I don't remember because I really don't care. All I do know is that I, Ed Calkins, was to play an unwilling role in it, and that made me feel very important. I was key to the plan, but I had to be groomed to fill my role. Evil infected me early in the form of Father Chokey, one of the Prime Evil's lackeys. In that way, "Enable" used the sin of its rival and became lazy, believing that its corruption would play out. But when that Prime Evil visited the prison where I was to be executed for my many murderous crimes, it found that not only was I not there, but I had never been arrested or charged. Still worse for "Enable," I had never committed any of those evils that were so within my potential.

What had gone wrong? Father Chokey knew right away, having his own experience with John Simons and his bride, Bryony. Ed Calkins had failed to realize his demonic ambitions because of his obsession with a tender-hearted woman, who should have never taken up with the likes of such a malicious force. How many young men fall from infamy into the charms of a female lover?

All was not lost. Father Chokey had sampled the blood of the young Ed Calkins to ensure his life's end would bring him to that undead kingdom and another chance to claim his evil potential. All that was needed was a few heartbreaks at the teeth of his rival Father Chokey, who was known to the rest of the world as Kellen Wechsler. Ed Calkins had a plan. John Simons had a different plan. All was well and good...er...evil, because Kellen knew of those plans and had countermoves that would work perfectly. Glorna was in his back pocket. Kellen could compel the old fool by proxy, so no one could tell it was him pulling the puppet strings...if only Kellen had understood the nature of dyslexia!

"What could you possibly be laughing at?" Glorna objected, waking me from my third person trance. "I had you under my power, and I told you to put your granddaughter in Cage Mary. Kellen is going to savage her!"

"Under your power, huh? Why do you think that, since that ball, you do everything I tell you to do?"

"You must have bitten me."

"A wood sprite? I don't think so. When you thought you were looking into my eyes, you were looking into your own eyes. Grant it, I was looking into your eyes as well. What actually did you tell us both?"

"I said, 'From this day forward, you will do whatever I say you will do. You will hear and obey.' I'm sure I told you that…except…"

"…and when you said that, who did you mean by 'I' and who by 'You?'"

"Obviously, 'I' is the speaker and 'you' is the spoken to."

"You were looking into your own eyes, Glorna. You where hypnotizing yourself. So you probably assumed that 'you' was the hypnotized and therefore, 'I' was the other person in the room, which was me. From your perspective, you compelled yourself to do my bidding; something I wished I understood when you showed up with loaded silver bullets pistols while I was being 'dealt with' by the mob."

"You told me to put the guns down and…"

"I wanted you to do anything but that. I was counting on your characteristic disobedience."

Glorna stamped his foot in frustration.

"But don't you get it," he demanded. "I was compelled to be there! Also, I was compelled to be there at the party and now here. We've been played! I was at the party to hypnotize you. I was at the apartment to keep you alive long enough to put your granddaughter in the wrong cage. I ordered you to put her in Cage Mary, and I did so very clearly."

"Glorna, did you ever wonder why I like you? You and I have one thing in common. We don't follow instructions very well. You don't because you don't like being told what to do. I have no problem with being directed, other than understanding what it is I'm being instructed to do. So when you told me that I was to do whatever you said I was to do, I heard I was to do what I said I would do. I thought you were telling me not to be a hypocrite. When you just told me to put Michaela in Cage Mary, I understood you to be joking. And, yes, Glorna, you did stab me, but not in time. I was already dead. Whoever compels you has failed."

"Who killed you first?"

Dyslexia. But I didn't say it aloud.

We did check the cages that were left. Clearly, it was Cage Kilroy that was missing, but I had to be sure. I knelt inside both, trying to get cut with the blade in Kilroy's cage, which would only be visible when it tasted my blood. I got no such cut. I found no weapon despite my efforts through Glorna's chatter.

"So, I guess it's really convenient for you," he muttered when my inspection was finished. "I have to do everything you tell me to and that's going to include being inside a changeling robot. I guess I really fell into that trap, didn't I?"

I stood up to face him, staring right in his eyes.

"I hereby release you from obeying me," I told him. "Do whatever you wish from this point."

"Really? You're not going to make me be John Simons' son?"

"No. I will ask you to volunteer. That baby growing up in that electronic womb could use your help, I'm betting."

"I will volunteer, but I might get bored. Who knows what I'll do if that happens? And, Ed, you don't have to do whatever you say you'll do anymore. I release you from obeying yourself."

"Thanks. Now get in my shirt pocket."

He actually seemed eager. In no time we were four years in the past and at the threshold of Eircheard's Emporium.

Dr. Rothgard and John Simons were just pulling up one second before I did, which might appear to them that I'd been waiting. Time is tricky when it's used for trickery. Should I pretend that I'm meeting the pair of them for the first time? Everything depended on one of them not remembering the true way this meeting would end.

"Dr. Rothgard, I hope you will not take offense," I chanced. "I will need to have a word with Mr. Simons and the shop owner after we wrap up our business here. It won't take long."

Not long....just eighteen years.

Dr. Rothgard looked suspiciously at John, who shrugged that he had no idea. I hoped to keep it that way.

Eircheard had aged since I had seen him last. I eyed him discreetly, but carefully, as so much depended on what we would not be discussing here. By now, the shopkeeper would have inherited a personal history to match his presence in this part of space/time, and I wondered if that included medical conditions that might interrupt my bargaining chips.

I did not like how he limped.

John was his impatient self and quickly broke the greeting portion of this historical meeting.

Eircheard locked the store and told us, "This way, gents."

What creatures was he talking to?

Stone steps led underground where a forest might have been before this ancient structure was created. There were plenty of tree stumps. Each of us found one to sit on.

Once seated, we waited, measuring the 'man' that would be most credited for our joint creation.

"Your request departs from our established method," Eircheard hedged, trying to read our reaction.

"One you promised to fulfill, Eircheard, when you commissioned this project," I told him, unwilling to renegotiate any part of our deal.

Mostly, I wasn't given to accept any other conditions woven into our arrangement concerning Trudy. He studied me for a while, then seemed to realize that. Like a skilled pawnshop dealer who'd reached a limit on price, he sucked his pipe and changed track.

"John, have you the payment...blonde hair and blue eyes as I require?"

"I have such a child," he told him.

"It's here?"

That was Dr. Rothgard's department. He was also my future doctor. One knows how far one can trust his physician when you're first dealing with him involves stealing the infant of a mother that's to give birth and ensuring she never survives. I wouldn't let Dr. Rothgard treat a hangnail. Presently, he stalled, saying the child would be "born" within a month.

"What about the program?"

Eircheard looked to me.

What program? Was I supposed to write some sort of program? Is that my part of this whole thing? I thought I was going to give the group the service of a wood sprite to protect any tree they deemed essential. If it's a computer program they want, well, that will take time. Sorry John, you can have your changeling son when you turn one hundred and sixty.

That would have been funny, if any in this very tough crowd had any sense of humor.

I had been working with the electronic womb for several days, trying to write a subroutine that would save the changeling's memories should those imaged satellites fail or somehow lose connectivity. Also, I needed another subroutine that made this changeling able to play the piano. If I had failed in either of these things, John would be angry with me. So what? The problem is, he might love John-Peter less. That was the only thing that compelled me.

The electronic womb could produce its own storage unit in any form I requested, but I made the mistake of asking for a pair of toy leprechauns. I guess in the distant future, toys aren't understood as well as "virtual reality." That oxymoron dominates childhood play. The thing spit out two of the ugliest plastic knickknacks I could imagine. I cramped into its hard drive, every possible memory that could help a child navigate the failing of its human counterpart until connection could be reinstated, and Glorna wouldn't have to bluff anyone. Also, I worked the musical subroutine, but it had one flaw. The program could not make mistakes. John-Peter could only play flawlessly. I hoped that wouldn't be too suspicious.

I held out the first of the demented toys as if I were proud of it. Would Eircheard be offended? Did Eircheard even remember that he was/is a leprechaun?

John Simons produced the wood to be used. It was the oakwood leg of a very impressive grand piano. Eircheard promised that such a fine piece of wood could give his late model oak wood unit five times its normal life span of two years. That wasn't good enough for John. He wanted twenty. The doctor promised he'd find a treatment that would help prolong its life. I promised upgrades to the software that would do the same. I'm quite sure each of us knew we were lying, but John was only going to hear what he wanted to hear.

"My son," he told us, "should detest meat and only eat my blood and other plant sources as soon as he can be weaned. Then, when the boy reaches his eighteenth birthday, Dr. Rothgard will give the boy a transfusion of my blood, which as I've been told, will make him as human as any man."

As if to emphasize his faith in this absurd plan, John whipped out a pocketknife and cut deeply into his own hand. The blood that flowed from the wound was captured in a small wooden bowl.

"For blood is life," John chanted.

"For blood is life," we responded as if we agreed.

"And it's my bloodline that will survive - despite the betrayal of Henry Matthews."

I had to do something before John read my thoughts. Turning to the doctor, I asked as politely as I could, "Dr Rothgard, the three of us have private business. Would you mind departing? You need not wait for us. We shall see you at the end of the thirty days you need."

Both the doctor and John looked uneasy at my request, but he left the way they came. Even Eircheard seemed uneasy; possibly because he expected the good doctor to loot his shop on his way out.

Then I spoke into my shirt pocket. "Come out, Glorna. It's time for a reunion."

Glorna did, despite me asking him to. He no longer used his "cowboy" form, but one more familiar to the leprechaun. I could only describe this form as a cross between and elf and a squirrel with no particular body region dominated by either.

"Remember me?" Glorna chirped.

Clearly Eircheard did but didn't like it. When he finally looked away from the spot Glorna stood, he turned his contempt to me.

"You are going to let this wretch ruin my oakwood unit. Why would I even craft such a thing when it has no chance? A brownie would, at least, stay in my unit till it rots. I told you what I could do, but you can't make a man out of wood, and you can't make Glorna do anything good."

"I'm giving him to you now, Eircheard, because I might not be here in thirty days. I think you know why. If this doesn't work, it's on me. You can score retribution by telling my remains that you dislike me and will continue to do so for the next one thousand years.

That was code. The leprechaun forgot his objections and played the role we had rehearsed. John, hearing anything that sounded like "this may not work" was enraged. He stood his very tall frame to menace me with intimidating gestures that were having the desired effect. Unnoticed by him was Eircheard that moved behind him. I grasped at what had been prepared. Behind my stump was a note on a small piece of paper, a stake of wood, and a small rubber mallet. Despite my cowardice, I stood tall to view his belly with all the items. He had just the time to smirk when I thrusted all three things into his arms and pushed him as hard as I could, which is to say, slightly.

That's all that was needed. Behind him, a portable mirror was changing into a portal. It sucked him into the night eighteen years later when my granddaughter would stab Kellen Wechsler, and he would try to respawn from the coffin he would be buried in. If the note was legible, John would know that, to free his soul, he merely had to drive the stake home and three souls (his, mine, and Glorna's) would be freed.

Now, I could breathe.

"Moved against him already, did you?" the leprechaun observed. "Is it because the unit will never work?"

I shook my head.

"John-Peter is already a little boy to me. John Simons is about to take himself out of the picture as his cure for vampirism is failing. If the merchandise you're still testing allows me, I'm going to stay in that boy's life until his time expires. That will be eighteen years from the day your oakwood unit is activated, transfusion or no transfusion. The program in the electric womb only works for minors."

Eircheard had no way of understanding this. My plan for "John-Peter" was that the Matthews infant would stay inside that electric womb and have a "virtual" childhood without knowing his full nature. Glorna would help. I knew this. Glorna loved the boy as much as I did and would put a rebel spirit into his life that I never could. They would both forget that they were separate beings. In addition, should the connectivity fail between my imagined satellites in an ancient time and the very unlikely robot of mythical creation of a race that lives in my imagination, Glorna, also a mythical creature, could connect with the youth telepathically. Not being quite as crazy as I would become, I struggled to believe all this would work, even though I knew it already did.

Are you getting this? Did you actually understand what I just said? Look, I'm very glad you're still reading my novel, but don't do it to the detriment of your own mental health. I do worry about you. Trust me, even geniuses of literature have been known to develop psychosis.

Anyway.

Eircheard stood, watching a crazy man.

"And what of the ...merchandise?" A shadow passed over the leprechaun's face as he mentioned Trudy.

"She might destroy me," I told him.

"But you won't kill her?"

"It would void our deal if I did."

Eircheard choked up a little bit.

"I need you to promise me that you will not bite her. Failing in that, at least promise not to make her a vampire."

"I can't promise that. I made that clear when you asked me the first time."

Eircheard looked me in the eye. "Look, what does that plastic leprechaun actually do?"

I told him the truth. It ran on solar power, reported space/time locations by reading star formations, backed up the boy's memory including pre-John-Peter memories, and kept time in years, days, hours, minutes and seconds till the electronic womb would consider him an adult and expel him into the non-virtual world.

"What if I could make it do more?"

"Like what?"

"What if it could locate lucky stars and adsorb good fortune? What if it could grant good luck?"

Don't laugh. Leprechauns are truly skilled at luck. While we Fir Bolg have been inventing steam engines and electronic devices, the Tuatha De Danaan have been advancing what we lesser fold believed to be a dead end.

"No deal."

"That good luck will go a long way and last as long as the device itself."

"I'd love that, but I'd need another way to pay for it."

Eircheard looked ready to kill. I was about to turn my back.

"Wait, there is another way. The Cluricahns are actually…"

"Related?" I was stunned. "I had been informed quite forcefully that they were two different races entirely."

"The cluricahns are part of the Tuatha De Danaan," he admitted with a sigh, "just not the part we're proud of. Right now, they want nothing to do with us. But as the girls we stole grow into young women, they're going to want their share, and never mind how they were raised or educated."

"You want to traffic in girls that have come of age?"

"Yes, but only blondes with blue eyes. They all should be under the age of eighteen."

"I thought cluricahns didn't care…"

"They don't, we do. I want girls that are too young to be married as, at least, that will give them some time to learn about honest work. Cluricahns would make them whores and thieves."

"You're going to give them to the brownies?"

"Sell them," he corrected me.

I would have to be a monster to agree to such a thing. How would I find girls like that anyway? With a pain of regret, I realized how. The "Kiss, Kill, or Marry" program I had written would be discovered by minors, foolishly seeking the company of vampires in the "kiss" option. I would make a simple rule: no modern day minors are to be delivered to vampires….period. Brownies would buy them, Cluricahns could believe they were getting the girls, but John-Peter would shut the whole thing down before delivery ever happened by putting an arrow in my back. I would be a monster that John-Peter would prove his worth by slaying me. Perfect.

I tossed Eircheard the plastic toy. Then I tossed him the second one as I wouldn't need backup.

"No trafficking till ten years from now," I told him. "And I need that lucky leprechaun in my pocket before the night ends. Keep the other one as a wedding present."

He did not know what I meant.

My dear spy…er literary genius, we must now talk of endings. This may well have to be my last chapter writing to you directly in first person. I've done everything the future requires of me except meeting my best friend in a field of battle. It's not the combat I fear any more than the result. It's you, I fear. I fear you

343

will think badly of me for something terrible that I did while I was still alive with my own damaged soul.

The day I won the lottery...I behaved badly. Maybe you should skip the next few chapters and just read the ending. If you did that, you'd think better of me.

Whether or not you do, I must thank you. I know I was a jerk when you first started reading, but I didn't really believe that I could write anything worth reading. But you kept on reading, and I started believing. It's believing in you that helped me believe in me. Isn't it strange that a novel that asks both writer and reader to believe in wood sprite, leprechauns, and brownies and all sorts of other myths should find the hardest belief of all is ourselves? I find myself at the end of a story I thought I would never tell. I find myself finishing a story that is actually worth reading...except for the next part. Thank you for believing in me when I could not believe in you. Now, with your skills as a reader, a world of brownies, rainbows, clovers, lovers, and leprechauns are just one good dream away and, maybe, if you so grant it...one good laugh.

Fare thee well, reader. May you live as long as you want and never want as long as you live.

CHAPTER 22: BATHROBE

It was already evening when Trudy returned to the station, but she could see the light still on in Matt's office. A deep dread filled her when she couldn't shake the feeling that he and the suits from Detroit were waiting to interrogate her. When she let herself in, however, Matt, with his office door open, was all by himself and clearly upset.

"What? The oversight committee?" Trudy jabbed the officers assigned to "help" the sheriff.

"We found him, Trudy He's name is Eircheard, or something, and he speaks quite highly of you. He says he's been working late at his place of business, which is a little shop called Eircheard's Emporium…a kind of Irish variety store or pawn shop in Jenson. Yes, he told us who you were, but he seemed very evasive when the suits asked about his relationship to you, and why he didn't tell you where he was. That's not the worst of it. In plain view, he had a 44. The suits took it with them, suspecting it's a murder weapon."

"Is he a suspect?"

"No, you are. Any chance that 44 will have your prints on it?"

Trudy couldn't form words. Matt went on speaking when she didn't answer.

"You are their prime suspect, not that anyone they talked to gave them any reason. The victim's son thinks his dad was shot by the stray bullet of a poacher. That reporter at the wake had several suspects in mind, but not you. In fact, the only thing they have on you right now is the mothers, both his and yours."

Trudy felt her heart sink.

"I'm not surprised," she choked out.

"But they do have some tire tracks the size of the cruiser you drove that night across from Wraith Park where Mr. Calkins took the bullet. It would be hard to claim that anyone could have plugged a target across the way with the 44 they've recovered."

"We both know I could," she told him.

"Yes. We do." Matt stared back at her as if he lost his best friend. "Trudy, give me your service revolver, now."

She was shocked. This was not the way to disarm a murder suspect. Almost out of embarrassment for him, Trudy stalled.

"Matt, I need time. Trust me, I'll do the right thing. Tomorrow morning, I'll come clean, but I've got something to set right later tonight, and I can't do this right now."

"Trudy, the gun."

"I was drunk, Matt. I knew I was about to swing into a deep depression, and I knew how shorthanded you were, so I drank and kept drinking till I blacked out."

"You don't remember what happened?"

"I remember shooting him. I don't remember why."

Matt who seemed to expect a confession, looked shocked before he told her.

"I know why. You saw your friend about to be bitten by a vampire that intended to make him one, so you shot him to keep him from that fate."

It was Trudy's turn to be shocked. Was that right? It did fit the evidence. She did remember thinking that, at least, Eddie was at peace.

"Well, it didn't work," she told him. "I can't do this now because I've got to meet our victim at Wraith Park at four a.m. for a duel. Matt, I've got to do this. Afterwards, I'll do the right thing. I promise!"

"Trudy…your gun."

It wasn't the way it should have been. Matt made no move for his. If their roles were reversed, Trudy would have ordered him, by gun point, to slowly unstrap his holster and let it drop to the floor. Slowly, Trudy lifted her revolver from her holster, feeling the wrong of it right away. An empty pistol doesn't weigh more than it should have loaded. Just as carefully, she turned the weapon handle first and gave it to Matt, who seemed mildly impressed.

He opened the chambers. Trudy could see why the revolver was heavier than it should have been. Not only did bullets fall out, they were...

"Silver bullets," Matt told her, inspecting them closely. "Not the sort of thing a part-time law enforcement officer can afford. I'm betting your Eircheard had something to do with the design of these. Impressive."

Trudy could feel the heaviness on her holster belt too. She didn't have to look. The bullets were there, too, and certainly silver.

He looked up at her.

"Do you know why I hired you?"

Trudy meant to shake her head, but her whole body seemed to quiver. Always, that was an unspoken question between them. He had to know she was an alcoholic and a simple background check would flag her as bipolar. An internet search would have told of her dominatrix past, but he offered her the job without her ever applying for it.

Matt went on when she didn't answer.

"It's a large area we patrol, but a small population. We've had more than our share of serious crimes: mostly missing daughters, unexplained fires, and general larceny. Any rational police force would look into bored youth, and I'm sure that's part of it. But everyone that lives here knows that the problem is vampires. I can hardly write that on any report. I hired you because I trust your sense of when to use deadly force, even when there's no evidence of a threat. I knew you carried an extra firearm with you on patrol, which is as illegal as having an auxiliary police officer doing patrols on her own. I don't know why the State keeps cutting our budget, but I've made enemies in my long career by telling the truth. Now I'm in deep but not as deep as you. When they arrest you, I'm going down, too. I hired you because I knew you would do the right thing. I still believe that, but the right thing isn't always the most selfless thing. Consider not meeting your vampire friend tonight."

He reloaded the revolver with the silver bullets and gave it back to her. "You'll need this if you still do."

"Thank you, Matt," she sighed with relief.

"Something else," Matt said. "I don't think it's going to be our problem anymore, but the girls that disappear...have you wondered about that? Girls, and not boys, suggests trafficking, but all the girls have one thing in common."

"They'd have more in common if it was trafficking but go on. They all have blue eyes and blonde hair. What could that mean?"

"It means our traffickers value blue eyes and blonde hair. I'd suspect international foul play but…"

"Vampires!"

"Exactly. Eddie might know something. Maybe I can get him to talk before I free his soul. I'll see you in the morning, Matt."

But Matt shook his head.

"They'll have the results of the coroner's autopsy tomorrow. It's rumored they pulled a bullet from the victim's head. If that bullet matches the gun they recovered, there will be a warrant for your arrest."

"I'll see you tomorrow, Sheriff Matt."

She turned away to face her fate, but Matt shouted out to her before she was out the door.

"One more thing." He paused, gathering his thoughts. "I wasn't going to give you this, but the victim's son asked that I did…you know, the guy that thinks a poacher shot his father. He doesn't believe in vampires, but he did make this and asked me to make sure you had it so that you could test it. I didn't want to encourage you but here."

He pulled from the top of his desk a metal baton about two feet long with a trigger on its underneath.

"My guess is that it's pistol that fires wooden stakes." He looked at it doubtfully. "Fire the silver bullets first."

It seemed to Trudy that every light was on inside the old saltbox at the top of Pike Street in Munsonville, which had a spacious estate that merged with the vast woods behind it. She'd lived in alot places over the years, but the saltbox suited her more than the small apartment above Sue's Diner. She would have only a few hours with him before she met her fate. Then, if all went well, she'd have the rest of her life to spend in prison, and no one on the outside close enough to ever visit.

What was she going to tell Bathrobe?

The wrong of it hit her nose the second she turned the key

and opened the door. Bathrobe had been smoking inside the house. On another day, she'd count it as him being Sammy. In fetish circles, SAM was short for smart-ass masochist with Sammy as adjective for a "strategy for getting punished." Bathrobe knew better, but sometimes the need for attention corrupts the mind. Trudy's past with men told her all about that.

When she saw him sitting with his smoke and melancholy, she broke her role by withholding the question of "Where's your bathrobe?"

She knew a breakup when she saw one. Divorces weren't the worst because all of those were those slow-motion train wrecks that sounded so cliché until you realize that expression covered half of her friends and most of her life. More hurtful were the ones like now, when boys or men realized their lives were too promising to continue the play that, for her, had the appearance of love. There were no promises made, so none were broken. No hearts were engaged, so no tears should flow. How fitting for her last full day of freedom!

For a long time he sat there with his pipe as if he hadn't noticed her looking. The man was well dressed for his lack of height, bad teeth, and big belly. His orange pin-striped suit and matching derby hat fit his form perfectly, and the smoke from his pipe ringed him with a sweet, fruity smell. She stood there, drinking in the parts of him that she had never allowed herself to see lest she lose something she couldn't get back when he went back to his life, love, or wife - leaving her to start over again with no more than she was wearing. That wouldn't be a problem this time.

"I don't want to play anymore," Eircheard told her without looking at her. "It's not fair to you if I let this go on, and I find myself getting lost in our play while I should be tending to the future. From now on, it's my house, so it's my rules. If you go out that door tonight, you're not welcome back in."

"It was always your house," she told him. "We were just playing the game you wanted to play."

"They took my gun away this morning while I was working on it…said that they thought it was used in a murder. The gun has your prints on it, so I think they're after you. Does this have anything to do with that business at that bar in Detroit?"

"I killed a man."

"No, you didn't. I'll ask again about Detroit."

"It could. The guys that were with the sheriff have it out for me."

"I've got friends that can hide you well."

"I'm not going to hide. I've got to face what I've done."

Anger shot in Eircheard's voice so quickly and with so much force that Trudy almost reached for her revolver.

"Going to face that Ed Calkins fellow? Is that what you think, is it? Are you thinking that you got him once, and you can do it again? Lassie, you know nothing! Why am I telling you that? It's because you've been with the Fir Bolg for too long, you see. Now you're acting just like them, wielding guns and running bars instead of crafting words and wisdom. So you think you got him with my pistol, do you? You can't kill a fool with a pistol, darling; you have to kill him with his own foolishness. If you don't see that, he's going to kill you with yours. What he did about the lottery, forget it! I don't know what it was. Fools always get what the devil sees fit to pay them!"

"That's my friend you're talking about! He was there in my life before you, and he'll still be there after I've walked out your door for the last time!"

As quickly as it flared, his temper fizzled.

"Your friend is not your friend anymore," he told her sadly. "He may have a soft spot for you, but it's not in his heart or his soul, because now he has neither. He's turned into a monster with a ruthless desire for human blood. He'll take you down with him, too. I tried to get him to promise not to bite you...offered a deal he couldn't refuse... but he did, so I couldn't."

"What do you know that I don't?"

"I know the vampire is more dangerous then you believe, lass," he lectured. "There are stronger powers then you trying to end him. Forget about it all. Forget about me. Forget about the undead man you used to know and let the other creatures of the night engage him till they or him find what afterlife they've earned."

"I can't do that."

"You have to. The guy has done more since the last time he lived than anyone else in six lifetimes. We know a lot, but we don't know all. Remember Arkiens? He is the luckiest leprechaun among us. While we had to travel time slowly, waiting for a portal that's close enough to our time but far enough into the future to make a difference, Arkiens has been traveling time at will since the day a goat bit him. He favored Roman republic times because he could pass for the god Pan, Faun, or other names. While the ladies would have nothing to do with us unless we paid them, women for all cultures were catfighting to get his jewels. Anyway, he found an ancient scroll, but it was written in modern English, that detailed what Ed Calkins did to change time and inflict himself with Deep Time Psychosis."

"I saw that book in my dream! It was in limerick form. Arkiens implied that only six or seven limericks were of any value."

"Of any value to you, maybe. But the whole of the limericks is subject to interpretation. We don't know if it's fancy or true. Hard it is when the future depends on the tales of a madman."

"Couldn't Arkiens have gotten the same disease?"

"If he weren't so lucky, he would have. Also, some magi seer paid Arkiens well to end Ed Calkins' life when he was just a boy. Arkiens' luck saved him from succeeding and saved all of Ireland as we know it."

"Yeah, I played a game to find out how, but that was in my dream."

"You must not think that, because it's your dream, it isn't real. What did that fool of a therapist tell you? 'Every person in your dream is you.' That's no truer than believing that every person on your land is yours. Treasure the creatures in your dreams, lassie. Each one is a hero wanting and waiting to make you the true poet you were destined to be."

"One of those persons in my dreams was that fool of a therapist."

"I know that, lassie."

"How would you know that?" Trudy asked, showing annoyance in her voice. She wasn't used to being called 'lassie' and she didn't like it.

"I'm a leprechaun. I never learned half the stuff you mortals know, but the telling of what a person is and where they should be going is, well...star-reading 101. There was a time when you Fir Bolg studied it, but you gave it up too soon. That's also why you know nothing of luck, and that's why you mustn't go killing Ed Calkins just because he dared you. He wants to bring the Knights of the Red Branch back. He wants to bring the world to admit that everyone everywhere is actually Irish. He's not going to spare you just because he feels sentimental."

"If I forfeit, it would be an admission of guilt. I've done nothing wrong." But as she said it, she remembered holding the pistol and firing at the driver's side of the white van. How much of this was really about that?

"Look, our kind tried to end him ourselves. I wasn't involved, but I heard about it. Some of the cluricahns teamed up with a vampire named Mary Steward to find the right hit man to kill Ed Calkins when he wasn't in Tara. She contacted a vampire who runs one of the undead Mafia families and paid him good money to end him. Now, a guy like that doesn't get to control a piece of vampire organized crime without a good sense of danger. The guys he sent to do the job were too deep in juice loans to ever pay up. Perhaps the mob boss thought to cut his losses because of the rumors concerning a secret organization aligned with Ed. Whatever it was, the three brothers paid a visit to him but left without killing him. The next day, they wacked their boss and are now acting like they control the undead wing of the Mafia. Kellen might have something to do with it; we don't know."

"Why would cluricahns want Ed Calkins dead?"

"Lass, you have to understand. Ed Calkins can imagine any bubble in space/time. What he can't do is unimagine it. The only way to pop the bubble is to kill Ed Calkins when he's in it. If you kill him outside his imagination, everything he imagined remains. The cluricahns were promised new girls, just like the leprechauns, but they didn't see a reason to go venturing into the future the way he was arranging to send them."

"Wait, girls? Where did these girls come from?"

"Everywhere, lassie. Brownies have been robbing human infants for ages. They take them, raise them as their own children, and when they come of age, they intermarry. We leprechauns even craft changeling robots to trick human mothers, so they don't come looking for the infants the brownies steal. You can't blame them, lass. They have to intermix with humans to save their species."

"Does this have anything to do with why girls with blonde hair and blue eyes are disappearing from Beulah County?"

"It might. Brownies have an easy portal in this place and

time. But brownies don't care about babies having blue eyes or blonde hair anymore then they care about stealing a boy or a girl. It's we leprechauns that care about that. We don't have a need for male children. Of the proud De Danann, only men exist. Our women left us ages ago. We didn't treat them well, I admit. Some say they took up with the Milesians, but others say they've gone into the future as we have, trying to keep our race alive. Brownies that steal babies with blue eyes and blonde hair are interested in bonding through marriage with a leprechaun. It's lucky to have one in the family."

"So that's why you are breaking up with me? You're going to marry a captured bride when she's eighteen? How old will you be then? Sixty-three?"

The aged man puffed on his pipe with pain and regret in his eye. "It has to be that way, lass."

"No, it doesn't! By rights, I should arrest you for human trafficking!"

Anger reddened his ears. His hazel eyes seemed to shoot fire.

"Rights?" he shouted. "What of the Fir Bolg that ever knew of rights? Why, you imagine a country and think you've got the right to own everything and, let's not forget, everyone in it. We Tuatha De Danann were doing just fine without your stupid fences, properties, and rules about who works and who gets the profits. What are you going to do with me now, lassie? Steal my gold? Take me prisoner until I pay ransom and call that good luck? WE HAVE A RIGHT TO SURVIVE! YOU DON'T! With your wars and your slaves and your blundering science, you've done nothing good. Oh, I thought you were different at first, but you're becoming like your so-called Celts who couldn't farm with a shamrock and a plow horse. What do you think would become of you if the lot of us just left? I KNOW! GO FIGHT ONE OF YOUR STUPID WARS. Use that bomb you're so proud of. You'd be dead, and we need never come to the surface!"

"If your race is so great, why didn't it win the war against the Milesians?

"War! Do you think any leprechaun with half a wit has EVER fought a war? Yes, it's true that any true leprechaun wouldn't be afraid to put up his fists and fight his own battle, but killing by proxy is not going to impress us. We did fine underground when the

Milesians barely survived above ground. Call them what you will. We call them smelly! Couldn't bear the assault on our noses, so we left them to fight and kill among themselves, which they did and are still doing to this very day."

"You're kidnapping infant girls."

"And showing them a better way. The brownies teach them hard work and how to be happy. We will teach them the secrets of the world around them and how to be our wives."

"What can you teach them? How to make shoes? We have factories and sweatshops for that."

"No leprechaun ever has needed a factory to make anything! In fact no leprechaun EVER has worked for ANYONE but himself. Where you Fir Bolg ever got the idea that you can take the profits from the labor of someone else is beyond comprehension, but you think it means you're better than us! Stay with the Fir Bolg if you want but if you leave MY house tonight, you are not welcomed back! Don't try to sweet talk your way back to me if you don't respect my rule!"

"Do you think I'd want to come back? You're tossing me out for a blonde girl who could be your granddaughter. I think you've made it clear which of us you want as I don't have blue eyes or blond hair, you pig!"

"Lass, at least try to understand. The genes for blonde hair are recessive. It's just the same for blue eyes. But leprechaun genes are recessive to all other types. So, if a baby turns out other than with blue eyes or blonde hair, we'll know…"

"…that the mother cheated!" Trudy accused.

"…That the child is a true leprechaun! I already told you that we believe there to be leprechauns among you as children of our women that escaped us. We have to build our race again! If it was just about pleasure, lass, I wouldn't be breaking it off. Stay with me until I collect my bride. All I'm saying is we can't play anymore. Before I get married, I'm going to move to some remote community where my kind and me buys it up and all the land that surrounds it, so the girls don't take up with Fir Bolg ways. It's not good for me or you that we should fall in love."

"FALL IN LOVE? WITH A PIG LIKE YOU?"

Trudy could see the sharp pain hit his fire-spitting eyes. It didn't give her the satisfaction it had promised. Still, she was too angry and hurt to take it back.

"Pig, am I? Do you know what else I can make besides a changeling infant? Think about it, Fir Bolg! I can better replace you with a stick of wood!"

Hot raged filled her in a stabbing instant that would force her to say only the truth, even if it contradicted what she'd been telling herself.

"I GAVE YOU EVERYTHING YOU WANTED AND GOT NOTHING BACK BUT A REPUTATION!"

The door begged for slamming and shattered glass. Bathrobe was running after her, trying to take it all back, but she had seven steps on him and barmaid legs. The cool night air found her tears before she could find the outdoor stairs.

"It is a good thing," she tried to tell herself. Tears meant she was coming out of her episode, although she'd never quite been in it.

Note to self: Keep taking that new medication and never date a leprechaun.

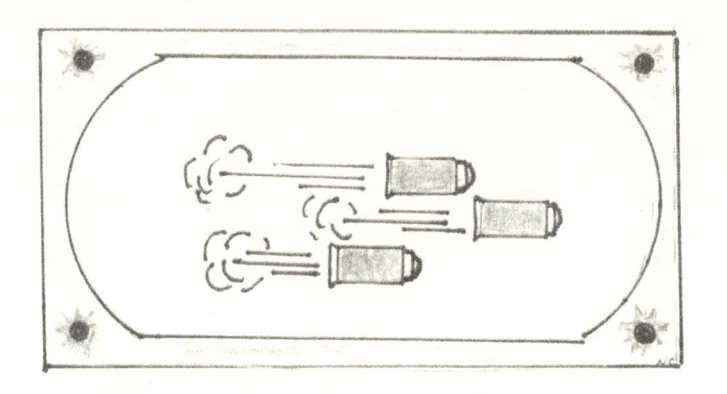

CHAPTER 23: FOLLY OF A GUN

She left, half-running, as tears flowed down her face. Bathrobe would never see those tears; she promised herself as much as she heard his steps and calling behind her.

"Trudy, come back! It's not like that. You can stay. We'll work something out. You can't leave with nothing."

She couldn't go back because he'd see that she had been crying. It was exactly like that, what they could work out was that she could stay as a whore, charity case, or some combination while Eircheard went on with his plans for his beautiful child bride. Leaving with nothing was the one thing that Trudy knew she could do as she did it every time.

This time, she knew where she was going. They wouldn't be letting her take anything with her to jail.

Eircheard was running now, closing the ground between them. The night was starless, and the even line of trees cast heavy shadows with the scant lights of street posts. His heavy breath, the steam from it and the sound of it, was his most identifiable feature, like the smokestack of a desperate train. It stopped at the point where it would have overtaken her, but his face showed no satisfaction…instead puzzlement, as if Trudy had become invisible.

How could he not see her? Was the darkness too strong around her concerning her location, life, or intention, or had she simply ceased to exist? His steamed breath frantically poked one way, then another, but sight did not seem to light his large face.

What?

He was close enough for her to touch him and almost did to

convince herself that she was there, breathing in the air he exhaled, but she did not hide, and he did not see her. Unable to do more, he gestured his frustration and placed his back to her, walking back to a life of marriage, children, and wealth.

"You were aiming for your own head and missed," Nalla had told her days ago.

She watched until his back blended with the darkness. That stray thought caught her off guard. She could lift the revolver to her mouth and pump a silver bullet, making sure not to miss this time. The thought missed its mark. There was no temptation. Whatever those pills were, she hoped the prison system knew about them.

She walked without direction and wept without comfort. It was a revisit to a distant memory of another breakup about her being inconvenient to marriage and family. The feeling was the same…exactly the same…except for the revolver and stake shooter she wore on her belt. That didn't belong. It was as if the fact of those two things made the circle of her life invalid.

"Folly of a pistol."

She heard herself say that out loud and wondered what she could mean by that. What did her gut know that her mind refused to see? And what about the bullets?

Strangely, she hadn't wondered where they came from. Was it just that so many strange things had occurred since she'd shot down Ed Calkins that this one felt too dull to contemplate. Or was she lying to herself again about something too costly to admit?

Something….strange of course, but dreamier than dreams themselves. It was like a morning beer buzz without any buzz or beer. With each directionless step, she was changing. How? What? Why? Where? None of it seemed to matter much.

Maybe she was walking time, but that's always. This was different. She walked, cried, and wondered, but some part of her was watching with a purpose and focus not explained by anything she could name.

"Folly of a pistol."

Again, she said it. Now, she knew something. She was getting lighter and stronger with every step. Was she a vampire? How could that have happened without her knowing about it? Besides, the change in strength would have happened all at once.

No! She was getting younger.

It was too late when she realized three things all at once. Now she stood in the middle of Wraith Park as the fourteen-year-old she'd been when she met Ed Calkins for the first time. This was the place of her dual with the same, and by now, it was four a.m.

She didn't learn how to shoot until she was twenty-one!

On cue, she heard the bicycle before she saw it. Its rider was a fourteen-year-old Ed Calkins with a bloodied face.

Cold gripped her, but that was a good thing. Without needing to think, she called her challenge.

"What kind of fool shows up on time to his execution?"

The young face considered that before answering with his own taunt that seemed as senseless as almost everything about him

"What kind of fool brings a gun to a limerick fight?"

Survival screamed at her to discharge her revolver before he dismounted his bike. She drew it, aimed it, but did not fire it. She watched warningly as he carefully kicked up his kickstand and place it out of harm's way before he would even look at her. They were not ten feet apart. When his eyes lifted to meet hers, she let the first round expel.

It missed. Did he dodge it somehow? Trudy fired again.

"Why are you aiming for me, Trudy?"

He did dodge it! She saw him. Holding firm, she did not let the target out of her sight while answering him.

"You said, 'Beulah County isn't big enough for the both of us.' Remember?"

"Have you looked at this county?" he scoffed. "It's not big enough period. Have you seen me lately? This county isn't big enough for my own ego. I don't think I can fit it in the state without a shoehorn."

Another two shots left the steady revolver. He dodged them both.

"Don't aim, Trudy. Spread your shots. Try to disallow any space between them that are large enough for my body."

Two silver bullets were left. She couldn't miss without being dinner. Holding firmly, she advanced.

"No, No! You'll miss if you do that. Take me from a distance, or I'll close on you before your finger can pull the trigger."

Trudy ignored him and closed fast instead. Sprinting harder than she should have been able to, she ran into personal range and fired twice, point blank.

Missed! He wasn't there. One moment she could have thrust the barrel into his chest, but by the first shot, he vanished. Panic threatened. She had to reload. Shaking, she opened the revolving chambers and steadied her hands enough to slip a bullet in each one without looking at gun or belt. The loading took longer than the countless times she'd practiced it. It could have done her in, but the target was nowhere she could see.

Scared and alone, she felt like she used to when she was fourteen, before she learned to fire a gun and be intimidating instead of intimidated. Then she remembered who her opponent was. Eddie wasn't going to lose his composure over gunshots. Gunshots didn't criticize or undervalue his person. Angry shouting did that, and Eddie was never more afraid then when those shouts came from a woman.

In a gunfight, the worst thing she could do was shout and give away her position, but this wasn't a shootout.

"Playing pimp are you!" she screamed as loud as she could. "Thought you could sell me to a leprechaun without my consent, did you?"

"Hardly a pimp. How could I sell sex when you're giving it away all the time!"

He shouted the insult, but she detected defensiveness. Moreover, she could gauge better than he, where the two of them were in relation to each other. She could do this if she kept him shouting.

"At least I could find someone willing to cut the deal. Nobody wants you! Never did, never will!"

"Well, I'm not pimping you, I'm selling you! He has to pay for you, you have to pay for him!"

Six yards away at least, a bush rustled when he shouted. Once she started her charge, she'd need to be silent. Get him thinking, fearing, and regretting. That was her only chance.

"Even if I wanted the leprechaun, why would I pay you for him? Why would he pay you?"

"Because without my help, you'll never seal the deal. If he doesn't walk from you, you'll walk from him, just like you've been doing all your life. Why would it be any different? What have you changed about you? If he doesn't leave you, you're going to think it's because he's not good enough."

Damn! He was smart enough to move, and she knew she had to do the same. He had already shown that he was much faster than she. Get to him, Trudy. Get him upset. Get him mad. Hurt him first, or you'll never kill him.

"Really! You're lucky I didn't sleep with her first, Eddie. I'm talking about your wife! You only got her because she didn't know enough to know how bad you are at lovemaking."

"She doesn't go that way, Trudy! Do you think everyone is going to drop their pants or panties just because you'll let them? Not, everyone Trudy, but certainly me. You could have had me, Trudy! You knew that! I made that as clear as you made it to me that you would only have me if you were ready to give up! But then the first time I fall for someone else, you come to me and propose. You proposed, but I had just gotten engaged! I guess you didn't want to lose your backup plan!"

Farther, but he was walking as he shouted. Big mistake! Lure him into long speeches, while keeping her own short and not moving while she retorted, that would give her this "limerick fight" that would end with a silver bullet. He was a wounded animal, already trailing emotional blood.

"You broke my heart, Eddie."

"How many times did you break mine? Did you ever even think about how badly I wanted you? How much from you I'd have put up with if you ever even hinted that you'd consider dropping the 'friend zone' restrictions? Every time we broke those restrictions… and by the way, it was once, not twice, it was because you were lonely or horny, not because you were being merciful."

His voice showed the hurt. He stopped just now. Where?

"You had me for forty-eight hours. I was your sex slave. You were the last man that ever dominated me."

"I was engaged to you at the time, Trudy. I really thought I was going to break it off with Nalla. You were the one that told me I was going to pick her over you."

It was true. She had dialed the number of where she was staying for him, even put the phone in his hand. She was on vacation. While she didn't expect him to break up over the phone, she expected something. Maybe just to tell her that they needed to talk when she got back. She knew it then, what he wouldn't figure out for another six years. He was in love. She knew about being in love. She also knew that being in love didn't mean "ready to marry."

Damn! She lost him again. Try Trudy. Try!

"I was a good friend, the best you every had!"

"You were…" he seemed to choke on his own words. He hadn't moved. "…the best."

It was working.

"And I came to recuse you, remember? You were too much of a coward to break it off."

"With you or her? I was afraid to get married. After you, it was break up with her and marry you, break up with you and marry her, or break it off with both and have two women angry with me."

Wow, that hit Trudy hard, but he must have been right. He even said that right, without mixing up any of the words. Thinking that, she lost his position.

"You said marrying me would be like winning the lottery!"

"I did win the lottery. The time I had being engaged to you was the best sex I ever had. The sex I had with you after we both realized I wasn't breaking it off with Nalla, that was even better. But I didn't deserve it."

Trudy, stop listening to his words and start shooting. Where was he now? She was just as upset as he was. Change tactics.

"How much for the leprechaun, Eddie?"

"You found out."

The seemed to stop him in his tracks. Four feet away, she could hear shoes meeting grass, sloshing on the nighttime dew. All she needed was a second to freeze him.

"You're the seller. What's your opening price?"

"I want February and January."

There! She fired twice.

"OK, OK. Just February and two silver bullets, but that's my best offer."

How was he still alive? Did he move? Silence. She'd never see him before he saw her. Bite. Bite or he will.

"How can I give you a month? Are we going to fix a price or not?"

A tree twig snapped too close to her left. She sprinted like she could back then. The safest place for her was the clearing near the sandbox. With gun pointed at the last direction, but eyes

361

searching everywhere, she made it.

"We already have March, you know."

He hadn't moved. Was he trying to draw her back near trees and bushes? When would this fire fight end?

Now, at least, she knew what he meant. March was often depicted with a shamrock because St. Paddies day occurred on that month.

"It's not a month, it's a day!" she shouted. "You only get that month because nothing else happens so far away from any interesting holidays. February is full. It has Valentine's Day, Eddie. It's also Black History month. You'll never overtake the heart-shapes that signify it. It's too deep in our culture."

"I said that was my final price. You'll have to find a way to pay it."

"Quit talking crazy, Eddie. I can't make your birthday a national holiday. Eddie, you've got to at least be reasonable."

Just for a second, she lowered her gun, overwhelmed by the fact that she cared about how the haggling was going.

At that moment, he was before her, already past where her arms held out the gripped pistol. She was beaten.

"Not with that," he told her. Their eyes were locked. Blue against the grey. Robert E. Lee could appreciate the way she felt now. Defeated, she spoke her folly.

"I brought a gun…"

"To a limerick fight." Eddie finished. "It's your verse I want. That's going to get my birthday celebrated. That's what will get you your leprechaun and make him forget the child bride he'll trade you for. I've got a younger man in mind to become her groom…and, yes, both her and him are going to pay me for it."

"I didn't prepare any sharply worded comical poems for this, but I assume you did."

"I came prepared. Now you shall suffer my verse."

"I'm sure I will," Trudy admitted, eyes already rolling. "Let me have it."

My exploitation netted two days of bliss
Sex that for the rest of my life I shall miss
But like a bathtub safari
I can't say that I'm sorry

But I do apologize for my Casanova-like kiss

"Wow." Trudy pulled a laugh. "I don't know if that's the worst poem or apology ever. Maybe both, I think. I'd need Arkiens to judge. The truth is that I didn't expect..."

"An apology?"

Trudy thought before she spoke.

"It's just that I thought we'd have bigger differences. Didn't we agree to forget about this."

"And yet we didn't."

"Is this why I shot you?"

"No, but that you think it might have been does tell us we left this unresolved."

"You didn't do much towards that end just now. I was less angry when you weren't smirking about the whole thing."

"I never explained myself." Eddie bit his lip bitterly and shook his head. "Trudy, the nights that we had, that was the best sex I would ever have. I really did think I won the lottery."

"But you threw away your ticket."

"No," Eddie was adamant. "The point is, it wasn't worth it. I always thought that I wanted as many lovers as I could get away with. A lot of guys think that. Most of them go through most of their lives lying, hunting, and covering their tracks trying to pull it off. Me? The first time I got to cheat was the best-case scenario. I got the best sex I could ever expect and cover because it was with my best friend who wouldn't tell on me. But it hurt. It hurt you because I rejected you. It hurt me because I did my best friend wrong. The year I was engaged, I got a lot of offers. I got even more after I did marry. It wasn't my conscience that kept me from trouble, it was the memory of how much it hurt afterwards. If I ever thought that the payoff might be better than the pain...and I kept hunting for that case...I might have been the player I always wanted to be instead of a husband; but it never happened. No one was going to be so good that I would risk feeling the way I felt. In the meantime, I saw guy after guy that was smoother than me, scoring girl after girl, and no good ever came of those guys."

"I assumed that you stayed away from me afterwards because you were preoccupied with a new love."

"No, I hurt. That was a good thing, except I should have let you know back when I was actually sorry. I'm just not sorry now."

"So I am the only loser," Trudy told him bitterly.

"Did you really lose?" Eddie challenged. "If you wanted me, I was for the taking....before I met Nalla. Before that, every girl I'd been with was handpicked by you. I told you that, for me, the sex was better than I would ever have. Can you honestly say the same?"

Trudy frowned.

Grey eyes met blue. Again, she lowered her eyes and surrendered.

"For me, it was just sex," she admitted. "At that time, I thought I had overlooked you, but there would have been other guys for me and other girls for you. I might have even allowed it that way because it would have been so exciting. I had it that way with so many lovers who were really skilled at lovemaking because of so much practice. Some were female, but the most skilled were male. Later in life, I would trade excitement for satisfaction if I could only have found it the way you did…so while we're confessing and apologizing, I have to correct you about one thing. You didn't get away with it. I was too hurt to be your best friend, and I told Nalla all about our night together. You were right to keep her, Eddie. Not only did she forgive you, she didn't rub it in your face. Maybe she knew you better than any of us, including you."

Grey met blue again. This time, she did not surrender.

"I'm not sorry," she told him. "If it worked out for you, and you stayed in my life, then I'm not sorry it happened the way it did. If we had been together as lovers, we'd be estranged by now. It's happened to me every time. What we haven't dealt with is why I shot you."

Blue eyes broke contact. Before she could follow where they went, she felt cold hands remove the weapon the Rick made from her belt. Panic shot. Was this not over? Eddie inspected it, then seemed to dismiss it. Trudy snatched it from him and poked him in the chest.

Eddie's smile was almost a smirk.

"What? Are you saying it won't work?"

"My son made it. I was hoping he would. You're going to need that weapon."

"But it wouldn't work now?"

The smirk wouldn't go. Ed was playing with her.

"Oh, it would work," Eddie allowed. "If you were aiming it properly."

"I'm poking your chest with it," she insisted, feigning confidence.

"No, you're not. You can't. It needs a modification. It needs sights mounted on the barrel so you can see where my chest actually is."

"Nice try." She poked to push as she spoke, but the barrel disappeared in the chest before her. At the same time, she felt his arms from behind her wrap around her. She could feel hot breath on her neck. All the while, blue locked in with grey. Eye to eye, she startled, the question asked in silence.

She didn't need his answer. This was the playing out of Plato's cave. Eddie was dead. She had shot the shadow, which should have killed both shadow and mortal soul, but the mortal soul had disbelieved it, and so the mortal soul never merged with the immortal one. Now, with no shadow to be visible to others, the mortal soul of Eddie had become a projection, more perfect than a shadow, but that projection was not occupying the same position on the cave's wall.

"You need this," Eddie told her.

He seemed to reach into his pocket and produce something flat and dark....really dark. It came up from behind her, raising and turning its flat side forward before her face. It was quite unsettling to see blue eyes…twice. One set was right before her. The other was within the black flat rock and belonged to the aged Eddie that she had aimed a pistol at six days ago.

"If you hit my projected self," Eddie explained, "that projection will do whatever you expect it to do. It might bleed as a man whose been shot would, or it will miss. What it won't do is kill me. To kill me, you have to hit me, not my projection. See, I'm the prefect predator, as you're back when you think you're fronting me. Right now, I can see the front of you and the back of you at the same time. If you shoot me with that thing, the stake will kill me, and a pile of ashes will be laying behind you. You have to look through the sights for my eyes and shoot with the barrel pointed backwards from under your arms. If you shoot or stab me with silver, you have to then stake me when and where I start to respawn. When and were by the way, is always right here in Wraith Park at four in the morning. As I respawn, a small tornado will gather my ashes until the remains of my body gather, and I am the most vulnerable. You need to know that."

Trudy was afraid.

"Bite me!" she told him fiercely.

"Trudy, I'm still trying to make the Divine Refrigerator. I need you to stake me sometime before I lose my humanity. It's just a matter of time, Trudy. My need for blood will make me a monster."

He placed the rock in her shaking right hand.

"No. I mean, bite me," she told him in a cold sweat. Trying to look tough doesn't go well with tears of fright. She campaigned, but it sounded more like begging…begging a vampire.

"Eddie, you've got to do this. It's what vampires do. Aren't you supposed to be ruthless? Think about it. If you sink your teeth into my neck, you'll have me as a virtual slave girl. Think of the fun. We could open a brothel. A vampire would make an excellent dominatrix. Nalla will forgive you. She did once before. Remember, wedding vows are only valid till death do you part. She knows you have to feed, Eddie. I'll make sure you don't get anyone else…"

Eddie just looked at her. Clearly, he was tempted…or was he playing some other vampire game with her. She felt he was toying with her but was too scared to be mad. She swished her shoulder length hair to expose her neck.

"Come on, Eddie. We did what was good for you last time. Now you have to bite. I need you to bite. I shot you! It's your turn Eddie. I need you to take me."

The projection of Eddie was unmoved by pity. Did his mouth just water?

"Hurry, Eddie! Can't you see you're being cruel? I'm scared, Eddie, and I don't like being scared."

He broke his silence with a frown.

"You're not going to prison, Trudy."

"You were right there." She pointed to the street. "I was in the cruiser right there. I rolled the window down. I don't know why. I shot. You're a vampire now, and they've pulled the bullet from your head. They have the gun. Tomorrow they'll match it with the bullet. I need to be dead by tomorrow, but you can make me undead."

"Let me show you what happened," Eddie spoke with the enthusiasm he used to have when he was the age his projection looked, and he was talking about chess. "It's a neat thing I can do with time. Don't worry about going crazy. It will be like a 3D movie that we watch disembodied."

The white van was on Tomas Street, just as it was. Even from here, she could not see the driver, but knew who it was. Then, she heard the sound of her cruiser pulling up on the other side of the park. She was in it and looked terrible.

"Let's get closer," Eddie told her. Time seemed to stop, and they appeared right beside the driver's side door of the white van. "You're going to have to live with this much."

The smell of alcohol dominated the air. So intoxicated she was now sweating, Trudy's former self aimed the pistol with a steadiness that didn't belong to anyone that drunk except her. The trigger squeezed. A shot rang out, but there was no flash from the pistol. Eddie stopped time and removed the gun from frozen Trudy's hand. Opening the chambers, he showed her they were empty.

"Maybe I knew the gun wasn't loaded," she guessed.

"What did you tell me? A gun is always loaded. No, Trudy. You did not know the gun was empty."

"Maybe I did. Who else would have taken my bullets? I knew I was going to have suicidal thoughts and…"

"No, Trudy. It wasn't you. If it were you, you'd have found those bullets somewhere in the house."

"Where else could the bullets have gone…I mean…"

"Eircheard's Emporium. He used those bullets to fashion the sliver ones in your belt and revolver. He was going to do the same for his 44 that you've seemed to have taken over. See, Trudy, he also knew you were about to entertain suicidal thoughts."

"But he broke up with me."

"Doesn't mean he doesn't care."

"Then, who did shoot you?"

Eddie's youthful projection took on a painful smile.

"I was having a really bad day," Ed grimaced then pointed to the van. "When that bullet struck my head, I was already a vampire who had just reanimated for the second time. Before that, I was stabbed by Glorna who was paid by Arkiens because it would have made me the king of vampires and under Kellen's, or Father

Chokey's, power. Before that, I died of dyslexia. After being shot in the head, I died of John Simons draining my blood. Sixteen years after that, I took an arrow in my back. But my son got the bullet part right. It was a stray shot for a poacher that happened to fire just as you squeezed your trigger. Four deaths within the first six minutes of being a vampire; I call that a bad day except it was a very lucky day because it made me unafraid to die."

"How can you die of dyslexia?"

"See that house over there? I delivered the paper on the day it started….and every day after, but they still called in. I was going to prove it. I borrowed a phone with a camera in it, finished the route, and waited for the sun to rise so I could take the picture. Then I realized I was on Tomas, but the start order and complaints were for Thames….two different names with three letters in the same place and only one different vowel. I had a heart attack in the rage that followed."

"But how did that make you a vampire? You need a violent death to become…"

"Trudy, have you ever seen me lose it? Trust me, you haven't. You can't get more violent than an Ed Calkins temper tantrum with no one to watch me."

"So, I'm not a murderer." Her relief was audible.

"Nobody is. The death right now is being ruled as a heart attack and the bullet, which, from my prospective, will be gone from my head in the next two minutes, will be ruled post-mortem. Even the poacher is off the hook."

"So what about you, Eddie?"

"I'm still dying from being drained of blood right now. In two minutes, I'm going to give a mother this plastic leprechaun that your boyfriend enchanted for her changeling son. It's supposed to be loaded with software, but it's just a life clock, star locator, and good luck charm."

"And after that?"

"I can sleep in for four days, just lying there like a good corpse. I've done everything that I have to do in the future already…you know, just in case you were able to kill me. But four days from now, which is tomorrow from your perspective, I need you to spread my ashes in this park right here. Meet me here every year and bring that stake shooter with you. The Goddess, that reporter you met, will know when it's time, but you can use your own judgement if you disagree. I'm not sure I wouldn't resist, so you'll have to stay sharp. If you grow too old to do it yourself, the Goddess will give the task to my oldest granddaughter. She'll already have two vampires under her belt before she takes on me. I'm sure she'll be up to the job."

As Eddie was talking, Trudy put the stake shooter under her underarm with one hand and raised the black rock with the other. She saw shock in the old vampire's eyes as the barrel touched his chest.

"Why not now?" she asked. "It's never going to be easier. You've said you've already done everything you have to do. Is this checkmate? Have I beaten you?"

It was Eddie's turn to be afraid, but he wasn't. The question seemed to reassure him.

"You have beaten me. And you're right. I have done everything required, but… there is a boy named John-Peter, who's not going to live beyond his teens. Even though there's two persons controlling his life, it's all the Mathews boy is going to know about childhood, and it's all Glorna's going to know about being human. I suspect he'll visit you in your dreams, by the way. He's grown fond of you. Trudy, I might not be the best male role model, but for the Matthews boy, I'm all he's going to have that doesn't hate him. The Simons guy will get himself staked before the boy is three."

"Ok." Trudy decided. She lowered her weapon. That was reason enough. But Eddie wasn't finished defending his future.

"And there's you, Trudy. If I'm gone, I can't sell Eircheard to you."

"Eddie, that bridge is burned," she sighed.

"Then rebuild it. Trudy, you're a hard sell, but he's the very best I could find. I know he's clumsy as a lover, but you can teach him. You can learn from him, too. He's very skilled and very rich without ever really trying hard. He loves you, Trudy. You can't say he doesn't. You're the best thing that's ever happened to him, and one of the things that happened to him is a guarantee of an eighteen-year-old beauty to marry him when he turns sixty-two. He's going to throw that away to have you."

"Maybe you don't know about the breakup. Eddie, I'm sure he means well, but the way he wants his sex is so….high maintenance. He wants to be cuckold, Eddie. Do you know what that means? He wants me to go to some bar, pick up some boy or girl, bring the catch home, and 'make' him watch."

"You were just offering to work at a brothel for me."

"I know, but that would be as a vampire and an alternative to prison."

"If you don't like his tastes in sex, change them. I'm sure you can pull it off. I can remember a younger Trudy that would have thought of this arrangement as the best case. You have sexual freedom; he's bound to faithfulness."

Trudy's face was still that of a young girl, but she showed every bit of her age with her frown.

"Look, it might have been different. I don't have the energy anymore. The medication I've been taking for my bipolar depression hasn't just damaged my sex drive, its destroyed it. For a while, I could still pretend and go through the motions. The truth is, I haven't had sex of any kind is the last six years. It's not fair to him. I've lost all the passion. I have no libido anymore."

"Really? I can fix that."

Eddie flashed his fangs.

CHAPTER 24: WON THE LOTTERY, DIED THE NEXT DAY

A new predator claimed the night. Agitated, itching, and aching, she could taste the rewards of her quickened steps along the ominous pines, willows, and maples that flanked her cinder path. She was middle age again, but the youth that commended her gave her no quarter.

Too soon, she was among the streets where people slept, and streetlights were vigilant watchers of walking heels. She avoided them. Instinctively, she avoided their scrutiny and favored the shadows. Almost dancing, she tapped on pavement of the perfect weekday time of night for feeding. It was past the time when young pleasure seekers had their dinners, drinks, dates, and dances, but too early for the morning risers to heed alarm clocks, bathroom lights, and closet selections to beat the daybreak. This was the time to begin savoring the catch of the evening hunt.

Too soon again, she was on the doorstep of a place she once called home and rang the doorbell as if she needed permission to enter. Could she hear booted feet rushing down the long stairway, or did she imagine it? The leprechaun should have been long sleeping now and almost ready to raise. His pawn shop was unique that way and opened early enough to sell freshly baked soda bread and other morning foodstuffs while other pawnshops wouldn't open their doors till the sun was warm and business warmer. Other shops

371

as large as his had employees.

Today, the shop would not open at all.

The porch light went on, startling her. Eircheard was already dressed in a fine colored suit and matching hat. He must have already been prepared for morning, but then she remembered he was still wearing the same clothes when she had left him. That could not have been more than an hour ago, she realized, but it seemed longer as everything had changed so suddenly.

He seemed relieved to see her. Fool!

He was the same height as she even though he was a short step higher. Their eyes locked. She made sure of it. Grey eyes commanding his unusually bright hazel eyes. She could feel him fumbling with two lines of conversation; one started with an invitation inside to renegotiate the conversation before. The other line was a simple question.

"You," she told him as simply.

Again, he fumbled, taking too much attention to comprehend that she was answering a question he had not time to word. The question might have been, "what do you want?" but too much talk robbed him of the bliss she commanded when she allowed gazing between them. If he'd just stared, he might have known all that was knowable. A full minute passed. Again, the leprechaun seemed not to know the rules.

"I haven't slept," he told her nervously. "I had to know… I don't know if I'll be opening the shop today."

"You won't. Don't ask. Quit talking. Just look into my eyes and learn all you need to know."

"Lass, you're scaring me. I can't stand on the threshold all day."

The problem was, he could. Her eyes! He wanted to drink it all in, but that desire made him fearful; she could see it. He tried to say something else, but before he could utter a breath, her forefinger touched his lips. He stood looking and losing all sense of time and space.

Trudy was satisfied and ready to move to the next level.

"Tell me why your shop won't be opening today," she ordered but not in the way of the roles they had played before. More, she was a teacher giving a quiz."

"I'm too tired, or you have too much to tell me?"

But that was a question. Trudy didn't have to tell him to try with an answer any more than she needed to tell him to try with the truth. When he did answer, he answered correctly, but it scared him to the point of panic.

"Because I'm about to win the lottery."

Without a sound, Trudy put her lips to the side of his neck. Eircheard didn't budge; that much impressed her. He had already made up his mind. Her tongue first tasted the salt, then lips and teeth made the well-practiced move. As she did, she remembered the flashing of Eddie's fangs. How quaint? How fitting? When Trudy completed her kiss that ended in a bite, she left on Eircheard's neck what should be a visible hickey.

"You're not."

"No."

"He didn't bite?"

"He didn't bite me," she corrected him. "We came to an understanding."

She didn't need to tell him, at least not the first night. Eddie used his teeth to bite himself. Using the razor sharp fangs, he pricked his finger to draw blood, then directed Trudy to catch the blood. She used two empty medicine bottles, filling each. Was it that he now had in him the blood of a teenaged boy, or was it the vampire's appetite that filled her libido? Whatever it was, it worked. She only drank a drop. The rest was for the rest of the year. Then, every year after, Eddie would get himself "killed" so he could respawn where his ashes would lie. There would be a built-in reason for the meeting. Eddie would bite himself again and fill Trudy with a year's supply of lust…if Trudy didn't kill him first. She would make it a habit to bring the modified stake gun with her, so that when she had to, he wouldn't be frightened.

"I should get my bathrobe…"

But Trudy shook her head no. It would be different now. It would be different forever. No more bathrobe, set roleplaying, or other people. From now on, it would be Her, Him, and a host of different games, pleasures, and fantasies as limitless as the time there was left. Toys would be allowed; Trudy was sure the leprechaun could make any they desired. She would encourage him, but he would always be the leading man in their play, and she would be the only woman.

She sent him up first, instructing him to lose the clothes. She went to the kitchen.

"Which?" she asked herself. "Champagne or martinis?" Another day. What about spicy bloody marries? Perfect for the first night if there was a small taste of actual blood. One drop for each drink and the bottles went into the freezer. That, too, was an explanation for another day.

He was ready! Not even touching the drink, he was about having her. Her uniform became a memory of four quick hands. It had been years since she last made love completely nude. Grabbing the cuffs from her belts, she slapped her wrist with one and the bedpost with the other.

"I'm yours until the morning," she told him.

Then she saw him. New Medication was lying on the dresser, elbow and hand propping his head up to watch.

"What about him?" Trudy asked.

Eircheard knew who she was talking about.

"He can stay," he decided. "But you'll have to find him his own breeder going forward."

Fair enough where first nights go. Eircheard was even a little better.

The afterglow was a little better than that. Trudy let her hand stay cuffed for most of it. Eircheard was very tired and did fall asleep but kept letting her know that he knew she was there. He slept very close, very warm, and very handy, stroking and caressing her as if he didn't know he was asleep. What was said? Less excitement, more satisfaction. She could live with that. How old was she now? Forty nine? More than half of her life was gone. Wouldn't it be strange, lovely, and ironic to fall in love for the first time right now after all the love affairs she had for the last thirty-five years.

Trudy's eyes grew heavy. By now, it was six or seven, maybe later, but the long day had reached its end. She dreamed again, but the troubled, imaginary world was outside a transparent dome of comfort. Creatures talked to her through the glass…too many to remember and little importance lie in what any had to say. There was Glorna.

"My name is John-Peter now, and I'm a two-year old," he told her. "Being a wood sprite is easier than a human boy. It's not as interesting as being a cowboy, except the piano. Did you know

I'm a genius?"

She would have talked more with him, but there were river nymphs and banshees that wished for her ear. Politely, she tried to assure a particularly high-strung nymph that she was not going to enslave her now that she ruled the stream that flowed on Eircheard's property. Pixies played and brownies worked. Banshees sang mournfully of an old paperboy who loved his wife, son, and best friend.

"I'll go to his funeral," she promised them. It seemed to help their mood.

"Why Steward not at work!"

The brownie seemed offended.

Because he's dead. Did she say that or just think that? Anyway, it should have been true, but it wasn't. Eddie had gone into the future to make sure the workload got done without any interruptions that dying could cause. Did she ever have a job like that?

The window shades could no longer keep the rays out of her eyes. It was afternoon, and she was ready to start her new life. Sleeping still, on his back, he had grabbed her hand and held it with both of his. Lips parted in a quite snore. He must have unlocked the cuffs sometime during the morning, for they were nowhere to be seen.

Matt hadn't called. He must know by now that there was no homicide to charge her with. Eddie had told her that. Maybe she couldn't trust him anymore, but that doesn't mean he would lie.

Bathroom!

She was with a man and that meant getting to her makeup routine before anything else. Still nude, she felt a sudden insecurity and raced to the adjoining bathroom before her leprechaun could see her. Shower, hair, and makeup…she could smell coffee. New Medication was making himself useful or perhaps just wanted coffee himself. Does a brownie dive into a coffee mug when he drinks it?

She thought of making breakfast and serving it in bed for him.

Then, she saw it. Eircheard's phone had a recent text message. She begged herself to leave it alone, but something tipped her off that the message was sent from the future. Was she hallucinating? It didn't matter. On a flip phone too primitive for pictures, she saw one…a nude blonde girl holding a blanket with blue eyes and an accusatory stare. The caption under her feet said: 'Number 42 on her eighteenth birthday, I just though you should see it again before you do anything rash. Your pixie friend, Owen…FYI, I don't think she saw me take it.'

The other nude hurt more. That image was in the mirror. She cursed herself for not dressing in one of so many fetish outfits that would have exposed the right parts. He might not care, but she couldn't stand to see herself like this. Even in her best years, she had never been pretty, but she could always meet someone that was interested in her seductive eye contact and straight talk about her wishes. But now, the best years for that were gone. She should be growing old with someone that she enchanted many years ago and stuck around because it had become a comfortable habit. Her grandmother told her long ago that that was the best any woman could hope for.

Comfortable habit! Grandma should have been a dominatrix or a nun. But what does a woman of her age do about a blonde beautiful child who rightfully belongs to the man she bought from a nefarious vampire who promised her that he was the best she could get? Vainly, a younger woman inside of her promised that it wouldn't be a problem. Everything he owned she owned, too, right? But no, it wasn't right at all. Not for him and not for her. She could think so many years ago when she was the girl that husband and wife shared, but she was young and stupid. If he were to take delivery, it would be to raise her, not have her and Trudy would fall in line playing Mom.

"He did win the lottery," she told herself out loud as she was buttering the toast. Making breakfast had always been his job, and he did it as if it was a privilege.

Tea for him, not coffee. She remembered that. Maybe she'd bring his pipe with his breakfast and see if he wanted more from her after that. Truthfully, she didn't care one way or another as long as he still wanted her in his life.

She opened the bedroom door and almost dropped the tray.

Breakups had a feeling to them. Was it a smell or a subtle sound? Whatever it was, it was the second time in as many days, and yet another man about to throw away a winning lottery ticket.

"What?" she demanded. Make it good, but don't lie to me. Tell me why the best you've ever had isn't good enough.

The man looked so sad, as if the very reason for life was draining from him. He had seen that look in her face, she knew. That fact softened her.

"Are you breaking up with me again?" she asked gently.

"Lass, try to understand the way it is with me," he begged her. "Did you think I liked everyone having a go with you, and I only get to watch? Yes, it was exciting but…"

"It's what you wanted. I was doing it for you."

"But don't you see, it wasn't what I wanted…it was what I needed…someone else to do what I could not… Now, I don't know what got into me this morning, but I can't do that anymore. I don't have the starch, you see."

Trudy tried not to smile. Did he think she didn't notice his erection problem? Did he think he was the only one? Men and their vanity. She knew to just listen until he was done talking. She wasn't going to brag about what she could do with a half masted erection or even about the blood in the medicine bottle…partly because it wasn't about that at all. It was about getting old.

"….and I know there be a lot of medication for my problem, but all of them have one thing you're not supposed to do while taking them and doing it can ruin the whole thing for life…"

"You're not supposed to drink while using erectile dysfunction medication. You're right. It can cause serious damage. If we were younger, I'd let you try it. We're not."

"I can't not drink, lass. I can't hold what you do, but I can't not drink. So, it's not fair to you to expect to be a full woman when I can't…I can't take her either. If I don't break it off now, you'll just leave me for someone who can. When I was young, if I'd have been better to your kind, you never would have left, and we'd have had eleven little leprechauns by now…but…"

Trudy used an understanding voice. "You still think I'm a leprechaun too?"

"A true poet can't be anything else. Didn't you tell me your father was Irish?"

She didn't think she did, but it was true.

"And aren't you going to tell me that your dad's eyes were as blue as his hair was blond? You'll be telling me that your mother had eyes that were neither blue nor brown."

It was true. The thought of her mother made her skin crawl. Her mother had grey eyes like hers.

"My mother was a fiend. She hated all human beings unless she could use them and hated all men even worse."

"I'm betting she hated leprechaun men before that. We gave her too much good reason."

Trudy put the tray on the nightstand and crawled into bed with her broken leprechaun. He turned away from her but did nothing to resist the spoon that she maneuvered into. Idlily, she stroked his red brown beard and pressed her too full breasts against his back.

It took a while, but some of the pain seemed to leave him. He was far from sleeping, but his despairing body was content to being held. She held her head up to whisper in his ear.

"What would you say if it turns out that all I need from you is what we're doing right now?"

"I'd call you a liar," he muttered.

"But what if it was true? I'd need this at least once a day for fifteen minutes…double that when I'm sad or lonely…triple that if you're mad at me and even more if I'm mad at you. Don't leave me, Eircheard. Don't leave me and see how loyal and loving your ex-mistress can be. What would you say?"

The leprechaun turned put his incredulous face next to hers.

"What would I say if I thought I wasn't hearing you correctly? What would I say if I thought I wasn't dreaming? What would I say if I actually BELIEVED what you were telling me? I'd say I died and went to heaven is what I'd say."

"My pet, you don't have to believe me. You've got fourteen years before you're supposed to marry that young girl. By then, I'll bet you know if I'm telling the truth or not."

"Ah, but if we wait that long, will have to pay the vampire. That Ed Calkins fellow is going to want everything we own because he'll know we've got to pay it. I gave my word, you know. I don't want to make the mistake my papa made."

"He wouldn't take everything we have, trust me. He'll only take everything we have that he wants. Your gold is safe."

"My soda bread! I'll be making the rascal all he can eat for the rest of his undead existence."

CHAPTER 25: A FULL CONFESSION

It was late afternoon when Trudy, still not completely dressed, got a phone call from Nalla, who was taking a break from the third day of waking her late husband. She had been going through some of Eddie's things and found some old poems that he had written. Eddie would have wanted her to look them over, separate what he'd have wanted discarded from what he'd want completed, and polish what she found of value. But Eddie never wrote anything down unless he had to. The best of Eddie's poetry was the verses he had shared with her back when he was trying to be a serious poet. That, of course, was many years ago, but Trudy was sure she could remember the best of it. Sill, stopping over to look through them seemed like a good idea. Also, she wanted to introduce Nalla to Eircheard who knew Eddie well as he sold him the soda bread Eddie brought to Nalla almost every morning.

The phone call ended with the plan for Trudy to stop at the sheriff's office first to brief Matt and give him the chance to fire her. For that reason, Trudy dressed in her uniform so she would have both if Matt asked for her badge and revolver.

It was hard to tell Eircheard's finest clothes from his everyday work clothes, because he was now dressed in a Lincoln green suit and matching derby hat. If it wasn't the suit he was wearing on the day he met her then he had two such suits. She remembered that New Year's day when he met her tending bar. He had come on to her with the worst line ever cast. Funny. The line had worked.

Eircheard drove the hatchback. He could afford better, but he was surprisingly frugal when it came to things not related to his business.

"I don't need to get messed up in any police business," he told her as they pulled in the department's parking lot. "I'll wait here. Take as long as you need."

Matt was at his desk. He gave her full attention as she walked towards him. Trudy took note that his right hand dropped below the desk flat as if ready to draw a gun.

"Is everything alright?" Trudy deadpanned.

"Everything is too 'alright.' Mr. Calkins was the victim of a heart attack, and the bullet taken from his skull came from a hunting rifle and got there after he died. There is no homicide to investigate. The suits left this morning in a hurry to get back to Detroit, and that reporter that knows too much about you and should be asking me embarrassing questions, is instead asking a set of different questions about our lack of funding to some very nervous detractors of mine."

"So, what's wrong?"

Matt didn't answer. He, just for the slightest second, took his eye off her and glanced. Trudy followed his eyes and found hers in the frame of a mirror that hadn't been there before. Did she just wink at herself? Whatever the case, Matt seemed to relax a little.

"Does any of this perfect day have anything to do with you and your vampire last night?"

"It's hard to tell," Trudy shrugged. "He didn't bite me, and I didn't hit him - although I lost more than half of my silver bullets trying. We came to an understanding. I don't think he'll endanger our area, but if he does, I've got a better plan than the one I had last night. It turns out that that stake shooter is the most effective weapon, but it needs modifications. Shall I get you one?"

Matt's face soured.

"Trudy, I'm looking forward to making my office transparent again. I'll let you be our department of mythical creatures, and I don't want to know we have a department of mythical creatures."

"So, I'm not fired?"

"No. Go bury your friend. We'll talk about 'promotions' after I get my new budget. Until you need backup, however, I don't want to hear about anything I can't put in a report…at least not while we're wearing our badges."

"Ok Matt, but there are things you're going to need to hear about. Most of the danger is to Munsonville but that's not going to lower our caseload. One thing though. When an unexplainable murder happens between two unlikely subjects, the dead one is the vampire. Explaining the crazy one with the weapon is somebody else's problem."

Matt just put his head in his hands and moaned.

In the car, Eircheard wanted to know how it went. His face drew a blank when Trudy told him she's taking over the DMC. He wouldn't have found it funny anyway.

Nalla had been crying.

On the floor of her impeccable apartment living room floor were boxes of pictures and other memorabilia. There were stacks of photos in one pile and scribbled, illegible writing on aged loose-leaf paper in another. As she suspected, most of it had been graded and less than kindly. Eddie never did his best work on paper.

"I don't have any pictures of Ed before I met him."

The lament was painful.

"That's because his life didn't start until you did. He said that all the time," Trudy offered. "This is my boyfriend, Eircheard. He's the one who made the soda bread.

"And he wouldn't have come to me if it weren't for you, Trudy. You were the best friend he ever had. You still are."

The leprechaun's eyes sharpened, and a curious look passed over his face.

"The brooch your wearing; I sold him one like that two years ago. He said you'd love it along with your bread and coffee. It was your anniversary, if I recall."

Nalla smiled through her tears.

"I never cared much for the bread; I liked the coffee."

"And Ed never liked the coffee but came for the bread," he finished.

Nalla nodded.

"It's a beautiful emerald in the shape of a rose," she told him.

Eircheard stiffened. "It was a ruby when I sold it to him. Who are you? You're not just human. You're something else."

Nalla nodded as if she expected the question. She told him

that she knew many of the things that Ed had bought her had magical qualities, with "magic" defined as natural properties not yet understood by the minds of the greatest human research and technology. Nalla was granted "magic" of her own, but she did not use it as freely. Most of the time, she forgot that she was any more than the daughter of two Polish immigrants who raised her well and accepted her when she brought a young man home one day who asked if he could marry his daughter.

"Eddie told that story differently," Trudy interjected.

"Yes. He claimed my father offered him all three of his daughters. I was fine with that, as long as I was the only one he slept with."

But Eircheard would not be distracted.

"You must know I'm a leprechaun."

"Dressed in green, that's hard to miss," Trudy joked.

"So, what are you? …if I may ask…but if I can't ask, I'll still suspect. We leprechauns are a suspicious type when dealing with the Fir Bolg."

"I'm only half Fir Bolg," Nalla told him. "But you have the right to be suspicious. Your kind knows a lot of things that lend itself to suspicion. I could answer your question, but will you believe me? I'm not even sure you should."

But Trudy had to know. "What's the other half?"

Nalla sighed before she answered.

"Angel…a minor variety. I hid it from him for years, but it was my singing while sleeping that busted me. He would question me ruthlessly when he was being playful and thought I'd let my guard down. You're not going to know more than him."

"The Nephilim!" Eircheard almost whispered, as if saying the word too loud might…

"Call evil," Nalla finished his thoughts. "There's no way for me to prove that I'm acting in the interests of the light or the darkness. You can't know until the undead life of Ed has expired."

"He claims you stole his soul," he challenged.

"Would that I could. Souls don't really work that way. You can't take a soul out of a person, but you can compel it. Ed was already being compelled by some dark source when I met him. I stole what I could from what was left, but that dark source was being very careful not to show itself. I also knew that Ed could handle the problem on his own if he ever became undead. That reporter friend you've made, Trudy, she'll know more than I'm willing to tell you. But know this: you were right not to destroy him last night. He has more to do...more that will keep the net total of undead on a downward trend. That dark force wants him to do the opposite. It's unlikely you'll have to kill him in your lifetime, but don't tempt him. His desire for blood will be all his willpower can handle. If the future stays as it is now, it's his granddaughter that will grant him peace. He won't bite his own granddaughter."

Trudy nodded before speaking.

"You know about that. We're good now. We had something between us that we never worked out. I'm speaking of that affair I told you about. We apologized to each other last night, but I never apologized to you. I should do that now."

Nalla smiled gently.

"There's no need. It wasn't really an affair. For two or three days, Ed changed his mind, and reluctantly agreed to marry you over me. Before that, Ed was a flight risk. He had never known a marriage that wasn't a hurtful disaster to everyone around it. After that, Ed had to marry or face the wrath of two women. That fear compelled him in a way I could not, forcing the choice: you or me. There was no chance he was going to get that wrong, because I had already snatched what was left of his soul. I'm only sorry about the pain to you, but not so sorry as to wish it went differently. You weren't wrong when you felt your friend was being trapped into doing something he did not want to do. In fact, you were part of the snare."

"You're as ruthless as he is." Eircheard observed.

Nalla seemed to enjoy that.

"But why him?" Trudy asked. "As a Nephilim, you could have snatched any man."

"I'm mostly just a woman," Nalla shrugged. "I fell in love with him."

"Before he fell in love with you?"

"Before he was born. Its more common than you think."

Neither one of them knew what to say to that.

There was one more place to go before the night ended. Trudy could have waited one more day, as Eddie's funeral would be tomorrow. Nalla had gone ahead with the plans to have the body cremated, despite the heated objection of Eddie's mother. It would

383

be a short service of eight which would include Nalla, Rick, Rick's hot wife, Eddie's two granddaughters, Trudy, and someone they should all meet: Eircheard. The poor leprechaun felt like a stuffed fish trophy on the wall, but he agreed to come. But now they were headed to keep a promise made what seemed a lifetime ago, but, in fact, it was four days earlier, when Trudy agreed to a full confession in exchange for that time of silence. They met at the Munsonville Library, the Goddess' suggestion.

Dressed in black with a black brimmed hat and overcoat, the Goddess sensed they kept the promise. She recognized Eircheard right away as the owner of the pawn shop that made soda bread, though he couldn't place her at all. She sensed that the full confession coming to her wasn't something that she could pitch to any newspaper.

Eircheard heard the alarm straight away but said nothing. This "Goddess" was also more than just a reporter.

Trudy spilled. It had been seven days since she held the 44 out the window of her cruiser and pulled the trigger. Trudy left nothing out. She told of the depression closing in on her, the dream of a road trip to oblivion, the incident with the mirror in the women's bathroom, her bar trip with Rick and the brownie that followed her back, the return to the bar from the last dream where she and Glorna were hanged, the roleplaying game where she was an eagle, and the shoot-out with Eddie, where she had mistakenly taken a gun to a limerick fight.

The Goddess listened and did not doubt, something that Trudy was getting used to. Was everyone in Munsonville so trusting, or did each one have their own history with the strange world of vampires?

"Good job with John-Peter," The Goddess told Eircheard. "I see your creation all the time. He's a wonderful boy who loves spending time with his father."

"Can't take all the credit. That vampire wrote the software."

The Goddess knew better but didn't say. If John Simons came to this very time and listened it, he might learn John-Peter was actually Henry Mathews' son, running the changeling's life remotely. And that would be unpleasant.

"So what happens now?" Trudy asked. "To the timeline, I mean."

"It's kind of like a divorce. Reality splits. In one reality, Ed Calkins is dead. The other has him, by all appearances, alive and continuing his life as if nothing happened. Nalla, Ed's family, and Trudy get the part where he's dead. Eircheard and several others get the part where he's alive. Once the vampire is no more, the two realities will become one, and everyone will forget the part where Ed lived past his heart-attack. I'm like the friend of the couple that gets both realities. Don't try to visit the other side. There are no fences around it. If you, Trudy, try to meet Ed Calkins in the morning at Eircheard's pawn shop, you might, but it will make things very confusing. Trying to keep track of space/time get very confusing, which is why Ed Calkins has become like a ruthless dictator that refuses to obey the laws of physics."

"A shame," Trudy lamented. "Ed wanted to be remembered. I don't think his life delivering newspapers was what he had in mind."

The Goddess looked at her, smiling brightly.

"Not so. Ed knew a famous poet whom he influenced greatly. She knows him well and will doubtlessly have much to write about him and his boundless imagination."

Trudy blushed.

"But what of the vampires?" Eircheard cried. "How will we stop the killing with so many vampires in our midst?"

"I've been keeping track of that," The Goddess told him. "There are six vampires that frequent modern-day Munsonville: John Simons, Henry Matthews, Mary Steward, Kellen Wechsler, Dr. Roslyn, and Ed Calkins. John Simons killed Henry Matthews a decade ago before killing himself in the next few months. Ed Calkins' software killed Kellen sixteen years from now. Mary Steward's first intended victim will be Ed's granddaughter, who kills her instead. Ed arranged for his own demise. The only loose end is Dr. Roslyn, who becomes a vampire willingly with the help of Ed's software, contracts Deep Time Psychosis while trying to reverse her conviction, and stops being functional when Ed is no longer around to treat her. Ed's son had made modifications to a stake shooter that neutralizes a great vampire advantage. The future is looking good for Munsonville."

"Wow," said Trudy. "With all you know, you should write a book."

The Goddess' eyes became uncharacteristically weary.

"With all I've tracked through the years, that would take ten years and more than five volumes."

The next evening, as the sun was just beginning to set, the six of them stood by the monkey bars. Trudy was crying on the chest of Eircheard, who pressed her hard into his body. Rick and his hot wife flanked the tearful Nalla, who held the ashes of her late husband's body. The two granddaughters could not have been more different.

The youngest cried out, "It's too sad, Daddy. Make it stop!" Tears flowed unabated.

"It's OK to cry," Grandma Nalla told her. "We'll all be together someday. You don't believe that, but I promise."

The oldest granddaughter was still too young. She stood alone with the weight of the world on her shoulder.

Trudy thought about the bullet that had annoyed him for…how long? Seven seconds, ten years, or as long as the universe lasts; it was just too crazy to think about. Right now, however, Eddie got the night off as he had the last few days when he filled in for his future self. When he did respawn, it would be without that rattling in his skull.

Someday, he would find peace.

Nalla opened the urn. Ashes caught the wind and scattered on the grounds at Wraith Park, where Trudy and Eddie first met, met last night, and would meet each year for the rest of her life or at least until she gave him that peace. He would respawn in a whirlwind that would gather his ashes and make him undead again. The Goddess would know when it was time to end that.

Nalla's last tear mixed with the ashes.

"It's been hard on the kids," Nalla told the hot wife, "Let's go for ice cream."

Eircheard whispered in Trudy's ear.

"Let's share a drop of vampire blood with our whiskey."

"Great idea," she whispered back.

Six months later, when it was too cold and too early…not yet one in the morning…

"Let's get this over with," Eircheard told the other Leprechauns. I don't like it either, but a deal is a deal."

Leprechauns had come from two realms, and both were in

Ed Calkins imagination of what Tara was. Brownies were also there but in a completely different mood. For them, night was work. Not so on this night, and that alone made it special. They jumped through the grass and rolled in their excitement, expressing their joy while waiting for the parade to start.

One of the leprechauns noticed Trudy, the only female.

"What's SHE doing here?" he asked in a harsh whisper. "Does Eircheard think that just because he has himself a girl that he can bring her to any Knight of the Red Branch functions? He's got nerve, he does."

"She is one of us," whispered the other. "She's the poet."

"THE poet? That's Eircheard's girl?"

"They say she's a sex goddess," another interrupted.

"Lucky dog! Maybe Eircheard is the luckiest of us after all, not Arkiens."

Brownies intruded on her overhearing. They were dragging a platform with two chairs fixed to it and bars on either side.

"Queen should sit here," a kneeling brownie insisted.

At least she and Eircheard would not have to walk down the long highway so perilously late. What about cars? Nobody was going to see the brownies or leprechauns as most people didn't believe in them, but what about her? Was she going to be struck by some bloke driving home from a pub?

Leprechauns lit torches and lined up, grumbling, in a straight line, except, of course, for lucky Eircheard, who sat in the chair next to her. It startled both of them when six brownies grew a size strong enough to have an easy time lifting the chairs.

Next year, they would do a little better. Merrows and pixies might be included. After all, a deal was a deal, and they had the rest of their lives to live by their commitments.

Arkiens, who was not in goat form, announced to the nonexistent audience.

"Ladies, gentlemen, and all the rest!" he called through the megaphone. "We bring to you the Calkins Day Parade."

The next evening was Valentine's Day…

Although they were both tired from the festivities of the previous night, Eircheard insisted that Trudy follow him to the "backyard" of his property, which extended for miles in all directions beyond the wooded area and patches of bush and grass plains. He took her to a clearing where a dug-out fire pit heated a transparent dome of plexiglass. "Be mindful of the creatures in the landscape," he had told her many times…any time she even hinted that he owned the place. Creatures own themselves, and they had the right to the trees and rivers as much as any, save those who endangered it. "Think of the trees that would gladly give you their fruit if you want something sweet. Think of the river nymphs that share their water to the thirsty or the stags that give their life, be it less then willingly, if you desire meat. The land is love, your highness. Never be too high to know that."

Now he looked back at her questioning grey eyes.

"Your office," he explained. "The land might inspire you as it does all true Knights of the Red Branch. Take your place in history and tell of the land that so loves you."

Trudy's eyes filled with tears.

But Eircheard wasn't done. Taking a knee, he held up the ugliest plastic leprechaun that Trudy had ever seen.

"Are you proposing to me with that thing?"

But he wasn't. Hushing her, he moved its position slightly as if searching with it. When she demanded what he was looking for, he didn't break his concentration.

"Star," he mumbled. "Be patient and watch."

"Starlight?"

"Ah lass, the light from the star we're looking for won't make it in time to see the world burn. No, we're looking for a gravity spirit."

"A what?"

Just then, the plastic leprechaun's eyes lit up with a menacing green.

"There!" He proclaimed. "I knew it. Here's our luck-bringer, lass. A star was born the day our love was. We've found our lucky star!"

Trudy fought with her skepticism, struggling to believe what her lover was proclaiming.

"I know you leprechauns know a lot about luck," she admitted.

"We leprechauns!" he barked.

That was hard to get used to.

"We have to recharge it with the luck the sky grants us. We

have to do it every six days or so. I gave that Ed Calkins fellow one just like it for the changeling we made."

"Really, gave it?"

"Well, no. I sold it. The price was quite steep actually."

He turned to her.

"Would you have said yes? If I asked you to marry me, I mean."

Trudy could think of worse answers to that question.

EPILOGUE

"Grandma!" The two girls, ages four and six, cried in joy as they charge forward; each grabbed one of Melissa's legs. She almost dropped her suitcase trying not to fall, as Jason, her husband and "Grandpa-Extraordinaire," dropped his suitcase to steady her. For a long time, Melissa had thought this vacation with her daughter, French son-in-law, and two grandchildren in the same hotel room in New Orleans during Mardi Gras would be a mistake. That feeling fell away as she dropped to her knees and accepted the love.

"Dad, Mom."

A young man hugged Jason, all the animosity that had built up while he dated their daughter melted away with the introduction of grandchildren, despite the theological differences that remained. Angela's hug would have to wait. As she attended suitcases, Jean-Pierre turned from Jason to hug Melissa.

"Thanks for coming, Mom."

It still pierced her heart when he said that. One could not fault the Frenchman for having the same name as her deceased son, nor could he be blamed for having neither a living father nor mother of his own; but an old loyalty resisted her from substituting him for the child she raised from birth. The pain of that piercing was dulled by the fact that Jean-Pierre, taller and fair of skin, did not resemble the memory of her master musician. Like Angela, he was adopted late in his childhood, but he'd kept his last name, Matthews, and close relations with his eccentric Irish uncle, who was to meet Melissa, Angela, and Jean-Pierre for a very late dinner in keeping with the Catholic tradition of Fat Tuesday.

Jason, wanting nothing to do Mardi Gras, the decadent parade, or the uncle who was a remorseless fabricator to his Christian grandchildren. The couple had yet to meet him, but Jason could wait.

"So, how is the arboretum, JP?" Jason thought the initials made his son-in-law sound more professional and less like a crazy vegan tree hugger.

"Dad, I'll tell you, if you get someone to pay you to do the thing you love most, you'll never work a day in your life. Most of the trees are healthy, despite the drought. The biggest threat right now is the Asian beetle. It's an invasive insect, but we're looking for natural solutions. I'm leading a research team while Angela stays home, video chatting with Asian colleagues. Our dinner conversations would drive you both crazy, but that's what you get when you raise a botanist who marries a tree nut."

"Jason, we can catch up with the kids later. I have a parade to attend and you have an evening with the grandkids." Melissa reminded her husband.

"I want to go with Grandma," Ruby, the oldest, whined

"Me too," Abby agreed. "I want to see the parade. Do they throw candy?"

Angela grabbed a jacket. "No, dear, this is only for grown-ups. We'll bring back any beads we catch."

"Aaaah."

"But wait until you hear about the great evening I have planned." Grandpa-Extraordinaire announced. "First, we shall close the pool, then we'll stream movies and pop popcorn. And then, since we're on vacation, there will be no bedtime."

"Candy from the vending machine?" Rudy asked, hopefully.

"No need, I have all the candy right here."

Jason showed the variety bag to the girls, then realized his mistake. With questioning guilt, he looked for his son-in-law's approval.

"I guess the 'no candy' rule is suspended. Save some for the rest of the trip," he told Jason, who nodded.

But that was enough for the girls to let the three adults to their parade without candy.

"Ready?" Jean-Pierre asked.

Melissa was confused. "Isn't your uncle meeting us here?"

"No, Mom. JP's uncle likes to wander around when he comes to a new city. He's meeting us at the restaurant."

"Do you think that's wise? That poor old man is suffering from dementia by the way you've talked about him."

Jean-Pierre exchanged a knowing look of confidence with Angela. It had been like that since the day they started dating. He was already a young man, but Angela had just started college. Always they acted as if they knew things that they couldn't say…good things, if not wonderful things. It actually galled Melissa and her husband. Angela was a junior the day they announced that she was pregnant. The same look passed between them while Jason went off about how she'd never finish school and how he would leave her for some girl without so much responsibility. The same looked passed the day of Angela's graduation, when Jean-Pierre asked for their blessing in a "pagan" marriage.

"I'm sure Uncle Ed will be all right," Angela told her mother. Was she trying not to smile? Melissa almost wished for the days when all her daughter knew was what Jason and she taught her. She was so easily frightened back then. Now, here she was, a fully grown woman who seemed to think that nothing could strike her down with her husband in tow. Did Melissa ever feel that way?

The parade was a fair hike from the hotel, but it was a cool evening with festive youths mixing with strangers like it was spring break. The energy was contagious. Saxophones cried, changing pedestrians into dancers. Angela and JP broke into a jitterbug as if no one else owned the world. Was Melissa ever that free? John Simons could protect her, but always seemed just this side of hurting her himself.

As she watched her children dance, she reviewed the strangeness of the decisions that they made together without any outside agreement. Angela Frye married Jean-Pierre Matthews, yet they insisted that their children bear the last name of Simons.

"It would heal an old wound." JP told them. Every time they

tried to explain their reason to Jason, they'd hit a wall, yet it secretly pleased her.

Angela started to perspire, and JP was breathing hard. So much for the dance, but the music went on, from street musicians to the marching bands that seemed to play their impatience for the marching to begin.

The high ground ruled the viewing. From hotel balconies, young men called their cat calls to young women, who responded will lifts of their blouses to show their breasts. On both sides of the cobbled streets, the old and very young sat on lawn chairs, held separate by police orders, and white gloved hands held out by blue coats, whistles, and silver badges. At some spots, intoxication begot pushing until law enforcement intervened. Clearly the police were on edge. An incident the previous night was handled too heavy-handed, so public approval was at an all-time low.

Finally Melissa and her company found an area behind seats where they could see the street without using tippy toes. Behind them, people were not so lucky. Finally, the band's restless music gave way to marching or dancing, and large floats filled in behind with elaborate themes of splendor. Strings of beads flew, beer from balconies spilled, and dancing in place consumed both the marching and the watching.

It was good, both the freedom of the festival and that Jason wasn't there to disapprove.

"Isn't that Uncle Ed?" Angela cried, pointing to a white-bearded man wearing a plaid kilt who had slipped from the police line and mounted a huge float bearing a double throne for the king and queen of Madi Gras. Police scrambled to intercept the old fat fool who'd broken through their careful barricade. At police order, the parade stopped, leaving the violated float right in front of Melissa.

Ed seemed not to notice the police mounting the float from the other side. He jumped down to the line of charging police and somehow past them, to shake hands of the line of stunned spectators.

"Thanks for coming, everyone! May you live as long as you want and never want as long as you live," he proclaimed.

Melissa hissed just loud enough for Angela to hear. "He's going to get arrested."

"Give him a chance," she said, dismissing her mother's

concerns.

Two cops were on the float owners, asking for information.

"He was just there, I don't know how," one was saying. "He seems to be quite happy because he thinks everyone is here to celebrate his birthday, even though we're a week late, but he thinks that's because we were waiting for him to get here. He's really no trouble; in fact, he's quite theatrical…look."

The float driver was pointing to Ed, on one knee in front of a middle-aged policewoman, who was about to subdue him. Ed seemed to understand her differently. He kissed the dumbfounded cop's hand and put something around her finger. By now, the crowd was eating this up, holding up cellphones out to take videos.

"Oh, aren't you sweet," she told the old man, bending down to kiss his forehead. Everyone in listening distance roared in approval.

The cop bride swung around to face them.

"I'm married now!" she shouted, holding up the hand that had the pop can ring Ed had placed on her wedding finger.

"That's my uncle!" Jean-Pierre called to a police officer near him.

"One second." The cop was on radio getting his marching orders. By now, both sides of the parade were captivated by the unexpected police response. The newly married policewoman produced hand cuffs, cuffed one of Ed's wrist, and then cuffed one of her hers. Instead of leading him to a cruiser, she mounted the stairs to the float, Ed in tow. The king and queen that were to sit on the two thrones surrendered their seats for the unlikely pair, who were both grinning as wide as the Mississippi.

"He's not in trouble," the officer told JP. "The police station is just north of here. Enjoy the parade then come there to get him. We'll take care of him till you arrives."

Melissa sighed in relief as the parade started up again. What a way to meet JP's uncle for the first time!

The parade continued for at least another hour, yet JP and Angela seemed totally unconcerned. A new energy seemed to overflow from each passing act.

Finally, it was quiet enough to check on Jason and the girls. He was excited but whispering. The girls dozed off after only half of the popcorn, a quarter of the candy, and a third of the first cartoon.

Swimming had tired everyone, including Jason. She didn't tell him about Ed; she didn't know how to begin.

Once in the police headquarters, no one had to worry about Ed's whereabouts. They didn't see him, but they heard him. He was sharing a birthday cake in a break room with the officers that worked the parade and expressing his thankfulness at their devotion.

"One second, husband," the voice of the officer told him. "I want to meet the in-laws privately before you go have your dinner."

A no-nonsense redhead moved to her desk and waved the trio to the seats before her. Without looking up, she gathered papers as they sat, Melissa feeling defensive.

"I get it," she told Melissa as she looked up. "That man is hard to keep track of. He got away from me three times to go shake hands and thank everyone. And I had him in handcuffs! He must have picked the lock and sneaked away before shaking hands and climbing out to reattach the cuff as if nothing happened. Do you know I'm wife number twenty-nine? He ranks his wives because I'm the sixty-fourth woman he married, but he liked me so much, he promoted me to twenty-nine straight away."

"Twenty-nine is quite an honor." Angela deadpanned. Or was she serious?

"Yeah, and that was while he thought I'd have to arrest him for bigamy. He says he lives in a small village called Munsonville, where he rents a small apartment by himself. Is that true?"

Melissa squirmed in her chair, but JP responded confidently. "Yes. He's OK, despite his delusions. He holds a job and supports himself with a certain dash, as we say in France."

"Well, do they introduce you to leprechauns in France? Your uncle introduced me to some of his closest leprechaun friends."

"Leprechauns?" Melissa asked, feeling strangely disturbed, like there was something about that comment she should remember.

"Yes, and some brownies, merrow, and pixies."

"Good thing he didn't introduce you to the cluricahns." JP sounded genuinely relieved.

"My husband's uncle sometime hallucinates, but he's completely functional." Angela added.

The cop looked at her. "Hallucinates? By that, do you mean he sees things that are not there?"

"Well, yes, but he drives. He never doesn't see things that

are there."

"Funny, because the leprechauns, brownies, and pixies that he introduced me to as his new wife; I saw them too." The woman wore a strange expression. Melissa could not be sure she was joking But she scribbled some notes and gave no indication that anyone was getting arrested this evening. Then she seemed to remember something.

"About this man living by himself in Munsonville: do they really have a St Patty's day parade there?"

"Munsonville is too small."

"…with all of the sidhe from a time forgotten?"

"Uncle Ed has the gift of imagination," JP explained. "He calls it the luckiest thing next to his first wife. I recommend folding to his madness."

"Sign here." She held out a clipboard. "He told me that even though we're married, I'm still free to marry someone else. If I want, I can date. I should date again. This one was a blast. Who knows; I might meet a man who doesn't have sixty-three other wives! Maybe I'll make the top ten with someone."

Ed was done with his cake. Smiling, he told the officers that "they were the best." He promised a limerick to make the police of New Orleans the toast of the nation for the next thousand years. As he spoke, he placed a red rose on his new wife's desk.

"Thanks, guys," JP chipped in. "You made my uncle's birthday one he will never forget."

"Husband," the officer said to Ed as he was almost out the door. "Try not to marry more than one woman at the Munsonville parade. If I come there, I don't want too many women fighting over you."

"Ah, but I do." Ed's eyes were twinkling.

The restaurant was dark, plush, and crowded. Ed had beaten the trio there and was kneeling in front of a woman who was at the bar, waiting for her table. Her male companion looked baffled. Neither one was drinking alcohol.

"Uncle!" JP shouted sharply. "What did I tell you about proposing to more than one woman per day?"

The woman, wearing a black brimmed hat and matching overcoat, was speaking to Ed. Melissa could swear the woman said, Rise, elf." But maybe it was something more sensible.

Ed stood up and introduced his family to the pair at the bar.

"This is my nephew, Jean-Pierre and his lovely wife, 42...er Angela. Meet my chief stalker, the Goddess and her husband Ron."

"Hi," the Goddess told them. "I'm 'the goddess' to him, but please call me Denise. I happened to be covering Mardi Gras for my podcast and whom do I meet but the ruthless dictator causing a scene."

Angela stumbled forward. "Uncle Ed, you haven't met my mother yet...this is Melissa Frye. Mom, Ed Calkins."

Ed looked pensive during the handshake. Finally, he asked, "Did you work delivering newspapers at any point? You seem familiar."

"I did for a time," Melissa said as she tried to place him.

"Ah," Ed said with a wink. "So many people come and go in the industry. I'm sure that memories repair themselves when vampires mess with the time-scape. Let me show you how to deal with the paparazzi."

Then looking at the Goddess he asked, "Would you be so kind as to join us? We'll need a table for six."

Thankfully, the Goddess accepted. Two complete strangers at the table made a dinner with JP's uncle more predictable and the conversation easier to follow. What did Ed mean about vampires? The thought nagged her memory. Melissa's life had been tragic. Both her husband and son had died from mysterious diseases, and her second husband had been murdered by a crazy woman. Now, there was this Uncle Ed. Would life ever get normal?

The food was spicy and flavorful with plenty of vegan options for her son-in-law. Melissa was relieved when the Goddess, who needed to leave the next day, offered to drive Uncle Ed all the way back to Munsonville. That save Ed airfare and someone having to drive him to the airport. She thought about her granddaughters. She looked forward to spending the rest of the week with them.

"So, Uncle," Angela asked after the long, pleasant meal with Uncle Ed insisting on paying the check. "The woman that my mother reminds you of: did you ever ask her to marry you?"

"I'm not sure 42...er...Angela. Women tend not to forget me. But I do believe I did ask her to marry me, but she didn't say yes. I doubt any good came of that."

The Goddess turned out to be an interesting woman with a

passion for writing and an understanding of ancient lore. Her commentaries added spice to Ed's long, drawn-out tales with the result that no one was bored.

As they talked, Melissa searched her memory. She did remember a man that she and her first husband worked with that had a vague resemblance to Ed. Her late son had worked with him too. Had anyone ever asked her to marry him, and she didn't say yes? A different marriage, even on JP's uncle's terms, might have changed her life, causing her less pain. But why would she think that? Another strange though came to her mind.

Later that night, when she was in bed with Jason's sleepy arms wound around her, dreams took her back to when she was quite young...before ever being a mother. It was somewhere in the time when anything seemed possible. She was at a Victorian-themed party with a handsome, tall, evil man in a top hat and suit who always seemed to snarl at her. The food was strange, yet wonderful, and music seemed ancient.

A white bearded, pot bellies man stuffed in a kilt came forth and asked her something... At first, she did not understand him. Then the warning came...too late. The cautionary tale could have saved her two consecutive tragedies.

Young women, please take my advice
Know that young love is a toss of the dice
And if Ed Calkins should ask
Be quickly up to the task
For to marry, he might never ask twice.

About the Author

Ed Calkins is a real, 60-something, proud of his Irish-heritage computer programmer and amateur writer who has also spent his entire life working in newspaper circulation. Years ago, Calkins invented a "ruthless dictator" alter ego, also known as "The Steward of Tara."

With Calkins' permission, BryonySeries author Denise M. Baran-Unland furthered altered him to create a minor character in "Bryony," making Calkins the first Irish vampire of any significance. Of course, Calkins claims "Bryony" is really all about him, so he's held his own book signings, which he is calls, "The Ed Calkins Tour." There must be some truth in his sentiments, because Calkins' plot importance does grow with each novel in the original BryonySeries trilogy.

Calkins is the author of "Ruthless" (his backstory) and "Denise M. Baran-Unland's Irish Genealogy." He also shares his writings on the BryonySeries blog. Email him at bryonyseries@gmail.com.

About the Illustrator

    Nancy Calkins taught art at Brodnicki School in Indian Springs District 109 in Justice, Illinois for 40 years. She taught different disciplines of art, including drawing and painting, to up to 700 students a week.

    Calkins also helped organize the district's teachers union, eventually serving as its president. When she retired in 2014, she received the key to the village of Justice.

    She grew up in Bridgeview and attended District 109 schools as a child. She graduated from Mount Assisi High School in Lemont without having taken an art class. Calkins also graduated from the University of St. Francis in Joliet with a Bachelor of Fine Arts.

    Calkins works in acrylics and continues to paint in retirement. Contact her at brushed1@aol.com.

Made in the USA
Coppell, TX
30 March 2021